After Brock

for

Steve and Ljuba Morris

Paul Binding
After Brock

SEREN

Seren is the book imprint of
Poetry Wales Press Ltd.
57 Nolton Street, Bridgend, Wales, CF31 3AE
www.serenbooks.com
Facebook: facebook.com/SerenBooks
Twitter: @SerenBooks

ISBN: 978-1-85411-568-3

Front cover by © John Lavrin, 'The Boy from the Mill' – oil on canvas
Typesetting by Elaine Sharples
Printed by CPI Group (UK) Ltd, Croydon

The publisher works with the financial assistance of
The Welsh Books Council

Part One

Nat's Adventure

One

Beginnings

The great waterfall gleamed white through the darkness, and he felt himself compelled to climb, to see where it began.

He craned his neck. The edge of the plateau from which the water tumbled down so fast, long and loud, was hidden from him, at least two hundred feet above.

What, right up there? It'd be like scaling a fucking wall.

He had no torch, it was past midnight, cloud covered the sky, and there was a night dew underfoot which would later turn to frost. He was alone, a stranger, without any mountaineering experience. As well as this he was a mass of cuts and bruises after the attack in which he'd lost the one friend he cared about. He knew his mistakes now for what they were, and those faults of his that were responsible.

He was dead tired and so very cold.

> *Come unto me all ye that labour and are heavy laden,*
> *and I will give you rest.*

Where had he heard that before? It was a command that was also a promise. And he wouldn't disobey. Up, up he went, in his jersey, jeans and sneakers, hardly appropriate for this place. Scaling a wall was about right, too. In front of him was a long vertical face of moss-covered stones and boulders with narrow slithers of soil between them. Bare, bent birch trees had their roots in some of these. Higher up, stark rock face confronted him. But he would surely find enough footholds to edge his way to where pine trees reared sombre forms against the night sky.

During his slow ascent, that sky often got blocked by birch or boulder or by flashes of the torrent itself, always audible, and always calling him on. Often he was on the point of slipping; the soil between stones was principally mud.

But his limbs had determination of their own. An hour's strenuous, patient, sometimes scary endeavour, and there he was. At the very top.

★ ★ ★

This waterfall is Pistyll Rhaeadr, at 240 feet the longest single drop waterfall in England and Wales. It lies in the Berwyn Mountains, north of Welshpool, east of Bala, south of Llangollen and west of Oswestry, on the Welsh side of the Wales-England border. Twenty-four of the Berwyn peaks are more than 2,000 feet high, Cadair Berwyn itself rising to 2,700. They contain Wales' largest stretch of moorland, many hectares of heather, cotton grass, bracken and peat bog, home to the famously elusive polecat, to foxes, squirrels, pine martens, otters and badgers. For birds, there are curlews, merlins, red kites, hen harriers, dippers, peregrine falcons and both red and black grouse; by streams you can see kingfishers.

It is in the Berwyns that tradition sites Annwn, that Celtic Otherworld with geographically traceable entrances in this one. The ruler of Annwn is Gwyn ap Nudd, head of the Tylwyth Teg, the 'good' or 'fairy' folk, elusive as any polecat, and his is a peaceful yet merry land. In the early seventh century Gwyn ap Nudd invited Collen onto his stretch of Berwyn moor. Collen was a devout local ascetic, later commemorated in the name of the nearest town, Llangollen (St Collen). The meeting of the two – as set down in Buchedd Collen (Book of Collen 1536) – ended ambiguously. For if Collen was never bothered again by Gwyn or the Tylwyth Teg and went on to sainthood, Gwyn himself continued his sway over his happy realm.

In September 2009, an eighteen-year-old boy disappeared into the Berwyn Mountains for more than five days. Then on the sixth day the headlines brought relief:

> Missing Berwyn Boy Alive
> Helicopter Rescue Drama
> We Didn't Dare Hope – Dad

But by the Tuesday of the next week, the story was changing:

> Berwyn Boy Mystery
> Was Nat Kempsey Really Lost?
> Doubts Grow Over Berwyn Story

And again:

> Nat's Dad's Secret Past

And, still more attention-grabbing:

> What is the truth of Dad's UFO Encounter?

Pete Kempsey was eighteen when he climbed to the top of Pistyll Rhaeadr at night, hoping to find a new beginning for himself. His son, Nat, was the same age when he vanished into the Berwyn terrain.

* * *

For a moment Nat's back there, bouncy, fragrant heather for pillow and mattress, and near his head a spring bubbling out of the ground. And far above him a lark singing to start the day.

Then he hears his dad clumping up the stairs two at a time, breathing heavily – he's become so out of condition these last two years – and Nat knows exactly where he is. In his room above High Flyers, his dad's kite shop in the little Shropshire town of Lydcastle. And in bed, under doctor's orders. And with a hard-on. Up there waking with one would be something to celebrate in a poem or song. But this wouldn't do for down here. Down here nature is something to disguise by rearranging the duvet. He has, he must remember, to be a paragon of virtue; that's how the kinder papers and programmes are presenting him, and he must live up to this image. Dad has now arrived in the bedroom doorway, with his most serious face on.

Pete Kempsey is thinking: 'I know even less how to talk to Nat now than before he disappeared, and I wasn't much good at it then.' And somehow things aren't helped by the boy looking so unlike Pete at that age: thin like a character in some cartoon, grey eyes and greyish hair that single him out from any known relative, and irregular teeth not really righted by that hospital operation. And every sentence he speaks bringing South London closer.

'Nat,' he says, 'another reporter's turned up. This one's from *The Marches Now*. Came here last week. Before we knew where you were.'

On perhaps the blackest of all those mornings, he nearly adds, when I was pretty much certain I'd never see you again.

'His piece came out on Saturday; I read it before joining the rescue operation.' How long ago that feels! 'He did a fair-enough job, all things considered, even though…' It'd be egocentric to quote that smart-arse phrase which so got to him, 'High Flyers is one of those New Age enterprises which still flourish in rural Britain, even though the Age has largely turned its back on what it once pronounced New.' Shameful enough to have even remembered this with so much else to think about.

'Even though?' persists Nat.

'Even though he did go off at a tangent,' says Pete, 'after all yesterday's hoo-ha, I was beginning to think the press would draw a line under your case today.'

After Brock

I wasn't beginning to think any such thing, he admits silently, so why say it? It'll only give the lad a false picture of what to expect.

'But this bloke downstairs,' he continues, 'is sure there's more media mileage in you, and he says it'd be better for you to talk to *him* than to the rest of them. But then he would say that, wouldn't he?'

Nat thinks: But I don't want a line drawn under my case. Has Dad really not worked that out? Maybe it's not only physically he's out-of-condition, what with living and working so much by himself. Aloud: 'Bad publicity's better than no publicity, Dad. All they print about me – about us,' for his father hasn't been spared, 'does High Flyers no harm. Quite the opposite.'

Pete Kempsey suppresses a wish to snap back at this crass observation. After an ordeal as gruelling as his you couldn't expect the lad to be himself, whatever that might be. Pete's all too aware that in the six years since he left London and Izzie, Nat's mum, for the Welsh Marches, he's failed to keep up conscientiously with the successive stages of his son's development. And by now… well, he's developed! Pete doesn't know what to make of how Nat's turned out, let alone of this big vanishing act gaining him so much attention.

'Nat, I can't keep this guy waiting much longer. I could tell him it's far too early for you to see him, if you like. Serve him right for barging in before I've opened the shop. I could even tell him that you're just not up to talking to anybody at the moment.'

Too early; not talking… shit, thinks Nat, what a strange life I'm living. Far stranger than life 'up there'. He mustn't, of course, downplay the health side of things; Dr Warne has told pretty well the whole reading, listening and watching world how Nathaniel Kempsey must rest and take a course of strong medication. In truth, Nat suspects, these later, slower starts to the morning quite suit his dad, for all his grumbing about the journo downstairs. But then, he thinks, I've fallen back to sleep twice since Dad brought me that mug of tea, and that's not normal.

'I've always said I'm available to the media, haven't I?' he doesn't mind sounding pompous, 'it won't look good if you say I won't see people after what they put yesterday.'

What he also wants to say is, 'And, you never know, this guy might actually talk money. At last!' Then a bitter little résumé flashes in his head, like an ad on the computer screen. 'Cash tally so far. BBC *Midlands Today* who have had two whole, *two whole*, interviews with me: zero. BBC *Mid Wales*, same: *Shropshire Star, Oswestry and Border Counties Advertiser*, likewise. *Western Mail* – well, they've gone so far as to say they're thinking of a feature; "We'll be coming back to you," But they've made it clear they won't be giving me a thing. And they haven't come back either. *Daily Mail* – mega-huge circulation! But all it managed was two miserable paragraphs talking about "the Herne Hill boy lost in Welsh desert" when everyone knows the Desert of Wales lies between Rhayader and Tregaron. You'd think they could get people to check that sort of thing, wouldn't you? Anyway, money from that quarter – once again, zilch!'

Pete Kempsey scratches the nape of his neck with his right hand. 'Nat, this man – this Luke Fleming – says he's got questions for you others haven't asked. He's coming from a different place from everybody else, to use his own words.'

At these last two sentences Nat's hard-on subsides and activity starts up in another part of his anatomy, his heart seems to double its beat. 'Well, let him ask,' he hits back. 'I'm good and ready, no matter *what* place he's coming from. After all – remember that sentence in *Shropshire Star*? "Nat Kempsey, in his own words, is a news-freak who's decided to turn newshound, and is to study journalism at the University of Lincoln." And anyway, *The Marches Now* is only a twice-weekly *regional* paper, and I'm someone who's been handling *national dailies*.'

That's just the kind of stupid thing I could have said at his age, thinks Pete Kempsey dolefully. 'If you call it handling to have ended up with that two-bit thing in the *Mail* that even got your location confused with some place else,' he retorts.

This Fleming guy's rattled Dad, thinks Nat. He hasn't got as much nerve as I have; I'm not sure he's got much nerve at all...

Nat has no idea of the battle I've been through while he vanished, his father thinks: the effort it cost to bother to wash and shave: the near-overwhelming temptation to knock myself out with a heavy concoction of whisky and Diazepam until at least some concrete information came through.

'Okay,' he says, 'I'll go and bring him up. But, Nat, you can stop talking any time you want. You'd be within your rights. He's not a policeman after all.'

'I've already been put through it by the police, and I'm still smiling, Dad.'

'Give me a cop any time over a journo. I never thought the day would come when I'd say that, but now I do. I'd shout it from the rooftops, in fact.'

Despite the bravado, his father's undisguised unease infects Nat. The rapid heartbeats are not slowing. A health course at school had told them that a good way of dealing with these is to gulp cold water. Which gives you a slight shock, makes you gasp. Well, he has a carafe full of water on his bedside table to help him swallow Dr Warne's tablets. So he pours himself a glass now, but his hand is trembling and, shit, he spills water onto the table, his own left arm and the duvet. The old Nat Kempsey's hands never shook when holding or pouring *any*thing. It's not, he thinks, his trials in the Berwyns that have changed him for the worse. It's all the grilling by press hacks, intent on catching him out, on presenting him as one more British youth whose good A Levels only illustrate declining national standards, and who won't be able to find any kind of job in the highly competitive global market.

And of course Dad's been well and truly grilled also. That's why (thinks Nat) he's let himself go appearance-wise today and yesterday; he's exhausted, knackered. Just as well he isn't showing this Luke Fleming bloke into his own room, bed most likely unmade, crumpled clothes all over the floor, a lingering smell of the dope he still smokes virtually every other day. Nat himself has a passion for cleanliness and order, which he now knows himself to share with most animals in the wild – though not with either of his parents or with a fair number of his friends, even Josh. But, give credit where it's due, Dad is amazing in the way he keeps his kite shop, scrupulous and appealing, changing the principal kites round at least twice weekly, so a customer's eye always meets interesting new potential purchases. And, in the public eye as it now is, High Flyers must be winning many a new visitor.

Nat takes another gulp of water, and back into his mind and body come the many times last week he bent down to streams or sudden little freshets on Berwyn mountainsides, his hands cupped. He can hear the two men coming up the staircase, which is steep as a ladder, for it's extremely old and made for earlier people and lifestyles. Nat can tell just from the upward drift of his voice and the impact of his tread on the uncarpeted wooden steps that this guy with the questions for him that haven't been asked before is still quite young, a deal younger than his dad anyway, who once, though you'd never know it now, was a fast sprinter and played rugby.

'Here's the invalid, Luke!' Dad says in that falsely hearty voice that he himself despises and which embarrasses his son. And he ushers in a guy of twenty-eight, no, more like thirty, reckons Nat. Fair, slim, bright blue eyes, not as tall as himself, at a glance the type who does daily work-outs at the gym. He wears a grey, two-button jacket, white shirt with black T-shirt beneath, blue chinos, and white Nike trainers and blue laces that match the trousers. All very different from Pete Kempsey's sloppy shaggy sweater, sagging jeans and dirty old trainers, and hair, though still dark and reasonably profuse, as unkempt as if he's the one who's been sleeping on mountainsides.

'Hi, Nat, pleased to meet you! Apologies for disturbing you at this godforsaken hour,' goes this unwelcome latest arrival. 'But then a man has to do what a man has to do.'

'A man has to…' fucking what does he have to do? Nat inwardly inquires. Men believe they have to do a great many horrible, revolting, contemptible things it'd be better they didn't.

This is more or less his dad's reaction too, though something makes him add to himself, 'You never know when someone who seems like an enemy will turn out to be a friend.'

'Quite a little snug you have here!' Luke Fleming is remarking breezily.

After Brock

'Glad you like it!' There's a touch of cheek in Nat's manner.

The word 'snug' has connotations for Pete, from his youth (and not unconnected with his own Berwyn adventure), and he rather regrets having heard it. He is also discomfited by the way the journalist has spoken the compliment. It sounds hellishly like a softening-up before he attempts the hard, not to say knock-out punches. Nat seems to be taking it straight, though; in fact he's smiling.

And Nat *is* pleased; he likes this room of his far better than his other one back in Herne Hill. It's nice too, now he's – temporarily – an invalid who mustn't budge from bed, that this room's window looks out over Lydcastle Market Square, lined by houses all with shops on their ground floors, and with façades painted cheerful greens, blues, light yellow, magenta. The façade of High Flyers is duck-egg blue but, needless to say, it badly needs a fresh coat of paint. (Another thing Dad should have seen to, his landlord having by law to pay the cost.) On Saturdays there are stalls in the Square, selling fruit, flowers, potted plants, cheeses, pies and pastries, and Nat is looking forward to seeing them. It's only Wednesday today, but a fair number of people are about, ramblers or other visitors, peering interestedly into shop windows, even though it's the last day of September, and the tourist season is coming to its end.

Inside, the room contains Nat's bed, a bookcase and a desk bearing his Dell laptop, and, pinned on the wall above that, some of his best photos: two ravens on The Stiperstones mating in mid-air; a collie confronting a hedgehog who's rolled himself into a ball. Then on the bulgy old cream-washed wall opposite the window Dad and he, only two months back, hung two favourite kites of his from the downstairs stock: a Balinese bird kite, made of bamboo and silk, complete with beaked head, and a Rokkaku, the famous Japanese fighting kite, painted with a picture of a carp. Perhaps, Nat thinks with a sudden irrational inclination to giggle, that's how it'll end up, this meeting between the guy from *The Marches Now* and himself – with a ritual kite-fight. But even with his prized Rokkaku he might, of course, lose to this fitness freak. Besides, how could he forget? He's *not* his usual energetic self, not at all, he's under the doctor.

Luke Fleming looks at Nat: thinking 'Even after all the photos I've seen – and his appearance on BBC *Midlands Today* – he doesn't really look like what I've been expecting. Nobody's mentioned how odd his smile is, as if somebody collected individual teeth from some dentist's and then stuck 'em all anyhow onto his gums. And then those grey eyes. Very bright too. Perhaps a touch of fever, I wouldn't be surprised. His eyes shine just as my Jared's did (though he's twelve years younger) when he was so poorly last March.'

Time to assert himself as the professional he very much is. No offence meant etc, he says to Pete Kempsey, and he thought he'd already made it clear downstairs (he knows he hasn't!), but he must speak with Nat alone. It's an axiom of journalists that, if it can possibly be avoided, an interview isn't conducted with a third party present.

Nat regrets this axiom on account of what Luke has already said to his dad. About coming from a different place. But his father – as his mother from time to time sadly observes – can prove pretty spineless in the face of opposition, and today he caves in without a show of resistance. 'Well, if that's how you work, Luke…!' he assents, though finishes this sentence with, 'Only don't tire the lad, please. He's had quite a time of it these last ten days.'

'I know that, Pete,' says Luke Fleming, matily, 'it's *because* of the awful time he's had that I've belted along over here to find out more.'

A race for my story? That's good to hear, Nat thinks, and if there's a race, mustn't there be… but he doesn't say the all-important word, even to himself.

'That's okay,' he says, and signals to his dad that this is perfectly true; he can be left alone with this man from *The Marches Now.*

I'm not a bully, I loathe bullies, Luke Fleming thinks to himself, but I must not let any fears of being one get in the way.

After Brock

Luke has, from the first, been convinced something's gravely amiss with Nat's story. And he's not the only one. He's compared notes with newspaper colleagues. But he can be surer than they, because now *he* has a trump card he knows for sure nobody else holds. And for a few seconds he feels almost sorry for the curious-looking boy sitting up in bed, ignorant of this last fact, vulnerable on so many counts, and already palpably on the defensive. Poor lad, the day might well come when both Pete and his son thank Luke Fleming for his insights and persistence, even for his very ruthlessness, but it could be a long time arriving. There'll be resentment before gratitude, and very possibly real anger.

Nat is saying, 'Won't you take a chair, Luke?' He feels that starting the first name business, instead of letting the older guy do so, is a good ploy. It's as if he's calling the shots. 'There's one over by my desk. See?'

'Best to be comfortable,' agrees Luke (ominously?) 'how *are* you feeling by the way?'

'*By the way*', thinks Nat, 'well, I like that!' Dr Warne certainly doesn't think his health's an incidental matter. And it was the police themselves who absolutely insisted he spend the two first nights after his rescue secure in hospital, being thoroughly gone over. Only after those was he allowed to come back to Lydcastle, and then with certain conditions.

'That twisted ankle of yours still giving you grief?' Luke Fleming's now seated himself on Nat's right-hand side, and is grinning away at him as though there's something humorous in his question. Humour!! If Luke was struck by the greyness of Nat's eyes, Nat is struck by the vivid blueness of Luke's, which doesn't make him feel a bit comfortable. Luke Fleming's eyes are like the lights of an interrogation cell.

'I haven't *got* a twisted ankle.' He sounds annoyed.

'Sorry,' keeping up the grin, '*sprained* ankle.'

'I haven't got *that* either!' What the hell homework into his case can this bloke have done if he's ignorant of so elementary a fact? It's been given out to the public a thousand times – by Nat himself, by his dad, by Shrewsbury Hospital, by the police. In truth any watcher of BBC *Midlands Today* could give a more accurate account of Nat's injury than this employed writer for an allegedly serious paper. Hasn't Nick Owen, that programme's chief presenter, spoken the correct words to well over a million viewers? 'I've got a *broken* ankle. That's hugely different!'

The expression on Luke's immaculately clean-shaven face is a question mark in itself. So Nat goes on. 'A *broken* ankle isn't at all the same thing as a *sprained* one. Ask any doctor. Ask Dr Warne here in Lydcastle. He'll be happy to put you in the picture. You have three bones at the ankle joint – tibia, fibula and talus – and I happen to have broken all fucking three of 'em.'

He hadn't intended the f-word but doesn't regret it.

'Just remind me how you got that injury, will you, Nat?' goes Luke Fleming.

Considers himself crafty, this hack, well, he considers wrong, is Nat's immediate response. But he's gone over this part of his history so often to so many different people from so many organisations that he's getting bored with his narrative. And that doesn't do the story itself many favours. But he can't get out of answering Luke's question, whatever he feels. 'Well I was out on the mountainside, wasn't I? and I heard this horrible little bang – sort of sudden loud pop, like someone shooting a rabbit. And then when I looked – well, the talus, the ankle bone, had broken through the skin. That's pretty serious, you know. But it only started to hurt a while after I saw it. Shock, I suppose. I still can't stand up or put any weight on my right foot. That's why they're keeping me in bed. That, and the after-effects of all the exposure.'

'Tough!' says Luke. His eyes don't exactly seem moist with sympathy. And he's pulled out of his jacket a neat little pocket recording device. At least, Nat thinks, he has the honesty to show it. 'Nat, I didn't ask *what* happened to your ankle, I asked you *how* it happened. So I'll put the question to you again: just how *did* you manage to *break*…'

And I don't like bullies, Luke rebukes himself.

'But this is in all the papers. Dailies, bi-weeklies, locals, nationals.' The boy's trying out a sick person's voice on me, feels Luke. 'I've told it all lots of times already.'

'Well, make this one more then.' And I don't like etc.

Nat gives a sigh which sounds, he knows, a mite self-pitying. 'I was coming down the mountainside rather too fast, I guess. Pen-plaenau; that's one thousand, seven hundred and seventy-one feet high, and there was once a Roman fort there, which explains some of the narrow furrows your feet keep finding. I tripped over one of those, and went sliding down a mossy boulder. After that I couldn't move much. So when I saw the helicopter all those days later, I found it difficult to stand up and attract its attention, let alone run and wave something at it. I was scared I'd just be left up there…'

Obligingly, as if in co-operation – or would it be corroboration? – Nat's ankle now resumes the throbbing that was so oppressive yesterday and which woke him up in the middle of the night. Maybe his first painkillers, taken with the early-morning mug of tea Dad brought him, are already wearing off? Luke notes this return of pain to the boy. That, at any rate, is genuine, you couldn't fake those involuntary winces. Makes him remember earlier sports injuries of his own, and the hell they used to give him, particularly when he tried to pretend he hadn't got them.

'So you were in the Berwyns all that time?' he says. 'Pen-plaenau is in the Berwyns?'

Nat forgets himself. 'Well, of course it is. Where else could it be? The Kalahari? New York City? The Berwyn Mountains are absolutely where I was. On my own. Where I was found. As the papers say.'

'So they do!' Luke Fleming is still smiling, 'where you were *found*. How could I have forgotten! Beautiful neck of the woods, the Berwyns.'

Nat warns himself: This guy is more dangerous that any furrow left by a Roman encampment. Anyway, as a reporter for the local paper, he must know all about Pen-plaenau. It's a Marches peak, and there's been a lot of interest in the place because all the archaeological work had to be carried out so high-up. Pen-plaenau tripped you up and broke your ankle, but, if you're not careful, this idiot's gonna trip you up and break your reputation – and for good! That's the difference between an ankle and a reputation, one mends quickly, the other may never mend at all. If this Luke Fleming makes a scandal out of all this, the University of Lincoln could throw you out before it's even let you in.

Luke's telling him, softly, meaningfully, 'I was in the Berwyns yesterday, Nat. Went and stood right at the foot of Pistyll Rhaeadr. Splendid spectacle! That's where your great adventure began, isn't that right?'

Luke tries not to remember American films of detectives entrapping their victims with casually delivered, seemingly normal remarks. He's actually never admired these characters, sees them as responsible for that disagreeable feature of US culture, its pervasive admiration of aggression.

'You know it's right!' Nat agrees, 'you must have read it enough times. I'd gone to look at that *splendid spectacle* before going up into the mountains. It's the longest single-drop waterfall in England and Wales, you know.'

'I might have heard something of the kind. And it was into the pool at the bottom of that huge single-drop that you had the great misfortune to drop your mobile phone. Which you'd had switched off all day anyway; we know that because your dad had tried to call you. That must have been an awful moment for you, seeing your phone go, plop! into that little maelstrom.'

'Yes, it was awful.'

'Still – with no mobile at all – you happily set off uphill for a good long mountain walk. Not knowing, obviously, that you'd be having an accident.'

This sneering tone isn't right, protests Nat agitatedly to himself, finding Luke's manner all too reminiscent of just such movies as the journo himself has been trying not to recall. This determination not to take anything he says at face value, this mockery of his Great Adventure that was also his Great Ordeal.

He mustn't just lie back and let it happen. 'This isn't fair!' he says aloud. Humiliating, but there's a lump in his throat like when you're about to burst into tears.

'What isn't?'

'You trying to say I never went to Pistyll Rhaeadr.'

Luke stretches the skin of his cheeks, which only highlights for Nat the fierce sparkle of his bright blue irises. The beams of his eyes are like weapons aimed at him. 'But I'm not trying to say any such thing!' he answers, half-offended, half-amused, and obviously trying to deflect Nat's erupted hostility with facetiousness. 'Why would I? I *know*, Nat, that you stood below Pistyll Rhaeadr on the day of your... well, let's call it, *disappearance*, on Monday September 21. Know it as well as I know that I'm Luke William Fleming, contracted to *The Marches Now* but also a contributor to other papers, including national dailies.'

He's trying to impress me, realises Nat. 'That's good!' he says, trying a new tack, 'always better if the interviewer trusts the interviewee.'

'Funny responses you have to things, Nat,' says Luke, 'aren't you curious about *how* I'm so sure you were there then? Late in the afternoon it was, I believe.'

Well, obviously he's curious how. But mightn't this shithead be bluffing?

'Well, you tell me, Luke!'

'I met Joel Easton.'

Nat sees a light of victory in those blue eyes, and triumph in the mouth now smiling more than grinning.

Joel Easton. Who on earth? The name means nothing to Nat, nothing. 'Name means nothing to me, fucking nothing!' he says out loud. He's beginning to take a full-scale 100-carat dislike to this reporter – and he doesn't care how many other papers he writes for! Could be *Paris-Match* and *The New York Times* for all it matters to him right now. He's endured more this last week and a half than many people go through in a whole lifetime, and hasn't Dr Warne told him to go gently with everything, however 'normal' he might be feeling?

'Joel Easton? Don't know him!'

'I think you *would* know him, Nat. If you were to see him!'

'How's that then, Luke?'

Fear's licking him now with its long, rough, stinking tongue. As it's done several times these last few days, face to face with nasty-minded, insensitive, pitiless hacks, of which this one sitting on *his* chair by *his* bed in *his* room is the worst. Does he really want to go to Uni to learn their skills?

'Because it was Joel you gave that package to on the Monday afternoon. You asked him if he would be so kind as to post it for you next day,' says Luke Fleming, 'you know the item I'm talking about? The jiffy bag you addressed to The Manager, The Cooperative Food Store, 59-63 Church Street, Lydcastle, Shropshire.'

His experiences out in the wilds, all the wind and sun, have left Nat with quite a tan. So hopefully his blushes won't show up like they normally would. Because he *is* blushing! What a strangely instantaneous response a blush is! Why can't a human have better control over the process? There is surely no equivalent in the animal kingdom.

He thought he'd taken care of absolutely everything.

Of absolutely fucking everything!

Think of what he was thoughtful enough to do…

Obviously Nat hadn't wanted any guy he entrusted the parcel with to know his name or where he came from. Therefore he couldn't put his dad's name on it, or that of the kite shop either. So he fixed on, as addressee, the manager of the Lydcastle store where Pete Kempsey was best known, being a hundred per cent sure, once that lady had opened it, and seen its contents, she'd take it straight up to him at High Flyers. As indeed she did!

So his helper was called Joel, was he? Name suits him, he thinks. Back he comes into his life, if only in the form of a memory flash.

He himself was standing on the metal bridge close by the little hostel-cum-cafe, Tan-y-pistyll. He had just thrown his mobile phone (item number one of his plan) down into the river which the waters of the great fall form after their descent from the rock plateau. And nobody had seen him do this. He let himself enjoy for a few moments the flying spray on his head and shoulders. And then he noted this guy roughly his age, perhaps a year or two older, coming onto the little bridge from the lower reaches of the Afon Rhaeadr valley. He had a dog with him on a long leash, the sort Nat liked best, a Border Collie, after so many centuries indigenous to the region. Black and white, but with tan on the legs and paws. Nat stretched out a hand and started to make a fuss of him. The owner was pleased at this, adapted his stance to suit Nat's attentions, and told him the dog's name was Mister. 'This valley's one of Mister's very favourite walks. We live just the Oswestry side of Llanrhaeadr-ym-Mochnant, we do, and we often get in the car and go for a good long walk out here.' Nat took to him, not least for talking about the collie and himself as 'we', and thought, 'He's just the reliable sort of guy I'm looking for.'

So there and then he asked him the favour, the wording of which he'd rehearsed so many times, hoping for a break like this. Though reality had exceeded hopes.

'I've been so stupid and selfish, I promised on my honour to send this parcel off today (it's already got the stamps on it), and then – can you believe it? – I clean forgot. I don't have a car, and anyway it's too late for the post office now, and I'm joining up with a friend in a minute for two nights' camping and trekking in the mountains. On the far side of this waterfall. You couldn't possibly be so good as to…?' Nothing odd or suspicious about all that, was there? Anybody could tell he didn't belong to a terrorist group, or form part of a perversion ring. Certainly the young man with the dog from the Oswestry end of Llanrhaeadr bought the story whole, didn't even blink. Untruths can flow out of someone as easily as (more easily than) perfect truths…

Nat's silence impresses Luke. It speaks the volumes he's been expecting and wanting from him.

I've already wafted my trump card in the boy's face, that journalist thinks, now I have to display it properly. A man has to do what a man has to do.

'The first Joel knew of your disappearance, Nat, was when he read my own piece last Saturday. As soon as he saw your photo, he knew what he must do, and he did it. He contacted me through the paper. Said he hoped what he had to say might prove helpful. You were still missing then, remember. You weren't found till later that day. Still, what he said set me thinking, even when all the jubilation at your being found was at its strongest. And yesterday morning when I read the other papers, I thought some more. Mean-minded sods those reporters, I'll grant you. Still they made some sound points… I'll pay Mr Easton a little visit, I thought. His home is not exactly the other end of the world from me. I'll see what joy I can get from him.'

Nat still doesn't speak. Judges it best not to.

'I guess you overestimated our wonderful, unequalled British mail services. Imagined – pardon the pun! – that what you sent would arrive in a *jiffy*! Well, you don't need to be told that it didn't reach the Co-op until Friday, after several days of people going frantic about you. There was a near miss even then, as I understand. Co-op Manager Joanne Gladwyn opened the package all right, but would have thrown the whole thing into the bin for recycling, had she not seen the name inside the notebook. Your name! Then, bless her, she raced up here, to your dad, where the packet and its contents must have come near to giving him – and your mum too, because she was here also – massive heart attacks. Shock and awe on a Quentin Tarantino scale!'

As if Nat hasn't imagined the scene a billion times. As if (worst admission of all) he hadn't taken it into consideration when he planned the whole thing. As if it hadn't nagged at him since – constantly. What if Dad had had a heart attack, or Mum fallen down into a faint, and hit her head on some hard surface and cracked it open!

Who does this smirking git think he is?

Luke Fleming now leans forward on his chair. Automatically Nat tilts himself away from the man, so sinking his head into the mound of pillows. Spells of dizziness are a major legacy of what he's recently been through. Whether or not he realises Nat is having a mild attack of these, this *Marches Now* writer is pleased to continue his pursuit. His tone is, if anything, lower and, more menacing, while paradoxically more relaxed than ever. 'So let's recapitulate, shall we, Nat?'

'If you must!' he mumbles, half into the pillow but still keeping Luke in focus.

'You leave Lydcastle early Monday September 21, morning after the town's Michaelmas Fair. Your dad's kept his shop open all weekend and till later hours than usual, so he's pretty shattered and is having a bit of a well-deserved lie-in, and might well not open up that morning at all. You leave him a note of what I would call the *cryptic* kind:

Dad, Heading for the Heights xx Nat.

'Of course,' Luke's voice has a purring quality now – he's so well pleased with himself he really does suggest to Nat the cat who's swallowed the cream – 'nobody knew what you could mean by your word "Heights". Which was, I presume, why you chose it, eh, Nat? I mean "Heading for the Heights" is not exactly a normal way of telling a father, or anybody else for the matter, where you're off to. Wouldn't you agree?'

Nat refuses to agree – or disagree. Yes, he's smart, this toe-rag, this prick, but maybe (he can only hope) not as smart as he thinks, or indeed seems, at this moment.

'Anyway your note gives the police a *high old time*, to coin an apt phrase.' And still he doesn't like bullies. 'Up they all go, members of the force and their helpers. To all those obvious heights near Lydcastle: The Long Mynd, Corndon, The Stiperstones. No trace of you there. Funny, that?'

Nat doesn't want to be assaulted by the beams from this guy's eyes any longer. So determinedly he screws his own tight shut.

But Luke isn't deterred by this childish response.

'Attention moves to take in The Clees, and The Strettons, even The Wrekin. Yes, Nat, you'll always, to the end of your days, be able to say you had the cops going *all round the Wrekin*.' He doesn't just smile here but actually laughs, and appears to have the nerve to think Nat'll laugh too. (As if his thoughts ran in this kind of way. This journo is judging others by himself, which, in his pathetic case, is a bad thing to do.) 'And then everybody was beginning to think. Well, if the boy isn't in the vicinity of Lydcastle, then mightn't "heights" apply to Snowdonia? Not too far away for a lively adventurous lad… By now operations must be costing police and tax-payers a pretty packet, I'd say. But then they shouldn't be thinking of anything so sordid as costs in a matter of life and death, should they…?'

'For Christ's sake!' For halfway through this q-and-a exchange – which has in truth degenerated into an 'a's session on the part of the questioner himself – Pete Kempsey, who was listening at the base of the stairs, has walked up them again to hear what his visitor's saying, and what Nat, as it were, is not. But this last comment about police expenditure (something which has been tormenting him these last days) has brought him to the closed door. And hearing the compound word 'life-and-death' is just too fucking much. He must put a stop to it.

The sound of his approach has made Nat open his eyes on the world again all right. There's his dad in the doorway, all red in the face, puffed and obviously furious. And to be reckoned with. Nat feels a rush not just of gratitude but of respect for him.

'For Christ's sake,' Pete goes again, 'lay off him, Luke. I won't have my boy given any more of this. He's not well, for a start. Can't you see that, you dickhead?'

His interrogator, he's glad to see, wasn't expecting an eavesdropper, which was a bit dim of him. (This is his dad's house, after all.) Got carried away by his own sadism. And now he does seem (gratifyingly) embarrassed at being caught out, like those blokes guilty of Special Rendition who've argued they didn't know what they were doing. Another thing – he clearly hasn't expected sloppy-seeming Pete Kempsey to speak as a man of moral authority.

Pete hasn't finished. 'Print what you like, Luke, in that arse-wipe you write for,' he goes, 'we can both stand it. The important thing is that Nat is safe and sound and here. With me. Alive. Compared with that, I don't give a toss!'

But Luke Fleming is far less disconcerted than Nat hoped. 'Agreed, agreed,' he says, 'I'm human, aren't I?' ('And what does *that* say in your favour?' Nat mutters to himself, for his thinking on this very subject has undergone a significant change up on the Berwyn Heights.) 'But every one of us, Pete, has a duty to be truthful. Otherwise we're done for. Accountability's the name of the game in this world, whether you're politician or – or a successful A Level candidate. And if the truth is hard to come by, then we must get at it, whatever it takes. Any journalist worth his salt will agree.

'So when we have the truth about Nat's whole story crystal clear before us, then yes, Pete, and a big yes: "Nat Kempsey's alive and well," we'll say and hold one mammoth party. Invite guests from all over the Marches, the whole West Mercia Constabulary included, and every member of the BBC *Midlands Today* team, right up to the great Nick Owen himself, and, obviously, every inhabitant of Lydcastle, down to the last cat and dog...'

Pete Kempsey gives a weary, wheezy sigh – like an old concertina being squeezed for the last time – as if he seriously doubts his ability to counter-attack here.

'But till that happy time...' Luke ends, 'the truth, and nothing but!'

Nat, well, he silently recalls: Joel Easton. After all the stuff he's been through, he's very nearly forgotten the guy's appearance. Curly red hair, freckled face, a button nose. Taller than himself. And a slight stoop too. But of course he was bending forward some of the time Nat was talking to him, to tickle his dog, Mister.

Well, Joel's proved as decent and kind as he appeared. Never occurred to Nat that precisely this decency and kindness of his would lead him to act, as it seemed to him, in his acquaintance's interests, but, in brute truth, clean against them. Joel went that extra mile all good folk are supposed to go. And he's likely done for the boy he befriended as a result.

That parcel. When Joanne Gladwyn burst into the kite shop and handed it to Pete, who of course recognised the handwriting on the label, he started to tremble so badly he felt his body was falling to bits. And his ex, Izzie, (who also at once recognised her son's scrawl) started to shake as well, despite years of training in calm through meditation. Envoys from the dead, they both said to themselves, trophies to stick on a shelf to prove their son, Nathaniel Robin Kempsey, once lived on this earth.

There were five items in the jiffy bag:

Map of the Berwyns
Postcard of Llanrhaeadr-ym-Mochnant
Postcard of Tan-y-pistyll
Teach Yourself Welsh
Journal: clothbound, unlined 'Paperchase' notebook

The map was in pristine condition. No sign it had ever been used. But both parents knew Nat to be a singularly neat boy, the kind that handles things so carefully they look literally as good as new. On the cover it says, bilingually:

Ordnance Survey Arolwg Ordnans 255
Llangollen & Berwyn, Ceiriog Valley / Glyn Ceiriog,
Showing part of Offa's Dyke Path /
Yn dangos rhan o Lwybr Clawdd Offa

There's a picture of two guys riding mountain bikes on a rough track with birch trees behind them, and behind those, an alarmingly dark night sky.

The postcards were of unremarkable views; they had obviously been bought for the sole purpose of being put inside the jiffy bag to be received as the longed-for key to Nat's whereabouts. In *Teach Yourself Welsh*, to judge by the red pencil marks, Nat had reached page 48, Chapter 4, Section 6. Both Pete and Izzie found it hard to imagine him applying himself to the sustained learning of any language, so were surprised he'd got so far.

After Brock

How old are you?

Beth yw eich oed chi or (lit.)	*What is your age?* i.e.
Beth yw'ch oed chi?	*How old are you?*
Rydw i'n un deg wyth	*I'm eighteen*

'Eighteen' was right, Nat himself turned eighteen on March 16. And for the last days Pete and Izzie had had to face the ghastly possibility this might turn out to be his last birthday. That he'd never go beyond the statement: 'Rydw i'n un deg wyth.'

And the final item? The journal. Pete had seen Nat writing in a handsomely bound book during his summer stay in Lydcastle, and wondered if he was keeping some record of his days and thoughts. The book was an unlined production of excellent quality, and Pete knew a lot about stationery because before the kite shop he'd first worked for, and later run, Sunbeam Press. Thanks to his godfather, Oliver Merchant.

If he had kept a Journal when Nat's age, and could read its pages now, might he not be better able to come to terms with his eighteen-year-old self, who – for obvious reasons – was haunting him now night and day. That eighteen-year-old Pete who'd left his native Herefordshire town of Leominster one bitter January night, with his friend Sam Price at the wheel, his mind, like his driver's, possessed by news of strange sights, and who'd ended up climbing a Berwyn mountainside beside the very waterfall shown on the postcard Nat enclosed.

The great waterfall gleamed white through the darkness…

He wouldn't go down that road yet. Would not remember his own adolescent eagerness to disappear and what had brought it about. Would postpone for a while the recognition of the invincibility of death, and the appalling, obfuscating greyness that made up its wake.

That notebook. It was by reading it that Izzie and he understood (as they were intended to) that the Berwyns were where they must search for their missing son. Like too many diaries, Nat's journal was very detailed for the first days of writing, and then trickled out into little more than a series of jottings, not all of them coherent. Still, Pete learned a lot from it, as much as he needed and far more than he cared to. And the police (to whom it had to be passed, though naturally Nat's parents made a photocopy for themselves) found it invaluable too.

Two

Secrets

Journal of Nathaniel Robin Kempsey

Yes, there *is* life after A Levels
Doings and reflections June–September 2009
Weather: assume temperature this afternoon is 80° Fahrenheit
To convert to Celsius:
Subtract 32 from your figure – that's to say, subtract 32 from 80
and you get 48
Multiply new figure by 5
5 x 48=240
Divide this last number by 9
Result 26.7
Temperature in Celsius!
Excellent for my first day of freedom.
But is that what it is?

This morning when I clambered off my bed, every section of me knew that in an hour's time I had to forget about my body and the whole being it housed, and just become a moving physical item that must tap out on a keyboard x number of words on y and z as they issued from the brain. Tomorrow I shall get up quite differently, restored to myself. And I'll let the sun pour through my closed eyelids, and imagine that when I open them, I do so as another sentient creature: a baby, for instance (was I really one once?) or an old man in care who can't stand up straight or see properly (which I may become one day, and that's impossible to accept too) or a cat, particularly the long-haired ginger tom who comes onto our balcony, or one of the many foxes in our neighbourhood (though, of course, early morning is when, after a night's adventuring, *they* slink back homewards to sleep).

Dad said, ring me when the whole thing's over, won't you, Nat? That's the nearest he's come to expressing any interest whatever in my exams. I've worked out that *he* must have taken *his* A Levels in 1974. Considering the heavy weather he makes of doing the accounts for the shop, I can't see him sweating away at revision – or even sitting in an exam room. But that's a failure on my part, I suppose. His amazing general knowledge must have come to his aid at some point in his school career surely.

Went home for shower and change of clothing, then took myself to the park near my school and my home. That's Brockwell Park which may well be the Centre of my Universe. Until I find another one, up in some mountainous region or other. I found a place free on my favourite bench by the lake with all the water-fowl, sat down and rang Dad (as requested!!!) on my mobile.

But was he expecting to hear from me? No, plainly not. Sounds like he's been dozing. Is he interested? Well, not much! No more than the next man (who wouldn't be my father). In fact I'm pretty sure he'd forgotten that it was today, Tuesday, that I finished. Typical! All he seems concerned about is me coming up to Shropshire on Sunday to start work for him. He sounds pretty wound up about a £600 power-kite he's got for some young guy who hasn't yet turned up to buy it, and not only can't be contacted by phone, but has failed to answer *four* emails. That's the twenty-first century for you, says Dad, and now is simply not the economic climate to be mucked around by macho retards with no cash. Well, I could have told him that straight off. He falls for these posers regularly... Finally (I must have listened to three full minutes by now) he does get round to admitting he knows what day it is, by asking me how I'm celebrating. Has Mum organised anything? Are me and my mates, me and Josh planning some grand piss-up? (Dad always remembers Josh, because he came up with me last summer to help in the shop, and went into the fields to try out new kites for him. You've got to do something that benefits him for Dad to take proper notice of you.)

I say nothing about Mum's plan for the evening, in case, without meaning to, I sound disloyal. I sincerely respect her good intentions here, but it'll be Doug, Doug, Doug again, I feel sure. Josh doesn't have *his* mega-party till Saturday night. And the morning after that, which may well be a 'morning after' in the usual sense, I shall risk Sunday train services, and travel up to Lydcastle to become my dad's right hand for a few weeks. And now of course he must tell me for the hundredth time that he can't manage the same wages as he paid me in the Christmas holidays. Oh, pay me what you can, I say, just make sure there's enough for us to eat. But he doesn't laugh, in fact sounds a little insulted. 'I don't think, Nat, malnutrition's a problem I'm much worried about at the moment.' Which is a morally wrong thing to say because malnutrition *is* a problem for millions on our planet right now. Then I appreciate it was me who made the 'joke' in the first place. Must watch myself here.

Dad's back to the shop. He talks about... Malaysian hummers, some good new Indian fighters (Tukkels and Tassel-tails) 'and two beautiful Barrolettas'.

'Barrolettas?'

'Nat, I told you about them when you came up at Easter.' Sounds aggrieved. 'They're kites made in one remote village in Guatemala – Santiago Sacatepequez, to give it its proper name.' (And Dad *would* give it, wouldn't he? Whereas I've just Googled it.)

'What do they look like?'

'Well, they look like cartwheels made up of hundreds of bits of brightly coloured tissue paper. The roundness and brilliance symbolise the sun which the old Mayan culture put at the centre of everything.'

'Well, isn't it? I wouldn't like to live without it.'

Dad doesn't respond to my little joke but goes: 'I've been trying since forever to get a Barroletta, then earlier this year I had a lucky break. Met this bloke from Central America who struck me as really 'simpático', Juan-Felipe. Knows Guatemala like the back of his hand, which remote village has this or that ancient tradition and so on. So he's bringing a pair of Barrolettas over for me. They'll cost me an arm and a leg, but there we are. Well worth stocking. Not that they'd interest the kind of customer I mentioned earlier, who's failed to turn up for his power-job. Or would they…? I wonder. One kind of kite man is potentially another kind, in my view.'

Dad does a hell too much wondering.

I let him wonder now without listening too attentively, second-nature to me once Dad gets going… Overhead is quite cloudless. Bright bars of sunlight stripe the still surface of the lake. All the people sitting or shambling about near me look as pleased with the afternoon as I am: the young mother with a toddler and her friend, both in burkas, the old coffin-dodger with a paper-bag full of stale bread for the ducks. They're like the original Mayan makers of Barrolettas: they're putting the sun at the centre of life. Not worrying their arses off whether Gordon Brown will be toppled by an insider coup, or whether the pound is holding its own against the dollar and the euro, or whether you have to get straight As in your exams to have even the faintest chance of getting anywhere in 'the precarious global job market'. Far better, we (they and I) think, to concentrate on the mallards on the lake, their bottle-green heads glinting in the afternoon brightness. But every now and then those heads disappear, these birds upending themselves to keep cool.

To change the subject, or rather to change it back, I say, 'What did *you* do when it was all over, Dad? Your A Levels, I mean. Was it hot like it is today? You go for a swim? Have a barbecue?'

If my dad hadn't deliberately fixed on somewhere as far away from London as the Welsh Borders when he left Mum and me, I might know the answer to this question, and others like it. Most guys know far more about their dads' life, and favourite pastimes, groups, books, football teams etc than I do about mine (and Dad's rather a talkative man, though he does also have unfathomable bouts of silence). But, 'I've got to get away,' he said to Mum and me, 'don't take this wrong,' well, how else could you take it? 'I badly need my own space…'

For a moment I thought my mobile had gone out of range, as it sometimes does out of doors. I was expecting some reply to my normal-enough son-to-father question. 'You still there, Dad?'

Dad goes, 'Yes, still here, Nat.' But his voice is faint. Then there's another pause.

The phone feels heavy in my hand and lifeless against my ear. Then he says, 'A swim? Well, hardly, Nat! I didn't take my A Levels in summer. I took 'em in dead of winter.'

'Bit unusual, wasn't that, Dad?' I say, 'at least for nowadays it would be.'

Dad answers me in the slow, remote voice I associate with the year I was just remembering, when I was twelve and he and Mum split up.

'"Unusual", Nat, is about right for my whole A Level year,' and his remoteness has, I realise, nothing to do with miles, or the quality of the line between South London and South Shropshire, 'and unusual years mean unusual measures…' I can tell he doesn't want to talk any longer. 'Well, give my love to Izzie – to your mum, won't you, Nat?' Yes, he's clearly dying to be shot of this conversation, and to return to his own thoughts, if not actions, about how best to get that macho retard to fork out six hundred quid for something he probably no longer wants. But then comes a little surprise. 'I know I haven't asked you if you've done well in your papers, Nat. But I don't ask that sort of thing. Not ever, as you must've noticed by now.'

Noticed? Well, yes!

'Give me a bell Sunday morning when you're about to get on the train at Euston, there's a good lad!'

Something in this talk bothers me. Why should anyone know when his dad did his A Levels and what the reason was? Whatever the reason in this case I now feel quite tensed up (probably a carry-over from this morning's exam paper), and I stretch myself out on the park bench which the old guy has now vacated, and go into relaxation. That means screwing my toes up tight against the sole of my foot (this is what Mum recommends from her own relaxation classes down in Camberwell), and trying to imagine myself into a peaceful state of being that contrasts with the present. Like an animal in hibernation or stretching out for a predator-free doze, such as badgers or foxes enjoy.

Nothing, I have found, is harder than trying to conjure up really different weather from what's around you. I attempt to picture my dad walking out of his exam room into the 'dead of winter' but can't. Sun's too strong, sky's too blue, strips of light on lake too dazzling.

I heave myself into a normal sitting position to write all the above. I'm making an effort to be literate – impressive even – I do want to be a journalist after all so I'm thinking about my readers all the time rather than writing for myself. Yesterday I went and bought this notebook. I liked the marbled cloth covers, patterned with birds and cones, and it's thick enough to last me till I go off to Uni (if I do). Reminds me of the time when Dad ran the Sunbeam Press and produced stationery and diaries for special occasions. I could have anything from stock I wanted, and often I did. That was my childhood, that was. Long ago. Mum said a funny thing the other day: 'It's not till you get to middle age that you start thinking about your childhood.' Well, I do think of mine sometimes already, how it ended, as everything around me did, when old 'Uncle' Oliver Merchant died, though Dad would often say – when he was winding the Press down, and preparing (as we now know) to leave Mum and me – 'It all came to a halt when Oliver married Rosie Roberts, and she decided she wanted to be a business woman rather than a chorus girl!'

Not much point in thinking about all that now. Dad's been in Shropshire nearly six years, back in the Marches where he came from, is independent of us, and running High Flyers.

11.30 pm. Yes, Night Thoughts, like the title of that famous old book of poems. Simply cannot settle down to sleep. Too warm and far too much to think about. Afternoon provided me with an experience I may have made sense of though I can't be at all sure. Writing it down might help.

From the lake in Brockwell Park I walked up to the big Victorian house in Tulse Hill where Josh lives. Wish I did too, well, much of the time I wish this. My mum worries about mortgage repayments, and all she's got for her borrowing is a small flat in a purpose-built block a bit too close to Herne Hill Station. Of course what's important about Josh's home is not its position or architecture or market value, though Josh will tell you these any time (partly because he believes that sub prime and the Lehmann Brothers mark the end of our 'capitalist era', and partly because he likes to). No, it's the house's atmosphere that counts with me. The man the kids call Strop and the woman they all call Strum in their private rhyming slang, but to the outside world Doctors Daniel Malinowski and Joanne Pargeter, of King's College Hospital, each brought children into this rambling place when they married (or whatever), so I'm never sure who's Josh's real brother or sister and who's a step-one. (An exaggeration, I know perfectly well.)

The hall of the house felt good and cool after the Turkish bath heat of the afternoon. There's a bay tree in a tub, and often I like to rub my fingers against its leaves and then hold them to my nose.

'Hi Matt,' said Josh's older brother, Rollo, as he let me in. Rollo often calls me this, not caring what his brother's (in fact *step-*

brother's) best mate is really called. From the little sitting room at the back of the hall came the strains of a violin playing the kind of music I think of as 'mathematics made sound'. It nearly always turns out to be Bach. The violinist had to be Josh's (real) sister, Emily, who doesn't go to our school but to a private all-girls' one nearby. Though younger than Josh and me, she can do many things very well – talk away in French and German, execute classical ballet steps – so that, for all her quietness, she intimidates me. And guys mustn't be intimidated, ever. I intend some time to do or say something that impresses, or at least surprises, her. Hearing this music had the same effect on me as seeing those ducks upending themselves in the water; it refreshed me, eased my tension a little.

'Josh, you know, won't be free to come downstairs for at least a quarter of an hour,' Rollo told me, 'he's busy.'

I went up to the bay tree, doing that thing with the leaves that I like, 'By the way Josh *did* text me just now saying come right over!'

'I know, I know,' said Rollo, 'I was there. He's finishing his black belt practice, his test's next Thursday.' He looked me up and down as if to ask where my training and ambition had deposited *me*. 'But Emily'll be finishing any minute now.' He gestured in the direction of the door from behind which the sweet mathematical sounds were still coming. 'She's having a private lesson with – with Dr Pringle, no less!'

'Really?' Only thing I could say.

'Many, Matt, would give their eye-teeth – and maybe their pudenda as well – to have Dr Pringle teach them. He's consulted by God knows how many high-profile musicians and organisations all over the world,' his voice lingered a little on these words, like it was he who was so famous, 'but he prefers just being a wandering violin teacher, bringing out his pupils' gifts to the full wherever he goes. So it's great for Em for *him* to be giving her lessons.'

Listening to too much brother and sister talk is a pain in the arse for an only child like me.

'Well, it sounds… er, beautiful. Bach?'

'Matt, who the hell else could it be? It's the *Chaconne* from Partita Number 2 for solo violin. In D minor.'

Was there anything this guy didn't think he knew? Standing opposite each other on the marble tiles of the hall floor, we both seemed to realise that the chance of the two of us having a good conversation was zero, so we listened in silence to the music for at least three or four minutes until it came to a stop – like some formula worked out to its close, or bird song that could end in no other way... Rollo, I should have said at the start of this page, must have timetabled leisure for himself this hot afternoon, because he was bare to the waist, and below that wore blue-and-green striped shorts.

'Em will be out now,' he said, 'maybe you'll get a chance to talk to her, Matt.'

'*Nat!*' Well, I owed it myself to remind him once, didn't I?

'Sorry?'

'Nat, N.A.T., short for Nathaniel. Not Matt, short for Matthew.'

Rollo threw his head back in amusement. 'I know,' he said, 'it's just that you don't look like a Nat – and I happen to know quite a few – whereas you seem like a *Matt* in every move you make.'

Luckily for him, the door opened, and first Emily, in jeans and a blue-and-white tank-top, and then this great Dr Pringle stepped into the hall, the latter carrying a violin case. I realised from his way of carrying himself and the sweat on his high domed forehead that the beautiful *Chaconne* I'd just heard had been played not by Emily but by himself.

'Dr Pringle, good afternoon! Em, an admirer of yours is here,' said the infuriatingly officious Rollo, 'he's called Nat!' and he gave me a little wink as he delivered my name correctly, 'these last minutes he's been standing here listening, spellbound.'

'Then it's Dr Pringle who's spellbound him, not me,' said Emily with the honesty I might have expected. She didn't, I'll admit, sound as if she cared whether she'd had an effect on me or not. I'm just Josh's undistinguished mate from down the road, Herne Hill way. 'He was playing the Bach piece as it should be played, I just fumble through it. For now!' She clearly had all her complicated family's determination to get things perfect... 'Dr Pringle, this is a friend of my brother, Josh,' (there we went!) 'Nat Kempsey.'

And on hearing this Dr Pringle did a double-take. I've read many times about double-takes but I have never seen one in reality. Now I was faced with the genuine article. For a minute I thought the man was going to fall backwards. He clutched at his violin case as if for support.

'Who? Who did you say?'

'Nat Kempsey,' repeated Em.

'Kempsey?'

'Yes.'

'Nat?'

'Yes, that's right.'

Were we going to go on like this for ever?

'Nat Kempsey!'

Well, it seemed we might... the man thrust his head forward towards me like a tortoise, his small bright eyes examining my face for... well, I couldn't guess what.

Not the usual reaction to my name, if such a thing exists. Feeling I should answer for myself now, saving Emily any further embarrassment, I said: ''Fraid she's right, Doctor! I'm Nathaniel Robin Kempsey, usually known as Nat.'

'*Robin?*' was Dr Pringle's weirdo response to this, 'Robin! Yes, it would be! Of course it would be Robin!'

I swear the guy looked and spoke like he was going to burst into tears. I will try and set down my impression of his appearance.

Tall and in his mid-forties (but I'm not good at older people's ages). Good head of hair, which I think is what's called strawberry blonde, with one or two grey streaks. Very pale blue eyes, like someone had taken hold of watercolour blue paint and then put in rather too much water (that's not original; some arty woman once said it about my grey eyes). Long, strong arms (short sleeves this afternoon) and hands with the muscular fingers you'd expect in a musician. Clothes – dark blue sports shirt and white chinos, both slightly rumpled; the man's clearly not an ironing fanatic like

I am. He has the face of a man of acute intelligence and many worries. It was now twitching with emotion. But *what* emotion? I'm reminded, as I try to bring him to life on this page, of one of those characters you often find yourself sitting beside on the tube or bus who's suddenly troubled by something: the train slowing down between stations, its lights flickering; the sight of a large unattended parcel...

Dr Pringle said: 'Nat, do you live in South London too? I suppose you must if you're a friend of Josh's.'

'Yup, just round the corner. Herne Hill. Close to the station.'

Dr Pringle appeared to struggle for a reply to this far from interesting statement. 'You a musician too, Nat?' was the best he could do.

'Not really, I'm afraid.'

'"Not really!" Why, this guy's tone deaf!' This was Josh who had, without us noticing, come downstairs into the hall. I was pretty glad he was there then because all the time I spoke I was aware of the violin teacher's colourless eyelashes blinking very fast, as though batting away some disturbing memory, and of a look of none-too-flattering curiosity in Emily's wonderful dark (near-black) eyes.

'Josh is being a bit unfair,' I said. 'I almost always know Bach when I hear it, and Mozart and Beethoven too (well, mostly). And some Shropshire mates of mine are members of a pretty successful band, The Tiger's Last Chance – called that 'cause tigers are nearing extinction, sadly. And there's an idea that this summer I'll write a song for them, to play at their gigs.'

But Dr Pringle, I could tell, was having difficulty in focusing on my words. Somehow the preoccupied look on his face reminded me of my dad when (as happens a sight too often) he's gone off on some mental trail of his own instead of concentrating on what other people are saying to him. And when this famous violinist replied, 'Certainly the tiger must be saved. It'll be a disgrace to humanity, if tigers are allowed to perish!' he sounded like he was hauling himself out of some quagmire, and the words weren't the ones uppermost in his mind.

Rollo evidently thought all this notice taken of me (not suffi-ciently important to be called by his right name) had gone on long enough. He said, with an odd concern for his sister: 'Em's playing brilliant as ever, Dr Pringle?'

'I am very pleased with her,' said her teacher flatly. Then turning to me he said: 'I have pupils of *all* different kinds, you know. Whether they're so-called "musical" or "accomplished" isn't a prime consideration with me.' This, one in the eye for Rollo, was said, I felt, because Dr Pringle was stopping himself talking about something else. 'Basically, Nat, I instruct pupils in the Kodály Method.'

This meant nothing to me, of course, although Rollo nodded and went 'Mmm!' But then he'd likely heard about it before, and from the same source.

'It's named after the great Hungarian composer, Zoltán Kodály who developed it for use in the schools of his own country. But it's spread everywhere since, long after he died in 1967. I tend to teach the method through my own instrument, the violin, starting pupils just as early as I can.'

I pulled my most interested face. It must have succeeded.

'But many Kodály teachers begin with no instrument at all – with just singing or chanting, or using hand gestures. We help children to feel their way into their natural birthright of music through their instincts and growing bodies.'

'I wish I'd begun with Dr Pringle earlier,' enthused Emily.

I maybe should have said something like that too, but couldn't think what. I've done a bit of drumming, but didn't say so here because even I know I'm not very good. My dad and mum would have approved of this doctor's ideas, if they could have taken off time from their own troubles to think about them. But to be fair, my dad always encouraged me, as a very small kid, to be free with the paint and paste and paper around the studios at the Sunbeam Press.

I had the odd and awkward feeling that the five of us, Dr Pringle, Emily, Rollo, Josh and myself, were shipwrecked folk marooned in the middle of this tiled spacious hall with its potted plants and basket chairs, without a boat to rescue us.

'I have one of my cards on me somewhere,' said the doctor of music, 'I'd like to give you one, Nat.'

Impressive though it sounded, he mustn't get the idea I was ready to start on this great Hungarian Method myself.

'Thanks,' I said, 'but like Josh here I've only just got shot of A Levels, and this Sunday coming I am going up to my dad's in Shropshire. For a working holiday!'

'Working after exams?' smiled Dr Pringle, clearly doing his utmost, given his very apparent agitation, to sound like a normal man talking to a normal lad.

'A working holiday,' I corrected, 'my dad's not too bad, though he does keep me pretty busy. Specially if I can save him doing stuff he doesn't like.'

Tiny bit unfair perhaps, and here Josh piped up from where he was standing behind me (wrong phrase – Josh has got a deep gravelly voice which some people say I've tried to copy): 'Nat's dad is a great guy, Dr Pringle. And I should know, because I've stayed with him. And worked for him too. He treats you like a mate, never lets stupid little upsets get the better of him. And he's interested in loads and loads of different subjects, always ready for something new to come his way.' Great of Josh to butt in with this nice portrait of Dad, though it's not the picture of him I would make. 'I'd leap at another chance,' went on Josh, 'of going up to Shropshire, and helping Pete in High Flyers.'

I was on the point of saying maybe then he shouldn't go off to Italy next week as planned but join me in Lydcastle instead. But before I could speak, I became aware that Dr Pringle was having what my mum's mum used to call 'a funny turn'. His face had turned so white it was now virtually green, with sweat breaking out of it. So strangely overcome did he look that Rollo shoved one of the basket chairs over to him so he could sit down. And he needed to. He seated himself cautiously, almost gingerly, as though afraid he might collapse.

Then, '*What* was that you just said?' he gasped, sounding more distressed even than over my name, '*HIGH FLYERS?* No, it's not possible.' He closed his eyes, as if he preferred blankness to seeing the people he was with. 'Whatever could *that* be? A travelling quiz show, I suppose.'

Josh stepped in, almost as if avenging an insult. '*Quiz show?*' he echoed. He obviously didn't mind being disrespectful to somebody of high reputation whom it was an honour for his sister to be taught by, '*High Flyers* is one of the leading kite shops in the whole of the UK.'

'…You must forgive me! It must have been what our forebears called "a touch of the sun",' said Dr Pringle.

Then he heaved himself up, a little shakily, from the basket chair, and valiantly tried to give us all a friendly smile. 'Here you go, Nat!' he said, and he took from his trouser pocket a wallet, from which he extracted one of the cards he'd spoken of. He kind of lurched forward, like somebody still not feeling himself, and handed it to me.

While the others made clumsy conversation to see him out and say goodbye-till-next-time in as ordinary a way as they could, I glanced at what I'd been given:

Dr JULIAN PRINGLE
B. Mus D. Mus. (Royal Academy of Music)
M.A. Kodály Music Pedagogy (Kodály Institute)
jul.pringle@yahoo.com

The address below was in Walworth Road. He lived within easy reach of my own home, a convenience I knew I would act on.

'Well, whatever was all that about?' said Josh, 'it was weird!'

'Just a bit.'

'Personal stuff, huh?'

My impression too, though I wouldn't admit this. 'Don't see how!'

'Skeletons in the old cupboard?'

'Not in mine!' I said.

'Well, these last ten minutes have been pretty fucking bizarre,' said Josh, 'so, Nat, why don't we go out into the garden, and, mate, you can test me on some of my martial arts postures.'

After Brock

Though this was handy for him, I could tell he was asking to distract me. (But from what?) That's what I like about Josh; he understands my moods, my states of mind, without prying too closely.

Mum was engrossed in making an Indian meal for my end-of-exam celebration when I arrived back, so I decided I'd keep my day to myself. I probably would have anyway. Mum likes life to be harmonious and 'stress-free'. South Indian food involves great quantities of tamarind and fenugreek, coconut, plantain and ginger, and the little kitchen was already smelling strongly and pleasantly of all these. The two of us, as I had guessed before-hand, were not going to eat by ourselves. Doug McBride would be coming round, as so often, as so *very* often. (I don't mind this as much as that last sentence suggests. I am indifferent.) Ever since Mum, who does admin in a primary school, went on a course about actual and ideal classroom sizes, where Mr McBride was giving a lecture, it's been Doug this and Doug that and Doug whatever. Though his head is buzzing with budgets and long-term forecasts (he's spectacularly unlike my dad in this, as in other respects), Doug does his best with me to be a laid-back regular guy. But he gives his true anorak self away in so many ways. Like: 'I can't help worrying, Nat, that all *three* of your A Levels are what we nowadays call s*oft* subjects. I wonder why your teachers didn't point that out to you. Those choices could go against you when whichever-University-it-is has to decide about its new intake.'

'Even the University of Bedfordshire?'

'I'm sorry. Why should that have different policies from else-where?'

'*Bed*fordshire. Beds are usually soft, aren't they? Unless they're futons.'

'Ah, I get it! But, seriously Nat, I have reason to think a number of top universities have "black lists" of subjects (meaning the soft ones). They tend to get lumped as things that only certain kinds of students take.'

45

'Well, I just went for the subjects I was any good at, Doug. English Language, English Literature, Media Studies. End of...!'

But tonight he was fairly bearable, talking away about India where he went some months back on a fact-finding visit. A lot of people would have found it interesting, but I can't say I exactly did because half the time (at least) I was aware of the rapt look on Mum's face. She was looking very nice tonight, had taken trouble to do so after she'd finished in the kitchen. She'd tied her sandy-coloured hair in a brief pony-tail, and wore her best peacock blue top. I don't look like either of my parents much, but I've inherited Mum's wide-apart set of eyes, though hers are a green-flecked brown, not grey. Doug greatly appreciated her appearance, I could tell.

The meal was delicious, as Doug said at least a hundred times. First we had *sambar* or vegetable stew, with aubergines, tomatoes and yellow cucumbers; then *rasam,* a soup made from tamarind juice and lentils, but Mum serves it up with rice and yoghurt-soaked fritters. Before we tucked into all this though, Doug produced a bottle of champagne to toast me and my results. So there we go! I still can't see why Mum prefers (at least I assume she does) a nerd like Doug to my dad. But then of course it was Dad who wouldn't stay with her/us, wasn't it?

Once I was by myself again and in my own room, I knew what I would do – I would go to the bookshelf on which stands the omnibus edition of *Sherlock Holmes Short Stories* which was Dad's as a boy. I knew I'd never thrown away that scrap of paper marking the whereabouts of that awesome story, 'The Speckled Band'. Quite yellowed with time it is. I took it out, and you might have thought I was deciphering code.

November 30 & Dec 7 1973
Violin lessons to Julian Kempsey given at
'Woodgarth', Etnam Street, Leominster
£7
Received with thanks Dec 7th 1973
Gregory Pringle L.R.A.M.

After Brock

The idea that comes to me is, to quote Josh, 'pretty fucking bizarre', and I don't know how I will get to sleep with it pressing on my mind. But I no longer have an exam to wake up early for. So why not, once Doug has left, and Mum is in her room, creep out of the flat, out of the whole building, and follow one of our local foxes – or better, a pair of them? Sleuth them to their dens, or stopping places? I love their slinking gait, their graceful muscular jumps of walls and defiance of gates or fences, their capacity for rapid movement while completely keeping their cool. There's nothing London foxes like better (this is hard fact) than fish and chips, so a good place to wait for them is the quietest spot near a chippie you can find. If you're properly patient, a pair will emerge from somewhere you've never suspected any creatures could be hiding, and – snap! – like lightning they've snatched a bit of batter-soaked cod or a few greasy congealing chips spilled from some wrapping. Then off they dance with their finds into the recesses of Herne Hill and Camberwell gardens and backyards. And I like to go with them.

Next morning, I didn't celebrate No School by dawdling over breakfast in the kitchen after Mum had left for work. Instead I left the building, crossed the road, and made for the 68 bus stop. Amazingly a bus came along as soon as I arrived. But traffic was heavier than normal and was held up for so long at Camberwell Green that I was tempted to get off and walk. But it's a long haul to where Camberwell Road becomes Walworth Road, and Dr Pringle, I knew from the number on his card, lives at least halfway up. And I didn't want to arrive at his home sweaty and breathless, but cool and collected, with both my curiosity and my social skills intact.

I could, of course, have rung him beforehand to check he'd be at home, but I hate speaking on the phone to someone I don't know well. And though I had his email address, I'd no idea how often the doctor looked at his messages. Mine might hang around in cyberspace a long time, possibly for the rest of the week, which wouldn't suit me at all.

His house was in a perfectly ordinary terrace on the Kennington side of the street, less well looked after than its immediate neighbours and, like every other in the row, divided up into flats. I guessed the doctor went out to teach pupils rather than saw them in this unprepossessing place. I felt nervous and bold, both together, as I walked up to the door. Above the second bell from the bottom I saw the name PRINGLE in handwriting, tacked on with a piece of sellotape.

'Yes? Hullo? Who is that?' came the voice through the speaker. It didn't sound quite like the voice I'd heard at Josh's yesterday, as it was speaking in a whisper, but on the other hand it didn't *not* sound like it either.

'It's Nat Kempsey!' Considering his reaction to my name yesterday, I couldn't rule out a strong response today. Perhaps he'd give a strange cry and faint dead away up there in his flat... But in fact his disembodied voice betrayed no surprise that it was me down there on his doorstep, which I found odd in itself.

'Nat?' he repeated, and this time he sounded, like, pleased. 'Well, you must come on up? I'm on the first floor.'

And seconds later the door gave a little squeaky sob, and opened for me.

The hall and stairs were as depressing as I'd expected from the house's exterior: lino and cheap drugget, and a faded brown wallpaper, torn in places, with a pattern of cream leaves.

Dr Pringle, dressed as yesterday, was on the landing outside his private front door, to greet me. In the stairwell's half light he looked younger than yesterday, but then, of course, he'd just finished playing, which must be tiring. 'I *thought* you'd come and see me,' he said quietly (and very nicely), 'but I hadn't, I must admit, predicted it would be first thing this morning.'

'Sorry about that!' I said, 'but there's no time like the present, is there?'

'Very true!' said Dr Pringle, 'and I wish more people acted on that principle... But – please come inside.'

After a hall with four other doors opening off it, we walked into a large sitting-room, not exactly cluttered, but as full as could be before that becomes the right word. It was plainly a practice room too. There were two music stands (well, maybe Dr Pringle did sometimes give lessons at his home). A net-curtained bay window looked out onto Walworth Road itself, the panes dusty. Otherwise the room, considering all the stuff it contained, was in good enough order. The walls were almost entirely covered by shelves holding books, CDs, vinyl records and scores, there was a shabby but comfortable-looking sofa and armchairs, a large desk stood by the window and on top of it were papers stacked in piles held down by glass paperweights, half-a-dozen framed photos and two potted yuccas.

'I can make you some coffee if you'd like some, Nat?' said Dr Pringle, 'and then we can talk. But we shall have to do so in a low voice. My wife is ill, you see.' He gestured to the wall. 'She's had a bad night. I'm afraid she often does!'

My mum's mum was ill for over six months; it was horrible. I should be less scared of ill people than I am.

'Sorry to hear it, Dr Pringle,' I said, 'yes, coffee'd be great.'

While he was out of the room, I went over to the desk and looked at the framed pictures. Two, wording at the bottom told me, were of the Zoltán Kodály Pedagogical Institute of Music, Kecskemét, Hungary. One showed a long, curved, whitewashed building approached by a walled flight of steps standing by which was Dr Pringle himself, even younger than now. The other was of a corridor inside, whitewashed, cool-seeming, particularly to a Londoner on a hot day like today, its arches revealing views of greenery. The music teacher was in *this* picture too, and, as if to prove his status, was actually carrying his violin case. This was the place, the institute, the degree on his card came from, I supposed. A third photograph showed the great man himself, Zoltán Kodály (I must Google his biography!), and a very nice face he had. Obviously the face of someone who cared about children having their natural musical heritage. Old and bearded and wise, eyes half-closed, right hand resting on the coat of a fair, charming-looking young woman. I guessed her to be, despite the immense gap in their ages, his wife, partly because, before all the rupture, my dad would sometimes put his hand on my mum's sleeve in just that contented way. Dad loved Mum at such times, I feel sure, but it's difficult to sort this stuff out.

A fourth photo showed a different woman, dark, plump-faced, sallow, in a black, high-collared coat. Though she looked many years older than him, I had no sooner turned my gaze on it than I reckoned this was the woman in the next-door room, the wife who was 'ill, you see', and who had just had a bad night, as she often does, he was afraid. For Mr Kodály a many-years-younger wife, for Dr Pringle a many-years-older one. I surprise myself with my intuitions quite often.

The sixth photograph was of a large old church, of dark pink stone, with a square tower. Underneath it, in old-fashioned, sloping, imitation script sprawled the words 'Priory Church, Leominster'.

Leominster, where Dad had been born, where he had spent his early years, but where he never (I'd noticed) wanted to go, even though he now lived and had a business not far away. He rarely spoke of his life there. When I'd told Josh I didn't know of any likely skeletons in the family cupboards, I wasn't being quite honest. My dad, unlike my mum, is a secretive person.

And having seen the photo I knew what my first remark to Dr Pringle should be when he returned. It was brilliant. After it everything would have to be revealed.

Coffee was certainly taking its time. I stood there by the desk looking again at each picture, and planning how the conversation might go after my opening gambit. But when eventually Dr Julian Pringle did come back into the room, with a tray holding two steaming mugs, a sugar bowl and a plateful of dark chocolate digestive biscuits, he started asking me about how many sugars I took – and, ridiculously, that threw me.

So what I came out with wasn't this piece of brilliance at all. But not all that bad. 'You said just now you *thought* I would come round to see you today?'

'I did, yes! And if *you* hadn't in some way got in touch with *me*, then I was going to contact Emily's parents this evening and ask for your phone number or email. But I'm very pleased it's *you* wanting to see *me*.'

I merely asked: 'Why are you pleased?'

Dr Pringle looked away from me. Balancing his mug a little awkwardly he sat himself down in the armchair nearest the window, then gestured me to take a seat opposite him. 'Surely you don't need to ask that, Nat? I would like to get to know you. You responded to the Bach so well, and the ideas of the Kodály method.' And he gave a quick nod in the direction of the photo of the composer with his young wife.

That can't be the real, let alone the principal, reason for him wanting to know me? I thought, somewhat put off my stride. Best for one of us at least to be more direct.

'I think you know my dad?'

'Know?' repeated Dr Pringle, now looking me full in the face, 'no, I'm sorry to say I do not.'

I was shoved even further off my stride now, and this made me oddly agitated. I stirred my mug with unnecessary vigour. 'But...' I began, then other words failing me, 'Leominster,' I said. And this time it was my turn to nod in the direction of a photo, of the great Priory in the Herefordshire market town.

Dr Pringle was, I now saw, every bit as ill-at-ease as myself. 'I said I don't *know* him. But I *knew* him. Of course I *knew* him – years and years ago, it all was.'

'I was sure of it.'

'How *is* Peter?'

Dad's always called Pete, he's quite insistent about this. He even wants *me* to call him Pete now. Well, he's better at being a mate than a parent, which is why Josh got on so well with him. So for a split second or two I didn't know who Dr Pringle was talking about. 'He's very well,' I said lamely, then remembering how the kite business was limping along, 'he's got worries, of course. Business ones, I don't know about any others. He and my mum separated six years back,' I added, in case he wasn't aware. Which he plainly wasn't.

'That must have meant hard times for them both,' he said diplomatically, after a pause. 'I heard you were born, of course, but otherwise – well – I have had no news about Peter's married or domestic life. Why should I?' Yes, why should you? I thought to myself. But again, why *shouldn't* you?

'Are you the only one?'

I didn't follow him.

'Only…?'

'Peter's only child?'

I gave a laugh as well as another over-energetic stir of the coffee-mug. 'As far as I know, yup! And I'm quite definitely my mum's only one too!'

For at least half my life I have regretted this. I've often envied Josh his brothers and sisters. Mine's been a lonely lot. I've never even had what I once pined for even more than siblings, the company of an animal in my home. Perhaps this explains my present habit of tracking of foxes in the night.

'And Peter's business in Shropshire? A kite shop, isn't it? Apologies to you and Josh for not having heard of it. Sometimes it's hard for me to know anything much beyond my music.' This I found easy to believe. 'And my wife and her sad condition,' he added quickly. 'But Peter's shop – is it really called High Flyers?'

There was a strange smile, or, more accurately, shadow of a smile, playing on his face. Which made it seem youthful. Now I could imagine he'd been a small boy once.

'Has been called that for five and a half years – since it started,' I said, a bit defensively.

'I suppose he named it *after* the quiz show?'

That was the second time Julian Pringle had mentioned this subject, and there was something about his manner that made me uncomfortable.

'I think that "high flyer" about describes a kite,' I said. 'There's a well-known kite shop in Chester, which Dad is in regular touch with, called Kites Aloft. Well, the name he chose for his shop follows the same idea.'

'But it was also the name of a highly successful radio programme in the early seventies,' said Dr Pringle.

First I'd heard of this.

'And was my dad connected with the programme?'

'*Connected*?' Dr Pringle looked positively aghast at my question, 'well, of course! A star, you might say. And can you be surprised when he was such an astonishing, precocious storehouse of knowledge? But surely you know about all this?'

Surely I did not.

But, as we were both searching for what to say next, a bell sounded – a harsh sort of ring, from the other side of the book-covered wall opposite me.

'Ilona, my wife!' said Dr Pringle, 'I shall absolutely have to go and see to her.' Indeed he would, for again the bell came, like an urgent cry, only seconds after its first clang. 'But this is a difficult conversation, Nat, difficult in the extreme – and for both of us. I'm a clumsy man in this sort of respect. Scribble your postal address down on the pad on my desk, and then let yourself out, would you? And I promise you that I shall write you a proper letter this very day. *Not* an email, definitely not that, for it must be a *really* private communication that nobody could spy on a screen or hack into. No, I shall send you an old-fashioned letter, even if computer written.'

And the bell rang a third time, loudly and more agitatedly.

I felt as though, if in the kindest, gentlest way, I'd been expelled from the Pringles', slung out of the premises by that awful pitched bell and, just when I was on the brink of knowing more, of having an evening and a night's disturbing speculations confirmed. I didn't feel like going back to an empty house – I almost regretted the lack of any exam to 'look forward to' – so instead, with this heavy, let-down sort of feeling in my stomach, I cut across from Walworth Road towards the Old Kent Road where I knew a good place to have (another) coffee and a pastry or two.

And all at once I remembered Oliver Merchant, Uncle Oliver as he was to me being my godfather, who had a habit of singing me some song about the Old Kent Road on his rare visits during my childhood to the Camberwell house we lived in then. Uncle Oliver was fattish with a protruding tummy and a mane of white hair, and a habit of wearing fancy waistcoats (which showed the tummy to bad advantage) and quite often a spotted bow tie. Uncle Oliver had been Dad's godfather too, and the founder of Sunbeam Press itself. So this was a song, in more ways than one, from pre-history, but somehow remembering it helped banish the disappointment and sadness left me by my call on Dr Pringle.

Well – Josh had his mega-party last night (Saturday, but it was two hours into Sunday before I got home). I'm writing this now in my journal book on the train journey up to Shropshire, despite a horrible headache, like I've had slithers of iron rammed behind and above the eyes. Easy to understand why they talk of headaches as *'splitting'* because my head really does feel it might break into two pieces (at least). Every now and again, like when the train lurches fast round a bend, I almost believe that's what it's going to do. Mouth and throat seem clogged with furry stuff yet extremely dry too. When that trolley comes round again, with that friendly guy not so much older than me wheeling it, I'll buy a *third* bottle of sparkling water, and hope it does more to rehydrate me than the previous two.

Josh called it, before, during (and probably after – though didn't see him after) *his* mega-party, to celebrate the end of his (our) school years, but really it was a family event with Josh's mother trailing through house and garden in a scarlet gown with a red rose in her hair, cooing at everybody, and his step-dad in shorts strolling from group to group like a man who thinks he's at once the wisest and the sexiest thing going. I went round to Josh's early to help set things up. There was to be a barbecue, lights strung through and between the horse chestnut and the crab apple trees, and a platform for the band; also long trestle tables had to be carried out of the house and placed on the lawn (looking pretty parched after so much relentless sunshine). Rollo, naturally, put himself in charge of operations. 'No, *not* at that angle, Matt, we should position it quite a bit further to the right. No, not that much further, airhead, that'd block access to the drinks table.'

I was surprised at the amount of meaty things on offer, stuff my mum and I, as vegetarians, would refuse. My disgust that so many dead animals and birds had been thought necessary for all these, mostly very well-heeled, guests gave me a sudden feeling of licence to behave exactly as I wanted. I helped myself from as many bottles as I could, as well as from the jugs of Pimm's, and opened more cans of both ice-cold lager and blood-temperature beer than I care to count. I discovered a tremendous pleasurable recklessness the further into doing this I got. In addition, I snatched people's glasses or beer cans when they weren't looking. Considering the length of time I was there, you will realise that I put inside me a mighty river, if not a great lake, of alcohol. I can't say when it was I understood this myself, but I thought it a spiritual condition more than anything else.

'Hi Em!'

As if it took her a moment to recognise me, 'Oh hullo, Nat!'

'Decided what you're going to do, Em, when this party comes to an end? Like all good things do.'

'Do you know, Nat, that you've said both those sentences to me already tonight?'

I was a bit taken aback to hear this, but wasn't going to show it. 'Worth asking twice, though, 'cos I badly want to know the answer.'

She looked heart-melting in her white dress which glinted in mesmerising places thanks to the play of the lights that I personally had put up in this particular section of the garden.

'We're only halfway through the party, at the very most. I can't think why you're bothering at this stage about what people should be doing in a couple of hours' time (or more). And, by the way, my name is Emily. Only Rollo calls me Em and it's a sort of private joke between us.'

Rollo – I didn't like that guy at all. 'Well, he calls *me* Matt,' I informed her, 'and that's even less *my* name than Em is yours. Fucking arrogant of him, I think.'

'Don't you think you should lay off the alcohol from now on?'

'Kind of you to suggest that, but no!'

With this I swung myself away from her, to appropriate the

glass of white wine that a very tall man with a distinguished beard had unwisely put down behind him, on top of the rockery.

'There are some matters too sad for words, Nat, and this (I admit defeat) is one of them. I got, on our two brief but (to me) immensely valuable and welcome meetings, the strongest impression that, whatever the differences you've had with him, whatever the regret you doubtless felt when he and your mother separated, you have a lively, ongoing, essentially affectionate relationship with Peter. So please understand and respect me when I say that I have chosen (once and for all) not to disclose the history of those early years in which Peter played so important a part in my life. And that, I am one hundred per cent sure, is how Peter himself would want it, in fact how he does want it, considering how much in the dark he seems to have kept you.

'In other words I prefer Peter to stay up on his Heights, and not to drag him back down into the lows we all, sadly, have to dwell in.

'That Ilona and I could have no children (or adopt them, for that matter) has been a great source of sadness to us both. We always have liked the company of young people. Well, I must do, mustn't I? – my work being what it is. If you can accept the above qualifications, I would be so pleased if we could both see you. Ilona's health is such a problem that it's difficult to make any forward plans. We have a system of minders, but even so it might be best for the two of us to meet somewhere away from Walworth Road at the end of some lesson of mine. I shall be here, I think, for the best part of the summer, then in September I shall go to Hungary, for my annual (at the very least) visit and, God willing, Ilona will be well enough to accompany me, and enjoy the landscape and music.

My good wishes to you, Nat…'

Music here in Tulse Hill was represented tonight by a Cajun group, reminder of a 'fantastic' visit to Louisiana and the Bayou country that Josh's parents had made after a 'fantastic' conference at a major New Orleans hospital (where they'd been called in to pronounce as experts on improvements after the city's great flood disaster). Well, the players suited the hot, strangely still evening all right: accordion swelling and subsiding in volume like someone half crying his heart out, half just letting himself go quiet, a fiddle singing alongside him, plangent (the right word?) in its vibrations, and guitar throbbing with the kind of pent-up sexiness I could feel there in my body for Em/Emily – and probably for a number of other girls here, like the one Josh had been talking to most of the evening. Over and again the Cajun melodies swooped and sighed: 'Allons à Lafayette'. 'Allons danser Colinda'. 'Jolie Blonde', streaming through all the garden's greenery and rousing many people old and young to dance, including the very white, very glinting Emily (with Rollo – of course, with Rollo). But not me, I wouldn't risk it, I'm a shit dancer. But tears came into my eyes and a lump into my throat. Sentimental, stupid. When the musicians paused, I went over to them, after having gulped another nicked glass of wine (red this time), and said: 'Why the fuck can't you guys play music from the UK?'

The fiddler (it was to his face I'd delivered the words) said, with a surprised, indignant look; 'Anything in mind, asshole?'

'Something in the nature of "Knocked 'em in the Old Kent Road"!' I said. And walked away towards where the beer cans were on the nearest trestle table.

'There are some matters too sad for words, Nat, and this (I admit defeat) is one of them.'
Well, maybe I won't bother with any more of the party. I'll just record the way it ended for me. No, I will just add one more thing. When Josh's step-dad and I literally bumped into each other and I nearly sent him flying, he asked: 'Where the hell do you think you're aiming?'

And I replied: 'At becoming a professional newshound! I'm a news-freak, you see!'

'Certainly a freak!' he mumbled, 'dead on the nail there!'

'Careful who you're insulting!' I called after him, 'I'm the son of a quiz-show star who was an astonishing, precocious store-house of knowledge.'

He obviously heard. I waited a moment or two then crept along after him to where he met up with his wife. 'Joanne, darling,' he said. 'What's the name of that unappealing boy who's a friend of Josh's, who often hangs about our house? You know, the one with the grey eyes and greyish hair, and a crowded mouthful of teeth? He's just been saying pretty loony things to me...'

Some time after this I sat myself down (with a bump and a thud) on the grass beneath the fine horse chestnut onto whose boughs, hours back, I'd tied the strings of red and green lights now indistinguishable from any exotic flowers that might have sprung up on this very English, very London tree. Josh came over to me and sort of knelt down beside me: 'You're pretty tanked up, you know, Nat.'

'I'm pretty tanked up, you know, Josh,' I said, 'and what are you going to do about it?'

'It's not me who's going to do anything,' said Josh, 'if I were you, I'd take yourself to the remotest corner of the garden – keeping out of the way of any couples – and start sleeping it off. I'll see to it you're left alone.'

'Remote corner of the garden?' I echoed, 'that's just given me an idea. There's a nearby fox I'd like to visit. Lives under a garden shed four doors away. We saw him last week, remember?'

'How could I forget? You're a bit of a fox yourself, Nat. Except a fox is quiet and stealthy and unobtrusive, whereas you've broken your usual party habits tonight. Badmouthing Rollo to his sister –'

'*Your* sister. *His* stepsister.'

'Step, then, and that's none of your fucking business, even if you do fancy her. A fox wouldn't deliberately collide with our dad and talk about freaks either.'

'It was him who called me one!'

Josh paused, crouched a fraction closer to me, and said: 'This is all about Dr Pringle, isn't it?'

Have I already written in this journal that Josh is perceptive as well as understanding about feelings? In hard factual terms I'd recounted very little to him of what passed between Emily's music teacher and myself in his Walworth Road flat. But I must have said enough for him to realise it'd had a strong effect on me. I quoted:

'In other words I prefer Peter to stay up on his Heights, and not to drag him back down into the lows we all, sadly, have to dwell in.'

'What's that supposed to mean? Who's Peter?'

'My dad. You and me know him as Pete.'

'Yes, I do. And Pete would give you the same advice as I just have, Nat. To take yourself off, and hide...'

'But I don't want to do that just yet, I want to visit my friend the fox,' I said, 'preferably not alone. I'd like to go see him in the company of a beautiful girl just like the one standing behind you now, wondering just what a jerk you've got for a friend. But then your step-dad thinks I'm unappealing.'

'As if!' said the girl – her name was Katey, I recalled. Josh had mentioned her to me long before tonight, which he'd spent talking to her for hours among the shrubs and even dancing with her on the lawn. She was not dark like Emily, she was fair, extremely fair, a blonde, 'Jolie blonde', like the Cajun song the band was striking up again, the fiddler double-stopping and bow-scraping like he'd soon go mad with longing for love. Katey went on: 'I know what a nice guy you are, Nat. But maybe you ought to sober up a teeny bit. Try getting on to your feet.'

'Easy!' I said, doing what she had suggested, 'in fact nothing could be easier.'

Adrenalin sped through me. Accordingly my legs felt steadier than they had for at least an hour. I seized Katey by the right hand and pulled her towards the nearest garden wall, and she, thinking it best to humour me, allowed herself to be pulled. We reached the wall's base. 'I'm going to climb up,' I told her releasing my hold of her, 'most direct route to Mr Fox.'

She made some genteel noise of protest, but I wasn't having any, and, surprising myself with my neat, effortless movements, leapfrogged onto the top of the wall. I half-cheered when I succeeded in my action.

Paul Binding

'It's great up here,' I called down, 'why don't you join me? The two of us can run along the tops of several garden walls until we've reached his den. Hope the noise of the party hasn't driven him away, but they're pretty resilient, foxes.' Also, of course, it was late, well gone midnight, and my fox, like many another, would be out searching for food more likely than not. 'He may not be at home, I will admit,' I went on, 'probably round and about scavenging at this hour, but we may get a glimpse of him on his way back. Foxes are much more scavengers than hunters, you know. People get them wrong. Of course they *do* take chickens and rabbits, and personally I wish they wouldn't. But truly foxes prefer finding things to killing. They mean us well, and we should mean them well.'

'I'm sure we should,' said Katey, 'but I don't think you should go looking for any foxes the way you are at the moment.'

'Leave him be,' said Josh, 'Nat always does what he fucking wants. He's not much of a one for reasoning.'

'No, I hate reasoning,' I agreed, and began to move away from the pair along the wall, swaying rather more than I liked, I have to confess, and some wide wobbles brought my heart into my mouth. But by fifty yards I had stabilised myself. Really the garden of the house wasn't so enormous as all their pride in their property made you think. I was out of it and onto their neighbours' wall in a remarkably short time. And, now I had left my hosts behind, I felt a new, most curious energy possess me.

I began to run along the wall, and then the wall after that. Fucking exhilarating, better than any dream, looking down from a height of more than three feet into gardens full of shrubs and brick-sided pools, and rose bushes, with bedroom lights shining down onto the darkened lawns, and a dog (or two?) barking up at me, but nobody anywhere taking a blind bit of notice of my moving presence. I might have had a Kalashnikov with me, after all. Above me London's lights met the night sky in what looked like a huge static barrage balloon and, all in all, though I knew I would pay for it all and in the near future, like now, it was the best night walk I have ever had.

After Brock

But I must have taken a wrong turning, or a wall too many; I hadn't been counting. I looked around me. The garden shed underneath which the fox lived – sheds are foxes' favourite habitat – was nowhere in sight. Been dismantled? Or maybe I'd got the location slightly but significantly wrong. Four doors away, I had told Josh, but I was now looking down on an alley-way. I would have to jump down into it, and cross over if I were to make for any next garden. And the only one I could see into from my eminence, on which my stance was decidedly shaky, was an extremely tidy place, with a big shrub, brilliantly blue in flowers, like a score of little alternatives to the darker night. No shed of any sort whatever. Far too regulated a garden for even the most Londonised fox.

I turned round to see if by any chance Josh or Katey had worried about me sufficiently to have followed me out of the press of people onto my wall-walk. However long had I taken to make it to here? Five minutes? Five hours? Five years? The party was still audible, though muffled, well beyond immediate hailing. Well, even if what was coming towards me wasn't the happy couple, *some* interest had been taken in me; I was definitely being followed along the wall. Nearby house lights were showing me a moving streak of sandy hair, attached to which were two little bright living lights: a pair of eyes without doubt, advancing towards me. Katey on all fours, maybe?

Just in case it was a guest from the party for me to impress, I had to do what the surge of excitement mounting inside me made virtually irresistible. I ripped off my shirt and threw it off the wall down into the entry below – the night was still warm, balmy – and then I let my jeans and boxers tumble to my feet (and thank the Lord I didn't go on to chuck *those items* aside). 'Hi there! *Salut!*' I called.

The being coming towards me stopped, astonished, in its tracks. It was, however, no person from Josh's mega-party, but a fox. Long light-brown proboscis with twitching nostrils; face inquisitive, sensitive, suspicious, valiant; pricked-up ears; eyes of a burning yellow, and a scent strong enough to engulf me in all my nakedness. S/he, I thought, is every bit as much an individual entity as me, and like myself, is driven by wants and needs hard to name.

I'm travelling up to Lydcastle the way I usually do (except I'm not usually hungover; in fact I've never travelled in this condition before!): that's to say, non-stop express from Euston to Crewe, where we invariably pull up at Platform 5. Then up the steps and along the covered bridge and down to Platform 6, to await the southbound train. This sometimes says it's going to Caerdydd (Cardiff), sometimes Caerfyrddin (Carmarthen), and occasionally for somewhere which always, in the English form of its name, makes me think of ships sailing off into cold distant seas, Aberdaugleddau (Milford Haven). Too often with far fewer carriages than the host of waiting passengers requires, this train'll take me through Shrewsbury (that has a Welsh name too, of course, Yr Amwythig) to Church Stretton in the Shropshire Hills. Here Dad'll meet me, as always, in his van (invariably dirty outside and untidy in, full of kiting clobber); most times he manages to turn up late. Then comes the ten mile drive over to Lydcastle, where 'I'm sorry, I should have got some food in,' Dad will say almost as soon as we've arrived 'home', 'but I didn't get round to it, I'm afraid. But there are a few eggs knocking about the kitchen, so could they – with a hunk of bread – do you for now?'

This time I'm coming to Lydcastle a different guy, armed with knowledge of Dad that he's withheld from me, his only son.

[Written same day, 10 pm]

I was right, of course, would have been astounded if I hadn't been. The Caerfyrddin (Carmarthen) train arrived at Church Stretton dead on time, but I had to wait a quarter of an hour for Dad and the dusty van to appear. (Didn't call him on the mobile; he hates being 'rounded up' and grumbles whenever he has been.) But though I minded this just a bit (all the other passengers who'd got off here, expecting to be met, were collected long before me), it felt good (and, in truth, *was* good for my 'morning-after' headache) just to stand still quietly in the yard outside the little country station, washed by the midday sunshine and to look up at the steep-sided hills that rise on either side of this town. I could then feel that those other hills of my life, Herne Hill and Tulse Hill, with Mum and Doug, and Josh and Rollo, and teachers and exams and 'whatever-will-you-be-doing-next year, Nat?' belong to a quite other dimension of the universe. Except that I have to carry myself through both, a being as unique and inscrutable (to myself that is) as that fox on the wall with the yellow eyes.

Obviously I know that lads of my age here in the Marches are having to deal with all the problems of courses and qualifications and 'suitable' jobs just the same as I am. But the landscape here was sending out the message to me that it's possible to see life with different priorities. I'd felt this even before my actual arrival, when the train was approaching Shrewsbury and I could see the high jagged green line of the Stretton hills in the distance, some miles beyond the red sandstone buildings of the town's castle and the grid of old streets that climb up to it.

I caught sight of Dad at the wheel both before and when he caught sight of me. His expression, a dull, heavy, serious one, didn't change a flicker. I found that interesting. You might think that the moment he saw his only son after several months, his eyes'd lighten up, that he might even smile. But no, not at all.

Nor did he apologise for his lateness. (Well, why should he? I wouldn't really want him to.) It's Sunday, the shop's shut, so he hasn't bothered about shaving, and has quite a crop of dark stubble on his face (which seems a bit fatter and redder than when I saw it last, at Easter).

'There you are!' he said in a sleepy voice. As if it was *me* who'd failed to be there in time for *him*. I've always been glad he isn't the sort of dad who throws his arms round you or, even worse, kisses you, but I wouldn't have minded a little more show of enthusiasm on his part. (When Josh came with me, I recalled, Dad was far friendlier in manner right from the beginning, which is why he speaks of him as a sort of mate. With me solo Dad doesn't feel the obligation to come out of whatever mood he's in.)

'Oh, hi!' I said, dead casual too, and jumped in. Underneath the front seat and in the compartment above it was any amount of torn crisp packets, sweet wrappings, used-up cans of Sprite, plus things impossible to identify just from looking.

'We won't be going home over the Long Mynd today,' Dad announced with some firmness. Though I'll be here some time, and will have other opportunities for being on this road, the news disappointed me. It's become an established tradition in my visits to Dad that we start off my stay with this ride, and it's one I relish: the long bendy climb up from Stretton, with the V of the Cardingmill Valley more and more precipitately below, then the journey along the heather-and-bracken expanse of the hill's great plateau, with its grazing sheep (and in some places white horses), and then the wonderful descent when you see Lydcastle on its hillside in the near-distance, and the ridges parallel to the Mynd, like The Stiperstones with its crest of rock piles.

'Why not?' And I probably sounded more put out than I really was.

'Because it takes longer, Nat. And I've got that jerk I told you about, remember, interested in that expensive power-kite, actually coming round to the shop "just after lunch", to use his words. And I literally can't afford to miss him. Why he couldn't have come on a normal week day beats me, but there we are.'

So Dad did have an excellent reason for taking the low road home, which is very nice also with its woods and little river and hill flanks. I'd been a bit hard on him.

'By the way,' he continued, 'I'm sorry but I didn't get round to getting any food in for lunch or supper. Co-op's open today, we can go along later. But there'll be a few eggs knocking about the kitchen, so you can make do with them, huh?'

'I have no fucking alternative, have I?' I could have said, but I didn't. Instead, 'Actually, Dad, I don't feel much like food right now. Don't feel like *any*, in fact. Went to Josh's party last night, and I guess I'm paying for it now.'

Josh, who'd given Dr Julian Pringle such a warm portrait of Pete Kempsey as a matey father, would have not recognised the man he'd praised – we were driving out of Stretton now, southwards along the

A49 with resort-like houses from Victorian times visible on the lower slopes of hills – in the uninterested individual at the wheel.

'It happens, doesn't it?' he remarked, 'well, that lets me off worrying about catering. I shall be really pissed off if this Darren Courtney guy doesn't show up, I can tell you, after having strained every gut in my body to make contact with him. Six hundred smackers, and not a penny less!'

I wasn't sure I wanted to hear any more about this. If Dad could groom himself into having a more impressive manner with customers, he wouldn't have half as much trouble as (apparently) he does. Anyway wasn't it time for me to keep to the plan I'd formed on the train journey up, and which I purposefully didn't write down in this note-book in case I failed to carry it out? (That wouldn't make for satisfying reading afterwards.)

'Dad,' I asked, guilefully, 'what are the comparative heights of the hills around us now? How does the Long Mynd compare with any of the Strettons?'

I must have been told this many times before, mustn't I? But as I don't have Dad's preternatural, enviable memory for facts, I truthfully don't know.

Dad didn't move his head so much as a fraction of an inch, took my question as a hundred and fifty per cent normal one, which it isn't, coming from me, and replied as if giving out figures was as natural as breathing – which it probably is for him. 'Well, the highest spot on Long Mynd is 1,693 feet, and Caer Caradoc – more or less opposite, and probable site of the last great battle against the Romans – is 1,506. But The Stiperstones, that favourite haunt of ours,' ('of *ours*' I noted, pleased), 'is higher still at 1,759. But pride of place goes to the Clees. Brown Clee, over there,' he indicated its whereabouts with a finger of his left hand, 'is 1,772 feet. You could legitimately call it a mountain in my opinion.'

'1,772 feet,' I repeated, 'thanks for the facts, Dad. I knew you'd be able to tell me them. You're a phenomenon, you know that. I've never met any guy who comes anywhere near you. You ought to go on a show. *Mastermind* or something?'

A side glance showed me no evidence of reaction on his face, but then we were approaching an often busy turning-off, and maybe he had to concentrate on that. But then: '*Mastermind*? I don't think so.'

'Why not? They're so popular, those programmes.'

'I thought Google did all that for people now. Anyway, my main reason for not going on such a show is that I haven't the faintest desire to waste my time in that sort of way.'

Dad's eyes were still fixed intently on the road, fuller of traffic than usual, but, well, it *was* a Sunday in the tourist season. And we were rattling along (Dad never has a van that doesn't rattle, so out of condition and cluttered up inside is any in his possession) to make sure we were well in time for this Darren Courtney with his £600... But then an interesting aspect of his reply, of his blank refusal to give quiz shows serious attention, struck me. Struck me so I had to say it aloud. I said, 'You don't deny that you'd qualify. And you're right. Anne Robinson could never find you the Weakest Link, not ever. You seem to know everything.'

Dad shifted himself in his driver's seat, a little uneasily, I thought. Probably realised I was getting at something. As I was.

'In fact, Dad, I have heard you were on a quiz show when you were young. Were a star of it, in fact.'

If anybody's face can ever be said to darken, then Dad's did then. He tightened his mouth so that his lips pressed hard against each other, and he narrowed his eyes. But he didn't brake, just drove on for a minute or two as though I hadn't spoken. In fact I almost wondered if I actually had done. The change of motion (van after train) had done nothing to help my hangover headache, to remove those metal splinters behind my eyes, but despite these pressures of pain, my body (and therefore my mind and my mouth) felt as if it didn't properly belong to me. So...

'Dad, did you hear what I just said?'

This time Dad did, for a nanosecond, move his head in my direction.

'And who the fuck told you about that?'

After Brock

I wasn't going to say who. Not yet anyway.

'I'm amazed at Izzie – your mother – breaking her word. I did tell *her* of course. When we set up together, I told her lots about my life, she was a good person to tell things to. But I made it pretty clear I didn't want anybody else in on them.'

'Dad, it wasn't Mum. Not at all. It was just a bloke I ran into who recognised my surname – your surname – from the radio back in the old days. And I went on Google, and found out that there was a programme called *High Flyers* – the bloke told me its name, you see – back in the seventies, with a quizmaster called Bob Thurlow.'

Dad did apply the brakes now, with an abrupt fierce jerking. He didn't, I suppose, do this purely out of emotional reaction to hearing this name from his past. But that, I have to say, is exactly what it felt like.

'But Google didn't mention *you*.'

'I don't suppose it did, Nat, no!' Coldly. 'I was just one of the many passing through.'

'But a star performer?'

'Enough said, Nat. Can't you sense another person's feelings at all?' This rather hurt me, for I pride myself on being able to do this. Dad's next sentences I wish I could reproduce in some special way other than in letters and words. For they came from him one by one, as if being painfully, slowly, deliberately, yanked out. Like thorns from his skin. Or obstinate hairs from a nostril.

'Of course it's impossible completely to block off something that was once heard by thousands of listeners. I guess I'm reconciled – well, just about – to bumping into folk who do remember my association – my very brief association – with the programme. For a long time I wanted to avoid doing that at all costs so never went back to The Marches, to the West Midlands. But time has passed now, and anyway my attitude to it all has changed.

'If I'd wanted, Nat, to tell you about it, then I'd have done so. Well, now you know. At least the barest details. Yes, I did appear on the show in the seventies, but more than that I'm not saying. Don't wish to. End of.'

Now the road came out from the shadows of beech and oak, and I could see ahead the forms of the hills, up the side of one of which Lydcastle draws its long steep main street. 'I hear what you're saying, Dad,' and truly I'd have had to be totally stone deaf not to have done so, 'but I'd just like to make one point.'

'Point!' repeated Dad, as if it was the most irritating word I could have selected.

'If you hate the whole memory of the programme, why did you name your shop after it?'

Considering the tone in which he had just been speaking, all disturbed and pent-up, I half-expected him to explode at my for-wardness. But the opposite happened. He physically relaxed himself in his seat, and, from this point on, his handling of the vehicle was gentler, and certainly far better for a passenger with head-pain and nausea.

'Because I thought that was the best, the only way, of exorcis-ing the memory,' he said. 'I thought – from its launch onwards the name *High Flyers* will refer to my business and nothing else. It was a good idea. I still think so.'

But it hadn't completely worked, had it?

'Which reminds me, if that Darren What's-it doesn't turn up this afternoon for his power-kite, and with the full payment, I shall hunt him down and fucking *murder* him.'

Once back at Dad's I took two Anadin Extras, which worked within half an hour, and inspected the shop's most recent stock. The Barrolettas were yet to arrive, but Dad said they surely would soon. But there was a new Maori bird-kite, with a sail made out of raupu-vine leaf, and crowned by an eerie big-eyed head; there was a Conyne or French Military kite, tailless, with a two-leg bridle, suited to flying in the most seriously heavy weather (in other words, not the best kind for these hot midsum-mer doldrums, but it looked appealing enough the way my dad had strung it above the window), and an extremely colourful Chinese butterfly-kite. Because I know these are the kites Dad likes best, would really devote himself to completely in his ideal world, I thought I'd postpone examining the other (more popular) items ('our cash cows') until later.

Dad had also put round the walls of the shop numbered posters – of his own design and printing, I could tell, drawing on the skills of his Sunbeam Press years presenting a 'World History of Kites and Kiting'. The first of the posters taught me something I didn't know (or hadn't retained from all the many factual goodies Dad had casually showered on me throughout my life).

We were, it said, in the twenty-sixth century of these 'gentle attempts on the heavens' by humankind. In 500 BCE the Chinese were not only flying kites but having kite festivals on the ninth day of every ninth month. A little illustrated story followed. A Chinese farmer had dreamed a dreadful calamity would befall his household the very next day. So what would be the best way for himself and his family to spend their last hours on earth? Why, flying kites, of course! So out into the fields he took them, to do just that. Meanwhile an accident destroyed their entire house. Kiting had not just relieved anxiety and passed time for them enjoyably, it had saved their lives. And that had all happened on the ninth day of the ninth month...

I was about to move onto the second poster, dealing with kites in Ancient Egypt, when I heard knocking on the door and saw on the other side of its glass, a man in his mid-twenties in motorcycle gear: the miscreant Darren Courtney. Not a bad guy at all, not the 'macho retard' Dad had decided on. The reason he'd been so hard to contact, Darren told us – not replying to *four* emails, for example – was that he and his partner had just had a baby (a splendid little fellow called Belshazzar). Oh, well, said Dad, this is *my* splendid little fellow here: Nathaniel or Nat as we call him. You're still interested in the job I got for you, I hope?

Well, he was, but would, I think, have liked to suggest he didn't pay the full amount outright, but came to some instalment arrangement instead. I think that Dad sensed this and, far from wanting to murder him, would have assented, relieved to get the expensive thing off his hands and to find its buyer was at least halfway honest. But here I stepped in. 'I'm taking over from my father now for some weeks,' I said, 'and, as I've only just arrived, this'll be my first bit of business. I take it you've got your debit card with you, Darren. Just let me set our machine in motion, and then you can key in your PIN.'

And less than two minutes later Dad had the welcome £600 in his system.

Despite this little triumph (well, not so very 'little' really) I noticed that Dad was uneasy with me all day. I shouldn't have tackled him so soon in my stay (within ten minutes of arriving) about his links with this once-famous quiz. Though why dissociate himself from something on which he'd been, as he did not deny, a 'star performer'?

That night I dreamed that I was back on top of those walls that stretched beyond my mate Josh's house in Tulse Hill. It was night-time, as it had been in reality, but my surroundings were lit up by the yellow fiery eyes of the fox pursuing me. Each pad forward this animal made corresponded to a possible answer to questions I hadn't yet precisely formed, even to myself.

A violin tune moaned enchantingly through my sleep, but it wasn't that Bach Chaconne, nor some plangent Cajun tune. 'It follows the Kodály method,' said Julian Pringle's voice, 'and you can hear it in the hills and mountains of the Marches.'

* * *

Reading through the Paperchase notebook now, It's clear that, already exhausted by exams, Nat had used up any energies left by writing so full an account of my life immediately after them. So he abandoned journal-writing proper in favour of largely random-seeming jottings, in deteriorating handwriting (laptops are so much easier) not always dated and probably making no sense to anyone else.

A great many entries concern the shop, its customers, its visitors who might, or should, or in some cases should not, become customers, its calling reps, its new stock, its actual sales. He also put these on a special computer file of his own, although he had Dad's password and inspected his files rather more often than he realised – though Nat *did* tell him! The names of supplier firms – T.K.C. Sales of Steeple Aston, Wind Designs of Ely, Cambridgeshire, Spirit of Air of Newport, Gwent – occur many times. But his private thoughts still went in the journal.

'Dad handled the rep this morning in a laid-back but pretty lazy way, I thought. Must have struck the guy as a pushover for anything he had to flog, and he didn't complain as strongly as we agreed he should do about those two Sky Lanterns that never arrived ('Romantic Chinese Flying Lanterns', which are ace to let float off at the tail-end of a barbecue party – and it's the barbecue season right now.) Why can't Dad see all this for himself? Why does he need me to tell him? And then sulk when I do?'

The same querulous mood prevails in the following regularly repeated, and heavily underlined, sentences. (Handwriting becomes neat again for these):

Kids' kites: single line. Average price £15-£30
Power-kites (adults and teenagers) Average price £150-£300

Wouldn't the obvious deduction from this be to concentrate on the latter?
   Pete Kempsey needs a really good shake up!

On the other hand...

'Dad said he was really chuffed by my hard sell today of the swept-wing sports-kite in general and the Sandpiper model in particular. So I said to Dad, "I'll take over the kitchen tonight, and I'll make a Quorn shepherd's pie." I burned the Brussels sprouts I served with it, and I apologised, but Dad said he hadn't really noticed, and anyway what did burnt veg matter. "It's a real treat for me you cooking dinner, and I appreciate it."

'July 18. Managed to Google a fantastically interesting programme – *Sixty Minutes* – from Australia (ABC) shown
yesterday (July 17). Watched it four times! Its subject's becoming
a hero, and I'm rather in need of one stuck up here a lot on my
own, and worrying about cash flow. What an ordeal this new hero
had, but what a reward! There's a dad round a son's neck there
too…

'July 23: 'Dad surprised me today by suddenly asking me, as I
was helping him clear out the yard, "Do you think Izzie is
serious about this Doug guy?" "Yeah, too serious!" I said, "and
the guy bores the pants off me!" Dad put down the white sack
the county has given us for garden rubbish, and said quietly,
"That's not fair, Nat, and I do wish you wouldn't say things like
that! I didn't meet the man for very long, but he struck me as a
thoroughly – as a thoroughly decent bloke." Isn't that what's
called damning with faint praise, I thought, but I had the wit
not to say this aloud. What I did say was, "Would you mind,
Dad, if you heard he and she had started living together?" (*I*
certainly would!) Dad said, "I haven't the right to mind anything
in that department, have I?" Which sounded unusually hopeful
as far as my own wishes went, I thought, though he immediately
spoiled it by saying, "And anyway I *wouldn't* mind! Not that I'd
say if I did. Haven't you taken it in by now, Nat, that I do my
damnedest never to pronounce on what anybody should or
shouldn't be doing?"

   '"Well, I suppose that has sort of struck me!" I replied.'

* * *

As Luke Fleming's investigations later uncovered, Nat made *two*
long stays in Lydcastle between June and September 2009. The
first ended on August 10 when he returned to London, to his
mother's flat. Then on Thursday August 20 he got his A Level
results. His journal would have you believe that on the morning
of that great day he didn't feel nervous but weirdly calm, as if,

whatever the results, good or disappointing, he had moved far beyond responding to them as an individual with a future dependant on them, but had, over the summer, turned into a different kind of person, with just enough curiosity about his own past to want to know how he'd fared.

He'd fared well, he found out, two As and a B. His place at Uni, the University of Lincoln, to study journalism, was now assured.

Both Dad and Doug were full of congratulations. No words from the first about the iniquity of exams and the ranking of people ('often for life!'), though it was unlikely his views had undergone any change, no words from the second about 'soft' subjects. Instead Doug told him that he'd heard nothing but excellent reports about the university of Nat's choice. Mum was moved to tears, but (according to Nat's journal) disconcerted him by saying, with eyes still moist, 'It's a tremendous relief for me, Nat, how you've done so well, and I really think some of the calming exercises we've done together helped you. I must be honest, and say I didn't think you'd make those grades.' She put a hand on top of his head – she was not a very demonstrative mother – and smoothed his straight, grey-brown hair making the feathered fringe in front tidier. 'You've been so difficult to know, Nat. Do you realise that? Perhaps if Pete hadn't left us, you'd have been a bit more forthcoming.'

'August 2. Decided I should let Dr Julian Pringle know my good news. But that strange letter he sent me hasn't exactly encouraged calling round again, even though it's full of good wishes and suggests we have a friendly future to look forward to. So I decided to ring. Dr Pringle sounded surprised to hear from me, as if I wasn't at all in his thoughts. But when he heard what I had to tell him, he was genuinely pleased (that was clear enough!). He really needed to hear things were going well for somebody, he said, as his wife Ilona had been extremely ill again. What was wrong with her? I asked; felt I had to. A pause. Then – "Leukaemia!" Impossible to know how best to reply, especially as I'm pretty ignorant about such things. But say something I surely should, so I managed:

"That's when white blood cells take over, isn't it?" Stupid really telling the man something he knows only too well but far more fully. He didn't answer directly but said that the two of them still hoped to be going to Hungary in ten days' time, but obviously it was far from certain. But on their return... well, things might have improved a little, and of course it'd be good for us to meet up. I really don't know why, after this, I asked my next question: "What did you mean by saying in your letter that you preferred my dad – Peter – to stay up on his Heights?" It was a mistake, saying that. There was an even longer pause than before, then, in a cold, firm, low voice: "I thought I made it clear I didn't want to go over all that past history. Let bygones be bygones." But I'm wondering if they are bygones either for him or for my dad.'

Using some of the money he'd earned, Nat joined three friends of his, including Josh (who'd only managed one A in his exams, though in the 'hard' subject of Economics) down in a rented cottage in Cornwall, near St Ives. They swam, they climbed the cliffs, they tried surfing. Nat wrote in his cloth-bound book: 'Hasn't riding the waves taught me that mastery of self is the key to life? And if an idea comes to you, but seems (at times) too hard to execute, then use that mastery to ride on the crest of it, as you would on an Atlantic roller... Never forget the hero of *Sixty Minutes*!'

Back to South Shropshire on Monday September 7. Jottings are far more numerous than during the London and Cornwall weeks, but, as before, they deal overwhelmingly with High Flyers matters. Still the same complaints that Pete Kempsey wasn't pro-active or efficient enough, but the tone, after the interval away, was more accepting, mellower. Not that Nat's mind had left its earlier preoccupations altogether. One page towards the end of those containing writing is, with hindsight, of particular importance to the Missing Berwyn Boy Case.

'At last my constant snooping has been rewarded. Dad has kept no papers or letters from before his marriage, and precious few from after it. I won't go down in history as a son whose smallest doings were of such vital interest to his proud parents that they hoarded away every memento of him they could. But I had hopes, remembering that yellowed little receipt from Gregory Pringle, of coming across something from my dad's past secreted (or just kept, preserved) in a book, and so went through every single old one in the house. And, just as I was thinking this far worse than the needle in the old haystack I found a volume of Wilfred Owen's poems, with a photograph, a news-paper cutting, and a letter inside, all between the two pages of the poem "The Show". The first four lines of this had been high-lighted in yellow:

'My soul looked down from a vague height, with Death....'

'The photo showed a youth on a summer's day, longish dark hair parted in the middle, bare arms, bare feet, and a shirt unbuttoned all the way down and worn over trousers turned up as if to aid paddling in a stream. He was sitting on a tree stump, and looking ahead of him, but what held the attention – as it obviously did his – was the white fox terrier between his splayed legs. This dog's pointed, bright-eyed face wore an expression of true content, as one who could envisage no happier, safer place to be than where he actually was. His back legs were on the ground, but his front ones rested and dangled over the youth's right thigh. This youth was my dad – no doubt about that. He had his left hand on his dog's rump while his other hand stroked his back. I'd never known the Pete Kempsey I was seeing here, and I don't say this just because I was born so many years after the picture. But I've glimpsed him, I believe, every so often, especially when he thought you weren't looking his way.

'There was something written at the foot of the photo, and I could tell it was in Dad's writing even though it was from way back. "Your former friend as he is now". Strange words!

'The cutting was from the *Wrexham Leader,* just a photograph headed:

Paul Binding

UFOs in the Berwyn Mountains – Anniversary Rally

Time and poor quality reproduction made people and bleak mountain almost impossible to make out. Attached to this by paperclip was a sheet of notepaper with, again, Dad's writing on it. No address or date, just "Sam, Got this picture through college where we can get copies of practically every goddam paper there is. Don't you think it's time we got together too? Whatcher think? And here's what I look like, with my closest mate, Pete." Then, after this the unnecessary words: NEVER SENT.'

'And what do *I* think?

'I think there's a very great deal about my dad's past I know nothing about. '

Trade was excellent throughout Lydcastle in the golden weather days leading up to and including the Michaelmas Fair of 2009; High Flyers did really good business. 'We're both rushed off our feet!' scribbled Nat, 'and Dad actually has sold (at a good price) one of his two beloved Barrolettas from Guatemala. He'll be sorry to see it leave, but he's happy too, and feels vindicated. He truly deserves to do well and yet – everything isn't as it should be with the shop, and he should understand this. How terrible if he went under!' These are the very last two sentences in Nat's Journal. As doubtless he intended them to be.

The Fair itself was a real cornucopia of entertainments throughout Lydcastle's cheerful old centre: Morris dancers (West Midlands style), Street dancers (New York subway style), toffee-apple vendors, three brass bands competing and an accordionist for the duration, jugglers, 'The Tiger's Last Chance' performing in the evenings on a platform underneath the early eighteenth-century Town Hall, and young, middle aged and old dancing to their rhythm in the streets while the moon climbed higher in the sky… Nat thoroughly enjoyed every moment of it all, and many is the person who saw and heard him doing so.

Yet the Monday morning after so much community fun, Nat disappeared. And did not re-appear until police operations found him stranded on a lonely mountain.

Part Two

Pete Kempsey's Adventure

One

High Flyers

'Our Midlands edition of *High Flyers* comes to you this evening from the old market-town of Leominster in the county of Hereford-and-Worcester. With me here, facing an audience of local folk, are six of the district's brightest and best, three boys and three girls to prove it as fertile in talent as in apples, hops and good pastureland. My name is Bob Thurlow, and it will shortly be my pleasure to introduce our contestants. But before I do that, a brief reminder of how our programme works.

'It's all a matter of sixes. So one accusation you can't make against *High Flyers* is that we are at sixes and sevens.'

Laughter, as anticipated.

'For our purposes the United Kingdom is divided into *six* regions: London-and-the-South; Wales-and-the-West-Country; The Midlands; The North; Scotland; Northern Ireland. We visit *six* different places in every region and, in each, *six* young people compete, first in general knowledge and then in a special subject of their own choice. Each region then has its own heat, in which its *six* strongest do battle. The winners of these regional contests then go up to London for the final, when we find the Highest Flyer of all. After which we makers of the programme have a well-earned summer break.

'And now on this golden evening in the county which boasts, not far from here, a Golden Valley, let me give you our latest High Flyers, selected after the most intense auditioning process man can devise.

'So – Miss Melanie Clarkson.'

'Good evening!'

'Mr Andrew Wheeler.'

'Hullo!'

'Miss Linda Rhys-Jones.'

'Hullo!'

'Mr Peter Kempsey!'

'Hi!'

'Miss Fiona Chambers.'

'Oh… hi!'

'And last but not least, Mr Robert Fitzwilliam.'

'A very good evening to all listeners!'

What a way of announcing yourself, thought Pete. He felt the agreeable prickling of the urge to win.

'It's a cherished custom of ours to begin with the six contestants introducing themselves. We like our listeners to *know* our participants; this programme celebrates comradeship as much as competition. Therefore I call on Miss Melanie Clarkson to give the opening self-presentation of the evening.'

The assembly hall of one of Leominster's chief junior schools, close to its Priory, was filled to capacity with people looking terribly proud that BBC Radio 4 had elected to honour their town on so popular a programme. Only Jim and Marion Kempsey appeared to be attending the show with visible reluctance; their claps, Pete could see from the platform, were mere token ones, palms barely impacting. When the 'recruiting poster' first appeared in public places, Jim Kempsey had said to his eldest son, 'You'll be just like those gullible young Britons in 1914, you know, Peter. They saw the picture of old Kitchener's face, and the words "WANTS YOU", and off they went, won over by flattery, to horror and death.'

'But some came back heroes,' said Pete. Neither parent denied the likelihood of his being chosen for the show, nor that he'd excel on it. They knew only too well that he was an extraordinary storehouse of facts. The explanation for this was something they repeatedly begged him never to disclose, but always Pete grinned and replied: 'I'm making no promises. Isn't there a saying, the truth must out?'

All other contestants in the show would have left home to volleys of good wishes. But not Pete with his younger brothers' words ringing in his ears: 'Mum and Dad are worried you're going to make an idiot of yourself this evening, Peter. They nearly stopped us coming along to see you perform. Thought you'd be a bad example for the two of us.' (It was Julian who spoke, of course!) But as Pete walked across the smooth stretch of lawn below the sandstone Priory in the early evening, he could not only sense September's tang of ripened apples but also an invitation to trust in his special gift, surely given to him for some great purpose. 'Tonight will be the turning point of my life,' he told himself, as he approached the red-brick, mock-ecclesiastical, late Victorian buildings of the junior school.

'…It's always good to remember,' Linda Rhys-Jones was saying in a curiously reverberant voice (sitting too close to the mic), 'that the poet, Robert Herrick praised our local wool, actually speaking of a "bank of moss more soft than Lemster Ore" (spelling the name LEMSTER).' This information, nothing to what Peter Kempsey was going to give 'em shortly, so charmed the audience that they spontaneously broke into a silly little burst of clapping.

'And now for Mr Peter Kempsey,' said Bob Thurlow. 'Sixteen years of age, and in his first term in the Lower Sixth at the boys' grammar school, Hereford. Peter's already told us his principal activities are day-dreaming and skiving off set work.' The laughter here was mild and muted, and his parents, Pete noticed, did not join in; indeed his mother lowered her head. Dad, in his best crested blazer tonight, was, after all, a highly respected accountant with an office in Leominster High Street and an open ambition to become a Liberal town councillor; Mum taught home economics at the comp. But someone more sympathetic to Pete's wit was sitting by his mother's side: his parents' closest friend, Oliver Merchant, founder of The Sunbeam Press, a bachelor who called the Kempseys' house, Woodgarth, his 'second home', and the only man in Leominster to accord Pete the dignity he deserved.

'So, over to Peter Kempsey who can tell us whether that is really an accurate self portrait.'

An icy cold wave of fear broke over and drenched him. Irrelevantly he noted that Bob Thurlow wore a toupee. What if he said this aloud? But, to his relief, he heard himself saying: 'It's as accurate as any, I guess.' He preferred the American 'guess' to the English 'suppose'. 'It's odd, I know, that a guy who doesn't particularly shine academically should want to take part in a brains challenge like this, and has already cleared the auditions with outstanding ease.' He tried not to take in the malign smirk of Mr Robert Fitzwilliam. 'But you see I have a secret, which I am going to make public for the first time ever.'

Well, he had refused to make any promise that he wouldn't, hadn't he?

'It was a hot summer afternoon when I was seven, and my mother's friend, the eminent educational psychologist, Dr Mary Smith, was staying with us. I didn't much like her visits because she always seemed to be investigating my faults. But on this occasion she decided to sit me down in the garden, and, without telling me what she was doing, give me the Wellerman-Kreutz Intelligence Test, a method of measuring brain-power she valued more than any other. I was just glad to be out of earshot of the horrible bawling new baby. When we'd finished, she didn't say anything to me, but went indoors into our kitchen and told my mother: "Marion, your Peter has just achieved an absolutely *amazing* score. The highest that I personally have encountered in a whole decade devoted to this form of IQ assessment."'

Could, Pete wondered, a child of seven really have absorbed such adult language? Her words must have been repeated to him later. Also was it wise to reproduce the psychologist's flutey, fervid voice? Some members of the audience were giggling nervously... 'The Wellerman-Kreutz test had given me an IQ of well over 160. Ever since, she's tested me regularly, and the only change has been upward. So here I am, a...' But what did his staggering IQ total make him? A genius? Surely not. A genius meant a Leonardo, a Shakespeare, an Einstein, and he didn't even *want* to be in their company.

No time left now for a more orthodox self-presentation. Later he learned that never in the programme's history had Bob Thurlow, experienced radio host that he was, felt such disquiet about what might be coming next. But he kept his cool. 'Quite some story, Peter! I don't think anybody's told anything like it on *High Flyers*. Well, listeners can judge this evening the accuracy of those tests. As for you, you'd better keep your fingers crossed; you're up against some mighty strong contenders.'

Why, the guy sounds as if I ought not to win, thought Peter, mopping the sweat now positively oozing from his forehead. Thinks I've overstepped the mark or something! Well, I'll show him!

During the first half of the programme he sensed that his visible public, a number of whom he knew personally, was against him. (About his huge invisible one it was best not to think.) Of his fellow contestants he had endeared himself only to Melanie Clarkson, who, with her long light-brown tresses, was the only one he himself had really taken to. During the rehearsal Melanie had surreptitiously whispered to him; 'You're going to be tonight's Highest Flyer, I know it!' The two were regularly to meet at a local coffee bar and at the town's liveliest Saturday disco throughout the following fifteen months. Those were bliss-ful moments when Pete stroked or ran his fingers through her soft hair.

'General Knowledge:

'Peter, which novelist wrote *The Idiot* and *The Brothers Karamazov* and what nationality was he?"

'Fyodor Dostoyevsky, and he was Russian.'

'Peter, which way do Earth's magnetic field lines go?'

'From south to north.'

'Peter, who was victorious at the Battle of Naseby in 1645?'

'Cromwell's Roundheads. Like in most Civil War battles.'

'Peter, approximately how many cells are there in the human body?'

'Approximately 50 million million.'

He gave his answers quickly but quietly, his manner belying the bombast of his self-introduction. Which he should never have made. Out there, in uncountable sitting rooms, kitchens and bedrooms of Britain people were doubtless preferring Linda and Robert to himself, despite his uniquely faultless performance. Why had he joked about skiving and day-dreaming? If he had given a different, more serious picture of himself, he wouldn't have had to counterbalance it by informing the whole bloody country of his electrifying IQ. Pete was burdened by this persistent feeling that he was neither liked nor admired, and so was over-compensating desperately.

'And for his special subject Peter Kempsey has chosen apples in Herefordshire. May I be so bold as to ask a personage of such high Intelligence Quotient as yours – *why*?'

Pete, detecting a sneer in Bob Thurlow's manner, answered straight. 'Because my native county has been famous for apples since way back. We produce what many say are the best cider apples in the world. And I love the sight of all the orchards round here, many by the banks of the river, especially at this time of year with the fruit ready for picking.'

He could almost hear the collective breaths of the audience changing into a different key, into a harmonious accompaniment to what turned out to be, again, a hundred per cent correct answers. His reply to Bob had brought him this approval because, with Britain's entry into the European Economic Community so imminent (January 1), there was a fear in the region that local-grown apples might be undercut by French or Dutch fruit. And with his awareness of this benevolent shift in his favour, Pete's own breathing became calmer, slower, lighter. In truth, as he supplied the facts that beaming, toupee'ed Bob Thurlow was eliciting from him, he knew he had never felt quite so glowingly well, so physically and mentally at one with himself, in all his sixteen years.

'How long should cider apples be left to mature after being picked?'

'One week.'

'What is a "scratcher"?'

Funny, but as he was speaking, the Assembly Room grew hazy, and he was half-*inside* those orchards close to the Wye, like a youth in some old print, armed with the traditional long-hooked pole and shaking fruit gleaming with red ripeness down onto the grass below. It was apple time now, of course and, like many of his school friends, he helped at weekends with picking in the nearby Bulmer's-owned orchards, for pocket money.

'A scratcher,' he was telling everybody with unalloyed, peaceful confidence, 'is what the apples are tipped into after that week for maturing. It crushes 'em.'

'What is the Foxwhelp?'

'The favourite Herefordshire apple for cider-making.'

'What apple is it said to have replaced in popularity?'

'The Redstreak.'

'Ladies and gentlemen, there is no doubt about tonight's winner, no doubt who is the Highest Flyer to emerge after this evening in Leominster, in the county of Hereford-and-Worcester. Peter Kempsey will now go through to the regional heat in Birmingham. Let us give him a big hand, but before doing so it is surely my duty to express a hope that he doesn't drink too much of his native country's excellent cider by way of celebration tonight.'

What fun, what attention then followed! In so many papers – *Hereford Times*, *Leominster Journal*, *Ledbury Reporter*, even, from over two different borders, *The Western Mail* and *The Shropshire Star* – photos of Pete appeared, all of them showing him to advantage, even as glamorous, some illustrating not-always-accurate articles. The best of these (thought Pete) gave the impression of a not only remarkably intelligent but a decidedly

Paul Binding

interesting, even sexy guy. Unfortunately the subject of his IQ cropped up in them all, but he did have only himself to thank for that. Just in case readers didn't know, journalists reminded them of Eugene Wellerman (born 1916) and Carl Kreutz (born 1917), American academics 'grossly under-appreciated' in the UK. Of course he got a hard time at school, but many there and in the town were impressed by such a public triumph – except, of course, for Jim and Marion Kempsey.

His parents were angry at him for 'flagrant, in fact positively brazen betrayal' of their trust, that is to say for telling the world about Auntie Mary's regular ratings of his brain. For them *High Flyers* wasn't 'something that counted' and scoring top marks in it was 'a flash in the pan'. Here Pete was able to fight back. Did Dad know what 'flash in the pan' meant, what it derived from? Thought not. It was *generally* assumed to come from the California Gold Rush, when prospectors would see something shining in their pans which sadly was not gold. But *actually* the expression originated in warfare: in muskets holding gunpowder in small pans; this powder could, and did, flare up without an actual bullet being shot. 'But in both cases the end is left open, don't you see?' said Pete, 'after all, after the flash, you might find a heap of gold or shoot your enemy to death. Never use a phrase, Dad, unless you know the history behind it.'

Dad, so often preoccupied and invariably irritated with his eldest boy, just said: 'It's a pity there's got to be a semi-final in these shenanigans. I think we've all heard enough about high flying by now; I wonder if you've been thinking about anything else. But if there must be another round, we shall just have to grin and bear it, I suppose.'

'Grin and bear it?' Another cliché which could be explained away, but this time Pete didn't bother. The fact was he was hurt by his parents' attitude, and sometimes this hurt took the form of painful rashes on his skin.

Bob Thurlow personally signed the letter to Mr Peter Kempsey of Leominster announcing the time and place of the semi-final – Pebble Mill Studios, Birmingham, Wednesday, April 12. His parents did not want Pete to go on his own, so they went with him, and of course his younger brothers, the Brats, came along too. It was a day when sun and shower followed each other rapidly and sweetly, so that all the blossoms in the small towns and countryside, cherry, almond, Japanese quince, shone in their whites and pinks, while newly fledged leaves shimmered in a variety of gentle greens. Not much of all this beauty was conspicuous in urban Birmingham. Inevitably Dad and Mum brought out their memories of the city before their war-time evacuation ahead of the bombs, and, considering that by a tragic coincidence, both lost their parents in these assaults (no Grans or Nans in Pete's life!), they could surely be forgiven for doing so. Less forgivable was Dad's having worriedly to go over last year's triumph in Birmingham (at Saltley) for the striking miners masterminded by that dedicated troublemaker, Arthur Scargill. He was even moved to repeat their successful rallying cry of 'Close the gates!' as if involuntarily he were still impressed by it. What should an honourable liberal's response to the situation be? Nonetheless this trip to the second city became a day to remember. Though they couldn't bring themselves to articulate it, even Pete's Mum and Dad felt a certain excitement before the event. And then, too, Oliver Merchant was there.

Earlier he'd insisted – 'No, I mean it, Jim, and if you value my friendship, you will let me have my way!' – on giving Pete money, and a not inconsiderable amount at that, expressly for him to buy new clothes for the show. 'You deserve them,' Ol told him, 'so mind you choose not so much wisely as well.' Catch that dreary couple, his parents, saying – or even thinking – such a delightful thing. So, in Hereford's most trendy shop, Pete bought himself – well, not a lamé suit or a satin-quilted jacket, let alone a rhinestone-studded shirt – but some pretty good items which suited his own brand of dark good looks: bovver boots, flared jeans, a tie-dye shirt all manner of reds and greens and, naturally, a denim jacket.

Now why would Oliver Merchant do such a thing? There seemed no end to his anxiety to do the Kempseys kindnesses.

The Midlands Heat was, compared with the Leominster edition, both more enjoyable and more endorsing of Pete's rapidly mounting high opinion of himself. His rivals came from every corner of the region, from Gainsborough in Lincolnshire, Alfreton in Derbyshire, Banbury in Oxfordshire, Thetford in Norfolk and Birmingham's own Castle Bromwich. His special subject that evening was Toys Through the Ages. Massing facts on this topic was like walking through colourful booths at a fair, and finding that, whatever ball or gun you used, you could knock off its perch every coconut, every box of sweets, every piece of interesting bric-a-brac you saw. Toys – what information about their long history had he not enticed into his receptive head?: the wooden figures which performed antics as second millennium Egyptians tugged at the attached strings; the tops that delighted children in medieval France, and the kites, stilts, hoops and air balloons with which their sixteenth-century descendants amused themselves; the sinister little toy guillotine given to a later gener-ation of French children by revolutionary-minded parents. And surely he'd have an opportunity to use toys-history names like 'thaumatropes' and 'praxinoscopes' from the technology-conscious nineteenth century.

The questions were tough, much more so than those asked him back in Leominster, and once or twice Pete hesitated, though less often than the others. But by the end of the evening he (nobody else!) was Midlands' Highest Flyer – and by a clear head. Yet more congratulations, yet more press attention and promises of good things ahead, as well as a silver cup and a gen-erous book-token. Ol Merchant was, 'more chuffed than I've been by anything in many a long year.' Dad said: 'Perhaps we can allow real life to begin now. At last!'

After the Midlands victory came the London finals, on an unusually hot June Wednesday. Pete went up to this event alone. Special subject – Flags of the World. His first choice had been his favourite group, The Grateful Dead. He was so proud to be a 'Deadhead', Jerry García and Phil Lesh were such great intel-ligences, who openly rejoiced in their powers – rather like himself. But this year, on March 8, the Dead's harmonica and organ player, Ron 'Pig-pen' McKernan had died of alcohol abuse. (Pete had worn a black tie for him.) Perhaps it was this scandal that made Bob Thurlow reject the group as a suitable topic for the programme. A pity, for in truth Pete hit upon Flags (which Bob at once enthusiastically accepted) almost arbitrarily; flags had never meant all that much to him. Not so surprising therefore that he blanked at two of Bob's questions, though he scored first-equal in his general knowledge. Result – he came second, was the runner-up High Flyer, no conceivable form of disgrace or even disappointment, as everybody agreed. (But his title of Midlands Champion, 1972-1973 was his till the end of his life.) Bob Thurlow said in a personal talk with him that though the programme wouldn't, of course, be visiting Leominster again, he'd find a way of having him on the show a fourth time.

Two

Enter Mephistopheles

Christmas 1973 was gravely overshadowed by New Year 1974. People talked of little else but the social and economic troubles ahead, they did not feel festive. Oliver Merchant even reported a (mild) slump in demand for Sunbeam Press's greetings cards.

A Sunbeam Press card that Pete himself received was from Bob Thurlow. His mother was looking over his shoulder as he read: 'Hope you are in good spirits despite all the gloom. You should be, because I've persuaded the powers-that-be to agree to a special *High Flyers* for those six highest-scoring regional winners who fell short of the final accolade. The programme wouldn't be right without *your* contribution, Peter, and I hereby invite you to participate on my show on January 31, 1974.'

'Well, you must do the polite thing, Peter, and send Mr Thurlow a card back?' Mum breathed her injunction down Pete's neck so its syllables tickled him. Pete raised his head to confront his mother, bathed in the morning sunshine coming through the red-and-green stained glass of the front door. 'And why wouldn't I?'

'Saying No always requires diplomacy,' Mum said, with a sudden, hard smile, 'when you refuse an offer of this kind...' she might have been dictating notes on hygiene to her Fifth Form girls '…you must sound at once firmly unambiguous and appreciative.'

'But I don't want to say No,' Pete objected vainly. Sometimes Pete could identify only too easily with poor 'Pig-pen' from the Dead, and a dullness, a heaviness, a lethargy could fill him for many hours, both at school and in his spare time. This made him unlike the Brats, especially Julian the leader, who filled every waking hour with activity, music and merriment.

On his father's desk, Pete discovered more Sunbeam Christmas cards, and from these chose one featuring Brueghel's 'Hunters in the Snow'. A wonderful picture (why hadn't he taken it in before?); cold and silence, peace and threat rose up from it. Above its human and animal figures, a dark bird, crow or buzzard, ominous and downwards poised, was intent on its own sombre business. Inside this card Pete wrote, in a hand more careful than usual: 'Dear Bob, Hope you like this fine picture, an old favourite of mine – and thanks for yours. Am delighted to accept your offer of a place on January 31 *High Flyers*. Best wishes, Pete Kemspey.'

He felt not a flicker of guilt when he announced just before tea. 'By the way, Mum, I did as you said and sent Mr Thurlow a card. Found one on Dad's desk. Made the midday post too.'

But his mother was reminding herself of some point in the libretto of the Gilbert-and-Sullivan opera with which she was involved, before turning to the Brats' tea and their favourite hot buttered scones. She merely nodded acknowledgement, as if what Pete had just referred to was of no importance to her. Through the long years afterwards Pete would see so clearly that uninterested expression on her pretty, symmetrical, tension-ridden face. He wanted to forgive her for it, across the gulf of time and tragedy, but the very sharpness of the image always prevented him.

In Leominster the Lugg Valley Players' production of *The Mikado* dominated the run-up to Christmas. The last of its four performances was on Saturday December 22. Pete went to this by himself, as Dad and the Brats, who went the night before, were at a Civic Society's Children's Party.

The whole country needed cheering up. Prime Minister Edward Heath had failed to resolve disputes with the miners, and now declared a National State of Emergency: five days' worth of electricity consumption up to December 30, and in the New Year, if need be, a three-day week. The very phrase, obsessively reiterated, sent people's minds (and tongues) agitatedly back to the War and the black-out. When his parents had come to Leominster as young Brummy evacuees, limits on light and heat and food supplies had been the norm. Now, in this era of prosperity, these had returned, and even television, that contemporary solace, was shutting down at 10.30.

Whoever would have thought that Mum, the cautious, the reticent, the ever-correct, would have so taken to the Lugg Valley Players? It had all begun with her playing a landlady in a Victorian melodrama last spring, which friends and neighbours had praised. 'We wouldn't have guessed Marion had such – fire in her!' But Pete, still smarting from her lack of enthusiasm for *High Flyers*, had not enjoyed her performance which, for indefinable reasons, made him uneasy. And here she now was in *The Mikado* as Katisha, harridan daughter-in-law elect of the Japanese monarch, determined to marry the handsome, missing crown prince despite his distaste for her. An undignified role.

It was not only Pete whose spirits had dropped this year. Jim Kempsey was visibly over-working, as a senior partner in his accountancy firm and in his public life too. Next month there would be a vacancy on the town council which he was favourite to fill. Dad knew that he had something serious to offer Leominster, but throughout this year, he was beset by the kind of anxieties such as, Pete gathered from half-heard conversations between Mum and Ol Merchant, had dogged him earlier, in his National Service and his early training. While he believed it his duty to take part in civic life, join discussion groups, be on committees etc, he was not naturally sociable, found dealing with other people hard, and sometimes downright painful. How he'd ever managed to get himself married was a question Pete increasingly asked himself.

A strawberry-blond like his second son Julian, he had a still-youthful appearance, an unlined face and energetic walk which not infrequently broke into a run, and few detectable bald patches. These features only added to the general impression he gave of some grave schoolboy overburdened with studies. A passionate internationalist like any good liberal, he strongly supported Tory Heath's belief in the European Economic Community. As someone who'd been a teenager in the war, he shared the PM's hopes that Europe could use its past conflicts and sufferings as leverage for the creation of a uniquely prosperous, peaceful continent. But as a local citizen and professional man, handling the accounts of farmers and rural-based businesses, he agonised about its effects on agriculture.

Compounding these divisions was the Chancellor's melancholy announcement last month of the country's woes and of the dire measures needed to restore its health; all this went to Dad's already troubled heart, for any responsible person involved in politics should have an answer. So his thoughts were constantly and heavily elsewhere, and only could be assuaged, and that but occasionally, by games and conversations with his younger boys, in which Pete was not included. He didn't disguise the fact that he found the Brats far more congenial company, and he listened to Julian scraping away on his fiddle like one privileged to hear a rare musician.

Dad's preoccupation created this gap in Mum's life which the Lugg Valley Players now filled. And behold her now, on the last night (thank God!) of the show, capering with unseemly abandon across the stage partnered by – who else but genial old Ol, one of the players' mainstays, as Koko, Lord High Executioner. The applause was so fervent, so boisterous, that they had to perform the duet declaring their weird compatibility all over again!

Before the show began the producer had stepped forward to say: 'Well, hasn't our good Chancellor told us that we're living in (and I quote) "the gravest situation by far since the end of the war". So I reckon we need a little G & S, even more than a little G & T,' sycophantic laughter here, 'to cheer us up. But we are all good citizens, here in the Lugg Valley. We have scaled down the lighting on-stage, without detriment to actors or sets. And house lights tonight must go off at the same hour as TV shuts down – i.e. 10.30. So we ask you all to leave the Assembly Room as promptly after the entertainment as possible…'

And this, *this* was judged likely to brighten up the spirits, Mum padded out in ridiculous robes and made up like a hag, carrying on a travesty of flirtation with old Ol, in light purple kimono with an obi round his over-expanded waist. Pete cringed in his seat as he watched them, just as Mum and Dad had doubtless cringed in this selfsame spot, while he'd told the whole listening nation from the rostrum how brilliant the Wellerman-Kreutz tests had found him.

'If that is so,
 Sing derry down derry!
 It's evident, very,
 Our tastes are one!
 Away we'll go,
 And merrily marry,
 Nor tardily tarry
 Till day is done!'

The final bows of the cast brought forth no fewer than four curtain calls, and then the producer emerged again, first to say a big thank you for such a heart-warming reception, and second, to remind everybody to leave the hall speedily because the lights simply had to be off in five minutes' time.

Pete had just reached the gangway when Mrs Richards, wife of a High Street dentist, tugged at his jacket sleeve. 'Marion – your mother,' was what she had to say, 'was *wonderful*, wasn't she? So can you be a love, Julian, and take this to her backstage?' 'This' was a bouquet wrapped up in holly-patterned paper.

Irritating to be confused with the elder of the two Brats, when Pete had always preferred the younger one, Robin, dark-haired like himself. His feelings for both had been grossly undermined the day before yesterday when he'd overheard Dad saying to Mum, 'I know Peter comes out so well in Mary Smith's tests, and can answer any number of useless questions on Radio 4. But Julian and Robin are, in my view, far abler boys. To listen to Julian at his age talking about music, to hear his command of the technicalities of notation...' His voice trailed away in sheer admiration.

'Abler boys', '*far* abler', the words stabbed Pete cruelly at the most inopportune times: when in the middle of an answer in class, while being offered a plate of sandwiches by a friend's mum, even on the toilet...

'Well, I could...' said Pete.

'That's where real actresses receive their tributes, isn't it? Backstage. And your mother's as good as – well, better than – most professionals.' Mrs Richards, oblivious of his lack of enthusiasm, thrust the flowers into his arm. 'So sweet of you, Julian! Marion absolutely adores freesias!!' and scuttled off to join the general exit. By now the Assembly Room had, in compliance with the producer's note of urgency, all but emptied. But Pete felt it'd be as much as his later life was worth not to carry out this request, much as it went against the grain being part of any compliment to such tripe as that he'd just sat through. So now, moving in the opposite direction from everybody else, he made his way to the swing door leading backstage, where actors and orchestral players would now be changing. And just as he'd reached this, all the lights went out.

Those few folk still in the Assembly Room, though forewarned, gave out little gasps and cries of vexation. But for Pete the bouquet in his hands acted like a rudimentary natural torch, the flowers giving out a gold-and-white glow and a heady fragrance, providing a lead through the darkness ahead. He was moving down a white-tiled, concrete-floored corridor which, yards later, turned sharply to the left. This new section terminated in a large changing room, announcing itself this evening by a flotilla of flickering candles – and audible talk and laughter. Pete might be bold enough to give a cheeky self-presentation to a visible and an invisible audience on a radio show, but he loathed entering social gatherings where people knew each other better than they did him, especially if clutching a poxy 'floral tribute'.

Off the left wall of the corridor three doors opened, and what made him peer through the gap in the last one? Into a space not much larger than a toilet, seemingly a repository for kids' missing boots and shoes. Plus two canvas chairs, a low table on which was guttering a candle in a lemonade bottle – and two human figures, Mum as Katisha in her splendiferous robes, and Oliver Merchant still dressed as Titipu's Lord High Executioner, locked in an embrace of a physiologically extraordinary kind. Even in the stinky gloom of this cubby-hole affection (or lust?) was having its way! For a moment Pete couldn't get his breath. Then he made himself look more closely.

Oliver was sitting on one of the two chairs, head between his knees, while Mum pressed a hand hard on his face. Presently (though how could they not be aware of his panting breath and the sudden sweet waft from his bouquet?) he realised his mother, crouching over, was firmly gripping Ol's nose with the right thumb and forefinger.

If the nation hadn't been ordered by its government to use only five days' worth of electricity per week, and this junior-school-acting-as-arts-centre to switch off lights when it wouldn't normally have done, Pete would have seen instantly that Oliver was having a nose-bleed with Mum tending him. But at first sight it had seemed they... would it be cunnilingus? Or some grotesque Kama-sutra act Pete didn't yet know the name of? Then he heard Mum say: 'Your nose must be held a good ten minutes. Usually the sufferer's too giddy to do this, so it's just as well for someone else to oblige.'

'Particularly if that someone is you, Marion,' came Oliver's voice, strangely nasal because his nostrils were being blocked, yet, because of the position of his body, also sounding as if it came up from his groin, through the unsteady candlelight, 'always so kind and good.'

'Aye, aye! What *is* all this?' thought Pete.

But Mum hadn't taken Oliver's words amorously. 'I do teach Health and Safety in my Home Economics classes, you know, and most of my girls would be infinitely better informed about your little trouble than yourself, Oliver. And keep your head *absolutely* still. Otherwise you might swallow your blood, which could lead to vomiting.'

Spare me the details, poor Pete said to himself, waiting to make his entrance. But, 'Always so kind and good!' reiterated old Ol Merchant.

'Really? Always?' thought Pete, 'only to someone infatuated by her she is!' (And how did you explain 'Uncle' Oliver's odd family status otherwise?) Well, his mother was 'good', he supposed, because of her many admirable qualities: patience, putting others before herself, sense of duty, industriousness. But 'kind' – no, not so you'd notice, not to himself anyway. And in that measureless, unbounded period before the Brats' birth, to be recaptured only in patches now, she had been, if anything, less kind still. Perhaps she'd resented the inquisitive, graceless, independent infant he'd been.

And then, despite himself, he recalled, even in the split seconds of getting ready to announce his presence, that tricky situation between himself and Mum, of which he alone was aware. His lie about the Christmas card he'd sent Bob Thurlow...

Up to this moment he'd felt no guilt. Now, witnessing his mother's administrations to her 'friend' ('lover'?) he belatedly experienced that softening of the guts which registers this emotion, recalling earlier occasions of being caught out in mischief or deceit. Poised in the doorway to this stupid little boot-room, and now on the point of sneezing, thanks to the flowers so close to his face, he forced from himself an exclamation, 'Ah, there you both are!'

Mum gave Oliver Merchant's head a vice-like squeeze. 'It's only Peter, Oliver, so please don't move a single inch, otherwise you'll undo all my good work... Oliver has just had a nose-bleed,

Peter. But it's the common anterior kind, thank heavens. Not the posterior variety which one would treat differently. Just the bursting of a blood vessel in a nasal septum.'

'As if I care!' thought Pete, though aloud he said, 'Good, good! What shall I do with the bouquet, Mum?'

'Put it on that little table there – where else? I can see that the roses and freesias are hand-tied together beautifully. I couldn't have made a better job of them myself.'

'They're richly deserved as well,' said Oliver Merchant from his seated position, his voice, still adenoidal, still bizarrely issuing from his crotch, 'and very thoughtful of you, Peter, to have brought it round here, amid all the confusion of this wretched lights-out. You are a most kindly lad who doesn't mind inconveniencing himself on others' behalf. Unlike so many young people of this "me" generation.'

Mum should have said that, shouldn't she? Rather than someone not flesh-and-blood. A mere godfather, and one not a whit bothered by his godson seeing him so intimate with his own mother. Pete knew he should now add something about the show itself, but couldn't find the words. He was seeing again Koko (without nose-bleed) and Katisha (not playing nurse) capering hand-in-hand to their sprightly tune arousing laughter, just like – well, like a husband-and-wife team. That was why he, Pete, had felt so discomfited watching them as well as – well, something not so far off insulted. Oliver Merchant might be Leominster's nearest to a saint, but he was decidedly flabby, as Pete could see tonight like he'd never quite done before – yes, even in this semi-darkness. Whereas Jim Kempsey was a *real man*, however abstracted and pompous, and even though he believed the Brats to be 'abler boys' than his first-born of the phenomenal IQ.

It was as he was having these surprising but instinctive reflections (as he was long afterwards to remember) that the door to this cluttered shoe-room opened a little wider, to show a young man who drawled out: 'His Royal Highness the Mikado of Japan – otherwise known as Trevor Price, my father – has sent me to inquire after the Lord High Executioner's health, and asks if his Daughter-in-Law Elect needs any assistance.'

For thirty-five years, Pete has said to himself: 'If it hadn't been Sam Price, wouldn't it have been someone else? Without consciously knowing it, I longed for a transformer of the soul. And here came one I could not resist. Maybe I even needed a Mephistopheles, with temptations so sweet and alluring, that they appeared like divine refreshments. What else did I have in my life to sustain my dreams and hopes except *High Flyers*? And Sam was as resourceful a friend over that as I could have hoped (or not hoped) for. For me now his entrance that evening from the dark, white-tiled corridor is indissoluble from the development of my life.

'Youth my own age in black bomber jacket, red scarf and tight Levis. Sleek dark hair framing the oval of his face, and curling crisply upwards at the shoulders. A pervasive aroma of patchouli, which I'd already planned to use myself in my life-away-from-home in the autumn but which was incompatible with Woodgarth. Said to be a real come-on!'

Pete identified the entrant from his facetious speech as Sam Price. He had seen him about Leominster occasionally over the years but never spoken to him. Though a contemporary, he had been sent to boarding school when very young, and so was out of the circles in which Pete himself moved. Trevor Price was owner-manager of Price's Menswear in the High Street. As it happened, he had in fact spoken to Pete on his last visit to the shop about his son. 'He's a sophisticated lad, if you get my meaning,' he'd said ambiguously, as if not quite approving of this attribute, 'and clever too, even if he's not a High Flyer like your good self.'

Well, this sophisticated, clever lad had now edged himself further into the junior school shoe-room. He peered at the seated Oliver Merchant with frank but not detectably sympathetic curiosity, as he might have at some rare zoological specimen with an interesting malady. 'The cost of talent!' he pronounced, 'my Old Man says of actors, the bad-uns swoon before and during, the good-uns swoon only when they've done their duty.'

'Mr Merchant did not *swoon*,' said Mum coldly. Pete could tell at once she didn't think Sam Price knew his place. 'He's suffered a nose-bleed.' And, with schoolteacher's precision, she gave Sam the same information she'd given her son.

Sam Price was not to be put down. Had, he asked, Mr Merchant's blood gushed out in a stream or fallen in big drops? Did he feel giddy like you did after a ride on the Big Dipper at the fair?

Mum's answers were perfunctory, but, 'In my opinion Mr Merchant needs at least five minutes more of sitting completely still, with his head well lowered. I'd be glad, Sam, if you told Trevor this. We'll join him and the others just as soon as we can. Nose-bleeds are not the trifles they may seem.' She clearly thought the messenger was underestimating their gravity. 'And Peter, I don't think there's anything for you to do down here, so why don't you leave with Sam? The two of you do know one another, don't you?'

'The whole world knows Peter Kempsey,' said Sam returning to his drawl, but unexpectedly proffering Pete a right hand, 'he's the cleverest man in the whole Midlands, is he not? Wow, if I'd known Peter Kempsey was to be down here, I'd have brought my autograph book along. His signature'll be fetching a mint in a few years.'

Hard to know in what spirit to take this, but Mum put a stop to any more of the same by saying, 'I'll see you then, Peter, back at the house. Depending of course on how long it takes Oliver to recover.'

'A true Florence Nightingale!' enthused the blocked voice from Oliver's loins and nose. Pete couldn't help thinking he might have come up with a compliment a bit more original.

So out into the dim corridor Pete followed Sam Price, who, disconcertingly, stopped, gave the kind of laugh that's really a snort, and then sang right into his left ear:

After Brock

'I laid a divorcee in New York City,
I had to put up some kind of fight.
The lady then she covered me with roses,
She blew my nose, and then she blew my mind.'

He chuckled lewdly. 'Not that I'm casting aspersions on your mother's virtue, mind. You get it, don't you? The Stones, "Honky Tonk Women", second verse. That little scene just put it into my head. We won't ask what "blew my nose" means to Mick Jagger, will we?'

Sam's breath tickled the entire shell of Pete's ear, while up his nostrils floated the scent of the liberally applied patchouli. Pete thought it didn't become him to show amusement. He drew apart from the speaker, unsure what his next move should be. But already the Price boy's blend of self-confidence, insouciance, impertinence and languor was having an effect on his blood, was proving a come-on like his lotion was supposed to be. But a come-on to where? Pity to part from this intriguing character the minute they'd met!

Sam was continuing in his thick whisper: 'I'd better relay your mum's words to my father, hadn't I? And then we can get out of this place, can't we? It's a tip!'

Wasn't that an invitation of sorts? Pete watched him go into the changing room, and talk briefly with Trevor Price. The fleet of candles illuminated them, so ludicrously unalike: Trevor was stout, Sam lean, Trevor florid, Sam sallow, Trevor bald, Sam long-haired. Pete had never much cared for the garrulous, pompous older man with his habit of holding forth to captive customers, and had never made his wanting to get away asap from him secret whenever he had to buy school uniform or sports clothes at his store. Odd to feel flattered now by the overtures of his son.

On his return Sam kept up his curdled whisper: 'No need for us to traipse all the way back down the corridor, you know, Peter. There's a door out into the car park just here, I've been using it all day, in my forced capacity as errand-boy.' And so there was!

Sam worked its long metal lever, and released the pair of them into the slapping coldness of the night air.

God, what a blessed relief to receive those slaps! It'd been such claustrophobia sitting in the Assembly Hall through the tedious, unfunny opera, on a chair hostile to bum, balls and thighs – and then, to cap all that, to witness Mum's attentions to her partner! All right, all right, he wasn't a partner of that kind! At least not provably!

'Well,' Sam had edged up close to him again as they took stock of a yard quite remarkable in its darkness: scarcely a light on anywhere nearby, the Priory at its back not flood-lit as normal, street lamps, by government decree, shining at forty per cent of their strength. The parked cars here, thought Pete, looked like so many rows of turtles which might crawl away into further deep shadow. '*Well! To* think I'm actually standing beside one of the Lugg Valley's few celebrities: Mr Peter Kempsey in the flesh. How did you enjoy that little Yuletide entertainment we've just endured?'

Pete couldn't do better than: 'And how did Mr Sam Price enjoy it?'

Sam gave another of his snort-laughs: 'Whatever fool do you take me for, man? It was a load of shit, was it not?'

'Can't disagree,' Pete said.

'Speaking of shit, do you fancy any? We've got enough time and…' he gestured ahead of them, 'plenty of space. What with Mr Merchant's gory ailment and all the TLC your true Florence Nightingale of a mum is giving him, not to mention my Old Man's tendency to hold forth at the drop of a hat, the Lugg Valley Players won't be leaving their makeshift Green Room yet. We'll have the car park to ourselves, and can be "out of sight" in more ways than one!'

'Meaning?' asked Pete.

'Come off it, man, you know what I mean full well.' Sam's deep-brown eyes glowed like little gig-lamps in the dark. 'I've got the stuff right here, on my person,' Sam was assuring him, 'don't like to be without for too long. But the two of us should not skulk here so near the main building. Despite the prevailing murk, we can be pried on by any townsfolk of Titipu who emerge. Let's find ourselves some remote nook or cranny where we can safely get stoned if we want.'

Pete did not get stoned. But he inhaled that evening far more deeply than he'd previously done. How could he not when the spliff was being handed him by someone so 'sophisticated'? Soon a welcome warmth was easing an unresisted way through his whole body, separating the basic or profoundest part of him from all the surface irritations and discomfort of the evening so far. Beyond him little fleeces of vapour rose in the chilly air from between stationary cars to float over brick walls and beyond, where they sought out larger vapours hanging over the town's water-meadows. Watching these gave Pete a pleasant sense of being anchored, and anchored in company appetisingly differ-ent from anybody else's in his life. The corner the two youths chose to occupy was blocked off by Lee T. Webster, Electrician's parked van.

'So this is something of a red-letter day for me, Peter, meeting you,' Sam told him, 'I need to talk to guys with brains, you see, otherwise I'd perish here in my parents' house, wouldn't I? And how could I do better than talk to your brainy self. Assuming I'm up to it!' Pete, suspicious he was being sent up, noted the asym-metry of Sam's oval face, mouth crooked on the right-hand side, one eye possibly a tiny fraction of an inch lower than the other.

'Pete, not Peter,' he stalled, 'I'm never Peter to friends. Never!'

'Keep cool, friend, not a matter of life and death surely! But I'll be kind enough to comply. So tell me, *Pete*, doesn't it feel strange treading the streets, going in and out of public buildings, riding trains and buses with the common herd, all the time knowing you're the cleverest person the region has to offer?'

For all his bravura on the programme Pete did not consider himself this. People might think he did, but he didn't. Paradoxically his two radio victories had made him doubt his intelligence more than at any other stage of his life. 'Only the cleverest among volunteers,' he corrected.

'But I heard your June performance, man. Wow! Three times wow! And I was actually present in the audience for your first show, yeah, right there,' he jerked his thumb behind him, to the school buildings, 'back in September '72. My Old Man felt we ought to do our local support bit, and so he dragged me along. Those tests you told us all about – they must be quite something.'

'True, true... but,' said Pete, marvelling that Sam had remembered this, 'but... but...'

He was being given an opportunity, he suddenly saw, by this brazen young man who was arousing his spirit and his flesh in about equal measure, to put right his relationship with Leominster, with the region, the country, the world, with his parents, his brothers, himself. Get himself on a decent, realistic footing with all that. These 'buts' could mark a tentative beginning of his doing this...

'But *what*, man? It's a fucking fact, as I see it.'

'It could just be a happy coincidence that the things I shine at are what those two American shrinks value most. That's what my parents believe, I know. They don't say so outright, but it's obvious. Mum's always loyal to her old college friend who gave me the tests, but I'm pretty sure she agrees with my Dad who thinks...' painful to get the next words out, but Sam's presence, and the spliff, stimulated – or relaxed – him into managing them, 'who thinks I'm not even as clever as my two younger brothers.' He shivered, not with cold nor dope, but from feeling afresh this injustice, this mistake in computation. He looked round him, before going on with what he now had to confess to this new friend of only minutes' duration.

'I've got myself up shit creek in all this *High Flyers* business, Sam.'

And after daring his deepest and sweetest inhalation of the evening, Pete described his deception. 'So there it is, the BBC is expecting me to participate on January 31, while my parents think I did as they wanted, and declined.'

Sam gave out a low hoot of conspiratorial interest. 'Well, they're lopping your balls off, aren't they? And you can't have that! Parents! Mine were determined I went to a swank public school, to prove how much dough they'd accumulated over the years, and chose Darnton,' he spat out the name in hatred, 'and I couldn't be doing with life there. It may have traditions that go back a thousand years and have ace connections with the law and the church and the army, even with the pearly gates themselves, but it wasn't for me. And I told 'em so enough times, and others told 'em too, but did the fuckers listen? Did they hell! So in the end I was forced to see to my own removal, wasn't I?'

By now Sam was standing even closer to Pete than before. So much so that, leaning against the meeting of two brick walls as they were, it felt as though they were lying upright together, two mates side by side in some natural outdoor bed, in an intimacy that intended to go further than just the exchange of youth's miseries. 'Now listen, Pete, you've fucking well got to act on your own behalf, just as I did. And I know just how.' His eyes had a fervid, almost hysteric sparkle. 'You're going to write straightaway, this very evening when you get back to your abode, to Bob Whats-his-name. You will tell him to address any and every communication to Mr Peter Kempsey c/o Price, The Tall House, Bargates, Leominster, Hereford-and-Worcester. You will explain you're staying with us while your parents are away. I'm now living at home – going to a crammer's in Hereford in the New Year so I can take my A Levels in the summer – and I'll get downstairs to the morning post before anybody else does. But to be on the safe side, I'll spin Mother and the Old Man some tale – oh, that I've agreed to enter some competition in your name because – well, are you eighteen yet, Pete?'

'Not till January 7,' said Pete, now a-bubble with an elation he couldn't name. Behind those stammered 'buts' of a few minutes ago had been the longing to extricate himself from his brain-box status – and his apparent need to live up to it in his own community (as well as to a nationwide audience). But now, with the aid Sam was proposing he passionately wanted to vindicate it. And bugger the whole lot who doubted him.

'Well, *I* turned eighteen in September. So there we go, my friend. Parfait! Perfetto! I've entered the competition because I'm eighteen whereas you are not. Obviously I'll let you know the split-second anything comes from the BBC. How d' you feel about it?'

'Sounds pretty watertight! Yes, I'm up for it!' Anyway hadn't he a moral duty to take part in the January 31 special edition? Bob Thurlow might well have decided on this extra edition of his show primarily to give a further opportunity to Peter Kempsey whose brilliant earlier performances he so admired. What other course was there for him but subterfuge?

Or rather, *more* subterfuge.

'This spliff's been great, hasn't it? Made us a friendship,' said Sam. And if it were physically possible for him to inch further towards him without the two of them actually melting into one another, he did just this. Patchouli and the caressing fumes of dope engulfed Pete, banishing the car park's plague-wraiths of night mist – and with them his martyr's humiliations. 'Something to be pleased about, huh?' That lopsided grin of his widened. 'Oh, and another point! Don't tell your parents a goddam thing till the actual date.' He articulated the next words in a loud whisper right into Pete's left ear-hole. '*Not till January 31 itself!*'

Pete said, 'Christ, you've thought it all out in no time! I reckon you're a bigger High Flyer than I am, Sam.' He couldn't pay anyone a greater compliment.

Their talk went onto more general things, and every sentence seemed to Pete confirmation of Sam's own reading of their situation: yes, the shared joint had made them a friendship. They only stopped when there was an irruption of torches into the gloom of the yard followed by the voices of their carriers. The cast of *The Mikado* and their helpers were finally leaving the school premises from the side door that Sam had revealed to Pete, a ragged aural army of chatter, laughter, hums from the ridiculous show, and best wishes for the festive season. Sam put a finger to his lips, and the two of them remained in their corner so motionless that even Lee T. Webster, Electrician did not see them as he came and drove his van away... Here was Trevor Price himself, self-importantly swinging his arms, as if he truly were Emperor of Japan. And now – Pete's mouth emptied of saliva at the sight – came Mum and Oliver Merchant. Considering the intense and varied proximity the pair had enjoyed all evening, their present movements were remarkably circumspect, not to say chaste. Mum walked independently, holding her bouquet of freesias-and-roses like a torch, as Pete himself had done earlier. Did he feel a little disappointment as well as relief at this? Did he want to get in Dad's good books at last, as his filial defender?

Sam was saying, 'Coast clear now, thank the Lord! I'd invite you back to mine, but the Old Man will have arrived in Bargates before us, and he'll be wanting to gas on and on about the triumph of the show.' Not half he won't, agreed Pete inwardly. 'He wouldn't let us just sneak off to my snug by ourselves. I'll walk with you as far as yours instead. Where is it exactly that you live?'

Great that Sam, so early on in their knowing each other, was volunteering to behave like any other mate. Yet Sam's last question, and the tone in which he'd spoken it, was annoying. He'd implied that wherever Pete lived it would be socially inferior to the Prices' Bargates house. And Pete Kempsey felt inferior to absolutely nobody... But, the two new friends made their way through the Priory churchyard and across the Priory Green, in a Leominster never so dark since World War Two.

They made plans to meet in a coffee bar this coming Thursday, December 27 (when, as Sam said, 'this farce of a festival will be over'). Pete cast, as often when out after dark, many a glance up at the strong sandstone tower of Leominster's Priory Church of St Peter and St Paul, almost willing its protection.

Etnam Street now; Pete could already discern the form of the Christmas tree in the front bay-window of Woodgarth. 'The Old Man's getting me a car first week of New Year so I can drive myself to my studies,' Sam was proclaiming, 'so you see... opportunity knocks for us, Peter – *Pete*, I apologise! We can go places together, have another spliff or three, listen to some good music.'

Pete said: 'Great. Let's do that!' Then, '*good* music,' he thought, and 'Do you like Jerry García by any chance?' he asked as casually as he could, and avoiding the very name 'Grateful Dead'.

Sam snorted out: 'Jerry *García*? Why, the man is quite simply a genius.'

'But when the great "Pig-pen" died earlier this year…' began Pete, to test his new friend further.

'The whole world seemed to come to a fucking end,' said Sam with a loud, sad, self-conscious sigh, 'but then the Dead's new album, released in October…'

'Wake of the Flood,' put in Pete hastily, in case Sam might think he didn't know.

'Turned out their best yet!' both boys said in unison.

Satisfied with such likemindedness Sam made as if to walk away, towards his house in Bargates, on the west side of Leominster's town centre. Then he clearly had a change of mind and swung round back to Pete. 'Do you want to hear something that happened to me shortly before I left Darnton? Do you know what Darnton even looks like?' he asked.

And though Sam's tone of voice here unpleasantly resembled that in which he'd asked where Pete lived, the reply had to be: ''Fraid I don't.'

'It's an old foundation and the School House actually dates from the sixteenth century, but most of it's Victorian Imperialist stuff run along medieval lines. Darnton town's pretty dismal, at least I think so, but countryside round it isn't bad. Ordinary fields, grazing pastures, little woods – typical Midlands. And it was out in the country there that I had my big experience.'

Bigger than being on *High Flyers,* I'll warrant, thought Pete.

'It was the last Wednesday in September. I'd just had my eighteenth birthday, and, by way of celebrating it, a little sermon from my Housemaster about not putting my shoulder to the wheel work-wise. I was really glad, I don't mind admitting, to be out on my own, on a long run. I've always enjoyed long runs, other people can get on my nerves so I like the solitude you can have on them. "How can I put up with another year of Darnton?" I asked myself, and Pete, I'm ninety per cent sure I spoke the words aloud. I'd come almost to the end of one field, and raised my head to look at the shape and size of the next one, and there, Pete, it was…

'In the sky, about sixty or seventy yards off. Resting on the air just a little higher than the tallest trees nearby! Circular object, two feet across. Joined to one end was a box shaped like one of those old magic lanterns, and this box was pointing right down *at me*. "Whatever are you? Have you come to my call?" I shouted out, "I need your help!" And before you ask, no, NO, I hadn't been smoking a fucking thing. I may have been known at Darnton as the Spliff King, but I promise you I hadn't been near one all day. And do you know what happened next, Pete?'

How could he? Pete was a-tremble with anticipation.

'This weird object moved so that the box part of it jigged up and down. It was like it was acknowledging what I'd just shouted out, and assuring me of something. Of my own powers, I guess. It must have stayed there nodding in mid-air at least a minute and a half. And then the entire contraption…'

'Burst into flame?' from Pete who felt as if he might do so himself, with the thrill of this anecdote.

'No, it disappeared. Melted into the golden afternoon. This may be hard to believe, Pete, but I wasn't afraid in the very least. You see, I felt *I* was part of *its* experience rather than t'other way about. Wherever it had vanished to, it was taking a little section of my own self with it. Understand? Now, Mr High Flyer Kempsey, what do you make of that? What do you think it was that I saw that last Wednesday in September?'

What could the mesmerised Pete reply but: 'A UFO?'

'You've said it, man, you've fucking said it!'

'I used myself,' said Pete, recollecting hours of boyhood reading, 'to be pretty interested in them.'

'Interested nothing!' said Sam, 'I've fucking *seen* one! And it's a pity more of us don't. We need UFOs in this goddam rotten world of ours. Happy Christmas!'

And with that Sam gave his friend a half-mocking salute, and then began walking up Etnam Street with big strides which – of all things – reminded Pete of Mr Trevor Price of Price's Menswear, as he made his way importantly about the town…

'Happy Christmas?' Hadn't the Prime Minister himself declared: 'We shall have a harder Christmas than we have had since the War'?

Christmas Eve, Christmas Day and Boxing Day – Pete awoke to thoughts about Sam Price. They may well have permeated his sleep also. He went over, with an obsessive, painful thoroughness, every divisible minute of their time together after *The Mikado*. How quickly Pete had felt sure enough of Sam to tell him about the parental opposition to the next *High Flyers*! Pete loved, warm in the security of his bedclothes, to linger on the expression in Sam's tea-brown eyes, the grin on his crooked, down-turned mouth, the saliva that had collected on his lips while he drawled out his advice (which Pete had now acted on).

But – here was the thing – no sooner was he rejoicing in his new friend's boldness, style, and sympathy for Pete himself, then absurd little misgivings would start bothering him. It was like having an itch, which you knew you could not deal with in public, but which furiously, tormentingly increased. The jeering low tone in which he'd quoted from 'Honky Tonk Women', the boastful look on his face as he spoke of his old public school, Darnton – these and their like got in the way of some of his most admiring images or cherished sound-bites.

What if Sam forgot about the meeting on the twenty-seventh? Should Pete ring and remind him of it? Or (better idea!) give him a call which would go something like this: 'Having a good Christmas and all that crap, Sam? Just wanted to find out! Still on for Friday? Just checking!' But he didn't do either.

Oliver's presence at Christmas feasts hadn't really improved them. And Julian and Robin, at eleven and ten, were not fit companions for himself, though inseparable from each other. Surely Pete had been more discerning at their age? The watchful, crafty Julian truly excelled (it was sadly a fact of life) at maths and music, yet this second Paganini could sit beside Robs, on the

sitting-room carpet, gaping not just at TV but at David fucking
Cassidy in the idiotically popular *Partridge Family*, singing his
Puppy-song.

'Give us a break, can't you?' Pete shouted. 'You're supposed
to be *musical*, Julian. Song's words don't make sense either. Why
should having a puppy mean Cassidy stays away from crowds?
Pity he can't stay away from Etnam Road.'

'Pity *you* can't stay away from it, Peter,' Julian retorted, 'you
don't like it here. You get nastier and nastier every day. You think
only High Flyers have the right to exist.'

The intense hostility on his nearest brother's face, the concentrated resentment in his unbroken voice took Pete quite aback.
He was to carry memories of them, in a rebuke palpably more
sincere than point-scoring, for three-and-a-half decades.

Well, Sam and Pete met, as agreed, at the 'in' coffee bar for
Leominster's youth, at 11 o'clock on December 27, and, gratifyingly, it had been Sam who rang Pete an hour beforehand to
remind him of their appointment. Sam didn't look quite as he
had these last days in the slide show in Pete's head. Not so tall or
broad-shouldered as himself, he was of neat yet sinuous build,
enhanced by that irregularity (more pronounced by light of day)
of facial features, by his gentle but unmistakable list to the right.
He was wearing a wide-lapelled suede blazer flaring at the hip,
and jeans flaring at the legs.

Sam told him, virtually first off, that, rather than be here in
Leominster, he'd like to be engaging in his favourite sports: ice
hockey, skating and skiing, both cross-country and slalom.
Economics and opportunity had made Pete a stranger to these,
and he surmised, rightly, that Sam didn't much care for team
games. Over Christmas he'd read Dostoyevsky's *Crime and
Punishment*, which Pete, who'd after all answered a question on
the great Russian writer on *High Flyers*, had not read. One day
perhaps…

'Which brings me to your own Christmas, Pete. Didn't you tell
me Mr Oliver Merchant, he who has a quite unearthly resem-

blance to our great PM, came to you for Christmas Day lunch. Not jetting forth any more of his precious blood, I hope? Your mother didn't have to play the ministering angel again?'

'No, not at all,' said Pete curtly, 'Ol was in the best of health.' And particularly pleasant to himself, he could have added, saying that there was nobody's advice he valued more than Pete's when he showed him a new design for a Sunbeam Press card. 'After lunch we all had a game of Cluedo.'

'Cluedo!!' Sam drawled the two syllables out so loudly many another coffee-drinker turned round, some friends of Pete's included. 'Cluedo? You don't fucking say. That kills me, man, positively kills me.' Somewhat vulgarly he blew across his cup of espresso to cool it. But then if you'd been to somewhere as posh as Darnton, you could get away with such abandonment of ordinary good manners. 'Have you never heard of the "weasel under the cocktail cabinet", Pete? Read Harold Pinter, man, read R.D. Laing, read Kafka and Dostoyevsky…'

His derisive attitude to Pete's domestic life notwithstanding, Sam asked if they could meet same time same place the next day. Naturally Pete agreed. He noticed that Sam did not go home straight after their coffee but along to Price's Menswear, in the same street. 'They're getting ready there for the January sales,' he reminded Pete, 'and I bet you're slavering at the lips already at the prospect of the bargains the Old Man is offering. I have to keep in with my Estate, because one day Trevor Price, though you may not believe it, will pop his clogs, so it will fall to me to manage it.' It shocked Pete to hear somebody speaking of a parent's death so lightly. On the other hand he himself didn't feel so close to his father that he would look in on his office, which was virtually opposite Price's. 'But I've got pretty thick these last weeks with some of the reps my father uses (good blokes for the most part), because don't please think that he confines his selling to those who merely walk into the shop off the streets of our town. Oh no, my friend, a thousand times no. He casts his net wide and cunningly does my Old Man.' This painted a picture of a very different man from Pete's father, with his high-principled worries about the state of the country. 'One guy among 'em you should meet one day. Don Parry, a real character, a card. He lives out at a place called Llanrhaeadr-ym-Mochnant, outlandish name but not outlandish to Don.' Nor apparently to Sam off whose tongue the syllables came with impressive speed 'He's really into the Welsh language, and things written in it: the *Mabinogion* and tales of Arthur generally. And he's probably had more women than any of those Knights of the Round Table, including Lancelot! That's what he'd have you believe anyway. And he can drink his rivals under the table... You must meet him.'

The next morning, December 28, they met again at 11 am at the coffee bar. Ever since saying goodbye to him the day before Pete had been unable to think about much else than seeing Sam again. His gleaming tea-brown eyes were like hooks to draw him into the world of his desiring. Was this a good thing? Should he try to resist it? He also learned today that Sam's A Levels were not in standard Arts subjects like his own (History, English and Art) but in Biology, Maths and Economics. This suggested sides of his personality he had not yet manifested. Also these were disciplines in which Pete was weak, unlike the Brats, Julian and Robin Kempsey, with their flare for mental arithmetic. 'Well, you'd better come round to tea at our house tomorrow,' Sam said, as they parted company in the High Street, Sam once again about to go off to his father's shop, 'last Saturday of the year, and all that, the Old Man will be shutting early, taking life easy before the rush of the January sales begins properly. I'm glad to be leaving 1973 behind – though our PM can't be, 'cause he knows next year he's going to be well and truly crucified, and next year starts Tuesday!! But the old year's brought a lot of suffering my own way, Pete, and I'm fucked if I want any more of it... Know where we live?' He was rightly assuming Pete would accept the invite. 'The Tall House, Bargates.' Pete heard pride in his enunciation.

The name Tall House was apt enough for this late Victorian villa. A flight of a dozen stone steps (slippery that afternoon with skeins of frost that had neither melted nor been scraped away) led you up from the pavement, past a steep little front garden dark with laurels, to the front door. Pete felt self-consciousness invade him as he rang the bell and heard its jangling chimes resound within. It was one thing speaking in a studio to a hundred thousand Britons or more, another turning up at a house which apparently looked down on your own.

Mrs Price answered the door bell. She switched a small smile onto her heavily made-up face, and tonelessly asked him in. The hall had rugs on the parquet floor and little tables bearing objects which Pete (whose vastness of general knowledge didn't extend to such things) immediately marked down as collectors' pieces; more of the same were visible through the panelled double doors to the left. Neither of his own parents came from backgrounds which passed on heirlooms, and Dad was unabashedly tight with his respectable salary, even though it was supplemented by Mum's more modest one. Had he not got three sons to bring up, and had he not to bear in mind the possibilities of a rainy day, possibly soon?

The Tall House, it was at once clear, was a household governed by very different values from Jim Kempsey's. Sam's parents had after all kept him until last term at a swank school where he'd been 'miserable', in deliberate contrast to a local one where he might perhaps have been a deal happier. Mrs Price looked Pete up and down with her somewhat bloodshot and bulbous eyes, as if to ascertain the cost of his clothes, not an item of which had been bought at her husband's store (used by Pete only for school gear). Then in a flat, guarded, but recognisably Black Country voice she said: 'Sam gave us notice only this morning that he had someone – you – coming round here.' She appeared to be as innocent of Pete's identity as he of hers. 'We didn't imagine you'd want to be having much to do with Mr Price and myself when you turned up. So we thought it'd be best if Sam took you into his snug. Conchita can bring your tea in there, in due course.' Her manner couldn't remotely be described as welcoming. Pete thought her words amounted to: 'Mr Price and myself don't want to have much to do with you, so we thought you'd best... etc.'

After Brock

Her son looked even less like her than than he did her husband, though her blue-rinsed bouffant hair was a greater barrier to spotting similarities than Trevor's baldness. Her complexion was unnaturally pale, not improved by savage application of powder, while her eye shadow gave her round face a disquieting, bruised look, as if she were recuperating from a fight. As Pete was seeking gauchely to assure her that these arrangements were fine by him, Sam himself appeared from the far back of the hall. His drawl sounded more languid than ever as he stated, with one of his most irregular smiles: 'My mother's afraid, you see Pete, the two of us will bore her and the Old Man with our demands for intelligent conversation when they're settling to their usual Saturday afternoon telly. So she's requested our latest skivvy to serve us tea in my little snug.'

All this talk about skivvies and snugs was making Pete feel well and truly awkward. And once inside the little sitting room that was Sam's snug – on the ground floor, to the back of the hall, and lit today by a couple of paraffin lamps – its owner was far less forthcoming than on their three previous meetings. Then Pete realised that his host was quite determinedly and watchfully leaving conversation-making to him, testing his powers while he himself reclined indolently on a BIBA sofa piled with cushions. There was plenty in his present surroundings to prompt remarks: an expensive-looking record deck (a Garrod?) and quadraphonic speakers (wow!), a backgammon table (well, that was a game Pete enjoyed and played well, and would condescend, when he was in a good mood, to play even with Julian) and a dartboard, plus a bookcase full of the classier Penguin and Picador titles, novels by Hermann Hesse, Franz Kafka, John Cowper Powys and Fyodor Dostoyevsky. Also on the walls were expertly mounted posters: of Genesis, and their albums *Nursery Cryme* and *Foxtrot*, showing Peter Gabriel in extravagant attire highlighting their anti-Tory number 'Selling England by the Pound', of the Dead (naturally!) and Jefferson Airplane – in the last case, a blown-up picture of the cover for 1973's own *Thirty Seconds Over Winterland* with its celebrated eye-catching squadron of flying toasters. (Flying toasters led Pete to think of flying saucers – for surely what Sam had seen in Darnton really did belong to this category?)

Also on the snug's walls hung four pictures in gilded frames, identical in overall design but strikingly different in colouring (poster-paints). Pete had never seen anything similar and was at a loss to place them in any context. In each an octagon of three-dimensional appearance was set within a diamond, which itself stood at the centre of eight triangles, but blocking their apexes. So often were Pete's eyes compelled back to this quartet of variants that eventually Sam, smiling, informed him, breaking the virtual silence: 'Jungian mandalas, to answer the question you're too shy to ask. They help me, you see.' Pete could find nothing to say back to this extraordinary statement. 'I did these pictures, after Jung's own model, when I was still at Darnton. There was one guy there, Andrew Smithers, who was far less of a bastard than the others, and it was he who introduced me to the whole world of the mandala. It's the inner world of all of us, of all humanity. But I expect you know no more about mandalas than my revered parents, who thought these paintings on the walls exercises from a geometry book which I'd decided, like a kid, to colour in.' He gave one of his snorts of mirth-that-wasn't-mirth with which Pete was becoming familiar.

At that moment there was a tap on the door, and after a word-less, affirmative grunt from Sam, in came a dark-haired, leathery-skinned, saggy-bodied woman in her mid thirties, dressed entirely in black and wheeling a trolley. Elegantly laid it might be but Pete, with a Home Economics teacher as a mother, saw at a glance it was all shop stuff (just as Mrs Price could assess the worth of his clothes): Warburton's sliced-bread for toast, a cheap make of strawberry jam, one Mum always avoided, a Lyons Victoria sponge cake. Only the most minimal commu-nications were made between the son and this – servant (?), who slunk from the room without even the shadow of a smile on her face. 'That was Conchita,' Sam informed him, 'my parents always get a foreign woman of a certain age and practically no

English to do their bidding, though they never stay long in The Tall House, and who can blame them? From time to time I wonder if Conchita is expecting me to fuck her, and whether I should oblige so she doesn't feel unwanted, but I haven't got round to it yet.'

Pete felt instant distaste at this remark; it struck a false note. Then his eyes met Sam's and he realised he was being tested again. This made him blush, and even if he hadn't then, he would have done when Sam said with a change of key, almost of register: 'I don't think we know each other well enough to talk about passion, do we? I have this damned feeling that passion's going to be my undoing, one of these days. Not so far ahead.'

As Pete felt disinclined, indeed unable to make any reply, Sam got up from the sofa. He went over to the trolley, from which he picked up the teapot. 'Perhaps you don't want tea?' he said, with one of his most twisted grins, 'perhaps you'd like some apple juice? Maybe, on a cold wintry afternoon like this, some *hot* apple juice?'

'Why ever should...?' began Pete, but Sam interrupted him: 'Because of your great feeling for apples, natch. Because of your gargantuan encyclopaedic knowledge of 'em. How did it go now? I'm afraid my memory isn't quite of the Wellerman-Kreutz kind – The Foxwhelp, once Herefordshire's favourite but now replaced by – yeah, got it! The Redstreak.'

Pete, not unimpressed, cut into this with a young man's version of that cool voice his mother had used to put Sam back in his place after the show: 'Tea will do me fine, thanks!'

'Pity we can't share some shit,' continued Sam unabashed, 'and I scarcely need to tell you that I have quite a bit in this very room. But there'd be a hell of a shindig if we were found out. And I don't want to go through that just at the moment. Ironic with Jefferson Airplane looking down so lovingly from the walls. That's the origin of their name, you know – Jefferson Airplane means a scrap of used paper split so it can hold a joint when it's been smoked too short, like ours was the other night. Stops your fingers getting burned.'

'Yes, I know,' said Pete, 'I guess I've read exactly the same articles as you.' Why was it better to be here with Sam than in some tea shop with Melanie, so unceasingly kind, so sensitive to his many moods? Why was he preferable even to the Brats, to be nicer to whom (after what Julian had so feelingly said) would be his 1974 New Year Resolution? Did he even *like* Sam? He was far from sure that he did. But that wasn't the point. This afternoon he felt more intensely held by him (and with no dope for excuse) than ever before: by the constant if shade-shifting dark brilliance of his eyes, by the asymmetry of his grins which appeared and disappeared like the Cheshire Cat's, by the powerful aroma of his patchouli, by the whole aura emanating from his fashionably clad, supple body.

'Well, it can't be *apples* again, your special subject on Jan 31, can it?'

'Obviously not!'

'So what are you going to choose? Got round to giving it any proper thought?'

The fucking cheek of him, thought Pete; whatever does he think I've been doing? But, truth to tell, (not that he *would* tell it to Sam Price in his present haughty mood), nothing he had come up with so far – breeds of dogs; giants from Goliath onwards; earthquakes (further localism this, for one of Britain's major geological fault lines runs through the Welsh Marches); currencies of the world; kites (surely the most original and pleasure-giving of the topics so far) – had seemed satisfactory.

'I'm still working on it.'

'You're not chickening out of our little scheme, I hope?' asked Sam, now back on the BIBA sofa and sinking himself deep into its cushions while balancing his tea cup deftly, 'let me remind you that you yourself said my idea was "watertight".'

'I'm sure it is,' said Pete. Didn't Sam realise that he was worried about other things than its efficacy, not least its eventual discovery? 'I've sent the letter to Bob Thurlow as we agreed – so let's wait till the letter arrives. Here at The Tall House,' he added.

'No, I don't agree,' said Sam in his drawl, 'I've got to have –

let's call it a return on my investment, haven't I? It was me who came up with the scheme?' And he waited for Pete's agreement, which, after a second's pause for surprise at Sam's attitude, he made, with a nod and a low, soft, slightly reluctant grunt. 'Well, then, I expect you to do your bit. You've got to be Highest Flyer by leaps and bounds, or else I shall feel cheated.'

'Cheated?' He had not once thought that his acceptance of Sam's proposal – made after they'd barely passed their shared joint three times one to another – had bound him to Sam, psychologically, morally if you liked.

'Cheated because I need stimulus if I'm to survive at all. The world around me – whether it's stuffy old Darnton or this snug,' and he waved a hand disparagingly round his comfortable, expensively fitted quarters, 'just isn't enough. I'm a superior soul. I know it; I guess I've always known it. And superior souls can't be expected to find much to interest them in inter-house cricket matches at school or small-town chitchat. That's why the idea of you as High (or Highest) Flyer was such a draw for me, and why I was so pleased when Fate – so to speak – brought us together.'

Pete didn't like hearing any of this much (if at all); on the other hand he was fascinated by Sam's frankness, and also (not without a prickle of guilt) recognised his own sentiments.

'You don't know many other guys, I'll warrant, who have seen a Visitant like I have. Like I told you about outside your house. Always remember that, Pete, it means I'm in touch with things in a way Mr Average simply isn't. There's only one person I can think of who may have the same affinities as me...'

'That bloke who works for your dad?'

Sam didn't look pleased at this interjection. *He* did the interjecting in any conversation.

'Don Parry, yup. And he's a good deal more than just a bloke working for Price's Menswear. Anyway, to continue! I can't be fucked around with or sold short. And now I've put myself on the line for you, I expect you to come up with the goods!'

What is all this talk of investment and selling and goods, thought Pete, when all we're dealing with is my special fucking subject on a BBC show? He applied himself to his cup of tea, which tasted stewed, like what you were served in cheapo cafes.

Sam may have perceived he had gone, for the present at any rate, far enough. He changed the subject, rather well, so that afterwards, looking back on this tea-time, Pete found it hard to recall just how offensive and bullying he'd been. Or whether even he'd been these things at all. 'I'm the world's greatest fan of the Grateful Dead and Genesis,' he was now saying, 'but I like other kinds of music besides, stuff that Jerry García and Phil Lesh would approve of, though: Yannis Xenakis, Pierre Boulez, Edgar Varèse, Karlheinz Stockhausen, John Cage. Know them?' As in so many other areas, it was only the names Pete knew (and not all of those!).

Sam saw Pete to the front door. Those panelled double doors into Mr and Mrs Price's antiques-stuffed sitting room, lit by gas fire and TV screen, were open sufficiently wide for Pete to have a good view not only of Sam's doll-like, blue-rinsed mother, now in a doze, but of his red-faced, hefty father seated in a winged armchair, a-gape at a Western, at the usual Stetson-hatted men galloping past the usual cacti and rocks. It was hard to imagine either of the pair having even a rudimentary flicker of interest in Boulez or Genesis. Sam saw Pete's appraisal of his parents, and Pete saw that he saw, and the beams of their eyes met in possibly their first sincere exchange of the day, even if non-verbal. Then Sam said: 'I'm so fucking lonely here, Pete.'

Pete surprised himself by answering: 'I can see that, Sam!' It was maybe a rude thing to say, considering Mr and Mrs Price had provided his tea, but Sam looked relieved that his admission had been understood, and more, accepted. Pete had understood that he'd behaved as he had this afternoon precisely because of this loneliness.

Then, 'Car is due to arrive on Wednesday. Second of Jan,' Sam told him as he undid the door-latch, 'the Old Man is generous to me in that sort of way, I have to grant him that! Doesn't spare expenses on me. I passed my driving test in November, first go, and straightaway he was talking about rewarding me, and how my own vehicle would help me in my new life at the crammer's. Once term's started, I can give you lifts into Hereford in the mornings if the times suit.' It was clear to Pete that Sam had already decided on this.

'Good idea!' said Pete. But he was not sure it was.

Certainly it was a real relief to be out of The Tall House, with the bite of the cold early evening on him rather than the Prices' heating turned on too high, and no longer under the control of Sam's mercurial, watchful, often assertive personality – and possibly too to be free of the discomfiting, experimental sound-world of Pierre Boulez. Pete decided not to make his way home directly, but via alleyways and paths which could give him a view of his native town at dusk. His feet knew for themselves the way to look-out points. He loved the position of Leominster – surrounded by farmland but with hills for all its far boundaries. Ordinarily visible from where he was now walking, these were – to the south, the long trapezoid form of the Black Mountains massif ending in the sharp slope of Hay Bluff; to the west, the austere, mostly bare uplands of Radnor Forest; to the north the conical rise of Titterstone Clee which has such dominion over Leominster's oldest rival, Shropshire's Ludlow. But so thickly did freezing fog lie across the land tonight, such a dearth was there, thanks to the PM, of street-lighting or road-lamps, that none of these familiar shapes could be seen. You couldn't so much as guess at their existence. If someone came up to you tonight and proclaimed: 'No, Leominster's situation isn't what you think, it's surrounded by a plain which goes on and on for miles and miles, like the Hungarian puszta,' you might be stumped for an answer. How could you convince the tiresome stranger otherwise?

From this thought, difficult to deal with for someone as whole-heartedly devoted to facts as Pete Kempsey, it was only a small jump – and his pulse beat the faster as he made it – to another. Was this not how disbelievers in UFOs conducted their arguments? Because the phenomena couldn't immediately be seen or touched or heard, because they couldn't (or wouldn't) reveal themselves at others' command, the cynical consigned them to non-existence. But all those saucer-like vehicles, those flashing lights, those moving boxes, witnessed by perfectly intelligent persons (Sam, for instance?) might they not well have (according to the rules of their own being) as firm a reality as, say, the Clee Hills, which he knew to be just over there though he couldn't see them tonight?

Accepting this as, for the present, unanswerable, Pete experienced a moment of inspiration which caused him – literally – to jump for joy, on top of a puddle covered by a film of ice, which cracked so that muddy water spurted out over his boots. 'Well, it can't be *apples* again on January 31, your special subject, can it?' he heard again Sam Price jeering, 'Any ideas of what you're going to choose? Given it any proper thought yet?' Well, now he knew. His next special subject would be UFOs.

UFOs would have enormous audience appeal and would be the greatest fun to research. And they constituted an important and challenging objective field of study. Sam – whose whole tendency was to look down on other people for the limitations of their concerns – would undoubtedly approve of Pete's sudden but definite decision. It'd be exactly the return for his 'investment' he was looking for, maybe expecting. For if Sam hadn't made his confession on the night of December 23, thus reminding Pete of his own boyhood interest, then Pete's decision tonight might never have been arrived at. For two pins he felt like making an about-turn to The Tall House and telling Sam in person.

But he did not.

Back at Woodgarth the first person he ran into was his mother. 'Rather later home than you gave me to understand,' she said in the flat voice that denoted her resigned disapproval where her eldest son was concerned. (Where was the high-spirited, cavorting Katisha now?)

'Does it matter all that much?'

'Only that we're having Gregory Pringle round.'

After Brock

'Gregory Pringle? Who's he when he's out?'

Mum contracted her mouth in tight irritation. 'Do you take in nothing that isn't to do with yourself, Peter?' she asked, 'Gregory Pringle is only the man who's been teaching Julian the violin these past eighteen months, and told us J was a young musician of real promise. And because they do everything together, and because he's already become quite familiar with his brother's instrument (*that* you've noticed, Peter, I know, because I heard you grumbling at him in your usual charming way), little Robin would like to start violin lessons now. That pleases Greg Pringle who's very caught up in this Kodály method which believes in teaching children instruments no matter how young. So we're giving Greg supper, as I surely *already* told you, so he can hear them both play.'

'Won't that be rather coals to Newcastle for him? Or, even worse, a busman's holiday? Here's the poor guy thinking he's coming round for delicious Saturday night fish-pie – I can smell it – and he's going to have to earn it by hearing the Brats making noises like those he hears every day of his working life.' In fact Julian played things like Boccherini's Minuet very sweetly, and Pete had little doubt his nearest brother was more musical than Sam, for all the latter's avant-garde knowledge.

His mother gave not a ghost of a grin at these sallies. 'Had a nice time at the Prices?' she inquired.

'Not bad, thanks!'

'Trevor Price talk about *The Mikado*? We should know our net profits by now, so Oliver said. Our box office takings, I understand, were better than expected for these dire financial times.'

'Old Man Price didn't demean himself to say hullo to me. Too busy, slumped like a pig in his chair, watching *Gunfight at the Okay Corral* alongside his funny wife who looks as if he's recently been beating her up.'

'I get daily more appalled by the sort of callous things you like saying, Peter, for the sake of being, as you think, funny. So it was just you and – that Sam?'

'That's right. "That Sam" and I sat around in his room, and had a bit of a chat.'

'*A bit?* – you were there for two and a half hours.'

'Well then, we had two-and-a-half-hours'-worth of chat. Time passed so quickly I didn't notice. We both had such a lot to say.'

'You surprise me! I mean, the end of the world would really be nigh if Peter Kempsey was at a loss for words: I don't know about the Price boy, of course, but as far as I can tell, he's another one with an over-ready tongue. Talk about women nattering; none of the girls I teach are half as loquacious as you and your pals... Oliver Merchant said Sam has given the Prices a lot of trouble. Apparently he has terrible rages, had one once when Oliver himself was visiting The Tall House. Ol said he'd never seen anything like it before. Trevor himself didn't know what to do with the boy.'

Best not to look interested here. 'Well, he didn't have any rages with me, I can assure you. We spoke of...' he was on the point of saying: 'What my next special subject should be', but mercifully stopped himself in time. Like grabbing hold of a runaway sledge before it hurtled riderless down a precipitous slope. But he blushed, as Mum saw, though doubtless she tumbled to the conclusion that the two youths had been talking sex. To disabuse her, but speaking with the other forbidden topic still unpleasantly and tauntingly in the outer layers of his mind, he said, 'Sam is very interested in the Wellerman-Kreutz methods.'

He could have hardly hit on a worse topic. As he should surely have known by now. 'Was he now?' said Mum, 'as if there aren't more worthwhile subjects to be interested by!'

Pete thought: my mum is a nice-looking, in fact a young-looking woman, always tastefully dressed – a black frock tonight which showed to advantage her slim figure – and so capable, so efficient, at everything she chooses to do. And a great many different people like her very much. Why then do the two of us not get on? Why are we always sparring?

Maybe he'd been stimulated by the sharp evening air outside because he dared to ask her (as he would for years recall): 'Why do you get irritated with me so often, Mum? What is it about me? Especially when I mention Wellerman-Kreutz...'

After Brock

In the brief ensuing pause Pete wondered if he'd managed a breakthrough (or, at any rate, a mini one). Wrong! His mother now quite literally turned her back on him and, making for the kitchen, said: 'I've really no time for such idiocies, Peter. Why don't you go upstairs and do a bit of long overdue revision, and I'll give you a shout after Greg Pringle has arrived...'

The syllables of the German-Americans' unforgettable names went on ringing for at least two minutes in Pete's ears after he'd, boldly and unwisely, spoken them, like the chimes of the doorbell at The Tall House. Wellerman-Kreutz, Wellerman-Kreutz.

On Monday December 31 Leominster's public library was open just for the morning, and there Pete took himself to embark on reading up for his exciting special subject. Whatever the tests meant, he knew his capacity for virtually instantaneous docketing of information inside his brain to be extra-ordinary (in that spelling!). Pete could positively *feel* his chosen facts (and many he hadn't consciously chosen) sliding, as if lubricated, into easy-to-find grooves within his head. He patiently worked his way through a large number of not always reader-friendly reference books. But he soon found himself on an enticingly long if steep and tortuous trail with new knowledge at every turn, every increase in gradient. And he was back in the library when it reopened (again for just the morning) on January 2.

Before long he appreciated that UFO sightings started with the onset – or, rather, the *perceived* onset – of the Cold War, with the coming down of the Iron Curtain. With these uncanny appearances was mankind being warned that it must not start off a Third World War? Though the term 'Unidentified Flying Objects' dated from 1952, what they referred to, mysterious 'astronomical' visitations, had been reported as early as summer 1946 when a high-speed wingless missile, cigar-like in shape, was reported from Sweden. Then a year later, in June 1947, Kenneth Allott, a serious-minded business man in Boise, Idaho, with 9,000 hours of aircraft flying behind him, mostly on Search and Rescue missions, saw *nine* brilliant objects flying over the

Cascade Ride, and thence across the face of Mount Rainier, Washington State, US. He took photographs of some of these, 'flat like a pie-pan', though one had a rear end shaped like a double crescent. They were 'flying as a saucer would', and in describing them so, Allott gave the world a new phrase, a new image, a new obsession.

In next to no time, flying saucers were, it would appear, whizzing earthwards just about everywhere. Even in the UK. In October 1950, the Ministry of Defence's Chief Scientific Adviser took the step of setting up a Flying Saucer Working Party. No case however made such an impact on Pete, as he sat there researching, as that of Lieutenant Thomas F. Mantell in Fort Knox, Kentucky.

This occurred on January 7 1948, and told the public that temporary celebrity was, tragically, not the only consequence of a sighting. Pete's heart increased its beat as he took in the date, for January 7 was his own birthday, he'd be eighteen in just a few days time, as he'd told Sam over their spliff.

The Fort Knox episode was especially interesting in that it wasn't the experience of one man alone: Lieutenant Mantell was with several colleagues when there appeared in the sky a brilliant white object (with, said some, a red border at its base) about 300 feet in diameter and moving westwards. Then it descended gently, to remain stationary (as Sam's apparition had) for an hour and a half. Men in the lieutenant's company noted a trail of green mist. When eventually it climbed back to approximately 10,000 feet, the airmen decided to pursue it. They dispatched four Mustangs, one piloted by Mantell himself. The higher this 'saucer' ascended, the higher Mantell and his plane climbed. When he reached 25,000 feet, he blanked out: his loss of control caused the Mustang to fall and crash, at Franklin, Kentucky. So Mantell's story is that of the first death brought about (if not intentionally) by UFOs. People said later that what drove the pilot onwards and upwards was the planet Venus, shining with greater-than-usual brightness that January 7. But there were those who declared that, on examination, Mantell's body showed marks of having been lethally fired at, and who could have done this but aliens? – an end so frightening the Pentagon used all its powers to keep it secret from the public.

Nor was that the only history the Pentagon held concerning the arrival of well-equipped extra-terrestrial beings. There was currently a belief that time was ripe for a new influx of similar arrivals, but would the CIA permit access to information and open discussion? Of course not.

Wow, what terrific material! Pete vividly saw himself relaying fascinating high spots from stories like these to his audience at Broadcasting House and to his vast listening public beyond it. He could imagine the look of stunned admiration on the face of Bob Thurlow, a letter from whom he awaited daily.

One reference book informed him that the great psychologist C.G. Jung had taken an interest in Unidentified Flying Objects, and had written about them in his autobiography, *Memories, Dreams, Reflections*. Remembering Sam Price's mandalas, Pete looked out this famous book and located it on the library shelves easily enough. Turning to its index, he found the entry: 'UFOs pp 239, 354 ff, 366,' and chose to follow up the middle one of these, to read the following:

'In one dream, which I had in October 1958, I caught sight from my house of two lens-shaped metallically gleaming disks, which hurtled in a narrow arc over the house and down to the lake. They were two UFOs (Unidentified Flying Objects). Then another body came flying directly towards me. It was a perfectly circular lens, like the objective of a telescope. At a distance of four or five hundred yards it stood still for a moment, and then flew off. Immediately afterwards, another came speeding through the air: a lens with a metallic extension which led to a box – a magic lantern. At a distance of sixty or seventy yards it stood still in the air, pointing straight at me. I awoke with a feeling of astonishment. Still half in the dream, the thought passed through my head: "We always think that the UFOs are projections of ours. Now it turns out that we are their projections. I am projected by the magic as C.G. Jung. But who manipulates the apparatus?"'

What – or rather, who – did *that* remind him of?

This piece of purloining nearly deterred Pete from his choice, for it showed him how thoroughly Sam himself had intellectually penetrated UFO territory. Wouldn't this make for difficulties? Wouldn't he be better off with one of his earlier possibilities? Kites, for example. And as it happened, when he got back to Woodgarth, his favourite of the two Brats was waiting for him in the hall, with a 'Bro, look at this!' Robin with his red cheeks and bright eyes did distinctly resemble the family's redbreast who held such winter dominion over their front garden. This human Robin was holding before him a sheet of blue paper which had been inserted in some Christmas gift book, headed 'How to Make a "Sled" Kite for £1.70.'

'Well, you haven't got a single one of the materials asked for, have you?' observed Pete, who never needed long to absorb a document, 'a sheet of heavy-duty polythene! Where will we find that? And a roll of "Cardoc" nylon cord, eh? Haven't noticed many of them around! Cheer up, Robs, we can get 'em easily enough when the shops open tomorrow, and then we'll have a go.'

'No, I don't think so!' came Dad's measured, cross voice, from disconcertingly near; Pete had forgotten that in the three-day-week he worked two days from home rather than in his office, 'Robin, your brother Peter has his A Levels to prepare for, if I am not mistaken. He certainly hasn't time to go traipsing round shops looking for special types of polythene, let alone spending valuable hours putting the contraption together... I'll help you to do that, Robin,' he added, giving away the real reason for snubbing Pete: that he himself would enjoy making the kite; it'd take his mind off his worries.

Pete wasn't going to let his dad have the satisfaction of a victory. 'Suits me,' he said, 'I was only trying to be brotherly, as you're always saying I'm not. It isn't as if I'm bothered about kites one way or another.'

Untrue, but there you were! Still he couldn't now go on and

choose kites as a special subject. He would just have to stick with UFOs, about which, he wagered, his knowledge easily outweighed Sam Price's already.

At half-past seven that evening the telephone rang, and soon Mum was saying in what her son thought of as her most Home Economics voice: 'Yes, and a very Happy New Year to you too, Sam... I'll pass you over to Peter, who is just in the middle of studying some A Level text or other.' (A barefaced lie!)

'Hi, there, dude!' came Sam's drawl, 'it's arrived, just as they promised. Right on cue.'

For a moment Pete had no idea what he was talking about. 'They' surely couldn't mean the BBC, and yet...'You mean...?'

'I mean, the new car my Old Man promised me, what else, moron? Not my latest Kalashnikov or my luminous, scented sheath,' Pete's blushes deepened on the spot, 'or my 1974 subscription to a Swedish girlie magazine, or whatever other desirables have just been flashing through your fertile, well-stocked mind. My new car – and tomorrow I'm going to try her out with my father – and then by myself, to see how I get on. But Friday afternoon, all being well, and if you're free, we could go out somewhere together. I can be round at yours at half past one, if you'd like that.'

'Great!' said Pete, 'great!' And so it seemed. This Friday heralded the last free weekend before the school term started. The whole British nation might be in financial straits, might be literally and spiritually groping around in darkness and in the seizures of bitter class warfare, but Trevor Price could still buy a new car for his maverick son. Pete had no difficulty in envisaging a drive worthy of a movie, Sam cool at the wheel and himself, snazzily dressed, in the front seat. His blood rose in him at the appealing picture.

At exactly one thirty that Friday (January 4) – a fine winter's afternoon, and not even as cold as the journalist doomsters had predicted – Sam turned up at Woodgarth. He was driving a VW Beetle, the 'Economy Car'. Pete felt both relieved and disappointed. Wasn't Trevor Price's choice of car for his son rather nearer what Jim Kempsey's might have been for Pete, had he felt like being generous in this respect (which itself took a good deal of imagining, his dad being such an unrepentant skinflint)?

'Before we decide where to head off to,' said Sam, as Pete sat himself in the passenger seat, '*this* came for you this morning. Thank your good friend Samuel Price that his plan worked. Remember what he expects of you too.' Pete shuddered here. 'You're more in my debt than ever now.'

'No need to fucking rub it in!' said Pete, tearing open the envelope.

As well as the usual details, the letter added:

'As this is a first in our programme – this friendly battle of the highest scorers who never actually became Highest Flyers at national level – we have decided it would be good to have another innovation. This time competitors will not undergo questioning on their special subject. Instead I will invite each of you to speak on the matter for five minutes.

'Ten members of the audience invited by the BBC and not by the competitors (and therefore without any personal loyalties) will be given cards bearing numbers from 1 to 10 to hold up after each talk. This score is then added to that achieved in the General Knowledge – and thus we get the total required for a winner. So please let me know your choice of special subject as soon as you can. Please find stamped addressed envelope enclosed.

Yours cordially,
Bob (Thurlow)'

Sam watched Pete reading with sly, keen, ironic eyes. 'Any joy?' he asked languidly, hands on the steering wheel as though he were in no hurry to be off. 'Any mention by the great Thurlow of the special subjects section for which he'll have to prepare those tricky questions to fire at you.'

Here was Pete's opportunity for admitting to – no, not '*admitting to*' (which smacked of guilt), for 'informing' Sam of his choice. In fact he could make it sound as though it were an inspiration of this very minute. 'Hey, Sam, don't you think *UFOs* would be a really ace topic. What you said about 'em has got me going again now!' But instead he clutched at the actual wording of Sam's question. 'Bob says there's going to be no special subject question-and-answer session this time.'

'Dear oh dear! Strike me pink! Revolution on Radio Four. Wherever next? *The Archers* will be moving to the Mile End Road before we know it!' said Sam, 'anyway, High Flyer, where do you reckon we should go? With the weather as good as this we should head for mountains.'

'Yeah! But mountains to the north and west,' Pete answered instantly. For the Malverns to the south-east and the Black Mountains to the south-west were Jim Kempsey's usual choices for family afternoons-out. Pete wanted, needed, a change.

'Suits me!' said Sam, 'Andrew Smithers, the guy I told you about at Darnton, thought one reason the dump didn't suit me was that there were no hills around – not like here. If there had been, it all needn't have happened. He could well be right. Had I stayed put in the Marches, I might have been like any happy sixth-former of the area. Like yourself in fact – except of course, you have a giant brain, which I could match with my giant soul. Who's to say?'

Pete wanted to ask: 'It *all*? *What* needn't have happened?' But he didn't; judging Sam's tone a tad truculent. As in his next sentence, a hipster's apology: 'No shit for this outing, I'm afraid. No nicotine either. Clean car, clean living – that's my motto for today!' Pete felt more relieved than sorry.

But as they pulled out of Etnam Street, he realised that conversation between them, in so confined a space, was going to be sticky; Sam clearly never modified moods for anyone else's sake. His present inclination to taciturnity with sporadic sarcasm made Pete, who, as his mother had stated, not only liked talking, but liked others to talk as well, physically uneasy. He shifted about in his seat until Sam gave him a sharp, reproving sideways look. Better if they had been bowling along in a Porsche or a Lamborghini. In prosaic reality Sam concentrated on driving his

VW with an earnestness suggesting neither confidence in his own abilities nor certainty of the Highway Code. Was this why he decided not to go along the A49 (connecting Leominster via Ludlow with Shrewsbury) but to take a country route in the direction they'd just decided on: over that puzzlingly named hill, The Goggin, the dense woods clothing it quite bare now, and then through the Teme valley, with Leintwardine and its large old church presiding above its north bank?

Home territory though this all still was, Sam didn't show himself at all familiar with it. Clearly Trevor Price had not been one for outings such as Pete's dad had taken his family on. And Sam had spent most of his life away at smart boarding schools. So Pete now had to prompt Sam about turnings, signposts etc and to volunteer info about the places ahead. Impossible not to notice at such moments Sam's dark eyes swiftly narrowing in irritation, so as the minutes went by, he steeled himself to abstain from any officiousness. Even so, only after Sam commented sarcastically, 'I take it you've already *got* your licence,' did Pete finally lay off. Sam's face had, he'd thought, been as cross, and as handsome in crossness, as a swan's when it rears its neck round towards you, to warn you off his particular stretch of a river path.

Once they'd crossed the county border into Shropshire the change in the countryside affected both youths, though neither spoke this aloud. Here it was emptier, less fertile – grazing land. Hills came higher, wilder, sheerer in their slopes, and closer. They were also more generously covered with snow from the night before. Villages were sparser, mostly hamlets made up of adjoining farms, palpably unlike Herefordshire's black-and-white half-timbered communities revolving round friendly greens or squares and with churches that told of centuries of comfortable prosperity.

As the great long natural bulwark of the Long Mynd, culminating in a weather-whitened plateau, showed more and more of itself on their right, Sam obviously felt that this little outing for the Beetle, this occasion both to test himself and to show off his dad's present, had already had some success. The muscles of his face relaxed, he became less like a cob-swan. 'We might as well go to – what-d'you call 'em... The Stiperstones, eh Pete? I chucked a map onto the back seat; take a peek at it, and find out what roads to take.'

Pete said: 'Stiperstones – brilliant! But I don't need to look at any map, I can tell you the best way off the top of my head.'

'Your mighty head!' said Sam, 'so unlike the head of anybody else!' Pete couldn't but be disconcerted by this, and the tone of its delivery. After all in the car park after *The Mikado* it had been Sam who'd defended the tests against Pete's own doubts.

'Some day I must look into these guys of yours more fully 'cause you don't seem too clued up about them yourself. Are they Freudians? Jungians? Adlerians? Kleinians? (Quite likely Kleinians since you were tested when you were only an ickle child.) But then they might be disciples of Wilhelm Reich, one of the greatest men to have walked this earth. But I doubt it. They're more likely to be common-or-garden arse-lickers of H. J. Eysenck, a man I utterly reject...'

Pete felt inadequate before this coolly delivered onslaught. Psychologists were clearly something Sam really knew about. He remembered the Jungian mandalas Sam had drawn, and the correspondence between his UFO encounter and Carl-Gustav Jung's of two decades before. About this last Pete didn't want to question him. A Sam Price mockingly quizzical was preferable to a Sam Price annoyed, and probably as capable of retaliation as swans similarly cornered. Anyway, before long, the heather-covered, snow-powdered west flank of the Mynd was forming one side of the narrow country road they'd taken, while on the other a breathtaking vista opened out. There, displayed against the sky, The Stiperstones stood, westernmost of South Shropshire's four great parallel ridges, five miles long, and unforgettable because of the long irregular line of huge quartzite tors cresting it, each different from its fellows in shape, each with scree at its feet, like shakings from a mason's apron.

Pete couldn't resist telling Sam the facts with which years later he was to impress Nat, 'The Stiperstones is 1,759 feet high and the rocks you can see on the top are 500,000,000 years old.' But Sam didn't snub him, as he'd half-feared, and after Pete had informed him that the biggest and most distinctive tor was called The Devil's Chair, his interest even seemed to quicken. 'And when you can't see the Chair from below – because of rain or fog or something – it's a bad omen; you should start to worry. But if you can't make it out from nearer to, then *real* disaster's on the way, so get serious. It might be World War Three. Or the end of the world itself.'

'You don't say,' said Sam, 'well, that shouldn't bother us too much.'

'What shouldn't?'

'The end of this world. It's not such great shakes as it is. I thought I'd made my views on that clear enough already.'

When Sam spoke like this, was it out of affectation or real deep-down dissatisfaction? Pete countered his companion breezily: 'Well, this day's the clearest we've had for ages. I can see The Devil's Chair standing out as sharply above the patches of snow as if some giant race left it there for us to find.'

He was to use almost identical words to these last when he went out here from Lydcastle on trips with his son, Nat. Whatever the merits of the conceit itself, it changed Sam's mood suddenly and entirely. Even during the best moments of their communion after *The Mikado* Pete had never seen him in such good humour. This presently developed into high spirits of a boyish kind Pete wouldn't have suspected.

Maybe it was the day's nipping cold or maybe, it being Friday, likely tourists were back in the workplace, but the beauty spot was devoid of visitors, and so swathed in silence. Neither sheep nor birds disturbed it – nor the red grouse, nor the two ravens in slow movement above the first significant tor in the long hilltop line, Cranberry Rocks. The boys did not impact on it either, walking uphill from the deserted car park. But when they reached, after the exhilaration of a short steep climb, that part of the main path which runs the length of the hill's spine-like crest, Sam surprised Pete by pointing ahead and asking in a stage yokel's voice: 'That there be The Devil's Chair, bain't it?' And by then sprinting off. *Really* sprinting too, though his feet, unlike Pete's own, had no knowledge from previous experience of all the pathway's treacherous little twists which skeins of black ice now compounded. Pete decided to let Sam have the freedom he so clearly wanted, therefore didn't take off after him. Soon, Sam was on top of the enormous quartzite pile which has fascinated so many over such a vast period, was standing against the deepening blue of the afternoon sky, in a black-leather bomber-jacket worn over red-and-blue Icelandic sweater and with a tasselled red woollen cap pulled over the ears but leaving long strands of jet-black hair still exposed.

Should Pete, now having gained its base, join Sam on the Chair? He'd have scaled it in next to no time had he been up here with Mum and Dad and the Brats (whom, especially Julian, he would have done his best to keep away from this tor). But what if today, for the first time ever, he were to miss his footing, slip, fall, something daft of that sort? How humiliated he would be! Also Pete sensed that Sam was positively relishing his own apartness against the great canopy of the winter sky, wouldn't want even those two ravens circling Cranberry Rocks to be given any indication that he and Pete were mates.

And were they? Pete couldn't, even now, decide. What he did know was that Sam Price was fiercely anti-sentimental, would never dream of expressing any admiration of his attributes or pleasure in his company... Oh well, that's how he was!

'Whoo-hoo! Here I come, earthlings!' And he did, bounding down towards Pete, arms stretched out straight like an animated scarecrow to preserve his balance in his precipitous descent of the huge, slippery pile of rocks, displaying an agility at least equal to (but not surpassing!), Pete's own on previous visits.

'Christ, view's fucking brilliant!' Sam exclaimed, 'All Wales lies on the other side, I know, Land of My Fathers, or at least of Trevor Price's,' and he gestured to behind the gaunt shape of the Chair he had just mounted, 'but what am I seeing from here? The Wellerman-Kreutz wizard can surely tell me.'

The ridges looked more like great beached whales than ever today, whales with their backs caught out of water by snow showers. 'Well, that's the Long Mynd directly ahead,' said Pete, 'and over there's Wenlock Edge, and the Clees. Brown Clee is in fact higher than The Stiperstones, though it may not look it from here.'

'I can't believe, friend, you're not going to supply me with its altitude down to the last fucking foot,' said Sam.

Ignoring any irony, Pete supplied, 'Brown Clee is 1,772 feet high. And if you try to look behind the Long Mynd, Sam, you can see the Stretton Hills, which are even more ancient than here: pre-Cambrian or Uriconian Volcanic,' he couldn't help his pride in knowing such things, 'well over 600,000,000 years old. And I'll tell you something else: The Stiperstones, all this extensive quartzite terrain about us, survived the Ice Age. So, had we been around then, we'd have seen only the very tops of the other hills peeping up out of the swirling seas.'

'Well, even now they look a bit like a school of whales half out of water,' agreed Sam, pleasing Pete with his quick analogy. Even though so many had made the comparison before.

But the very thought of the antiquity of the Shropshire hills spurred Sam into speaking again of the matter so dear to him.

'I suppose other planets – and obviously I don't mean just the planets in our own solar system – have histories as long and complex as Earth's and must have gone through just as many face-changes. So how can it be not just possible but *probable* that some of them (even if it's only two or three) have developed sophisticated forms of life – intelligences, if you like – which are curious enough about Earth to want to help it or to frighten it into averting further disasters? It's not a very happy place, our planet, is it?'

Pete winced, but he didn't want to disrupt this present, unprecedented, marvellous harmony between them. The right time would come later. 'Not happy?' he echoed, 'well, it looks terrific this afternoon, wouldn't you say?' and he swivelled his gaze slowly all the way from Shrewsbury, past the Wrekin and the rises of the Severn gorge right the way round to where loomed first the Black Hills, and then to their south, the Black Mountains, that familiar landmark on Leominster's own allotted sky.

'Yes, it looks okay enough on a day like this. It would fool anybody,' said Sam. He moved his head to look in the opposite direction from that Pete was surveying. 'When I asked you, before we set off, where you wanted to go today, you said "North and west". And that was fine by me. It's turned out well. So what's north-and-west of here?'

For a horrible moment Pete's mind was empty of an answer. And as he turned his head to the compass-point Sam had just mentioned, he didn't feel the usual smooth rolling of information from the well-oiled grooves of his mental chambers. Way beyond Shrewsbury the atmosphere was considerably thicker than else-where, with infiltrations of mistiness. If the West is the last direction to retain a day's light, it's invariably the first to manifest coming changes in the weather. A greyness piled on its distant and indistinct northernmost heights suggested showers, most likely of snow, soon to sweep eastwards over England – maybe even before midnight... then the wanted name slid, albeit bumpily, into Pete's head. 'The Berwyns,' he announced, 'over the Welsh border.'

'And?' Sam's face had gone a bit swan-like, a bit fierce again. 'What might they be like?'

But Pete knew nothing to recite at him. 'Pretty wild, I believe,' he said.

'The wilder the better. That's where we should go next.' Pete's heart skipped a beat with pleasure that Sam should be wanting not just a repetition of but a sequel to today, 'and hey, I've just remembered: I've told you about Don Parry who lives in Llanrhaeadr-ym-Mochnant. Well, that's over in the Berwyns, isn't it? To our north-west now?' Pete nodded assent. 'Well, there's a date for the two of us to fix: a call on old Don Parry. You'd like him, Pete, he's quite a character, a real card. Has no end of stories about the Welsh past. And the Welsh present too – at least where women are concerned...' The man has made a huge impression on Sam, thought Pete, what he's saying about him now is virtually word for word what he said before. 'But now we should be making tracks!'

Back in the car – and they were glad of its warmth after the sting of the winter air now the sun was in retreat – Sam said, casually enough, and in the drawl with which, Pete was beginning to notice, he protected himself against social awkwardness, 'I was a bit of a bastard all the journey here, I know. I'm feeling less of one now I've been in touch with my *mineral* self. I guess we all have mineral selves, coming as we do from… from all this rock! And I wasn't telling you the truth earlier either. I do have some dope here; shall we smoke some?'

They did.

Once down in the valley again it was already evening, its thickening shades in such contrast to the light still carpeting the hills to their west. Sam turned on the car lights, for the first time, he said, since his ownership. In terms of the amount of remarks exchanged the homeward ride was proving quieter than the outward one, but what a different atmosphere! Yes, Sam did have qualities Pete couldn't find in any other of his friends. Not one of them would have talked about his 'mineral self…' Also on this return journey Sam was handling the car rather more confidently.

So it came as a shock when, suddenly, he braked. The abrupt action bounced Pete alarmingly, jarringly in his seat. It needed quite some self-manoeuvring just to stay sitting. 'Shit!' Sam exclaimed with a loudness that bored through Pete's head, 'fucking shit! Did I bloody hit it?'

The outrage in Sam's voice was infectious. 'Hit what? I didn't feel anything.'

'Hit that badger crossing the road, idiot. Where are your eyes? I swear there was one, but it's hard to see things in this narrow lane. I'd hate to kill a badger.'

He stopped the car engine and jumped out of his driving seat into the dark of the minor country road. Then, 'Yeah! It's okay!'

he called back, 'Thank God...! Want to come and have a look, Pete?'

He was continuing, reinforcing that easy inclusion of Pete in feelings and actions which had begun in earnest only after he had come down from his solo scramble up the stern irregularities of The Devil's Chair. Pete hadn't associated him with tenderness towards animals. Was that another product of his rock climb? Or had the joint brought it out from under the several layers of his difficult, perturbing self?

Pete stumbled out of his passenger seat, and, without completely straightening himself – his movements must be stealthy lest he frighten the animal – he crept across to where Sam was standing stock still, as if mesmerised. And sure enough he soon made out the large shambling creature, dark-haired, much the colour of the evening itself, but with a broad white stripe on the head and further stretches of whiteness for cheeks and chin. About two and a half feet long and heavy in build it was – surprisingly so to those who didn't often see its kind – and short in the leg. Nevertheless it was now moving purposefully at a slow trot towards a clump of ferns beneath a modest outcrop of rock on the left-hand side of the lane. Pete was closer to it than Sam, but for the next four chilly minutes at least, both of them stood still side by side, so close to one another that Pete's right shoulder leaned against Sam's left. They hadn't enjoyed such proximity since the night of their first meeting. Only after the animal had gained the swiftly enveloping security of the ferns did they relax. They had seen the badger's long strong sensitive snout continuously pointing down to the surface of the road as if it might find something there to snap up, and the highly developed claws on its forefeet. Looked at closer to, the dark of its thick hair coat was not a uniform colour, but charcoal grey on the upper body and black on the throat, under-belly and legs. Its tail was short, efficient, and grizzly grey.

'Safely on the other side, huh?' said Sam, with a sigh of satis-faction, 'well, I guess we can bugger off now. It seemed to know where it was going okay, didn't it? So why didn't it wait till my car had passed by?'

'They don't seem to have evolved road sense,' said Pete, 'but they're intelligent in other ways. I reckon that one was a female – most often the females are the first out from the sett when it's dusk, like now – and she's making for what's called an "outlier", a sort of satellite sett. Generations of badgers have worked pretty direct tracks through the undergrowth from one to the other, but of course they haven't taken man-made roads into consideration... at least they are protected by the law since last year, 1973. That might well have been our badger's first airing in quite a while after so long a cold spell. They don't hibernate exactly, but spend days at a stretch underground in the winter, warm and safe, and with provisions of food.'

'Sensible!' said Sam, 'on which note we should get back into the warmth of my car. I might have known you'd be a mine of information about badgers like everything else.'

'In this case not a mine,' said Pete, following Sam back into the VW. It came to him that he knew next to nothing about the deeper pattern and texture of these animals' lives, not even how many years they could live. He should do something about this.

'Brock!' he said suddenly as Sam started up the engine again, 'that's an old name for badgers isn't it?'

'Yeah. When I was little I used to read the Sam Pig books, you can see why he appealed! And there was one called *Tales of Four Pigs and Brock the Badger*. I read them again and again; I must have really liked them for some reason.'

'And it's a bit sad,' agreed Pete, 'that school never taught us more about them. We should take seeing this brock just now as a reminder that we must learn from animals.' Instead of which, he thought, I've set about cramming my head with facts (to call them, that) about the extra-terrestrial.

After this things went even better, in truth went the best ever, between these two young humans. And the quiet Shropshire hill country through which they travelled homewards seemed to encourage conversation.

As Sam swung the Beetle onto the A49 just north of Craven Arms – because it was getting dark, he'd decided to go back to

Leominster by the highway – he said to Pete softly after a break in the talk scarcely long enough to be termed a pause: 'Things aren't a bed of roses for me at home, you know.'

Pete said: 'Well, are they for any of us?'

'Mine's a very different case from yours, I'll wager. Your parents are decent people; I don't think that description fits mine, for all my dad behaves as if he's living up to the first line of his song in the show: "A more humane Mikado never did in Japan exist!" But he isn't. He beats my mother up!'

Didn't I know it? Pete thought unhappily. Didn't I say something of the kind to Mum, only she wasn't having any of it. Blinkered as she always is against anything I say. But sometimes it's worse being right than wrong.

'And the terrible thing is – I don't always blame him. She's so disgusting and foul-mouthed when she's drunk.'

Pete felt too shocked to find suitable words. But he now experienced a rush of tenderness towards Sam such as he'd never felt for anybody in his life. Didn't Sam *need* his friendship? This was something Sam wouldn't ever acknowledge, which made the feeling itself easier to accept – and endure.

After his disclosure Sam looked like a cob-swan again, 'Anyway, Pete, now I've told you, we'll drop the subject. As I've said, I can take you into Hereford in the morning when term begins. And we'll have a Berwyns expedition too. I'll get in touch with old Don Parry, maybe even tomorrow… And you, everything's hunky-dory at Woodgarth is it? With old Oliver Merchant round every touch and turn. That man bats for the other side, doesn't he?'

Pete, not knowing this expression, said: 'Oh, yes, I expect so!'

Sam, realising his ignorance, which was also innocence, said no more here.

As they drew nearer their home town, both boys were struck by the roadscape not looking like its normal after-dark self. It took them a moment to understand why not. Buildings you expected to be lit up against evening were bleak, black shapes; of the string of lamps leading into the town, a fair number were not on at all, and those that were gave out the ghost-town rays of the new regulation wattage. Pete had to suppress a thought that this bore some resemblance to the change of mood between them in the last half hour. Sam's revelation of his parents' relationship had somehow darkened and chilled what, after Brock, had been so glowing and warm.

As he walked up the small front garden of Woodgarth he saw the family had started the evening meal without him. There they all were, at the dining-room table, the curtains not yet drawn (a practice Mum considered unfriendly before a comparatively late hour of the evening; 'We have a lot to learn from our neighbours, the Dutch,' she'd say, 'who think as I do on the matter'). Shimmering candle-light showed them to better advantage than the now proscribed electric lighting could ever have done: Dad and Julian, their strawberry-blond hair shining in the flickering beams, talking animatedly and smilingly away to each other (when had he, Pete, last elicited an animated smile from his father? Had he ever done so?), Mum leaning over the table to give Robin, the son who most resembled her, an extra helping of what Pete knew from the casserole dish to be Irish stew (with sliced carrots and parsnips, and dumplings – the best in the West Midlands). Good people, all of them, Trevor and Susan Price's conduct was unthinkable inside Woodgarth. And yet Pete felt as apart from it as, in physical terms, he now was.

That night he took a long time to go to sleep. His own fault really. After reliving the afternoon's 'mineral moments' with Sam, he'd gone downstairs to Dad's bookcase and taken out a book his father had bought, when a young man, to celebrate the Festival of Britain. It was called *A Land* by Jacquetta Hawkes, and was illustrated not only with extraordinary photos of petrified mud-cracks and ammonites and bivalves but with colour-plates by Henry Moore. It portrayed Britain as the result of a long process of evolution, not just political-historical, ethnic and cultural, but geological, natural-historical too. Back in his bedroom Pete turned to the Pre-Cambrian Age, 600,000,000 years ago, to which the body of the Long Mynd and major sections of the Strettons belonged.

'The young [Pre-Cambrian] world was without spring; it knew nothing beyond rock and water. There was the colour of open skies and of sunrise and sunset, but when the sky was overcast the landscape was sombre beyond our present comprehension. Colour had not as yet been concentrated in leaves, petals, feathers, shells. The only sounds came from the movement of water, whether of rain or streams or waves, from thunder, and from wind sweeping across rock. At long intervals this passivity was convulsed by erupting volcanoes and by the rending and falling of vast masses of rock, but silence and stillness prevailed. No one inured to the din created by our species can conceive the silence of a calm day on pre-Cambrian earth. I cannot use the word *hush* which perhaps best conveys the sense of a closed-in silence for it also implies a world of life that has fallen silent. This was a negative and utter quiet.'

And this terrifying scene (though there was no living being there for it to terrify) was stark reality once, and who was to say it might not be reality 600,000,000 years hence? To imagine sixty years hence, with himself no longer a lad with dark hair worn longish but a grey old man past the traditional three score years and ten, was hard enough. To imagine a future made up of 600 years was an impossibility: even 6,000 defied sanity, but 600,000,000...Yet such a world at such a date was as near to him tonight as that silent, sky-dominated world which Sam and he had gazed on this afternoon.

Where had *he* been all that time? Waiting in some cosmic wings, like Mum and Oliver Merchant preparing to come on stage? Where in all those hundreds, thousands and millions of years had any sign been given that one Peter James Kempsey would exist in the mid-twentieth century as a sensate flesh-and-blood-and-bone being that considered itself as important an item on the planet, not to say within the universe, as any other? Considered itself, moreover, unique. Wonderfully so.

'You were nowhere,' was the dreadful, irrefutable answer, 'just as in 600 or 6,000 years you won't be! The destination of every-body, everything, anybody, anything you've seen, or read or heard of.' Dead, deadness, death! His body broke out into a cold sweat, the first of several, to assault him in successive waves of clamminess. He longed to go downstairs and put his arms round his mother and father, for all their irritating ways, and round Julian and Robin for that matter, and assure them – but what? It was himself he wanted assurance for, and he realised they could give him none.

When finally he went to sleep, however, it was to dream very briefly, but accurately, of that badger waddling its (her?) way towards the ferns in the early evening. This didn't disperse these quite appalling reflections – which came back to him regularly throughout the next week or two – but it did provide a modest protection against them, an image of stubborn and, yes, beautiful life achieving a manageable aim. Snout held down and quivering with attention, stripe white against the encroaching evening, claws sharp and ready, short legs confident that the track on the other side of the road could not only be reached but trodden, despite all the density of the thicket, until the sett and safety were reached.

In the morning he rang up Sam. Half of Pete wanted to share with him the visions, the snapshots of universal truth that *A Land* had forced on him; the other half wanted his friend to say some-thing so diverting that these fell away, evaporated. But he had obviously rung too early. At half past ten Sam clearly hadn't been up long; a luxury forbidden at Woodgarth.

'Hi, Sam, it's Pete.'

'Well, I can tell that. Whatdyerwant?' This last, delivered as one ill-swallowed word, did not have a detectably friendly ring to it.

He could hardly reply, 'To stop thinking about what it was like six hundred million years back and what it will be like in six hundred million years' time.' Instead he said, 'To see how you are!'

'In fair enough shape,' drawled Sam, 'but I'm missing my Orgone Accumulator.'

'Your *what*?'

'No. You haven't got round to the great Wilhelm Reich yet, have you? You're unaware of the great value of an Orgone Accumulator.'

'I'm sorry?'

'You wouldn't even understand me if I explained it, you're such an innocent. But if I said name derives from same word as 'orgasm', perhaps you might have a bit of an idea.'

'I'm not sure I would!' Sam wouldn't surely be meaning what it sounded as if he were meaning. 'I just rang to see what you were doing over the weekend.' He'd like to have said something that referred back to the riches of the day before. But Sam was in one of his moods again.

'Following the social calendar of events that my mum and dad have drawn up. Probably won't meet any of *your* lot. But that's the harsh fate of us Bargates folk. But I'll be in touch Sunday night – or Monday, yes, certainly, Monday. And on Thursday next you might still want to take up my offer of driving you into Hereford instead of riding in on the train with the usual band of yobs…'

It's very possible that, had Sam not spoken to him in this affected, aggressive manner but had instead proposed – or even agreed to – meeting up that day or the next, Pete would have got off his chest his intended *High Flyers* special subject, and this whole history would be totally, unimaginably different. As it was, he was sufficiently hurt and annoyed to feel entitled to write to Bob Thurlow within the hour. And did so conscious he was dealing Sam Price some kind of blow. He popped the stamped addressed envelope that the quizmaster had sent him into the nearest pillar box within three minutes of finishing his letter.

Monday, January 7, one day before the school term started, was Pete's eighteenth birthday. At breakfast-time Dad announced he had opened a bank account for him, with £200 in it, a complete surprise (two hundred pounds from *Dad the Skinflint*). Julian and Robin had clubbed together to buy him a metal-framed Genesis poster (one, as it happened, matching Sam's in The Tall House) while, in the early afternoon, Sam himself dropped by, in the VW Beetle. He had remembered the significant date and, it turned out, had driven all the way to Hereford to buy Pete a present at its biggest bookshop: a Penguin Classics edition of Dostoyevsky's *Crime and Punishment*. Inside he'd written 'Happy majority, dude, January 7 1974. Your good friend, Sam.' Pete felt ashamed of his own meanness of mind.

His majority. Yes, now he could drive, though buying a cheap second-hand car would all but clean out his new account. He could buy alcohol and consume it openly in pubs and bars, though alas, the government hadn't legalised pot, which was better – and he could marry, though first, as the saying went, he should prove himself a man, and who with, for Christ's sake? Melanie? Hardly likely! And he kept away from those parties – some hosted by his own friends in this very neighbourhood – where casual sex was an accepted alternative to finishing a dance. Also he could vote, as eighteen-year-olds had been able to do since 1970 in the United Kingdom, the first European country to give them this privilege. But *who for*? Pete was weary of all the interminable debates about Heath and the (well-handled? mishandled? insoluble?) crisis, of the divisions inside the Conservative Party, the equivocations of Wilson's Opposition, the possible strength of Thorpe's Liberals, the anger of the Internationalist Left, including student bodies, the pronouncements (not always consistent) of the pundits. But, if the more contentious of these were right, the PM might well call a general election sooner rather than later to extricate the country from its knotted condition. So... the vote bit at least might happen fairly soon.

Before he left Woodgarth by its front-garden gate, Sam said to Pete in that low, sexy whisper only he could command: 'Like I said, you can ride into Hereford with me of a morning – though my term doesn't start till Thursday. Say yes, Pete, there's a good guy. I need the company, and to be honest, I'm pretty much dreading the crammer's. Better than being cooped up at Darnton, I know, but still not my cup of tea.'

'Okay!' said Pete. He could feel again, after its temporary absence, his desire to accommodate his unpredictable friend whenever possible. Had Sam not used the word 'need' himself?

Supper that night was a birthday celebration. Mum served up his favourite shepherd's pie, with a treacle sponge to follow, and Dad opened a bottle of Liebfraumilch, because, needless to say, Ol, the saintly, ultimately unfathomable Oliver (apparent batsman for the 'other side'), was at the table too – and indeed, as god-parent, presented him with a cheque for another £100 to add to what Dad had already put into his account. And after the excellent food Julian played a Hungarian folk-tune on his fiddle, collected by the composer Zoltan Kodály in a remote country village. It was beautiful in a plaintive way, and Pete told Julian he liked it very much.

Sam driving Pete into Hereford, far from requiring more sub-terfuge, even lies, turned out to be an arrangement others respected and even envied. For on January 10, to the consterna-tion of all Heath-watchers and the indignant satisfaction of his growing opponents, the train drivers went out on strike. Peter Kempsey was the only one of his friends who didn't have to bother about the bus companies: he had his own lift to school. Sam actually dropped him off there, before proceeding to the city centre, where his crammer's had its premises in a tall eighteenth-century town house (a bit like Ol's in Leominster) with a view of the Cathedral. Their afternoon hours coincided too.

How peaceful it was travelling with Sam those mornings of strife throughout Britain – from the valleys of South Wales to Lanarkshire, from Kent to the Pennines – through the gradually lightening pearly greyness, sometimes undercut by translucent envelopes of green and buttermilk pushing through the horizon, three or four mornings lightly filtered by snow scurries. Every morning they reached the city in time for sunrise so that its features – suburban roads, football stadium, Bulmers' great cider-factory, red sandstone cathedral, the spires of All Saints' and St Peter's, the banks of the river Wye in swirling spate as a result of snows on Plynlimon – were all recipients of a fresh-minted light. This lent each the patina of a daily discovery, a daily benediction which improved Pete's spirits – and even his school work. (He wrote a good essay on Wordsworth's *Michael*.)

Sam himself, as Pete by now anticipated, was unpredictable in mood, sometimes wanting to talk, sometimes wanting to listen to the radio, sometimes showing a careless masculine pleasure at having company, other times implying he was doing Pete one hell of a big favour just by taking him as a passenger. On the homeward journeys he was particularly apt to be edgy; he found classes at the crammer's a strain, and smoked ferociously in the breaks between them.

Some things about Sam became clear to Pete now (like the Black Mountains, white in the morning after a night's snow). Pete had assumed Sam's unhappiness at Darnton, to which he made countless bitter references as they travelled, had made him a strong opponent of public schools and their apartness from local, 'ordinary' life. Not a bit. When he remarked of his crammer's (properly a tutorial college), 'The guys there – both staff and student – are simply *not* out of the top drawer, just *not* the sort I've been used to associating with at Darnton,' Pete realised reluctantly that Sam largely shared the values of the school from which he had (but why? how?) engineered his own removal. It was only particularities and individuals he'd resented.

Pete's growing understanding of this led to him surprising himself. Every news the boys listened to on the radio intensified the generally accepted picture of a country nearer and nearer disintegration, chaos. Oil prices rising would mean petrol rationing (and, bizarrely, ration books had already been printed). Already there was the 50 mph limit. The train strike had caused disruption to many other services, at who knew what cost; for instance the post was now irregular in the extreme. (And here was Pete waiting for another letter from Bob Thurlow. And yes! when he had confirmation of his choice of special subject, then he would *of course* tell Sam all about it!) 'Our country can't go on in this fucking stupid way, can it?' said Sam after some news bulletin of further anarchy, 'why don't they call the army in to deal with the miners, for fuck's sake? Even the Old Man – who's as keen on profit-making as they come – goes a bit soft if you propose that. Remembers he has miner forebears down in the valleys, and all that crap. Well, sod the ancestors, say I. We can't be dictated to by a mob of oiks.'

'A mob of oiks!' Pete couldn't afterwards remember whether he really gave the disgusting words back to Sam or not. But definitely he spoke his next sentence aloud: 'I don't agree with you there, Sam. There was this bloke from the Miners' Union, the NUM, on the radio who said something like: "Why are you willing to pay the Middle East such fabulous prices for their oil and yet begrudge money to fellow-Britons working their arses off to get you your fuel?" And I think he was right.'

Sam jerked his head in quick astonishment to his left, then jerking it back to face the road ahead said: 'Well, *I* don't think we should be kowtowing to those Arab pillocks either. But that's another matter. What bothers me is – well, at Darnton I got to see some pretty big guys on parents' day: Sir Gilman Brand, for example, one of the men who really matters at Barclays, and Professor Maurice Weaver, the famous historian of the British Raj. (His son, Danny, was quite a one for a spliff, I can tell you, and his father knew and didn't mind.) And I fucking well don't see why all the sterling work men like that do should be put in jeopardy by the kind of shit we're getting now...'

The logic of this was not immediately apparent to Pete, but this was not the only reason he made no direct answer. Such a speech was wholly unsympathetic to him, and none of his school friends would have made it. But the fact remained – and oddly it *was* a fact – that Sam's company exercised a magic over him, theirs did not.

As if aware that harping on the distinguished parents of Darnton boys might have been a shade tactless, Sam, after switching off the radio and letting the stillness of the countryside prevail over roadway and car, said: 'Can't wait for a chance to drive over to those Berwyns and visit Don in Llanrhaeadr-ym-Mochnant. He's quite a character, you know, a real card.' (Were there no other ways of describing this mysterious guy?) 'He's as much a mine of information as your good self, but it isn't just facts, as it mostly is with you. Old Don's bristling with theories about – what you might call the seen and the unseen, the visible and the invisible.'

Pete was pretty sure that the dreaded term 'UFO' was imminent, but at that moment an Aston Martin did a nasty, and positively dangerous bit of overtaking, and after Sam's justifiably obscenity-laden outburst on its driver's recklessness, Pete was able to change the subject easily enough. And presently here was Hereford awash with sunrise.

That day, Friday, January 18, Pete returned from Hereford at half-past four to find his parents waiting for him in the hall. They must have heard his oncoming footsteps and positioned themselves. The fury in their faces would have been apparent to the most innocent eye, which Pete's was not. Behind them loitered the Brats both visibly trembling with excitement at the explosion they were soon to witness (which, needless to say, was none of their fucking business).

Mum waved an envelope at him, waved it so vigorously that a little breeze blew inside the close-carpeted, draught-proof hall. Before he could read anything printed on it, Pete knew its provenance: The BBC, Broadcasting House etc, etc. And now Dad was waggling his index finger fiercely above the typed address: Mr Peter Kempsey c/o Price, The Tall House, Bargates, Leominster…

Dad said: 'This is the *most* deceitful conduct, Peter, that I've come across since the sad case of Laurence Giles.'

It was good to have some obvious gibberish to seize on while preparing his defence. 'Laurence *Giles*!!' Pete repeated aghast –

and talk about melodrama, he splendidly outdid his mother hamming it in that Lugg Players' Victorian offering, 'and who might he be when he's out?'

It was an unwise rejoinder. 'I'm not at all sure he is out,' Dad said in a grim, quiet voice, 'Laurence Giles was the young clerk who appropriated funds from our firm, and got sent down – we were all surprised at the ferocity of the sentence – for eighteen months.'

Julian looked positively cock-a-hoop at this speedy verbal defeat of his elder brother. This moved Pete to say: 'If we are going to have to talk about this...' he gave an injured nod at the offending envelope, 'I'd prefer it if Jules and Robs were not around. It's nothing whatsoever to do with them.'

'That's for us to decide, I'd have thought,' said Mum sharply, and Dad backed her up by saying in a loud voice that wouldn't have disgraced a courtroom, 'It's everything to do with them. I want Julian and Robin here for every single minute of what your mother and I have to say to you. And to hear the pathetic kind of case you're doubtless going to make for yourself – in your habitual way.'

That 'habitual' was both below the belt, and inaccurate. Pete exclaimed: 'Habitual! I like that! What precedents have you in mind, Dad?' His father chose (wisely) not to answer. His mother's eyes were stony. 'Can we not at least sit down?' Pete went on, attempting nonchalance. But 'No!' said his father, and 'No!' said his mother, and the Brats were pleased to add their own negatives (in unison of course).

Well, it didn't take a Wellerman-Kreutz big scorer to work out what had happened, and Pete could have kicked himself for not having foreseen it. Because of the chaos in public services, the postman hadn't called at The Tall House, Bargates until ten minutes to ten, whereas he usually called at half-past seven, had called indeed just as Trevor Price was leaving for Price's Menswear. So it was he who received in person the letter from the BBC addressed to Pete. He then recollected the garbled story Sam had spun him before Christmas, to which, little interested, he hadn't paid close attention – about the Kempsey lad preferring to keep quiet about some competition he'd entered for and using the Prices' house as a PO Box. 'Well, I thought in these strange times we're living in, I should just bring the letter round to Woodgarth.' And when he did, he found Mum in, as bad luck would have it, the electricity situation having involved radical reorganisation of her cookery classes at the Comp. 'And I felt humiliated, I don't mind telling you, Peter!' she informed her son, 'because, I'm sorry to say, before I had so much as opened the letter, I understood what had been happening all this while, and behind our backs!'

'All this while? It's been barely a fortnight! And why *sorry*?' asked Pete, 'I'd have thought it'd feel good to have such accurate powers of deduction.'

'Sorry, because it meant that I had an eldest son who's perfectly prepared not just to fly in the face of decisions taken on his own behalf, for his own good, but to secure what he wants by underhand measures, involving lies to his own family as well as co-opting others to carry out his deceptions.' She could hardly have expressed herself more forcibly; her eyes were not stony, Pete saw, but ablaze with moral passion.

'Sam himself proposed that I used The Tall House!' said Pete, 'I never had to *co-opt*, as you put it, anybody. He was really indignant on my behalf at the lack of recognition I get from my own family.'

'Was he now!' said Mum, '*was* he now? And what form of recognition do you propose we should give you? That we chant a little grace before each meal about how lucky we are to have a champion in our midst? Don't make me laugh!' She appeared alarmingly far from doing this. 'As for Sam Price and his sympathy, the more I hear of that lad, the less happy I am that he's become such a regular companion of yours. Oliver was saying only the other day that he finds him watchful, supercilious and sneery.' (Pete, surprised by the asperity of the usually kind-tongued Oliver Merchant, thought, 'I wish that man would keep his moral reflections to himself'.) 'I know it's been very convenient, given the strike, your riding into Hereford and back with Sam, but I have noted a real deterioration in your general demeanour recently, and so have Julian and Robin.' The Brats nodded their assent enthusiastically. 'Heaven knows why he's so stuck up. So I for one wish you weren't having a lift in with that self-opinionated dandy. And please don't tell me that you don't enjoy the odd cigarette on your ride out, and I'd probably give a huge sigh of relief to find out that that cigarette contained tobacco…'

Pete's deep blush told her all she needed to know.

Dad did not seem much bothered about Pete's friendship with Sam; perhaps he needed Trevor Price's support, as that of a local bigwig, for some manoeuvres towards the Town Council. 'And there I thought we'd made such a good beginning to the year, Peter,' he said piteously, 'me putting that two hundred quid into an account for you…'

This was hard to bear, and Pete was afraid he might cry like a kid. Far easier to deal with Mum's schoolmistressy crossness. 'Dad, we *did* make a good beginning. You know how pleased I was by the new account and your kindness. I said so enough times, and I meant it… aren't we in danger of getting all this a bit out of proportion? And anyway what are you proposing to do? They expect me to turn up, the BBC; I've even chosen my special subject.'

'Yes,' said Mum, 'UFOs. Such a useful topic in today's fraught world! Typical!'

Before he could retort, Dad was saying, 'Well, obviously we can't now stop you appearing on the programme, and we'll see you go up to London and back all right. But you cannot expect us, after how you have treated us, to take any interest in it at all. Whether you do well or disappointingly is no concern of ours. We shan't even listen. Instead we shall do something we'd in point of fact been intending to do one day that week, take Julian and Robin into Bristol to see the production of *A Midsummer Night's Dream* that's had such good write-ups.'

Now Pete felt tears in his eyes, and no mistake: 'That sums up the relationship between me and my family perfectly,' he said, 'you infantilise me'. He had not been travelling into Hereford with an admirer of Jung for nothing. 'What you have just proposed is the sort of punishment you'd mete out to a small child. I know you don't think much of my intelligence, I know you think those two conceited little jackasses grinning away in front of me now are cleverer. Well, I don't care any more, do you hear; I simply don't care. I shall do my own thing in the world, in my own way, and it will be beautiful.'

Three

Unidentified...

Ping! That was the fifth or sixth pebble to hit Pete's bedroom window in the last couple of minutes. Was a freak wind blowing up those little stones Dad and he had laid last week on the pathway connecting front and back gardens? Very freak it'd have to be, for, though cold and cloudy, this evening of Wednesday, January 23 1974, it was also very still. As this was an electricity day by government permission, Pete's bedroom was warm and well-lit enough for him to persevere with *Reform and Renewal: Thomas Cromwell and the Common Weal* by G.R. Elton. 'If you show familiarity with it,' Mr Taylor at school had said, 'you'll impress any A Level examiner.' Pete had immediately envisaged this man, sweating out the July evening (when marking would be done) in some stuffy study, a pale-faced, prematurely ageing wreck, with a half-drunk mug of Maxwell House at his elbow, and an almost-empty packet of fags. Just as despair at his thankless task was becoming unbearable, his eye fell on a phrase: 'As the great contemporary British historian, G.R. Elton has written...' Whereupon the poor bloke would leap up and exclaim: *'Elton,* my sainted aunt! *Reform and Renewal.* Nothing but a straight A for *this* candidate!'

These were the last hours of Pete's Fifth Day of Disgrace, his parents persisting like the weather in general coldness, speaking to him only about household tasks and what work he'd been set for his A Level studies.

Ping! Another pebble. The sixth or seventh. Casting *Reform and Renewal* aside, he walked over to the window, the curtains of which he'd not drawn, and pressed his nose flat against the cold pane. Its moist chill on his skin sent him back to when he was a kid, and would envisage on the other side of the glass some visitor from Narnia or Middle Earth – Reepicheep the Militant Mouse, Puddleglum the Marsh Wiggle, or Gandalf and Frodo Baggins themselves – calling up to him to join them in adventure. And indeed tonight there *was* someone below, someone gazing up at him with bright imploring eyes: Sam Price, in tasselled woollen hat, red scarf, bomber-jacket, and jeans. He had in his right hand a fresh pebble, which he stopped himself from chucking upwards as soon as he caught sight of Pete's head and torso framed by the window. The relief he showed was like a parody of that emotion; shoulders sagged, knees splayed an inch or so further apart. Then he put the first finger of his right hand to his lips, and shook his head eloquently from side to side. He's telling me not to open my window and shout out to him, appreciated Pete, who mimed to him to come on in. Sam shook his head again, but now mouthed the words, 'No! *You* come down! *At once*! Important!'

Whatever was the time? The evening had dragged so in G.R. Elton's company he had little idea, but supper seemed long, long ago. Pete glanced up at the clock on the wall, a present from his parents on his seventh birthday, with an animal picture beside each number on its face. Only 9.15, squirrel minutes past camel. The evening had more of itself left than he'd supposed. Dad was out at a Civic Society committee meeting; Mum was in the sitting room watching a documentary about Kew Gardens, the Brats were up in their room. Nevertheless best to tiptoe his way down the thankfully well-carpeted stairs; only one of those naturalists who went in for recording bats could have heard Pete move. Whatever urgency could have brought cool Sam down in such stealth to Woodgarth? Was he in trouble? Had Trevor and Susan Price found the stash of dope in his snug and kicked him out? Or threatened him with the police? Or had some incident at the crammer's come to a head, comparable with whatever-it-was which had finished his Darnton career, and its Principal had phoned his parents? Or maybe – the worst possibility perhaps – his parents had had one of their violent set-tos.

Pete opened the back door with anxious caution, yet it squeaked and sighed. The hinges needed oiling, and Dad had asked Pete to oil them yesterday, but hadn't he performed too many penance tasks lately? So now he had to let himself outside into the zero temperature mighty carefully – to be immediately assaulted by Sam hurling his heavily clad body onto his. He pressed his brass-studded, leather-jacketed trunk and tight-jeaned thighs hard against him, and clapped a strong, gloved, determined hand over his pal's mouth. And into Pete's ear, in that sexy, creamy-thick voice at his unique command, Sam whispered: 'I've got the car parked a few yards up Etnam Street. If you don't come with me this minute, you'll regret it to the end of your days. No! Fucking! Kidding!'

On each of these last three words he gave Pete's right shoulder a vigorous shake with his free hand. And each shake felt to Pete like a sloughing off of stupid custom-bound restraint. He had, even in these nanoseconds, time enough to think: 'It's the school corridor and the car park all over again, but multiplied by ten, because of what's developed between us since. He led me that evening, and he's gonna lead me again tonight.' *High Flyers* apart, nothing mattered more to him than Sam's good opinion. His attitude to himself stood in strict measure to this, it grew in strength whenever he gained Sam's (usually unvoiced but nevertheless detectable) approval. For Pete was finding it harder and harder to dislodge niggling notions that he himself was essentially a nerdy, dull, unfocused, even conventional kind of guy, who would one day vanish 'without trace' into the vast crowd of his kind, the most unimportant of unimportant specks in the horrendous enormity of existence. Whatever his faults, Sam Price could not be so dismissed.

The two of them walked to the waiting VW Beetle, about a hundred yards off, in total silence. Cloudy sky, and wisps of mist rose from the ground in every direction. Sam, unlocking the car, said, without forgoing his tone of an initiate into mysteries which only he could disclose, 'Get in, Pete and I'll tell you everything!' Paradoxically Pete felt the stronger for doing as he was told. Only by compliance with Sam could he live up to the manhood his eighteenth birthday should have conferred.

Though – '*Everything*, mind, Sam!' he felt he owed it to himself to say.

Sam slammed the car door shut on the two of them and placed his hands on the steering wheel, but clearly had no intention of starting up the engine yet. With something of his usual truculence he demanded, quietly, 'Where do you think we're off to tonight? For this opportunity in a million?'

'But isn't that what you're about to tell me.'

'Guess, man, first. Use your imagination.'

'London?' (The Grateful Dead performing in some late-night gig that they might just about make with a bit of luck?)

'Wrong, man, utterly wrong. Though I wouldn't be surprised if London isn't on its list,' he added cryptically. ('Its'? '*Its*'?) 'You and me – we're headed for the Berwyns. Before schedule, you might say.'

''Streuth!' said Pete. 'Can I ask why?'

Sam just said: 'Dude, guess again!'

Pete tried again. 'That older friend of yours,' he recalled. 'The guy who lives in the Berwyns. Whatshisname!' And then out the required disc in his head slid. 'Don Parry!'

Over Sam's face, unprecedentedly tense though it was, there passed, unmistakably, a look of admiration. A look which, because involuntary and immediate, so touched Pete that he would treasure it, against darker memories, and sometimes against his wishes too, through the years to come. 'You've hit the fucking nail on the head! Yes, Don Parry. It's because of him we're going on our – what shall I call it? Mission?'

'We're going to rescue him?' Perhaps Narnia and Middle Earth came too readily to his mind.

'I don't think so, no! But that's a possibility, I have to admit... I've just had, you see, the most amazing phone call from old Don, and I've come here to act on it as fast as I could. Never in a million years could you guess why the old bastard rang me, why we've fucking well got to get over to Llanrhaeadr-ym-Mochnant,' once again the impressively smooth flow of Welsh syllables, 'pronto. Absolutely pronto.' And he thumped his right fist lightly against the rim of the steering wheel.

'Okay,' Pete still strove for nonchalance. 'First you ask me to guess, then you say I couldn't in a million years. For Christ's sake stop beating about the bush!'

But Sam wasn't exactly doing this, he was just so revved up himself he was unable to speak coherently, let alone compose himself sufficiently for a night-time drive. He might even benefit from smoking a joint, though the prospect of being in the power of a high Sam for the next hour and a half was unnerving. Was this erratic friend of his a touch crazy after all?

Perhaps not. Sam revealed himself as perfectly aware of his own state. 'Just give me a few moments,' he asked. And resting his tasselled, woollen-capped head against the back of the driving seat, he went through a sequence of deep breaths, drawing himself up so high he all but touched the lining of the car roof, then sinking himself so low he slumped down beside the brakes. It was an exercise which, if carried out by somebody less self-confident than Sam Price, might have made Pete giggle. But it worked, and presently Sam had steadied himself sufficiently to give the gist of Don Parry's vital communication in a voice very different from his favourite cynical drawl. 'Because, Pete, in the Berwyn Mountains, just over an hour ago, a UFO landed. And I'm speaking in earnest, man, in fucking earnest. Just as old Don himself was. Weird, isn't it? That you and me should have been both planning to go to the Berwyns, and chatting away about extra-terrestrial matters. Like we had second sight. And now we're off to what's maybe the turning point of our lives. Of human history too.'

Wow! Sam's ecstatic agitation (though the pupils of his eyes had contracted to those tiny pinpoints generally associated with alarm) had, rather to his surprise, produced in Pete himself a complementary calmness (for all the disagreeable resonance of the word UFO). Possibly this was a concomitant of shock: shock at seeing his worldly friend in such an explosive condition; shock that it was UFOs, that subject which both united and divided them, which had brought about Sam's abrupt, astonishing, clandestine descent on Woodgarth, shock too – as at certain other instants of his life, like seeing his dear tabby-cat fatally knocked down by a car; or facing his quiz show audience – at having to confront an ineluctable slice of reality. For this was clearly how Sam saw the event he had at last been able to name.

Though they'd ridden together in this car only that morning, Pete now experienced his most intense closeness to Sam yet.

'Where to start? The whole thing's so fucking shaken me, I don't really know where'd be best. How about reminding you that my mate Don – I guess I can call him a mate even though he's thirty in February – really plays the field where women are concerned.' The phrase didn't come out quite naturally; it was somebody else's, probably its subject's. 'Well, the main woman in his life at the moment – she's married actually, which is not without its problems – lives in Llandrillo, on the far side of the Berwyns from Llanrhaeadr.' He was speaking as an intimate with a region he'd never once set foot in. 'Well, this evening Don went over to Llandrillo to see her, like every Wednesday, staying till about a quarter to nine, fifteen minutes before her man comes back from shift work in a hotel in Bala. So there the two of them were, sitting in the kitchen – we won't ask what they'd just been up to – when, taking them absolutely by surprise, the house gives a great shake, and then another and then another. The floor was rocking under their feet, like, Don said, two people were pulling at the boards from opposite ends. Scary, huh? And that was just the start of the fun and games. The goddam table had a trembling fit. And the chairs too, one toppled over completely. And the fucking carpet curled up, and the kettle bounced about on the hob so it splashed scalding water everywhere, and the hearthrug flew into the fender

– and Don, who was trembling himself, only just rescued it before there was one almighty conflagration. And most of the plates and cups and canisters on the dresser – which his girl-friend, Susie, like every good Welshwoman is very proud of – fell off, many of 'em smashed beyond repair…'

Pete was increasingly sure he heard Don Parry's voice within Sam's, particularly when it came to that antiquated phrase about Welshwomen and the dresser so uncharacteristic of his companion did it sound. He couldn't prevent himself from interjecting: 'But all that sounds like an earthquake, Sam. Really does! We have quakes in this region, you know, only often not so you'd notice. In fact the most serious fault-line in all Britain runs the length of the Marches. Shrewsbury more or less stands on it, and it has a kind of tributary known as the Bala Fault.' His brain truly did come in useful at times, it wasn't only good for thrilling a radio audience! 'Didn't you learn about all that in…?' But then Sam, thanks to his parents' misplaced snobbery, had never been to a local school, where they taught you about such things with an enthusiastic pride. So he had no idea of any Marches fault.

But Pete's diagnosis in no way put Sam off his stride; he clearly judged it an irrelevance. 'You wait,' he said, turning his head so that those deep-brown eyes with their still contracted pupils could bore their beams into Pete's, and make him see events as he himself was seeing them, 'you just fucking wait. This bizarre shaking was just beginning to subside when they heard a bang such as neither of them had heard in all their born days. Ear-splitting, like the hugest load of TNT being tipped out from a great height onto the land. Susie screamed fit to bring the house down completely, (and this is a couple, Pete, who, for obvious reasons, try their darnedest to stay quiet in all circumstances!), and asked: "Is the planet breaking up?" Well, old Don couldn't simply say No, could he? He didn't know any more than she. Thought it was possible, because this was just how it felt. *That the planet itself was breaking up…*' There was real relish in Sam's repetition. 'Not your usual *earthquake* story, huh?'

Pete wasn't at all sure of this point, in fact those grooves in his brain could probably release not a few eye-witness accounts of the phenomenon (from Indonesia, Turkey, Iran, Japan) which might well corroborate Don's story, so placing the upheaval at Llandrillo decisively in that category. But he could see, from the bright glint of Sam's tea-coloured irises, that he had a lot more to tell, and that it would be sensational.

'The banging went on for some while, though Don knows only the time it began – which was 8.30…'

'But that's only just over an hour ago!' exclaimed Pete, for hadn't he noticed the exact time on leaving his bedroom? 'So we're talking about something that may not yet have finished…'

'That's why I'm here to take us to the Berwyns now, moron,' said Sam, 'so why not let me get on with the story, and then we can set off prepared? Don and Susie saw through the windows of the cottage that other people were hearing the bangs too. So pretty soon they went outside to join the crowd on the main street of Llandrillo, everybody scared shitless. For now they could see right above the mountain they call Cadair Bronwen – the Mountain of Love with the cairn to King Arthur at the top – a great mass of blue and orange lights, with irregular white little dots of brightness at its edges.'

'Fucking hell!' said Pete, 'And all the others in Llandrillo noticed this – this *mass*?'

'Every man jack of 'em,' Sam assured him, 'and among them the very guy Don and Susie least wanted to see, Susie's husband, Tom. Jealous pillock, with one hell of a terrible temper. Don judged it best to scarper as quickly as he could. Otherwise, as he wittily put it, there'd be another kind of almighty bang at ground level, and he didn't want to hang around for *that, thank you very much*! But before he managed to get into his car and take off, he realised – like all the other witnesses – that this brilliant mass in the sky was pointed in the direction of Corwen and the north. And he heard from a babble of voices that many folk watching had actually dialled 999, and were expecting the police to arrive any minute. A young farmer friend of Don's, John Roberts, said to him: "I've heard a lot about flying saucers, and there is one now, going through the air…"

'Flying saucer, that's what old Don had had in his mind all along. All the shakes and noises were just signals of their arrival on Earth… Anyway he's now left Llandrillo to head for home where he lives with his mother, wondering how she must be coping. For if you could see this huge thing in the sky from one side of the Berwyns, wouldn't you be able to see it from the other, the Llanrhaeadr-ym-Mochnant side?'

'Sounds a fair assumption,' said Pete.

Sam withdrew his flesh-stirring nearness, and shifted his bum in his seat so that he was once more the driver – if imminently rather than actually. He's establishing his own authority, his special relationship to these happenings, thought Pete – and, sensing this, he couldn't suppress a resentment against his friend for his (habitual) insistence on superiority. No, he told himself, I won't tell him about my own involvement with UFOs just yet. I'll wait till he's in a slightly more modest, equalising frame of mind.

'Convinced so far, my friend?' Sam was, condescendingly, inquiring, 'Don would hardly have bothered to ring me up (and in a pretty sane manner, all things considered), to tell me of events in his neck of the woods if he hadn't felt something big was occurring. Something he felt Yours Truly should know. "One of your UFOs!" he called it, *our* UFOs, you might say, eh Pete?'

And then, of course, despite his thoughts of just the moment before, Pete did feel guilt for his continuing deception. For Sam to say 'our' – and about this of all topics – wasn't that as great a piece of generosity as he was capable of? Didn't that speak of some warmth for Pete in his cool soul?

'Now you get the gravity, don't you? So I think we should head off right away. There's a lot more to tell you, but I can do that as we go. We'll never ever forgive ourselves, my friend, if, when we get there, it's too late, and the… the *visitation's* ended. Evaporated… though I think that unlikely,' he added ominously, as one speaking out of further, undisclosed knowledge. On edge he might still be, but Sam Price was, no doubt about it, enjoying himself pretty well. Just like when swooping down solo from The Devil's Chair. He always needed drama, didn't he: an apparition on a long run, a spliff, a rock-stack central to a frightening legend, and now this! Sam Price's constant enemy was boredom, and he clutched at what would best dispel it.

(And, whispered an inner voice, can't something of that accusation be levelled against yourself, Pete Kempsey? Why else all the pride in your IQ and radio appearances?)

'Well, here I am, Sam, ready for the off!' Pete said aloud, thinking 'Ready? I have no coat with me, no jacket, no scarf, no money, and only sneakers on my feet. But what can any of that matter when flying saucers have landed? And virtually in our backyard.'

Because it was mid-week and late in the evening, because there was this prevalent fear that petrol would soon be rationed, the A49 was emptier of traffic than Pete had ever seen it. They shared their northward stretch of it principally with long-distance lorries travelling well under the regulation 50mph. After Craven Arms they'd turn north west towards Welshpool and then Llanfyllin. This small town with a square at its centre is the Gateway to the Berwyns from the south. Had they not been travelling on so misty and cloudy a night, they would then have seen the range they were headed for looming against the (invaded?) night sky. But in truth they were to have little awareness of the proximity of the mountains until they had actually gained their destination, Don Parry's home-town of Llanrhaeadr-ym-Mochnant...

And how would they both respond to whatever was awaiting them there, above their heads or, even more alarmingly, before their very eyes? What figures would they cut in future UFO annals? Would they be classed with those Swedes who ushered in a whole era by looking up aloft at a cigar-shaped trajectory? Or with the Mustang-flying mates of Lieutenant Thomas F. Mantell who perished through following an irresistible shining whiteness – which might have only been the bright shine of the planet Venus? Or would the historian place them with Carl-Gustav Jung who didn't mind whether his UFOs belonged to the dreaming or the waking world?

For the first ten miles of their northward journey, Sam was in full narrative spate: 'So there's old Don Parry making for home along the B4391 worrying not only about what he's left behind in Llandrillo, but about what lies ahead in Llanrhaeadr. All the tremors and explosions could well have scared his poor mother out of her wits! Anyway he couldn't be sure they'd come to a stop, could he? Still wasn't when last he spoke to me…

'Once, Don says, you've left Llandrillo and the Dee valley, it's high and really desolate country until you descend to Llangynog and get back down into the Tanat Valley. So he's going across the southern flank of the Berwyns: treeless moor, not a house in sight, only rock. And he thinks to himself, so where's that bloody blue-and-orange mass gone to? Is it still hanging above Cadair Bronwen? By now he's nearer the other great peak of the range, Cadair Berwyn, which is higher still. So what does he do but park the car? He's got guts, Don has.'

So much had Sam absorbed Don Parry's intense relation to his own experiences of an hour back that Pete, by this time somewhat disoriented himself, began to wonder if this 'character' hadn't taken over Sam's body, voice-box and all. 'Yup, Don not only parks the car, but gets out of it, looks up into the sky. As you can see for yourself, it's not clear tonight, but this UFO – and maybe that's what we should start calling it, Pete – was so goddam brilliant its light pierced the cloud layer. Don says what he saw was about 1,500 feet up, and moving ever-so-slightly along. More orange, even orange-red, than blue, and shaped like a rugby ball (which would please old Don, who's a Wales aficionado). At its base those very small lights he'd noticed earlier were twinkling and dancing about in zigzag formation. Don just stood there beside his car watching them, hardly knowing whether he was frightened or happy.'

'Fucking hell!' said Pete again.

'But by the time he'd got back down to Llanrhaeadr, he couldn't see this any more. On the other hand lots of people were out and about in the main street. Practically everybody he bumped into had met somebody from Llanderfel and Llandrillo, or spoken to 'em over the phone, and were gobsmacked at what they'd heard. Llanrhaeadr itself had felt some shakes and bangs too, though not everybody there had done so, and never as badly as at Llandrillo. Quite a few in the district had rung the police – in fact the cops must be fucking inundated this night with all the 999 calls they've had. And Don himself felt he had a duty to tell as many people as he could asap about what was going on. That's why he got in touch with his new young friend, Sam Price. He knew he'd be the guy to take his news seriously.'

Pete's head swam as Sam his ventriloquist came to the inconclusive end of Don Parry's tale. Were they really out on something as prosaic as the A49? Was it the mapped workaday world of road signs and traffic lights on either side of the car windows or had he exchanged it for another that Sam Price and Don Parry's fused imaginations had brought into being? Small towns, villages, hamlets, farms, lonely houses, were all entering that state of rest supposedly central to night times – even though, were he still at home, he would not have gone to bed yet, would be still, maybe, struggling with Thomas Cromwell as viewed by G.R. Elton... Would his parents have noticed his absence yet? Now he was in the doghouse, they'd even stopped calling out: 'Good night, Peter, sleep well!' as they always had done, his life long. (Or had they, after all, gone on wishing him this, and he'd not heard them, because he'd shut his ears even more determinedly than he had his bedroom door, over which he'd now hung a sign: WORKING. KEEP OUT. THIS MEANS *YOU*!)

Don't think about Woodgarth, he told himself, it's too late now. What's done's done! 'Tell me more about Don Parry,' he asked Sam to distract himself. If the land around him was really under the dominion of this magnetic guy, he might as well be better informed about him. 'Apart from his sexual prowess.' This was the right note to hit; Sam grinned collusively. 'Does he *only* work for your father?'

'Hell, no – though the Old Man thinks highly of all he does for us.' Pete noticed (not for the first time) Sam's casual, unconscious use of the first person plural when talking about Price's Menswear. 'He does all manner of freelance work, Don does: for a local builder's, getting material at low costs, because of all his many contacts; for a bakery shop in Llanfyllin (which we'll be passing through later); he's quite an expert on flour. But his real interests are artistic. He's the creative type. He wants to make a huge mural of the King Arthur story, with glass and minerals inserted in it, and install it right in the middle of Llanrhaeadr. Minerals, because they're basic to Britain, and glass, because it shines with promises for both this world and the next.' More ventriloquism, obviously.

'Why the next world?' queried Pete. This nocturnal expedition smacked too much of that already, he thought. After all hadn't even the UFOs chosen *this* one for their activities?

Sam turned to him with a knowing smile of curious, uncharacteristic sweetness. 'Because the next world *starts* near Llanrhaeadr-ym-Mochnant, my friend. At the waterfall above the town, Pistyll Rhaeadr – a 240 feet drop, highest in England and Wales...'

Pete grunted impatiently here, implying it was unnecessary for Sam to tell him this sort of fact. ('Peter Kempsey, what is the name of the tallest single-drop fall in England and Wales?')

'You could describe the fall, to quote Don, as Nature's equivalent to the Pearly Gates. Climb to the top of it, and you could find yourself in Annwn.'

'Annwn?' Here was a name Pete did not know, here was info he definitely didn't possess.

'A.N.N.W.N. Annwn. The Celtic Otherworld. The Land Above the Falling Water. The country ruled benevolently by Gwyn ap Nudd.'

'And who's *he* when he's at home?' He felt a decided pang of jealousy. Sam had clearly been spending a deal of time recently with this Don Parry character, had been the recipient of many of the guy's more unusual stores of knowledge (as well as of his tales of women) which – until this minute – he had not thought fit to share with Pete. Besides it was just a tad irritating that Sam should be now addressing him as some expert on Celtic lore when he was no such thing.

Yet who knew better than Pete how you can feel at home with a subject after a very short acquaintance with it?

'Gwyn ap Nudd is the head of the Good Folk (or to give them, as Don does, their Welsh name, the Tylwyth Teg) and that made him a natural for the ruler of this realm, though he had competition for the post. It's all feasting and fun in Annwn, no kind of disease or misery…'

'Like Heaven!'

'Yes, very like Heaven. But whether it actually is Heaven or not is a moot point, Don says. You just go there when you've kicked it, as far as I can make out; no question of judgement, or whether you're worthy. Well, that isn't the traditional Christian view, or wasn't at one time.'

Pete had never been quite sure what this Christian view entailed. He'd long noticed that newspaper announcements, as well as the Sunbeam Press's condolence cards and the subsequent gravestones, spoke of folk who'd just died as going straight to their eternal rest, as being under God's good care, so perhaps the alleged judgement wasn't as severe as some were pleased to make out.

'The Berwyn's local saint – St Collen, who gives his name to the town of Llangollen – was a bit of a puritan, I gather, a hermit-like bloke, and he believed that there *was* a strict test for where you went after death. But simultaneously there were all these arrivals into Annwn, just down the road; not over the rainbow but over the waterfall. So he thought he'd better do something about it, and suggested Gwyn ap Nudd and himself had a meeting. Which they did. The Church has it that Collen came off better in their debates, but Don Parry says it's a toss-up about who came out top, and in fact posterity has given both of them crowns.'

'I see,' said Pete, 'and this Annwn itself…?'

'Is the place of utter peace and joy. For any and everybody who goes there.'

'I get it!'

And he did. For though he was positive he had never heard the word spoken or seen it printed, what lay behind its two syllables was surely something he had known about all his life, even before he could speak? But it alarmed him to think any more like this.

To help him move his mind on he inquired: 'And – what does he look like, this Don Parry bloke?'

There followed a pause, during which Sam let a Long Vehicle overtake them. Perhaps he hasn't heard what I just asked, Pete thought, and anyway it doesn't really matter because I'll be seeing him for myself shortly. Then – 'You're not going to believe this, Pete,' Sam said, 'but he looks like you. Oh, I know, he's twelve years older, and he wears a small beard, while you've just turned eighteen and ain't got no beard, though with your kind of stubborn stubble, you might think one day of growing one. But otherwise I reckon you look pretty alike. Same build, same colouring, same habit of slouching, and of stooping when you run.'

Pete was astounded hearing this. Never had he imagined that this hero in Sam's eyes would resemble himself. He could think of nothing appropriate to say back.

Anyway Sam had, for the time being, worn himself out with talk. Shropshire was all about them now. Hills swept upwards to culminate in vapours rolling down from the sky, farmhouses presented themselves as randomly spaced dark shells of one-time habitation, which might or might not reassert their normal activities when, many hours later, morning broke. If it ever did!

Woods were fringing the country roads now rather like reeds do ponds. Shropshire has far fewer real woods than the boys' Herefordshire; night accentuated this, while making what woods there were seem denser, more inimical. Once an owl flew out, with a fierce, intent, insouciant face, a surreal white for the seconds of his visibility to them by the car's headlights – and probably both boys thought of the badger which had lumbered to safety not so very far from here on their previous drive through this territory... And then here, almost on cue, came another of its kind. Once again Sam had to brake while the animal, his great white stripe all but glowing in the darkness against the black of his long-snouted face, moved across the road, but at a far greater speed than his cousin of January 4. On this occasion Sam, his head full of Don Parry and his tales, was less interested by the creature though just as concerned that it crossed the road unscathed.

Pete, on the other hand, positively welcomed the badger. And in retrospect was to welcome it even more heartily. This sight of this animal, eager to get over the road, to reach the safety and warmth of his or her sett on a raw yet damp night on which extra-terrestrials might or might not have visited the planet, gave him a needed sense of perspective: there was clearly satisfaction to be found just accomplishing little tasks essential to preserving existence. Once again he resolved that when this adventure was over, he would pay badgers the kind of attention he had hitherto given to less sensate subjects. There were lessons to learn from even a glimpse of so self-possessed a being.

The boys half-expected Llanfyllin, which stands within sight of the Berwyn Mountains, to have some, if not all, of the atmosphere of a town on the edge of a danger (even a war) zone. Police cars (hadn't Don Parry said that the constabulary had already received an overwhelming number of frantic calls?), ambulances, a taxi or two bearing eager newshounds, reporters and photographers ... but where were *any* of these? Answer – nowhere; this could have been any freezing January night, with every right-minded person tucked up in bed. Even so, as they drove three or four miles away from the town along the B4391 and then exchanged this road for B4580 (by means of a sharp, ill-signposted turning that Sam very nearly missed), expectations of seeing preternatural lights in sizes and shapes that would blow their mind assailed them – and how could they help this? Their gaze moved constantly to the partially fogged-over massif that was the Berwyn Mountains. Nor could they refrain from speech. 'Hey, wasn't that a ray of red light? Just over there? To our left?' 'No, look straight ahead, Pete – I'm sure my eye just caught – well, something like the bright *zigzag* in Don Parry's story? Gone now, fuck it!' 'That doesn't mean, it won't come again. In fact, if you…' 'For Christ's sake, moron, let me keep my eyes on the road, can't you? This is hardly the M1 at high noon, you know.'

Very true, it certainly wasn't. The road was taking them over a little bridge, beneath which audibly rushed the swollen waters of the River Tanat. This formed the long awesome valley separating the Berwyns from their lower foothills. The sound of the river was good to the ears, sweet, musical: Pete liked it. It made him experience a rush of gratitude to Sam for having brought him all the long way out here, even if they never were to see a UFO – and God knew, there was a quite reasonable chance that they might not. A bigger chance surely, for all Don Parry's story, than that they would.

But just assuming they were fortunate enough, if that was the right expression, to be granted a vision, wouldn't it be far better for Pete to have got off his chest the matter of his subject for *High Flyers*? Of course! A hundred thousand times 'of course'. He repeated to himself but more emphatically his earlier sentence: 'After we've arrived in Llanrhaeadr, I will fucking *force* myself to tell him!'

He himself was not as clued up about the mountains in front of them as he had been about the Shropshire hills, though he did know quite a few facts… They were not so staggeringly ancient as sections of the Long Mynd and the Strettons, yet ancient enough in all truth, from the Ordivician age, 500 million to 430 years ago, and the Silurian, 430 to 410 million years back. They had seen much violent volcanic activity, and contained many examples of tuff – rock formed from volcanic ash. They contained no fewer than twenty-four peaks of over 2,000 feet, and the two highest (the two Cadairs above which this mysterious brilliant mass had been seen) neared 3,000 in height. As Sam had already reminded him, their famous waterfall, Pistyll Rhaeadr, had the longest single drop of any in both England and Wales, at 240 feet, and was situated at the back of the township that was their destination, and was now at last visible as an almost lightless huddle, Llanrhaeadr-ym-Mochnant.

And at some point on the range you could apparently wander into Annwn, even when still living…

'Next task! Finding old Don. I've got the address of his house, don't you worry, and its whereabouts, I gather, couldn't present less of a problem. Right in the main street just before you get to the turning to the right which says 'Waterfall'. Don said, more than once, for us not to worry what hour we arrive. Someone or other, probably himself, will be up and around, even on a shitty night like this, so help us! He was bloody fucking insistent we came, believe you me, Pete! But in fact, we've made really good time, I've done us all proud. I'll become a chauffeur if all else fails me. Fourteen minutes past eleven.' Pete looked at his own watch on which you could press a little knob so it was luminous in the car dark. Yes, truly, fourteen minutes past eleven it was. 23.14. Three hours one minute since he'd crept out of his bedroom at Woodgarth.

By now surely his parents would know he'd gone out? Were they worried? Mystified? Angry? Dad certainly would be home from the Civic Society; he might easily have taken it into his head to bid Pete a stiff if kindly good night. Or again the wretched Julian might have noticed the complete quiet behind the shut door, and come into Pete's room to investigate; he was the noticing, prying sort all right. Would make a fine private eye! But did Pete care about all this compared with the great adventure still ahead? Like hell he did! Had the family shown care for Pete in the only way that mattered, understanding of his temperament and tastes? They had not. So why should he bother himself about causing them a few minutes' anxiety?

The little town proper of Llanrhaeadr was heralded by a Victorian school building after which the road swung right, then left into the main street. 'Girls' and 'Boys' said the letters over the doorways, bringing back bad old days when the children of the place were rigidly separated by gender and not allowed to use words in their own first language. Even if anarchy was about to descend on the UK because of governmental stubbornness and incompetence, even if this part of the country was being disturbed by aliens, there were a few things, Pete thought, to be said in favour of being alive now rather than back then...! Unlike Llanfyllin, Llanrhaeadr was not deserted, despite the hour. Men and boys stood in talking groups in front of the grey-stone, slate-roofed houses of its principal street, with only a few women among them. All turned round as they heard – loud enough in the dead quiet of the hour – the engine of Sam's Beetle, as though, thought Pete, they were afraid an extra-terrestrial might be driving it. Or, failing that, the Head of Scotland Yard himself with tidings of further visitations... Off the very tarmac of the street worry, insecurity, fear rose up, and these qualities had also barricaded the houses, so that their drawn curtains looked like so many metal portcullises.

Sam parked the car without difficulty, but with many troubled, curious eyes playing on him, parked it right opposite the last house but two in the row before the sign 'Pistyll/Waterfall'. Pete's heart beat faster. There returned that feeling that he was enacting something long planned, that he had known all his life that this Pistyll Rhaeadr was a place in his destiny. But this knowledge had risen to the reachable surface of his mind only these last cold minutes.

Don Parry's house stood a few feet back from the pavement and was approached by a short path. The date 1845 was engraved over the front door, and above that, set in the wall, was a plaque bearing some commemorative words in Welsh; Pete couldn't even make out the lettering, and obviously none of the sense of this. 'You'd best stand away while I beard the Parrys in their den! Don won't mind you being here at all, but I can't answer for anybody else...'

Pete had rather assumed that Sam would have told Don that his great mate was accompanying him. But perhaps he had judged it better not to tell him. Pete observed that a public-school assurance had spread itself over his friend as soon as he switched off the engine and prepared to disembark. That Darnton education? Or simply the result of having access to a bit more money than most youths his age? All of a sudden Pete felt what he surely was: a junior partner in a madcap enterprise, Sam's less sophisticated shadow.

Both boys crossed the road, but while Sam walked up the diminutive path and knocked on his friend's front door, Pete went and stood near a little gaggle of men, by the window of a general store named GREATOREX in capitals. Established in 1935 its lettering proclaimed, followed by the announcement of 'Drinks, Bread & Cakes, Wines and Spirits'. Soothingly humdrum commodities (even if the shop selling them had shut many hours back) on such a night of near-apocalypse.

Sam was having the door opened to him by a woman in her mid-sixties, tall, with wild, woolly, grey hair. She was wearing tortoiseshell-rimmed thick spectacles, a fluffy pink cardigan and a long plum-coloured skirt which didn't disguise legs of an extreme thinness; these gave her the appearance of an animated Dutch doll. She didn't have the worried look of most faces out in the main street. On the contrary, considering she was confronting a total stranger at gone quarter past eleven on a night already distinguished by the uncanny, she appeared quite remarkably unfazed, you could even say, at ease.

Pete had positioned himself so he could hear everything the pair was saying.

'Mrs Parry?'

'You'll be Trevor Price's boy? That right?'

'That's right.'

'Yes, I've been expecting you, though I didn't think you'd have made it over here so quick. I can see for myself you're who you say. You have a look of your dad about the mouth. Don drove me over to Leominster before Christmas, and introduced us.'

Sam flushed, but didn't look altogether displeased.

'Is Don in?' Sam asked.

'Don's gone out; some of the lads press-ganged him into going with them, and he's never a one to say no to anything,

my Don. So you have two options, Sam (it is Sam, isn't it?).
You can wait in this house with me for him to return. Or you
can go out somewhere to see what you can.' She made the
occurrences, thought Pete, sound like a fall of snow or the Tanat
overflowing its banks.

Sam said, 'I think that we – that I'd like to have a sighting, Mrs
Parry.'

'Sighting?' repeated Mrs Parry with a quizzical smile, 'Yes,
that's Don's word too. This evening's tailor-made for him, isn't
it? He's still a boy like yourself, even though he's pushing thirty,
and he's been wanting something like this to happen his whole
life long. Even when we were still living in Wrexham.'

'What do *you* think's happened, Mrs Parry?'

Mrs Parry had obviously answered this question that night
many times before, mostly in reply to herself. 'Well, when we
heard the loud bangs round half eight, and then saw the sparks
flying into the sky, what I thought was – those bloody soldiers at
the camp in the mountains are doing their exercises again and
have gone too far this time. I've never trusted the military all my
days, and even less this last year when they got official permission to do whatsoever they like up there. Dangerous! Asking for
trouble sooner or later!' She peered over her convex glasses as if
half-suspicious that the lad before her in the bomber jacket and
speaking with a classy English accent might be in league with
the British Army. Then, as if reassured, she went on: 'All I know
is that the strange things that Don saw over at Llandrillo where
he was visiting his nice young friend,' and from the way she said
this Pete surmised she knew of Don's liaison with Susie, 'that big
mass of light, with the little ones twinkling below it – were all
seen by other folk from Llanrhaeadr who were over that way too.
And many far less full of wild fancies than my Don. Bill
Edwards, two doors down, came back here, about an hour ago,
with the strangest story yet.'

'Really? And what might that be?' And Sam stretched forward
his neck towards the elderly woman, again like a cob-swan, as if
to snatch this story from her lips.

'He was over in Bala, Bill was, having a drink in a hotel, and into the lounge there came a posse,' she seemed proud of this word, but probably it had been Bill Edwards', for she repeated it, 'a real *posse,* of men in black. All looking alike, and all telling the receptionist their business was urgent. Men in black, eh? Same time as all the noises and apparitions in Llandrillo. What do you make of that, boy? Bill said the lot of them gave him such pip he was out of the hotel in two shakes of a lamb's tail, and driving home – along the B3491 if you please – like a speed-hog to get home and dry as fast as he could.

'But me – I'm a dull old woman really – I expect there's an ordinary enough explanation. Sanitary inspectors most likely, checking up to see whether the hotel meets the health and safety regulations. Or maybe,' she chuckled, '*tax* inspectors. That'd frighten the management far more than any aliens, daylight robbers that they are... Anyway I can see you can't wait to be on your way.'

This was certainly true. Sam was visibly wriggling in his impatience to be off – somewhere, anywhere, not to miss even the faintest glimpse of these goings-on. And Pete had already stepped forward from Greatorex's window in readiness... 'But on our way *where?*' Sam couldn't quite check the exasperation from his voice, for really Mrs Parry, while kindly and hospitable, had been unhelpful in her vagueness about her son's whereabouts.

'We-ell, I would think the waterfall's where you might think of looking for him first. High up it is. Just right for meeting people not of this world.'

For a moment Pete suspected she was teasing Sam, even having him on. But then he thought: 'She just doesn't know how best to behave in such abnormal conditions.'

'Meeting people not of this world? Annwn?'

'Anyway I think my Don spoke of going up to Pistyll tonight?'

'Well that's where we – where I'll go! I just follow the sign, I take it...?'

'Scared, Pete?' asked Sam, as they jumped into the VW, 'did you hear all that?'

Pete nodded. 'Not yet,' he answered, 'though I dunno how I'll feel when we encounter a posse. A posse in fucking *black!*'

'Me neither,' said Sam. 'You can't know how you'll react before something's actually happened. We might well shit ourselves but I was anything but afraid on my last sighting.'

Yes, I keep forgetting about that, thought Pete, though I don't know how I could do. Sam's always one major step ahead of me in this strange game we're playing, instigated by him, and organised too. Which might well turn out no game at all. 'I can't recall when I was last afraid either,' said Pete. Nor could he! Quits!

Sam turned right, as signposted, at Greatorex's shop, drove past the British Legion Hall outside which another bunch of men were talking (comparing notes?) and then swung the car to the left. Soon Llanrhaeadr was behind and below them. The road to Pistyll Rhaeadr follows the downward course from the Fall of the Afon Rhaeadr. It's narrow, and every now and again climbs uphill, but mostly it keeps to the valley. To the boys this seemed unknown country indeed, and, for all the houses and farms here, charged with arcane power. On their right the mountain slopes looked mighty in the darkness; further ahead these turned into cliff faces. And beyond?

'Crikey! What a place!' Pete forced himself to exclaim aloud, though he was sincere enough, 'and what a story all this will make for *High Flyers*!'

He felt like he'd thrown himself off the highest diving-board at a pool, in some swimming exam, as he should have done a long time before. At last he'd managed it!

Sam's voice was low-toned when, after a pause that quickened Pete's pulse, he inquired: '*High Flyers*, what has that got to do with this waterfall?'

'Not the waterfall as such. Unless we're lucky enough to have a sighting there. I mean, the whole thing itself. Our journey in search of an Unidentified…'

Why was he unable to continue the sentence? At the back of it was only a stupid radio show when all was said and done. Compare that with the thrilling reality of two true mates bonded by delight in each other's company fearlessly travelling towards the Unknown. Sam, even though they had just rounded the bend of a tortuous road he didn't know at all, was slowing the car down radically, and his head, which he turned to Pete, maybe at the cost of control of the wheel, was his fiercest cob-swan's yet.

He had understood anyway. As his very next words made clear. 'Do I take it you've made UFOs your Special Subject for your Jan 31?'

'Yes, Sam, I thought I'd already made it more or less clear.' ('More or less'!?)

'Like *fuck* you did!' Sam hissed, and now he'd stopped the car and turned the engine off. 'I've asked you about it, directly and indirectly, I don't know how many sodding times. Until I thought I'd best stop, because you might have chickened out of the damned show altogether, and just not wanted to say.'

'I promised you I wouldn't chicken out, and I've *kept* the promise, Sam. And I couldn't have a better subject than UFOs, could I? You of all people must agree?'

'Me of all people... too fucking right, Pete. UFOs are *my* subject, man, *my* experience, *my* passion. You little arsewipe, you pathetic cocksucker, you shrivelled-up cunt, you can't go stealing from me, and expect me to take it on the fucking chin! You *know* you're a thief, you *know* I'm right to think you one, I can tell from your fat little common face... I bet you've already told them your choice? The BBC crew?'

If Pete couldn't remember when he was last afraid, he most certainly knew he was now. Sam's viciously spoken language – way beyond the normal locker-room obscenities of young male talk – had appalled him. 'Well, I had to tell them, didn't I?' he protested, 'but we're doing things differently this year, as I remember explaining to you. No more questions and answers. Instead each competitor gives a brief talk and is judged on that. Good idea, don't you think?'

'Oh, I think it's a marvellous idea, a perfectly fucking *brilliant* idea.' Pete felt as he heard and saw Sam's uninhibited fury that – whatever peculiar bodies were manifesting themselves in the sky above, whatever animals were prowling or running or hunting or grazing in the wild around them – reality for him right now was confined to one object, Sam's irate head spitting hostilities at him in the inescapably confined interior of the VW. 'Mr Pete Kempsey – who's never seen a UFO in his life, and who never gave the matter serious thought before the two of us shared that spliff one month and one day ago – for that twat, that shithead, that spunkless prick, to get up on his hind legs in front of all Britain and talk about *my, my* greatest interest – which I share with the wisest man of the century, Carl – Gustav Jung – yeah, that's such a good idea I feel like getting up and fucking dancing on the roof of this car for sheer joy.'

Swans angered on riverside paths not only hiss at and threaten irritating intruders, they strike them with their wings and poised beak. And now Sam, leaning over Pete with rage in his deep-brown eyes and with his handsome head jutting forward, laid into him with his fists. Pete, hoping to avert a full fight, received the blows without retaliation.

'Nobody deceives me, friend, fucking nobody,' Sam informed him, 'you don't know why the hell I left Darnton, do you? You'd have been more careful if you'd known.' It was not one of Bala's Men in Black or any other unidentified phenomenon that was going to make Pete shit himself in terror; it was this youth from The Tall House, Bargates, Leominster who was now forcing himself astride him.

'Sam, I've always wanted to know,' said Pete with difficulty, from underneath this strong, electrically charged body, 'and on the programme, I'm going to tell them all, the whole of Britain, what a great guy you are, the greatest I've ever come across, and how it was you – and you only – who gave me the idea in the first place, and how you've actually seen…'

Impossible to go on any further because down came Sam's right fist – probably not caring about its aim, but landing on his nose. Hard. Extremely. And Pete couldn't but feel his head was spinning round and round and might well part from his neck and trunk. Tiny little stars appeared sparklingly before his eyes.

All this, before pain – multiple pain – properly registered itself, and the blood flowed down over his upper lip and so into his mouth which had gained some cuts of its own.

'You haven't heard me out, you scumbag. I'm now going to tell you why they made me leave Darnton.' Pete, the appalling loosening in his bowels beginning the filthiest realisation of what Sam and he had ruefully suggested as possibilities for this last stage of their adventure, attempted to wriggle out of Sam's hold. But his own greatest asset in any combat – his feet, with which he'd aimed many a successful kick on the sports field – were pinned down by his companion, who weighed more than he'd have suspected. 'I tried to top myself. Understand? With a knife, in full view of those guys I thought had most to answer for. I'd absolutely had it, had it fucking up to here, in Darnton with people letting me down, and deceiving me. Stealing my ideas. Betraying my friendship. God, I resented those two guys – Rogerson and Lawley, I'll never forgive them – going for me two against one, and forcing the knife out of my hands. And let me tell you something, Peter fucking Kempsey, you've behaved worse to me than anybody, you dickhead you. You make me disgusted with life all over again. And then some!'

'Don't kill yourself because of me, Sam!' Pete got out, 'I mean, I *like* you!' ('And perhaps even *loved* you, though not again after this.') He was aware more blood was pouring from him; his nose had not been the only victim of Sam's fists. And now, still unable to move from under Sam, the inside of the whole car, and what he could see of outside it, was tilting back and forth as if some earthquake was starting up (and maybe, like at Llandrillo this very evening, it actually was). Faster, faster. Faster, everything rocked.

'Don't you fucking faint on me!' Sam was, just about audibly, saying, 'we'd better get you into the fresh air, hadn't we?'

He stretched his left arm out to the back of Pete's head and with his hand pushed open the passenger door behind him. The impact of the night, through which rain was beginning to fall in chill gusts, dealt another blow to battered Pete, but it was welcome too – insofar as his swaying, throbbing, bleeding body could welcome anything.

'Let me help you out, friend!' said Sam, his voice suddenly gone soberer, softer, mellower. 'I'll get out my side of the car, and then help you out yours.'

'Well, his fit is over, thank heavens,' thought Pete, 'truly dreadful though it was while it lasted. And I pretty well deserved it too, didn't I? Not coming clean with him earlier, though I only spoke the truth when I said I always intended to praise him on the programme. I did, I did. Always, always…'

'Easy does it, dude!' said Sam, in this new, warm, greatly preferable tone, his strong hands moving under Pete's shoulders and lifting him with impressive ease out of the front seat onto the tufts of moorland grass that formed the shoulder of this unfenced road.

Pete couldn't help crying now. Pity, but he couldn't switch this humiliating process off. He was not crying from physical pain, though he had plenty of that – he'd always been reasonably brave – but because of the intensity of Sam's bad feelings towards him, which he now could share only too easily. 'I've been a complete pillock, I know,' he gasped to the figure standing by the open car door, 'I should have told you ages before, I do see that! I guess I always knew you wouldn't like the news. But I've always meant well towards you, Sam. Everything I've done has been with real…' But 'real' what. 'Admiration'? The unspeakable word 'love'? But his mouth was now starting to pulsate with hurt so much it couldn't cope with another word.

'Glad to hear it, friend,' said Sam, who was now slamming-to the passenger door, 'so let me wish you a very good night. Sleep well, won't you?'

He ran over to the driver's door, then banged it shut, firmly, and started up the engine. No doubt what he was going to do… Pete could barely raise his head to watch the VW move on out of sight. And then back in sight again. Sam had obviously found a little gateway into a field in which to turn the car round. He drove on, down past him.

Amazed, distressed, incredulous and guilty, Pete stretched out his body, bloody, mucus-ridden and sore in the face, all ache and bruise at the back of the head, and jabbing with pain at the shoulders, thanks to Sam having shaken him so furiously. And filthy at the bum too. With maximum caution he edged his way so that, still recumbent, he had a small moss-covered stone for a pillow. And there he would lie, he told himself, and banish all thoughts of any kind, all feelings physical or emotional as thoroughly as he could. Sam had deliberately abandoned him to the night…

Before long Pete appreciated that where he lay was more or less at the head of the Afon Rhaeadr valley: the waterfall Pistyll Rhaeadr could not be very far off. Another car – maybe Don Parry's was – might be making its way down from there, and its driver would for certain see Pete, lying there in his blood and shit, with his feet splayed out, and come to his rescue.

But no car appeared.

Infinitely venerable these shanks of the Berwyns looked tonight, in their desolate wintry coat, with patches of snow on the higher moorland. If Pete shifted round he could see to his left those stark black cliffs in the direction of the fall which suggested wilder terrain beyond. The night sky was still overcast. Pete realised that though spiritually he couldn't recollect any comparable desolation and misery, bodily he had suffered many similar injuries, and probably worse ones – playground fights years back, and that time when three thugs had jumped on him from the Priory walls back home and beaten him up for the sake of his wallet. At the time awful, but not amounting to anything so very serious!

Taking courage then from these occasions, when he'd overcome what had been inflicted, he now, slowly, gingerly, hauled himself onto his feet. Arrows of agony shot up the length of both legs, but… He would find a stream, and, after wiping his behind and legs with ferns, he would wash his whole body thoroughly. He told himself: 'You're not gonna die. There's nothing for you to do but walk up to the waterfall. Unaided.'

After Brock

The great waterfall gleamed white through the darkness, and he felt himself compelled to climb, to see where it began.

He craned his neck. The edge of the plateau from which the water tumbled down so fast, long and loud was hidden from him at least two hundred feet above.

What, right up there? It'd be like scaling a fucking wall.

He had no torch, it was past midnight, cloud covered the sky, and there was a night dew underfoot which would later turn to frost. He was alone, a stranger, without any mountaineering experience. As well as this he was a mass of cuts and bruises after the attack in which he'd lost the one friend he cared about. He knew his mistakes now for what they were, and those faults of his that were responsible.

He was dead tired and so very cold.

> *Come unto me all ye that labour and are heavy laden,*
> *and I will give you rest.*

Where had he heard that before? It was a command that was also a promise. And he wouldn't disobey. Up, up he proceeded, in his jersey, jeans and sneakers, hardly appropriate for this place. Scaling a wall was about right, too. In front of him was a long vertical face of moss-covered stones and boulders with narrow slithers of soil between them. Bare, bent birch trees had their roots in some of these. Higher up, stark rock face confronted him. But he would surely find enough footholds to edge his way to where pine trees reared sombre forms against the night sky.

During his slow ascent, this sky often got blocked by birch or boulder or by flashes of the torrent itself, always audible, and always calling him on. Often he was on the point of slipping; the soil between stones was principally mud.

But his limbs had determination of their own. An hour's strenuous, patient, and sometimes scary endeavour, and there he was. At the very top.

As it rushed over the edge to form the celebrated fall, the silver-

shot dark water of the little river, Afon Disgynfa, instantly turned
white. It was incredible to think he had been standing down there
in that gulf of blackness a mere hour ago. Only venture a few
inches closer in, and he'd be part of this 240-feet tumble, and
arrive in the whirlpool beside which he had had the urge to
climb. But 'I wouldn't do any arriving, would I?' Pete told himself
caustically, 'I'd have leaped myself out of life, as Sam wanted to
at Darnton, with a knife for the purpose which those guys
grabbed from him.' That kind of exit was never to be his course,
he suddenly understood, however miserable he was. Anyway,
hadn't he, thought he would begin afresh up here? He swung
himself away from the great drop into the abyss, and instead
looked towards the land from which the river was issuing.

Quite featureless it seemed too, the Afon Disgynfa itself the
principal giver of light on this clouded night. The marshland on
either side was a bumpy spread of obscurity above which tall
reeds or grasses protruded in colourless clusters, and in which
big stones and bigger rocks were anchored. Eventually, on both
sides, this marsh – Pete could tell – gave way to firmer ground
(though doubtless many a patch of bog punctuated it, to pull any
foolish night-time walkers down, or suck them in). This ground
rose to meet hillsides hung with mist, especially to the west, in
the direction of Llandrillo and the alleged celestial intrusion. But
Pete felt the only direction for him to take was that of the source
of the river. He was surely right to feel he had reached some
objective, the heights above Tan-y-pistyll; it was here that he
would find whatever it was that was right for him. So, from now
on, Afon Disgynfa would guide him, with its calming sheen of
surface, its fleetness of motion, its quiet campanology of notes.
Deliberately he didn't check the time by looking at his watch.
Exactitude of hour wasn't important now.

But with saying goodbye to watch-time, he said goodbye to
progress. On and on upstream he walked, but the same stretch
of moor and marsh continued to lie ahead of him, the same
bends of the mercury-streaked Afon Disgynfa, and the same hill-
slopes on either side of it, clad in the same, never-unveiling mists.

After Brock

Could it be that he had now attained a curious stasis of both time and space? That ought to be frightening, but somehow this was not. Could it be that he was inside Annwn? The Land above the Falling Water.

Part Three

Pete and Nat

One

Confessions

'So you made it into the Berwyn Heights same way I did,' says Nat, 'up the side of the great waterfall.'

'T'other way about, I'd say, wouldn't you, Pete?' observes Luke Fleming, 'Nat went where *you* did! '

By now he's so reconciled to Pete's presence in this room that he's turned his chair round to face him. He finds the father easier to relate to, and deal with, than the son. Pete could be a mate, but there's something strange, deliberately elusive – or is it evasive? about Nat that's disconcerting. But if he's proved correct about what the lad did – and he's sure that, sooner or later, he will be – then he has guts in quite alarming supply. Pete Kempsey's cut from rather more ordinary cloth than Nat, and as for his 'wrong-doing', well... who was he to cast the stone here? He himself, after all, swore to his mate, Justin, on the *Shropshire Star* that he'd keep those rumours about the new development area in Newport to himself. And didn't. Made one of his own most successful stories out of them.

Nat thinks: Any consideration Luke shows me will be because he's taken quite a liking to my dad, has thought better of him for springing to my defence. For all his moodiness there's a matiness in Dad which gets to people. I don't have it. 'That's shit, that is!'

he hears himself saying, 'How could I fucking know Dad went into the mountains via Pistyll Rhaeadr years ago? Dad's never told me about this part of his life before this very morning. It's all been news to me! Isn't that right, Dad? You tell him!'

Pete doesn't answer. He's read Nat's Journal after all, and knows that his dreadful escapade of January 1974 wasn't completely unknown to his son. Luke has sussed this out too.

Nat closes his eyes as if to keep what he alone has knowledge of safe behind his closed, if sun-filtered, lids...

After he discovered that newspaper cutting from *The Wrexham Leader*, secreted inside Wilfred Owen's poems, he carried out the most tirelessly thorough Google search about the Berwyn UFOs. He found himself more fascinated by the territory of the sightings than by the alleged events – surely a mid-twentieth century not a twenty-first century preoccupation, and interesting because people had once believed, or half-believed, in them. Llandrillo and Llanderfel were the Berwyn places most reports concentrated on, but Llanrhaeadr-ym-Mochnant featured regularly as well. He wanted to visit the region, and maybe strange emanations would arise from rock and heather and tracts of marsh...

The very next day Nat went to the local newsagent's, and bought that Ordnance Survey map he was later to post back to the Co-operative, Lydcastle, in that tell-tale jiffy-bag. By the time he did this, he had the territory pretty well fixed in his mind, so that, when up there day after day, he had the clearest mental picture of the relationship between Berwyn streams, expanses of moor or forestation, high peaks, and so on. But from his very first inspection of the map Llanrhaeadr had struck him as the place to aim for first. He liked the physical shape of the valley leading north-west from the town up to the waterfall. This last, lettered in blue, in both Welsh and English, and honoured with a star, seemed to beg for full attention. That's where I'll begin, he told himself.

He'd never heard anybody speak so much as once of Pistyll Rhaeadr.

After Brock

'I've never heard anybody speak so much as once of Pistyll Rhaeadr!' he says aloud, principally to Luke but with a near-accusatory side-glance at his father. And could the moods in which the two of them confronted the great fall before climbing up to where it began contrast more radically?

'Well, Nat, I think we should both thank your dad for being so free and forthcoming with us,' says Luke, as if reprimanding the younger for implicit criticism of the older, 'and it so happens I can vouchsafe the accuracy of everything you've said, Pete, about the 1974 UFO sightings. They crop up, you see, pretty regularly at the paper as part of our regional history. So in my time I've watched quite a few YouTube clips – showing various local guys swearing blind that lights they saw flashing above their heads were from another world. And how there was a huge government cover-up afterwards. How Whitehall arranged, at about two minutes' notice, for a whole horde of coppers and squaddies to come belting on up to Clwyd, nab all the extra-terrestrials on the hillsides, handcuff 'em and haul them off to some deep underground prison somewhere in the south, where (apparently) they still are. Well, if you can believe that, you can believe anything!' Then, as if recognizing the possibility that he may be doing himself out of a juicy tit-bit for his publication, he adds, 'I take it you *didn't* see anything out-of-this-world that night, Pete?'

'Not *see*, no! Or hear either, come to that!' And yet it was not a night like any other. Annwn clearly means nothing to either Luke or Nat. Luke, thinks Pete, is one of the increasing number who would come to High Flyers for a power kite but not an art or ethnic one. He'd fork out good money for a little buggy to draw him and some traction job along the sands of West Kirby at a fair old speed, but he wouldn't give a Barroletta, with all its centuries-long tradition behind it, the time of day… Funny thing is, I don't dislike him! Even though I caught him giving Nat the third degree. Even though I suspect he's here in this room as the enemy.

Yet he wonders how much more he can take from him, or any other prying journalist, given he has any choice in the matter.

Which he surely hasn't. This last week anxiety has loosened his tongue far more than was wise (shades of the bad old days of that quiz show!), and he's already made himself, as well as Nat, a target for investigation. When he joined the police expedition to the Berwyns almost one hundred per cent certain that this was where Nat would be, he foolishly told other members he'd been here before – 'in the UFO time'! A clever cop had already, of course, noted the cryptic reference in Nat's notebook now in police possession) and an equally clever press hack was listening to their conversation! And so what he said had become:

Dad's Long Ago Brush with the Bizarre

But should this have surprised him? Already, by Wednesday last week Pete (and a few million others) could read this sort of despicable crap about himself:

'A picture is emerging of an unstable family background for the missing bright young boy who, says his Headmaster in South London, "never failed to hand in assigned work exactly on time, and with the confidence of someone who knew he'd done the best he was capable of."' (Oh, really! It was certainly news to Pete who, over the years had built up a picture of Nat as a pretty indifferent pupil. But then he was that bogeyman of the righteous press, an absentee father.) 'Nat's dad, who grew up in Leominster, Herefordshire, is remembered in that town somewhat differently. "Oh, yes," says a prominent senior citizen who knew him well back then, "he was a bit of a lout. Of course he had his moments of glory, on that old Radio 4 quiz show, *High Flyers*, and didn't he let the world know! Went clean to his head, we all thought. In reality, he was much the same as any lad in those days when so many of them were living on benefits beyond the country's means, and leading the life of Riley. Of course tragedy came his way later, and we all hoped it would make him re-think his ways. It certainly made him decide to leave our town for good. But there you are!" finishes this anonymous member of the Leominster community, "we're all a mixture of good and bad, aren't we? I don't suppose he's much worse than most of us, and he must have suffered terribly what with the worry and guilt.'"

'Knew him well, huh?' Whatever old fart had the paper managed to corral on the street and make talk? Pointless to ponder; he'd never find out. He probably did have many a hater as a schoolboy, and deservedly too. Beside this guff the paper printed a picture of 'Peter Kempsey at 18,' then of Woodgarth, Etnam Road etc, his hair long-flowing Renaissance-style, like boys wore it in the seventies, in those far-distant days (regretted by many of his generation) of glam rock and a state actually proud of itself for looking after the needs of those who made it up.

'Which reminds me,' says Pete slowly, but he can he face it? 'I haven't come to the end of my story. I've got the worst part still to tell you, I'm afraid. But I guess, Luke, if you and Joe Public are to make sense of the whole Peter-and-Nathaniel-Kempsey saga, I've no alternative but to press ahead. Without any further ado!'

'Well, of course you must, Pete,' says Luke, with a breezy kindness. 'Take it easy, man. We've got plenty of time to spare for you, haven't we, Nat?'

That, thinks the boy he's addressed, is the first time this guy's used my first name in a light, natural way. Are things looking up then? Well, the sun is higher in the sky, the sky itself is a brighter blue than before. It'll be a fine afternoon. Up there he'd have stretched his limbs out on the heather and surrendered to the warmth, and later gone picking cloudberries.

But Pete who's about to take him back in words to those mountains Nat now thinks of as his own, is casting his gaze downwards, as one dreading what he yet has to relate. There's no going back for him now. He's turned his shop-sign round to 'Closed', believing Luke Fleming's his best bet, as far as both accurate and reasonably friendly unravelling of Nat's tale's concerned, and of the history behind it too.

Paul Binding

When it's my turn to come clean about everything (assuming – a big assumption – that I allow myself to agree to this), I shan't be anything like as submissive as my dad, thinks Nat. Mum's right about him; for all his awkwardness and independence, he's only too apt to choose the line of least resistance. Unlike me, who, when still at Junior School wrote a poem about myself beginning:

'My secret is my own person,
Because my own person is my secret…'

But he listens to his dad now as if his whole life depends on it.

Pete's upstream nocturnal walk beside Afon Disgynfa might not have yielded the usual signs of progression through a landscape, and his sense of stasis might have been reinforced by the measureless calm all round him on those uplands. But there came a point when sheer bodily exhaustion informed him 'Enough is enough!' And when, combating a surprising reluctance, he eventually did stop in his tracks, to his heartfelt relief time and place established themselves again.

However many ready facts about natural history he had at his disposal for quiz-shows, Pete was not one of those boys who identifies birds or plants as he looks about him, was, in truth, ignorant of the appearance or habits of, say a peregrine or a merlin, a buzzard or a hen-harrier, all birds for which the Berwyn Mountains are famous. He wasn't even sure in what seasons these were to be seen. But most walks in every part of the Marches bring you into contact with sheep. And bleak and remote and hallowed by Celtic mythology though this plateau might be, it is also very much sheep country, and many of those humans who do bring themselves up here do so on sheep business. Strips of barbed-wire fencing as well as stone walls run across this bare moorland. And, as he halted, overpowered by his most intense weariness yet, by the ache of his every limb and the smarting of his every sore, Pete could see, hanging over an uneven strip of fence a huge black, layered shape. As he peered through the night at this, a word came into his head, almost as if Bob Thurlow had asked him for it. Tarpaulin.

'Tarpaulin', he said aloud. And – in the interests of finally lying down for sleep after the most extraordinary nocturnal activity he'd ever indulged in – he forced himself to inch his way to it, stepping carefully from larger stone to larger stone, so as not to sink feet into soggy and chilling marsh... With the temperature having been so low for such a long period, these great folds of material were frozen weightily stiff. But realising the use and, beyond the use, the unspeakable comfort, the material could be to him, Pete tugged and tugged at it, till he had hauled it off the wire completely, and onto a suitably hard strip of ground. Then he set to and began patiently, systematically to stamp the stuff into some sort of manageable flexibility... How long did these endeavours take? He never knew. He still refused to look at his watch. And his determination to succeed was so powerful, so consuming of the whole of his bruised, battered self, that he surely could have endured all of them, and worse, for twice, if not thrice, as long – if it were to end with achieving his life-saving purpose.

The tarpaulin, he had seen at first glance, was both big enough and long enough for him to wrap himself up in it several times over. Even one folding would blissfully do the trick, let alone the four or five that, he soon appreciated, he could in fact manage. Beyond the fence Pete had already spotted a little stone cairn, protected by two incomplete, roughly constructed walls, part of some sheepfold long since abandoned.

His brand of energy, originating in desperation, in a grasp of the seriousness of his situation, did not forsake him for so much as a second. He dragged the now pliable canvas sheeting over to the cairn, again having to tread carefully because of the wet treacherous slipperiness beneath his feet. He chose the side of the shepherds' rude construction least vulnerable to the wind, protected to some degree by the unfinished walling. Turf here was comparatively dry and therefore free from the night frost now setting in by the minute. So, after lowering himself down with anxious caution, Pete wound the tarpaulin round him even more times than he'd reckoned possible. Then he let himself slump inch by inch down to the ground, and wriggle into a now-yearned-for horizontal position.

A little saying of Mum's came into his head, one she'd used when he was younger (and employed to the Brats even now): 'Snug as a bug in a rug'. Well, somewhat improbably, this was his condition now.

As he felt himself borne into unconsciousness, he involuntarily envisaged Sam Price beside him, also safe from the winter cold inside the black, rank-smelling canvas, his feet touching his own, and his eyes fixing their beams on his face, not with the fury and loathing of their last moments together, no, nothing like that, but with forgiveness, understanding, satisfaction in comradeship…

He was never to forget what he dreamed of in those tarpaulin hours. He was making his way back to Leominster, not by the slow slog of road in whatever vehicle, but through the air. He simply put his hands on the string of a huge kite, the plain old diamond-shaped sort like his brother Robin had wanted him to make, and floated effortlessly off this shank of the Berwyn Mountains to home and safety, a high flyer with the best imaginable goal for his high flight. Possibly this was the first time that particular play on words occurred to him – asleep on a stretch of Welsh wilderness.

When he was sufficiently awake to poke his head out of his tarpaulin cocoon, it was still dark and cold on the Disgynfa plateau. A dark which was nowhere relieved by any luminous flying object in the sky. Had there ever been such a visitant to these mountains? Perhaps only those saw who deep down wanted to see. Sam Price did want to see, fervidly, so maybe he'd met up at last with Don Parry (clearly another bloke who wanted) and had been rewarded with a brief, bright glimpse of some balloon-like form hovering overhead, little twinkles of light playing on its underbelly. But Pete himself, he did *not* 'want'. Somehow the great peace on these Heights, which had enabled him to sleep so deeply these past hours had taken from him any desire for extra-terrestrial encounter. In truth this had been Sam's desire, not his own, and he had borrowed, not to say appropriated or stolen, it. Surely, after all their joint quest had brought him – Sam's obscene, hostile words and his vicious blows, which still hurt, to say nothing of his feelings of guilt and loss – it would be best for him to abandon UFOs once and for all. When he got back home to Leominster, he would write to Bob Thurlow and tell him, sorry, but he'd had a change of mind, and would instead go for...

No. That wasn't enough. He must inform Bob Thurlow that he was, regretfully, unable to take part in the show. He still felt, of course, 'honoured and appreciative' etc etc. But the pro-gramme – under this waterproof canvas he suddenly understood – had brought him nothing but woe. What success it had bestowed on him had, even at its best, its most dizzying, been hollow – and it had always met resistance from those closest to him. Better by far to let the whole thing recede.

His parents would rejoice at his decision, would think it showed moral maturity; he could scarcely bear the wait before informing them. It'd be a while before this would be practicable. He looked at his watch for the first time since he'd lain down: almost half-past five; he had slept, he reckoned, for at least four hours, and probably longer. High time to be off and away, and sadly there was no likelihood of any kite coming to bear him back to Herefordshire. He had a horrible cramp in his right arm and right leg, indeed the whole of his right side was uncomfortably stiff, the consequence of the foetus-like attitude in which he'd slept. With every minute of fuller consciousness, he was more horribly aware of his profusion of bruises and cuts. As well as of the hideous truth that Sam had left him with injuries beside a quiet roadside to – well, to bleed to death for all he knew! Or, apparently, cared!

Bringing this improbable, almost impossible fact to mind enabled him to find the strength to crawl out of the canvas, lurch his shaky body upright, balance and support it on feet very wobbly at first, and then take forward steps. He must look like some flesh-and-blood scarecrow placed by some crude joker by this broken-down, dry-stone sheep-fold. Well, a fixture in this gaunt, frozen landscape he was not going to be. How he was going to explain himself – even on his homeward journey, let alone on arrival at Woodgarth – was a thorny matter to be postponed until he'd got properly started... His mouth tasted unspeakably foul, and even spitting out disgusting globules of yellow phlegm into the nearest clump of bracken didn't relieve it. There was an emptiness around him beyond any past experience of night or countryside. For the first time since his arrival above the waterfall, he felt fear at the sheer scale of where he was. If this really were Annwn, then he was perfectly happy to quit it (though grateful for having stayed unscathed in it). He did not belong here; the Overworld was what he'd settle for.

Few other ramblers in the Berwyn Mountains scale the side of Pistyll Rhaeadr as he had done. Official notices oppose their doing so; there are other, far kinder and safer ways of getting up to the plateau from the base of the fall, and of coming down too, to end up where they began, in the hostel and café of Tan-y-pistyll. From here the tarmac road leads down the Afon Rhaeadr valley to Llanrhaeadr-ym-Mochnant, which Pete now felt he'd visited in another life. Pete took far less time to reach the normal path to Tan-y-pistyll than he'd anticipated. Could it be that, however remote and arcane his sleeping-place had appeared to him, in geographical reality he'd never been all that far from where other people could, if they wished, walk without any feeling of entering wilderness? That his psychological state had created the sense of great space? Anyway soon he was back in the world of recognisable sounds. Among the trees and bushes he was now passing there was, at this pre-dawn winter hour, enough rustling, scurrying, wing-flapping, to have given him at least a few frissons, had he been suddenly placed down here among them. But, in his fervent resolve to make for Llanrhaeadr and means-of-transport home as quickly as he could, he was scarcely bothered by these noises, not all of which he was able, first off, to identify. Tan-y-pistyll, like the farm houses beyond it, appeared still rapt in sleep. Pete however strode forward defiantly in the direction of his goal, with something of the spirit in which, against common-sense, he had scaled the side of the waterfall.

But he still felt he had to sing to keep up his spirits, particularly as he would soon pass the place where Sam had stopped the Beetle and assaulted him viciously. When he did actually pass it, he deliberately swivelled his head to the opposite side of the road, lest rage rise too strongly in him.

He made himself remember happier things, and went through the successive verses of many songs until – really not so far now to the little town of last night! – he'd reached the junction of the road down from the waterfall and the road down from the village of Llanarmon Dyffryn Ceiriog; clustered houses were imminent, thank heavens!

But now from the direction of Llanarmon DC (as most signposts call the place) a car was coming, to Pete at this moment a more unnerving sound than any late-hunting owl's hoot. Though what else do you expect to hear on a road? It was, in point of fact not some little Beetle like Sam's, nor anything remotely rustic, but a black Volvo, obviously bound, like himself, for Llanrhaeadr. Pete judged it best to take no notice of this intruder – perhaps, he told himself only half-facetiously, it's driven by an alien? And he walked on, purposefully looking straight ahead of him.

The ploy didn't work. The car was drawing up alongside him.

It seemed to Pete now a truly immense while since he had seen another human being. The night had thoroughly removed him from his kind, with all its capacity for hostility and treachery, and he'd been glad. But now he felt a stab of pleasure at seeing an indisputable *man*. Especially one so utterly normal-looking as the bloke now leaning across the empty passenger seat, and winding the window down. Expressly to address him, no doubt of it. He was about his own dad's age, with dark, curly hair, and, would you credit it, wearing a formal suit. Talk about swallowing pride, Pete would accept the lift the chap was surely about to offer him.

'Morning, young man!' the latter said, with the play of a smile (rather than an actual one) on his round, red-cheeked face, 'unusual sort of time to be taking a walk!'

His face expressed only too readably the unsuitability, the sheer unlikelihood of Pete's gear for a pre-dawn Welsh mountain road. 'Well, it's not a walk,' Pete answered, breezily all things considered, 'I'm just heading home after a night out.'

'Quite a night out too, by the looks of you,' said the man. To Pete's discomfiture he now switched off his car engine, 'did you enjoy yourself?'

'Well… I found a good place to kip down,' and that was no more than the truth, was it now? 'which was all I was wanting by then.'

'After your fight with your mate over a girl? You lost, I suppose – and took yourself way up here to lick your wounds?'

'Sort of!' A little less than the truth, but on the right lines, more or less, 'in a way!'

'Perhaps you gave as good as you got? Let's hope his wounds are crying out for a good chunk of beefsteak on 'em as much as yours?'

'I'm not sure,' answered Pete, his hand involuntarily going to his face which indeed felt a mess still, whatever the overnight improvement, 'I don't know how he is now.' The man's interpretation of his condition flattered him more than somewhat, made him feel he'd come of man's estate, at least in the world's eyes. But he didn't want to hear any more of it. He could not suppress a violent shiver. Just after six on a January morning in mountain country doesn't make for comfortable loitering in talk, and temperature was certainly below zero.

'Buried his body somewhere nearby, have you? Your mate's?'

'No, of course I haven't!' said Pete, realising as soon as he'd spoken that his indignation was not wise. Also it made him sound as if he really had disposed of Sam, along with his own shit-soaked underpants, somewhere on the waterfall road. Anyway, his tone impressed the man unfavourably enough for him to slip a hand into his jacket breast-pocket and take out a printed card. This he flashed at Pete with a professional's expert gesture, following it by enunciating himself the all-important words on it: 'Jim Maddox, CID. Hop in, young sir, if you will be so obliging!'

Pete was too bemused, and too grateful for the warmth of the Volvo's interior, not to be obliging, though he also appreciated he couldn't very well not comply. He felt curiously light-headed, what's more. His whole body was now telling him that he hadn't slept long enough to be properly ready for any challenges the day might bring. 'Jim's my dad's name,' he heard himself say, to his own surprise, as the guy started the car up again.

'That's nice to know? A Tanat Valley man, I presume?'

'No, he's not!'

'Know you're out here? And not in your bed about to get up for breakfast and school?'

'No! Not at all!'

'I reckoned not! Probably doesn't even know you and your buddy go out with flash girls and then brawl about them?'

This was true. 'No, he doesn't know that. He's a well-respected accountant in Leominster.'

'I can well believe it,' said the CID man, 'and I expect he'll be very far from pleased to find out what his son has been up to behind his back miles away from where he should be. What will please him, I've no doubt, is seeing you at home in one piece. If that's what you can be said to be. You look a right dog's dinner to me!'

'Yes, he'll be relieved to see me!' Pete agreed. He could see lights ahead of, as well as below, the road: the town that had been last night's destination, home of the mysterious Don Parry. Fires were now being lit in households to start the morning, fathers would be polishing shoes and boots, mums setting out breakfast things on kitchen tables, maybe even frying mushrooms and sausages. And, of course, making tea (he could use a cup of that himself, right now). Newspaper boys might be starting their rounds, bringing tidings of 'Aliens Have Landed in…' Well, very possibly right here or as near here as damn-it – here in – the lightness in his head made him, uncharacteristically, hesitate over the little town's name. But Jim Maddox was telling him something...

'You're aware, are you, that all behind us, between Llanrhaeadr-ym-Mochnant and Llanarmon, and on all roads over to Corwen, there are scores – bloody scores – of my colleagues, plain-clothes and otherwise, plus a few of our military friends just for good measure.'

Fear stirred in Pete's stomach.

'Thought not! The road I've just come down is chocker with the force. Thanks to our efforts no one's allowed to stray onto Cadair Berwyn or Cadair Bronwen at all. Not so very far from where you had your kip, I'd reckon... Any idea why there's all this fuss?' His tone was the light casual one he must have used, with success, on many a dubious-looking character on many a chase. Pete fell for it.

'The sightings?'

Jim Maddox gave him a quick, interested, appraising glance. 'To coin a phrase!' Jim Maddox said, 'but then everyone else has been bloody coining it since about...'

'Half past eight yesterday evening?' ventured Pete. The man mustn't think him (that favourite term of Sam's) a moron.

Another dart from the assessing eyes. 'Exactly! Do you know I wouldn't be surprised if, along with the lassies, news of aliens arriving here didn't play a part in your nocturnal fun so far from home base? I didn't arrive here myself till gone half past bloody midnight. None too pleased at having been summoned out here either... These godforsaken mountains are, at this very moment in time, as big a hive of activity as anywhere in Britain. Probably as anywhere on the bloody globe, since we all seem to be thinking in inter-planetary terms...'

'And have you,' Pete struggled to sound calm, mature, and what he thought of as 'natural', 'have you actually found any...' What word would it be most dignified to use here? Well, why not the one Detective Inspector Maddox had himself employed? 'aliens?'

After Brock

'Just a few of the blighters. Here and there, you know. Usual types. Green skin, blue hair, three horns growing out of their foreheads, forked tails.'

'In other words – nobody?' Was he disappointed or relieved? Or just hearing what he'd have expected all along.

'Sod all as yet. Not that I'd be allowed to tell you owt about it if we had found 'em. Anyway it's not been for want of trying, or for want of time,' he glanced at his watch, 'or money, come to that. What's being spent on this bloody lark, at a time of national financial crisis, is anyone's guess!' He snorted with derision. 'Now in a moment we'll be in the main street of the metropolis that goes by the outlandish name of Llanrhaeadr-ym-Mochnant. Me, I'm heading onto Llanfyllin. Can that be of any use to you?'

'It could be a lot of use,' Pete said with a rush of enthusiasm he couldn't control, 'though Sam may still be down right here.'

'Sam? The lad you've been fighting with?'

'Yeah!'

'Well, I think we might leave him to steam in his own belliger-ent juice down here in Llanrhaeadr. It'd certainly be against my professional instincts to liberate you just so's you can have another set-to with this local Sonny Robinson... I didn't quite catch your name, I'm afraid.'

Best not to give his real one. But he didn't feel like telling a complete lie either. This was a decent man he was lucky enough to have encountered. Well, Mrs Richards, at *The Mikado*, had confused him with one of the Brats, the one who in the past had irritated him most, so why didn't he give the name of the other one? 'Robin,' he said, and then added, 'Price'. Practically every other person in The Marches (not only Trevor, Susan and Sam) was called Price, so he would be believed.

Enshadowed houses, still wrapped in the night's cold, with roof-tiles whitened by frost, showed themselves on either side of the street... 'Well, Robin, on to Llanfyllin, where I am going to meet up with reinforcements for this madcap operation, but where I'm told there's an excellent café, serving its own bread, famous for miles. We might grab ourselves a bit of makeshift

203

breakfast, and I'll try to grab you a lift back to Leominster. It is still Leominster, isn't it?' He implied that someone as patently shifty as Pete might well have changed his destination already.

'Yes, of course, Jim!' Bit forward to use a first name to an inspector from Scotland Yard perhaps, but Pete had warmed to him. And the man himself didn't appear to mind, seemed pleased rather than otherwise. Clearly he resented at having been sent all the way out here – on what he thought a fool's errand which would devour already ill-stretched funds.

Several times on the way to Llanfyllin, Jim Maddox slowed down to talk to fellow-cops in cars travelling in the opposite direction, to cheer them on, or inquire if they'd had any fresh news from Bala or Llandrillo in what he called the 'night's shenanigans'. Pete found it difficult to construct any clear picture of these. Often the operations mounted sounded as complex as for a Soviet invasion: men sent to Bala, men sent to Corwen, men just arriving in Llangollen, men who hadn't turned up in Llanderfel, but others well in place in Llangynog and Llandrillo, 'and a bloody tough bunch too, thank the Lord. Unlike some of the other wankers they've chosen to send along!' Perhaps the arrival of non-human beings, the very sight and sound of whom were total unknowns, made more demanding and alarming task than facing any number of Russians. To deal with whom you could at least have found interpreters.

But then after Annwn this whole business – though a true schoolboy's dream, and full of matter to arouse the curiosity – felt less important than Pete would ever have guessed it could.

By the time they got to Llanfyllin, the morning was beginning, in stripes of green and orange at the base of the sky to the east of the little town, in the direction of Oswestry and the North Shropshire plain.

The café-cum-bakery, for which, after parking the Volvo, Jim made a beeline, assailed the two visitors warmly and wonderfully with its smell of yeast, sugar and coffee, and was already quite full, its clientele at this hour entirely male. Even with so much else to worry about, Pete was possessed by a child-like fear that the delectable-looking doughnuts would have all been snapped up before their turn came round. Jim Maddox, with his manly manner, vocabulary, neat, dark (if cheapo) suit and telltale badge, commanded immediate respect, and while Pete kept a place for them in the queue, he stepped out of the line to exchange words with men who seemed positively honoured by his doing so. Only two customers away from the counter at which a young man and woman were frantically meeting the orders, Pete caught his own name in one of these exchanges, well, not his own name exactly but 'Robin'; he'd be heartily pleased to see little old Robs again after this weird time away! He glanced to his right, and saw two heads, Jim's and another man's, jerking forward. Good old Jim, he must be finding him a lift. Doubtless too was telling the possible driver, who'd clearly already noted Pete's facial scars, that he'd suffered in a punch-up over a lassie last night, as all lads will. The new man grinned – in fellow-feeling, Pete thought. He was maybe thirty, dark wavy hair, broad-shoulders, black beard of the short-haired kind fringing the face from ear to ear, and slightly too much of a tummy for his years. Probably a rugby player who didn't always keep himself in trim as he should, and enjoyed celebratory or commiserative rounds of drinks a bit too well. Pete liked the look of him, hoped that he would be the man taking him at least part of the way home.

It turned out he was actually going all the way to Leominster itself. 'You've found yourself a guardian angel, Robin,' Jim Maddox said, 'isn't that right, Joe?'

'Don't think I quite deserve to be called that,' said this Joe, 'but I'm happy to play the part for the duration!'

So there it was: the two of them travelled down to Herefordshire for an hour and a half, in Joe's cream-coloured van with the words Watkinson Poultry and Fish and a horrible little picture of a chicken, done in red and black, on its sides. 'It's not my own vehicle, actually, but a good mate's,' Joe apologised, 'it's got far more space for my goods today than my own old banger would have!' He was noticeably disinclined to talk, had nothing of the bluff friendliness of Det. Insp. Maddox. Rather he appeared sunk in reflections that periodically he had to haul himself out of, and with some effort, to give necessary attention to his duties as a driver. For his part Pete felt overcome by an exhaustion greater than any he'd ever known.

Only when the van had got onto that old friend of Marches folk, the A49, did this van driver rouse Pete with words... 'Well, Robin, you look a bit readier for the civilised world than when I took you on to please that plain-clothes dick friend of yours,' he said, on entering the rail-and-ribbon-development that is Craven Arms, 'and I reckon you've well earned all the snoozes you've been having. But you're not going to feel too much better, are you now, till you've hit the bathroom and bed at your home. And my advice to you, pal, especially after hearing you speak – you've a nice, honest, frank sort of voice, you could go on a radio show with it – is this: Don't, please don't, not any more! Give it up!' He himself had a nice voice, lively, rich, recognizably Welsh.

'Don't what?'

'Go chasing after girls you have to brawl for! You think all that's your passport to manhood, don't you, but it's no such thing. It's giving in to the weaker side of you, if truth be told.'

In all the many errors of Pete's vision of life so far the notion that Joe was repudiating had never figured. But he wasn't going to say so.

'Some of us,' Joe went on, giving him a meaningful sideways glance, 'and I say "us" as probably shouldn't, are cut out to be virtuous. And if we are, then it's virtuous we should be. No matter what this rotten modern culture of ours says.'

'I wouldn't have (indeed I hadn't) marked this man as some hot gospeller,' said Pete to himself, 'but he's certainly speaking like one.' 'How d'you mean?' he said, aloud.

'How can a man be virtuous, Robin?' said Joe, rhetorically, 'well, surely you can work that out for yourself?'

But Pete was too clogged with sleep to be able to phrase any reply which suggested he was capable of doing this.

'Be kind to others. That's the golden rule, wouldn't you say? Be kind, be considerate of their rights and feelings. So the only way for a man to treat a woman is with the utmost gentleness and respect. And that means honouring the promises they've made to another. Unless, of course, that other person is really giving them grief. Which may not be the case at all.' He seemed, thought Pete, to be seeing scenes from his own life, or from a life he knew as well as his own – in addition to scanning the roadway itself, with the perpendicular, much-admired tower of Ludlow's St Laurence's rearing up in the near distance. 'That's not what you've been doing, eh, Robin? Maybe you tried snatching some-body you fancied from a lad, who, in his own clumsy way properly loved her. And maybe she him; that's often the part hardest to take. Well, you can't blame the lad for lashing out at you, I think you're understanding that already. Take yesterday's wounds as elementary lessons, pal.'

It was obviously impossible for Pete to tell this bloke the (almost humiliating) truth: that he'd come nowhere near such a situation, that he was a virgin who had not even had a proper girlfriend, his relationship with Melanie being almost absurdly tepid and irregular in meetings. On the other hand he could see still more fully than on those approaches to Annwn that he'd done Sam a real wrong with his concealment. (And where was that stupid guy now? Probably about to tuck into a good country breakfast at the Parrys' house!)

But he had missed something his lift-to-Leominster was inquiring of him: 'What do you make, man, of all the happenings in the Berwyns yesterday?'

Too tired not to be completely candid, Pete replied: 'I'm afraid I don't know enough about them to make anything!'

'You weren't in Llanrhaeadr yesterday evening then?'

'Yes,' he stalled, 'but…'

'But were otherwise engaged, as they say. I get it, man, I get it…Well, me, I don't know now what we all did or didn't see. But I can tell you this, Robin – I think the whole show, the whole celestial display, if you like to put it like that, came to us as a warning, as a lecture from on high, if you get my meaning! A kind of drubbing-down in bright colours. From now on we have to be good, and it's up to us folk of the locality to start the ball rolling. Like Yours Truly. That's the message of whatever lights came flashing above our mountains or whatever men in black popped up over in Bala! Take it from me, my friend, because you're, I'd say, ten years younger than me, and so you've got an extra decade that you need not waste. And you will not waste it if you try your darnedest to be *good*.'

Pete was so astonished at this homily that all he could think to say back was, 'I understand what you're saying.'

'No good just understanding, pal. In the end only action counts.'

Pete could do nothing about the sequence of great yawns that followed.

'Yes, I know, you're well and truly knackered, man, I can tell. Well, that's nothing I daresay a good morning's sleep won't put right. Wherever was it you eventually laid yourself down last night?'

All Pete could answer was, 'Somewhere pretty rough and ready, but I did find some old tarpaulin.' Of the peace of the heights he would say nothing.

'Well, I didn't have too good a night myself,' said Joe, 'scarcely slept a wink, to tell the truth. Still I had this load of wares to take to a man I do a lot of work for in Leominster, and I hope to goodness it doesn't all smell too much of old Will Watkinson's bloody fish... Oh, we'll all be a heap better when this morning's over, I reckon.'

Pete knew the road from Ludlow to Leominster so intimately that he let himself slip into slumber once again. This must have lasted ten minutes, because, when he opened his heavy-lidded, furry-edged eyes, the houses and allotments better known to him than any of their kind anywhere on earth were presenting themselves before him, like the Kempseys' neighbour's tree always did through his bedroom window after a dream. And, not only this, but his driver, this Joe guy was digging him awake again with his elbow and asking him, 'Where do you want dropping, pal?'

Pete thought: Well, not Etnam Street – there were always other residents about, who might pester him, if not now, then later, with censorious questions about his extraordinary appearance and how was it he was turning up to his home (when he should be off to his school in Hereford) in a fishmonger's van? He didn't think he should confront his parents just yet, and in this state, for how was he to explain where he'd been and how he'd got so beaten about? 'Oh, as near the Priory Church as you can get,' he told the driver, 'I live close by.'

For there was always, it occurred to him, Oliver Merchant's house in Church Street, and he would be able to confide at least something of the night past to him as he could not to Mum and Dad. And – best thing of all right now – Ol had a most luxurious bathroom. 'Thanks, Joe, for all your help.'

The man gave a little nod, a little laugh. 'My name's not Joe, that cop of yours got it wrong. But it'll do as well as any other for this morning. Another little lesson in humility for me.'

'Well, thanks, anyway!' Really their leave-taking was as laid-back and run-of-the-mill as if Pete hadn't been delivered from a Welsh mountain town with a legend of an otherworldly realm at its back, as if there had been no involvement of any kind whatever with UFOs which now looked like warnings against sinful conduct.

Yes, better to wake up Oliver than Dad and Mum. So Pete stumbled up to the front door of his godfather's elegant, mellowed brick house, the one with the fanlight above a maroon-painted front door. Lights (still well needed at this hour of a winter's morning) were already on in the beautifully proportioned, high-ceilinged front room on its right-hand side. This acted as both studio for the Sunbeam Press and reception-room for Ol's many friends and visitors. From the doorstep Pete fancied he could smell the logs he could see burning away in the fireplace – cherry and apple, those were the woods Ol favoured most. Security might be dull after his protracted taste of time-transcending Annwn, and sadly this would probably irk him again sooner or later, but just for now, it was welcome.

He gave the door a vigorous thumping with its brass, dolphin-shaped knocker.

Ol himself came to answer him. Why, whatever was up with the bloke? He was looking quite aghast at Pete, an incongruously wild look in his – bloodshot – eyes, wholly inconsistent with his usual bearing. 'Dear boy, where have you been? Where on earth have you been?' He leaned forward and shook his godson as if to prove he was still flesh-and-blood.

Pete knew straightaway that this shaking – a common enough expression of anger – was in this case no form of rebuke whatever for his night's roaming.

'Do you know, dear Peter?' Ol seemed at one and the same time to be shouting these words and merely mouthing them, 'have you heard? We've been desperately trying to find you.'

'Heard what?' he asked.

But maybe he knew already.

'Dead!' Oliver Merchant told him, 'killed! Your whole beautiful, wonderful, lovable family... Well, not Julian. He's in a severely critical condition in hospital, though, and we can't know yet whether he'll pull through or not. But the rest – gone, Peter, all gone. And I loved all of them so much. What are we two going to do? How can we possibly bear to live without them?'

Nat averts his gaze from his dad's face consumed by inner devastation. Where or when did he last see him wear such an expression? Then he knows.

It's an August afternoon in Kensington Gardens, just over six years back. The undulating lawns, after so much protracted dry weather, look like stretches of raked-out Shredded Wheat. Sprinklers are making no proper impact. The waters of the Serpentine are low, still, opaque, and a little rank-smelling. Even its boats appear sluggish in their movements; in fact the whole cityscape – Knightsbridge Barracks, the Row, the distant towers of Park Lane – is burdened from above by the low white-grey depression of clouds that create haze but will bring no rain. Dad normally likes watching boats – his suggesting an afternoon trip to the park came as no surprise – but today he quite obviously has no attention to give them.

'I'm leaving London, Nat,' he says, 'I'm leaving you and your mother. I hope this doesn't come as too big a shock.'

Nat doesn't know whether to tell him, No, actually it doesn't. Mum, eyes moist, upper lip quivering, informed him yesterday but said, 'Dad will want to give you the news himself, in his own way. It's really for the best, including for you…' etc, etc.

Dad is now providing plenty of etc, each sentence adding to the burden of the heavy loaded air through which the two of them are dispiritedly moving to the brim of the lake. Afterwards Nat will wonder if Pete ever said what his head has retained from the conversation. 'I bore your mother, you know, Nat. It's best for her not to live with a man who bores her… I suppose I've always tended to bore people, Uncle Ol apart, ever since I was a swollen-headed schoolboy.'

'You don't bore me, Dad!' But maybe Nat never gives his father this assurance.

What he does come out with, to his own astonishment, is: 'Don't you love Mum and me then?'

A moment's silence, a moment's speechlessness, then Pete shows his son just such a ghastly face as he has now, at the climax of his tale. But can't manage an answer, any more than Nat now can manage an adequate comment to what he's just heard.

'The newspapers have already been pleased to tell the great British public some of all this these last few days,' Pete is saying, now out of breath and trying, for his part, to look not at his audience but at the bright sky above the Market Square outside the window, 'so you both knew how my story was going to end. Were waiting for it, I guess, though you couldn't know from what angle I was going to come at it. Anyway the whole appalling thing's in the Herefordshire archives, for any researchers worth their salt to read, to use against me now.

'Regional papers in 1974 went fucking wild over the story. Can't you imagine? "Father and mother of three and their ten-year-old son killed on the A49 at 12.50 am on the morning of January 24. Lorry skidded and jackknifed into the Kempsey family's Rover. Lorry-driver – working overtime for Bulmers' of Hereford – not killed. Will face prosecution." As the wretched bloke did. Not that I was there when he faced the Law, or cared much about the justice of his sentence, I have to say. In fact Oliver Merchant kept me from a hell of a lot of unpleasantness. That's almost the biggest of my many, many debts to the man.'

'Uncle Ol,' says Nat to himself, seeing in a flash of clarity that pink-faced, white-haired, flabby elderly man to whom his dad had been so devoted. And yet who had frequently made him edgy, impatient. Incongruously Nat can hear, the faintest whisper on the morning air, the old man singing to him.

'Ol was my protector in more ways than I can even begin to name,' Pete continues, his eyes, to his own annoyance, watering, 'starting with what we should tell the world about myself and where I was that fatal night. It might be widely thought I had quite a bit of explaining to do.'

Luke is quick off the mark here. He's not an ambitious journo for nothing. '12.50 am!' he goes, 'when the accident happened, you were halfway up the side of Pistyll Rhaeadr?'

'Yes. I was.'

'Had your folks gone out to look for you, do you think? To find you and bring you back from wherever they thought you were?'

'It's one obvious explanation, isn't it? Though it was a fucking odd hour to be doing that. The car crash happened about four miles to the north of Leominster, direction of Ludlow. It doesn't tell you a solitary thing about where they were bound. Even though they were actually headed north, how could they possibly – possibly know about my being in the Berwyns? News of the UFO sightings hadn't even percolated through the media to the outer world then.'

'But,' says Luke, 'there was a survivor? Your brother Julian.'

'Yup, Nat's uncle,' and he gives a quick smile at his son as if to confirm a likeness between the two of them, which doesn't per-ceptibly exist, 'his uncle whom he has now met, as I know from his own journal. Julian had pretty grave head injuries, poor fellow. Was on the danger list for four nightmare days. Then the worries changed from whether he would live to whether he would be permanently mentally impaired… Oh, it was a sojourn in Hell and a half, I can tell you. But, when he came fully to, Jules could remember nothing of what had happened to him, nothing. Doctors tried, police tried, Ol tried. But with no result. His blankness bewildered Julian himself as much as it did everybody else.'

'Wasn't that a bit of a relief for you, Pete? In the circumstances?' Luke asks. Impertinent of the guy really, but – maybe through his seriously mounting weariness – Pete isn't as offended by it as you might think. There's a little kernel of truth in his question after all, as he's had to admit to himself over the years. Not that he was going to do so now…

'If it's a relief to think you might have brain-damaged your nearest brother as well as killed both your parents and your youngest brother, then I guess you could say so, yeah…' But it comes out sad rather than sarcastic. 'Oliver was adamant what I should say and do from the very first. He was my parents', and therefore my own official next-of-kin, even though no sort of blood relative, and so had been contacted pretty soon after the bodies were discovered in the wreckage and identified… "For the time being, Peter," he said to me, "I don't want to learn a single thing more about your activities last night. You've told me more than's good for me to hear as it is. There's all the time in the world for me to hear the rest. If I want to. What most people here will think is that you were out on the town and only emerged from your pleasures in time for a late breakfast. Typical lad of eighteen, in other words! You've got all the right scars to show it too. And we're going to keep to that. It will make people sympathetic towards you rather than otherwise. There's hardly a person in the world who hasn't a similar story to his credit – or discredit. And I should doubt that Sam's going to talk. He's going to learn the dreadful truth pretty soon – all Leominster will be gossiping about it. I hardly think he's going to add to the drama by revealing he chucked you out of his car onto a lonely mountain road in Wales. But just to make sure of things, I will pay a call on Price's Menswear later on in the morning."

'When he got there, Ol found Trevor Price stunned by the news, but under the distinct impression that his son had had a rotten night out, was now feeling a bit poorly, and wouldn't be going into the tutorial college that morning. "Them that ask no questions get told no lies, eh, Ol?" Sam recovered enough, apparently, to go to London a few days later, because it was from there I received his condolence card. It said: "So sorry about your sad news! Pity we haven't seen each other these last weeks! My life's about to take a curious turn; I'm going back to Darnton. Forgive and forget's their motto they say, and I think it's a wise one. Yours, Sam." That was telling me in fairly clear terms what line I had to follow, wasn't it? Would you not agree?

'Unlike his parents Sam didn't show up at the big funeral – which was put off and put off until the police were satisfied with everything. It was a big occasion, in the Priory, both my parents were well respected, even popular, and of course the whole acci-dent – with its unsolved mystery (i.e. why *had* they gone out at that hour?) – had mesmerised the entire county. I recall – stupid, blind young bastard, that I was – looking round repeatedly during the ghastly, interminable service, thinking, even hoping Sam might have come on his own to show support. But no. Of *course* he didn't show up. In the end, some time in early March – I remember the daffodils were just showing in all the gardens, and they made me think how happy the sight of them always made my mother – I did get a postcard from Darnton, that famous old public school of his (it was of the Old Quadrangle and Chapel), to prove, I suppose, that he really was there. Sam had written to me, "Good to be back at the old dump, whatever its faults! Hope all is going better for you, with good wishes, Sam."

'"Hope all is going better for you." Like fuck it was! I was des-perately trying, every hour of those weeks, to understand the un-understandable: that I would never, never see Mum, Dad and Robin again, never be able to tell them that, appearances often to the contrary, I'd been fond of them. Hadn't ever imagined existing without them. And I was feeling... well, like Judas

Iscariot himself, as it seemed to me. And we know what *he* went and did… And nobody mourned him! Instead they passed his story on down through centuries of history as a byword for ingratitude and wickedness.'

Both Luke and Nat want badly to dissipate the mood that this last sentence – urgent with dark past self-conviction – threatens to establish. But it is Nat who provides the means of doing so: 'And Julian – my uncle Julian. What about him?'

If, he thinks, I hadn't, that first afternoon of freedom from exams, arrived at Josh's house at the time I did, I never would have known I had a flesh-and-blood uncle, let alone one I can actually like. In the same way, if I hadn't followed an unremarkable-looking path up the mountainside, for no obvious reason, I never would have had my own great Berwyn experience.

Julian was in intensive care for several days in Hereford County Hospital, and then transferred for another two weeks to a priority two-bed ward in the same institution. Slashed and swollen and pale almost beyond recognition, his journey from unconsciousness to semi-consciousness didn't alleviate the distress the onlookers felt at his condition. Rather it taunted them with new proof of the fragility of human communication. Jules might as well, Pete would think, be dead like Robin for all I get through to him. Perhaps it'd be better – for his own sake – to perish right now, and join the others, rather than survive as this cruel travesty of a living being and a banished member of his firmly bonded family. Yet even as he silently articulated this thought, Pete knew he didn't subscribe to it, that he wanted his only remaining sibling to survive. As he did – and indeed there turned out to be no lasting damage to the brain, though it was possible he'd suffer throughout his life from acute headaches.

Pete travelled into Hereford by train several times a week to see Julian. Hearing him mouth his not always consistent grasp of what had happened, and of whom he'd lost was not the least anguishing experience of that near-insupportable period. (Pete would replay scenes from it for years afterwards.) No details of the car crash itself had lodged in his head…The injustice of their (related) different fates made Pete, sitting beside the hospital bed, exclaim: 'It's not fair, Jules, is it? I was there up on the Heights in Wales, and they took care of me after my accident. But you – well, you got away, unlike the others, but – trapped in the car and now trapped in bed!' It hardly bore looking at, let alone thinking about.

And Julian opened his blue eyes, and gave him an inquiring, disquieting look, to haunt him for years. Which would haunt him maybe forever.

But their ways were to diverge. Oliver Merchant set about looking after the family he loved in their deaths and precarious fragmented survival as earnestly as he had attended them all in life.

Pete of course never took part in that special January 31 edition of *High Flyers*, never had to write any get-out letter to Bob Thurlow. Ol contacted him instead. On the programme Bob spoke to the world of 'Peter Kempsey's unspeakable loss', and the audience broke out into an ovation of sympathy, probably louder than any they would have given his successful answers. Later Bob sent him a Complete Shakespeare as a keepsake.

Recovery wasn't so swift, and soon school became a problem too. Oliver fixed that he should sit his A Levels, not in summer, like most people, but in the winter, when the healing process, if only tentatively, should have begun. He himself – few widowers can have grieved for their loved one more than Ol for Marion Kemspey – proposed to move Sunbeam Press out of Leominster and back to London, the South London he had come from. He would take Pete with him.

Julian, once his recovery was established, was another matter. Pete at eighteen or nineteen would be going to college and entering independence, Julian was still a needy eleven year old. As Julian improved in mind as well as body, he turned for comfort to the music he had always excelled in making. It was Gregory Pringle himself who proposed that he and his wife Ros adopt the lad, as companion to their son, Dickon and their daughter,

After Brock

Amelia. It was a proposal that, insofar as anything could, made Julian happy, feel that a new and interesting life might stretch out before him. So he became (legally, and later emotionally) Julian Pringle – a Kempsey no longer, though he'd been the favourite of Jim Kempsey whose distinctive strawberry blond hair he alone of his children had inherited. Greg Pringle had just moved to a new house in the nearby Herefordshire town of Bromyard, and that is where Julian went to live.

When Pete reviews that strange first half of 1974, and his own state of being then, as gradually, improbably, it moved towards summer, it is whiteness that first comes to his mind – or rather blinding flashes of it. Scarcely a day went by that he did not suddenly see the void blazing in front of his eyes in the form of bursts of pure white fire, sometimes engulfing, sometimes systematically devouring objects or persons surrounding him. But other times the whiteness was visible as a distant, threatening, burning mass, advancing inexorably with cruel, colourless intensity. It's this that's behind the world, it announced; not dark – or blackness – because that's readily identifiable. Back up on the Berwyns, inside the tarpaulin, didn't you yourself, Pete (eventually) find the dark soothing as well as daunting, a perfectly right and proper element for rest? But with this whiteness you can know no rest. It dazzles, it torments, it destroys, it's the terror behind life which we so rarely deign or dare to acknowledge. It makes nonsense of any idea that rewards and celebrations, whether for doing well at school or for answering correctly the questions posed to you, have any importance whatsoever...

In May that year – and a more than usually beautiful and full-blossomy May it was – Pete received in the post a redirected envelope sent from Pebble Mill, the BBC's studios in Birmingham, visited that happy day when he became Midlands Champion. (His address now was Ol's house in Church Street; Woodgarth was already on the market, expected to fetch a fair price.) This was not the first letter he had had from this provenance. Since his very first appearance in Leominster's commandeered Junior School, quite a few fans had written to him, some asking for his photo, some wanting to be his friend, some plainly off their trolleys, and several more critical folk into the bargain; one writer informed him that Somerset, not Herefordshire, was England's greatest cider-apple county, another complained of his 'common West Midlands accent which will have a deleterious effect on impressionable young listeners'. More recently had come, as a result of Bob Thurlow's explanation to his audience on January 31, letters of often truly affecting condolence. These would make him cry, as tributes from people he actually knew hadn't done... But today's letter had been written before that date, Pete saw at once; someone in the BBC office had just forgotten to forward it:

'Dear Peter Kempsey,' it said,

'Before you go on air again as competitor in *High Flyers*, as I see from the *Radio Times* you are shortly to do, I must ask you to spare us all your boasts about your high scores in the Wellerman-Kreutz tests. For a start, they will not do you yourself any favours. Such standing as Eugene Wellerman and Carl Kreutz once enjoyed well and truly slumped some four or five years ago, after it was found out that Dr Kreutz had used family members, whose talents he was naturally aware of, to prove his dubious theses. He has now been obliged to leave his academic post, and to set up as a private practitioner only. The reason that this did not create more stir – in fact was virtually ignored in UK media – is quite simple. Already their book written in tandem, *Psychometry: the Vital Statistics of Intelligence* had been consigned to the dustbin of intellectual history.

'Its origins, as you may or may not know, lay in the one-time popular approach to foreign language teaching, long since exploded, which holds that the learner's most important task is to acquire as extensive a vocabulary as possible, since without names you can't converse or read, and which correspondingly ignores the structure of the language. I hope you can see, young though you are, the callowness of this mistaken thinking. Similarly the acquisition and retention of mere facts, taking no

notice whatever of their context, of the wholes of which they
form mere parts, are neither indications of a particularly competent or creative mind nor sensible guides for satisfactory living.
This is not to say that yours is *not* a mind capable in due course
of worthwhile things. But while you yourself rate it so highly for
a fundamentally trivial and unimportant capability, you are not
serving yourself well, nor setting a good example to others…'

Mum knew all this, was Pete's second reaction to this letter (his
first was that visceral dismay that always follows being 'found
out' and then 'told off'). Maybe she only suspected the American
psychologists to begin with, but after a while her suspicion
turned to rejection. Only she couldn't bring herself openly to
confront either Dr Mary Smith (probably still a devotee of
Psychometry etc) or his poor deluded young self. Though in the
latter case, she did try… maybe a little too harshly at times.

'It won't make me sound much of a person, I know,' goes Pete,
'but then I'm likely not much of a one anyway, but, even set
alongside all the other terrible events of the year, this letter,
whose truth I didn't doubt, made me reel; it knocked the bottom
completely from my world, and left me dangling. My individual
identity was inseparable from my belief that mine was a quite
remarkable intelligence, and here I was being told I was no different from some idiotic twat who knows the French for, let's
say, 'chimney pot' or 'bellows' but can't form a single coherent
or grammatically correct sentence… Of course I might not have
reacted the way I did had the other… the other tragedies not
occurred. But as they had, this was the last straw. I can honestly
say I've never been the same since.'

And not even a wife and a son could change that for you,
thinks Nat, almost self-reproachfully, for hasn't he somehow
sensed something of the kind about his father?

Well, thinks Luke, there was a time when I thought that
Wolverhampton Wanderers might spot my talent and snap me
up young. The notion of Luke Fleming, Wolves' most famous

striker, wasn't just confined to beach or bed-time fantasies either; I was even unwise enough to mention it to others. But reality – well, eventually – did set in, and now I'm all set to be a premier-league journalist! On the backs of exposure cases like this one conducted in a boy's bedroom hung with kites... trouble with me right now is I'm starting to identify with both father and son. Is that what a career journalist should do?

Nat's thinking: light green (turf), dark green (clumps of woodland), light purple, deep purple (all the heathers), brown (bracken), grey (the shale) – these colours make up Berwyn mountainsides, and often up there I thought, those are the colours of existence itself, representing my own stubborn self trying to hold its own. When the light in the sky dims, then they start fading, and you realise that nothing but nothing can maintain itself for ever against the rules governing life. You think this even more strongly when the night wins, and the colours cease to be themselves, to such an extent that your inner eye can't even reproduce them so prevalent is the darkness. But when, many hours later, slowly, slowly the dawn begins, and you see in the sky all those, at first rather diffident shades, of green and orange and rose-pink, then you know the colours on the mountainside will blaze again. Dad left his sheepfold by Afon Disgynfa long before the sun came up; he never knew the wild land, superficially barren but in truth heaving with different lives, asserting itself, telling you that, whatever its limitations, existence is something not just to cling to, but to relish and uphold...

But, in all that time up there, did I ever properly acknowledge the power of Death? I don't think so! Dad didn't either, and yet there it was, waiting for him, at the bottom of the A49...While I sat there in the mountains, owls killed the small rodents whom Nature, for its own unfathomable reason, doesn't permit to live safely or long, and both buzzards from the air and wickedly fast-moving little weasels, with their weird hissing and trilling noises, robbed rabbits of their lives. Perhaps I should have mourned every addition to the rank of the dead. But I let my sense of the beauty of existence bear me on past it all, through to the joy of sheer survival.

Dad did the same really, did he not, thinking the Disgynfa plateau might be this odd Annwn place. But it wasn't, of course. Couldn't be! There's no room for Annwn in any truthful reading of the Universe. Even his imaginary Annwn didn't shield him. Except that I haven't yet quite built it in myself, that cancellation of the living, that extinguishing of breath and pulse and blood-flow. But Dad, when he joined those search parties for me, on land and in the air, was forced to recognize its ongoing, merciless presence once again.

And that, God help me, is the worst thing I've done to the man I've been wanting so hugely to help...

It's hard to miss the increase in anguish in Pete's voice now, as, having found his second wind as narrator, he continues, addressing himself – or some invisible jury – more than the two individuals in his room: 'Just think of me and my life! Until the kite shop here in Lydcastle I've never been present at it, I don't believe – not since January 1974. And it's doubtful whether I was adequately present then. I know that sounds a dreadful, even an immoral thing to say, but... God help me, it's the fucking truth.' And here he can't, masochistically, resist casting a glance at his audience, to gauge their level of shock. He doesn't find it. Maybe his self-accusation is no more than what they think about him anyway from his story – Luke from a pressman's swift ability to assess anyone he meets on a professional job, Nat's from his insider knowledge. And certainly it is Nat who's moved to inter-ject, in an assuring, rather than an aggrieved, voice, 'I know it's the truth about you, Dad, I've known it a long time.'

'I can't doubt it!' Pete says.

Possibly he should stop talking here. But having switched himself on at such length (or been switched on, by pressure of circumstances and Luke's insidious power of persuasion) he can't, and won't, switch himself off. Not until he's released some statement about what now appears the second great dark climax of his feeling life.

'I was glad of the move to South London (Norbury) that Oliver Merchant and I made. He'd always pronounced himself impressed by the way I inspected and commented on new designs, new lettering for his cards, a service I rendered him from age ten or eleven upwards. So when he suggested that I actually entered Sunbeam Press, as chief assistant who would quite definitely become a partner, and maybe one day – a heady promise then for any young man! – managing director, I said yes, Ol, yes, that's the best future for me I can see. Ol arranged for me to sit my A Levels that winter in a South London school, and I didn't do so badly. And, with these results, the London School of Printing – looking on me kindly because of my family tragedy – allowed me to start my degree course a term late.

'One really thoughtful thing Ol did for me, the Christmas after the exams, was present me – to my astonished joy – with a dog. From Battersea Dogs' Home. We never knew exactly how old he was, a couple of years they reckoned. A white smooth-haired fox-terrier (well, that's as accurate a description as you could come up with). I called him Baron, I don't know why; name just came to me, and he seemed to like it from the first. He was very clever, very sharp of hearing, very loving, wanted to go everywhere with me – and to an amazing degree succeeded. I even smuggled him into college classes, and he became quite a party-goer, and saw a lot of human nature which most 'pets' don't, but it never fazed him. He slept at the foot of my bed, but he'd always edge up to the pillow by the time I woke up in the morning.'

Nat sees with sudden, moving clarity that photo of his father when still a youth, long hair parted in the middle, and a white dog between his firm hands. The Pete Kempsey of that picture was as capable of devotion as Baron, he reckoned.

'And he lived to a good enough age, though his death, when it came, tore me up, I don't mind admitting. I was going out with Izzie when he had his last illness, his heart. She helped to look after him, and that drew us even closer together.

'What kind of student was I? Well, a pretty average one, I'd say, no high flyer at all, better at some things than others, but at those competent and steady (believe it or not). As for life-style, well, again much as you might expect. (I daresay you can match it, Luke.) Some pubbing, some clubbing, some casual sex, some dope-taking, some protest marches for good causes (a big and enjoyable one on behalf of Allende's Chile, I remember, on which I met a girl I went out with for about a year), some playing rugby until I got fed up with the amount of practice-time it required, some trips to good gigs and exhibitions (most of which have slipped into mental oblivion years since) – all singularly unre-markable. In fact, my painful past history apart, I suppose that my having Baron as a constant companion was the only out-standing thing about me. It's strange to reflect on now, but I never once went back to Leominster. Refused to do so. Hence the abyss that opened up between me and my brother, Julian Pringle. And Sam I banished to the horrors of the past.

'Baron and I lived with Ol, in his large, comfortable terraced villa in Norbury, which was often pleasantly full of visitors, as Ol was hospitable to any people who worked in any capacity for Sunbeam Press. He allowed me to bring friends there too, but I mostly chose not to. Why? (Apart from the fact that he might smell dope!) Well, I've probably already made myself out a shit, so why not do so further? I came to long for freedom from Oliver Merchant, and cherish any I got. (And Baron was something of a bulwark against him too.) You see, Ol was over-kind to me, over-solicitous; there was no getting away from him, and yet I wasn't – still am not, I guess – the kind of guy who stands up for himself with strong words or shows of temper. Far from it! Mates of mine, usually after too many drinks or smokes, said: "He's an old pouff, isn't he? A jealous, fussy old queen!" Well, I wasn't having any of that; I was loyal to him – but also, of course pro-tective of my own reputation… And, you may well ask, were my friends right? Yes and no's the answer. I would take my Bible oath he never had sex with another male, and I would even go so far as to say he never wanted to. My mother he'd adored from a safe distance for more than twenty years, entrusting her with confi-dences, listening to hers (whatever they might have been), paying her compliments, singing her praises, and Dad, obviously, hadn't felt a flicker of threat. After their deaths the sentimental fondness he'd already developed for myself – partly as his dear Marion's son – occupied his emotional centre, and that could be a burden for us both. Particularly when I took girls out. He definitely got jealous then, which took the form of fault-finding first with them, then, if I persisted with my friendship, with me. He hoped, he'd say, I wasn't going to slacken in my Sunbeam Press work, there had been a case of a complaint from a major shop, a long-valued customer, and so on and so forth. And wasn't Baron enough of a companion for me? The dog surely had more sense than… well, than whoever was on the scene at the time! Such tensions were usually resolved by me stopping seeing the girl in question. Weak, I know, but there you are! Until, Nat, I met your mother. I fell in love with Izzie so overwhelmingly there could be no reining me in. After a month or two of sulky remonstrations Oliver had to swallow his pride, and later of course he was Unselfish Aid personified when it came to helping the two of us buy a house. (We'd buried poor old Baron by then.) You came into the world, Nat, eighteen months after our having moved there, as a happy couple.

'Except that we weren't one, not really. Oh yes I was pleased to be a father all right – I never quite understand what the phrase "a proud father" means, because one thing that I felt right from the first, Nat, is: Here's an individual, with a life before him, who, for all his dependence on others at the moment, is utterly sepa-rate – from all others even from those who have brought his life about, who has ways and desires demonstrably and absolutely his own. Possibly I've felt that too strongly. Possibly it's a form of evading responsibility – or of my difficulty in receiving another person's life. I felt my own separateness encroached on by my householder existence, though I never ceased, Nat, to feel that you and your mother were the two people most important to me. And I…' he resents the painful lump that's come into his throat, 'and I haven't changed in that respect either. But I haven't got enough, I reckon, to spare from that separateness to give out to others. Izzie said all I could really manage to tell the outside world about was my own pursuits. Greeting cards and now kites. Sounds comical, doesn't it? And that's why finally I bored her, I guess, but from my point of view... Well, I don't know I really *want* to tell anybody about much else. I am, and must remain, the text books would say, a loner. Some of us *are* loners, some of us aren't. And only sorrow follows when you read yourself wrongly.

'Funny thing is Oliver Merchant – Leominster's most prominent bachelor, said Sam Price once – came firmly in the second category. He was not a loner. He started – ludicrous though the word may sound for one of his age and mannerisms – dating women. In South London, as back in Herefordshire, he got involved with Am Dram, and I even think he capered comically over some Norbury or Dulwich stage as Koko to another Katisha. (I did not go to watch!) And he and one of these women, Rosie Roberts – who, far from being a lead-part in these shows, was merely a member of the Chorus – got on so well that they married. The proverbial feather wasn't in it when I heard, but of course I said I was glad to hear it. I wasn't. Not a bit! I'd guessed that Rosie would start taking an interest in Sunbeam and work her way into it as shareholder and Board member. Still the actual settling up of the company's affairs after Ol's death wasn't as fraught as I'd once feared. For by this time – I'm truly sorry, Nat, for you to hear this in such black-and-white terms – I knew for definite that I couldn't sustain a family life any more, that I'd bring more unhappiness than happiness to my wife and son if I stayed. I remembered what joy I'd had from kites – my little brother Robin had always liked them, and you, Nat, long before the move, enjoyed flying them on Clapham Common and out on Box Hill, when we made those expeditions into Surrey. So I bought myself out of Sunbeam, saw that Izzie was well provided for, and then came out here to The Marches, my native region after all, to look for some property in which to establish a kite shop. And the rest, as they say, is History.

'Some history, I hear you thinking!'

For a moment both Luke and Nat think he's finished, that, in a surprisingly flat way, he has got to the climax of this last part of his story. But just by looking at his flushed face they see that they are wrong. Pete is just bracing himself for what he still must tell them.

In Nat's head those Berwyn colours repeat themselves – light green (turf), dark green (clumps of woodland), light purple, deep purple (all the heathers), brown (bracken), grey (the shale) – all to be subsumed now in the variegated blackness of night. Which denied them their power.

Pete is going, 'When, after being unobtainable by mobile all day, all fucking day, Nat didn't return on the night of the twenty-first, I went spare; do you both understand that? I didn't know what to do, where to put myself, who to be with, how to eat, how to sleep – from that time on, right up to my going into the air with the North Wales Police, Heddlu Gogledd Cymru, taking off from Wrexham… Hard to decide whether I felt worse before or after receiving the jiffy-bag from the Co-op here! A case could be made for either, and, take it from me, these last few days I've made both. Before last Friday I thought Nat might just have buggered off on some giant escapade that could lead him half-across the globe, that those Heights he mentioned in his note were emotional or psychological ones – a bewitching girl, quality-time sex, 'Ecstasy', the chance to travel to Arctic Norway and Sweden before the winter begins – any of these! But the devil in all that was, however were Izzie and I ever to get in contact with him? Assuming he was alive. Then when those items came to us from Llanrhaeadr, then, yes, we now knew at least where he had undeniably *been*, and therefore where we should start looking.

'But both Izzie and I, at our most despairing, thought what we'd got could well be farewell tokens. Either sent by Nat instead of the conventional suicide note – never a satisfactory form of leave-taking – or else found in a little heap somewhere, with no owner visible or traceable, by some kind busybody, and then forwarded – though why to the Cooperative here in Lydcastle we couldn't explain. We got to the stage, you see, when we couldn't feel a hundred per cent sure of the handwriting on the package;

it was all in Caps, and rather wonky ones at that, and as Nat has never been a great communicator, neither of us could even remember the last addressed envelope from him we'd received or exactly what the lettering on it looked like.'

Nat is inclined to chip in here: 'I sent the things partly because I was keen you *didn't* think I'd topped myself, Dad.' But he doesn't; it would be a little less than the truth. He'd inwardly provided for the possibility that the world might well think that was what he had done. And had gone on with his scheme.

'Izzie was too frightened of what we might discover on the Berwyns to go into the police helicopter, and that's the first time in all the years I've known her that I've seen her show fear. Anyway there was barely room for a fourth person in so small a space on such a ghastly journey. When I say "ghastly" I mean from the point of view of my spirits, my appalling fears. Remember I am someone who knows what it's like to have close ones, dear ones, taken from me. In another frame of mind it would have been a journey of great beauty, one never to forget, flying above the heather-covered Berwyns on a sunny September morning, able to see all the contours of the mountains below.

'We went up in a Eurocopter EC 135T fitted with a day camera with a zoom lens, and the guy beside me, Islwyn, was in charge of the map reading. And I remember thinking "I know many a lad in Lydcastle who'd give his eye-teeth (and perhaps more) to be in this helicopter. But me, I can't properly see for the dread throbbing behind my eyeballs, and the whirr of the machine is almost drowned out by the loudness of my own fast-beating heart. If we discover Nat dead down there, well, then, *I* will die too. I shan't think even about poor Izzie or the kite stock or any unpaid bills or my pals in Lydcastle, or any other hopes I've been daft enough to harbour these last years. I'll force myself out of the aircraft, so I'm dashed to pieces by whatever rocks catch me. And good riddance, I would say...'

'Dad!' Nat can't help himself crying out, and as for Luke: 'When I first made a journey in a Eurocopter, I was like a kid, over the moon. Except literally, of course! I thought well, now

I'd really fucking arrived as a full-blooded investigative journalist. But if we'd all been searching for our Jared...' It doesn't stand thinking about.

'Over and over those peaks, round and round the massif we circled until I thought I would go stark staring crazy. I could not have believed so many gulleys cut their way into the slopes, nor how many outcrops of rock obscure exactly the natural aperture the crew thought we had to peer down into. We flew over not just Cadair Berwyn and Cadair Bronwen, but over their rivals, Moel-y-Henfaes and Moel Fferna. Until we passed over Pen-plaenau. And there we saw...'

But he can't continue. Anyway both his listeners know what they saw. On Pen-plaenau both the police team and the father were rewarded with the sight of Nathaniel Robin Kempsey standing on a slope, looking up towards them, perfectly alive, and – with the pilot's eminently reliable expertise and patience – perfectly rescuable.

Pete, to his own dismay, is not merely weeping now but sobbing, a kid's sobbing, his head resting against hands held up as if in prayer, sobbing to the point of breathlessness, as he has never done during the past days of either loss or discovery, as he never did even after learning that all his family save one had been killed.

Luke says, with a tender gruffness he doesn't know himself capable of: 'This has been a rough ride for you, Pete! A good part of the morning's already gone. Why don't we get some lunch?'

Pete, trying to compose himself and sound ordinary, says: 'Why not?'

'No! Not yet!' Nat's voice is so loud and urgent it startles both Pete and Luke, 'not till... Dad, please leave the room. I want to have time with Luke Fleming.'

Pete is wiping his tear-spattered face, and trying to recover his normal breathing rhythm back. Old Nat has been right about him all along; he truly is out of condition, a man shouldn't get as short-of-breath as this when only in his early fifties. He feels he must resemble some clumsy dog who's tumbled in a cold pool by mistake on a country walk, and is now sorry for himself. 'I dunno if I *should* do what you're suggesting,' he says.

'Dad, please!'

'He'll be okay with me, Pete, I promise,' says Luke Fleming. Where's the Reuters' wonder now, where the methods of the 87th Precinct in those American detective stories he devoured once in a holiday guesthouse in Rhyl?

So Pete leaves the room, shutting the door behind him. He walks down two stairs before returning to the landing and listening outside the door. Nat, preparing himself for the last and worst haul of them all, recites: Light green (turf), dark green (clumps of woodland), light purple, deep purple (all the heathers), brown (bracken), grey (the shale). And it's full sunlight, a splendid midday. Just see the strolling people in the Square below, enjoying it all. And with their dogs with them, including Harvey, my favourite border collie from Bull Street...

'Luke,' begins Nat – best to stick to the first-name approach, 'I did it all for Dad. You've got to know that from the very start, and keep it in your head all the way through. Now I've heard everything he went through at my age, all those things I truly didn't know about, I can't feel the same about my action – even less so now I've learned how he suffered when I went missing. Which is why I want to get it all off my chest, especially as it seems to have backfired! Otherwise why would you be here, Luke, in my bedroom, come to hear me make a cock-up, to spill beans you've probably already counted up, like a Spanish Inquisitor getting his heretic? But when the idea first came to me – well, it seemed brilliant, I don't mind telling you! A stroke of genius.

'As I sit here now, it feels not brilliant, just plain stupid! And unmindful of its true effect on other people. The decision of an idiot really – even though I've nearly brought it off! All except one extremely important aspect of my plan, which hasn't – shall we say, materialised at all.'

'Money?' says Luke, but his grin isn't of his former gloating kind. Is this because, after the dad's breaking down, triumphalism of any kind isn't in order. The boy knows he's been rumbled, but instead of being sorry or angry, is, on the contrary, pretty fucking glad.

'I've always said, haven't I, I'm a news-freak who's going to be a newshound. I never had any doubt what course I wanted to take at Uni if my A Levels were good enough to get me there: journalism. I'm still headed in that direction. Though the way you press guys have set yourselves at me and baited me, like dogs attacking some shackled bear, has made me more than once, these last days, have second thoughts about joining your pack. Well, it all began, my Big Idea, with my getting excited about the story which broke in mid-July...'

'Of Jamie Neale. In the Blue Mountains of Australia?' hazards Luke Fleming, though of course it isn't a 'hazarding' at all. Luke's used up a hell of a lot of brain-power working the whole thing out. And he wouldn't have hurried over here to Lydcastle, ahead of his colleagues and rivals, if he hadn't been sure of his conclusion (though needing help from Nat himself about the stages leading to it). Only when the intriguingly strong parallels between the two boys' adventures came home to him had he appreciated just how right he (and certain others too) had been to have misgivings from the first about Nat Kempsey and the tale he told. The key to it, to its inconsistencies and difficulties, lay, he became convinced, in that other boy's experience. Meeting Joel Easton only vindicated his thoughts.

'Seemingly it's you not me that should be talking about strokes of genius,' says Nat, at once sorrowfully and admiringly. (Maybe he *will* follow in this guy's footsteps after all?) 'I must say I've been surprised that nobody yet has asked about that entry in my Journal after my trip to Cornwall. "Hasn't riding the waves taught me that mastery of self is the key to life? And if an idea comes to you, but seems (at times) too hard to execute, then use that mastery to ride on the crest of it, as you would on an Atlantic roller... Never forget the hero of *Sixty Minutes*,' I wrote! Though I guess I should have added "the hero, Jamie Neale, as I see him," for in my view there's really no good reason whatsoever to doubt the truth of what he told the world, like so many fuckers tried to. And the medicos backed him up a hundred per cent. You seem clued up already about the Jamie Neale/Richard Cass case, Luke, but you can't be as clued up as me; I could get a fucking PhD in the topic, I reckon. (Probably the only one I'm capable of getting!) So I'm going to run it all past you, even if it does mean telling you things you already know. Because unless you're familiar with what I read up and looked up on the web, then you won't fully grasp what I did – and why. I don't know how many times I watched the YouTube of that ABC programme on him. It became a true obsession.

'Jamie Neale's position seemed uncannily like my own; I thought that even before I decided to take him as a model. Like me he's a Londoner who got his A Levels, like me he comes from what's called a dysfunctional family (his mum and dad weren't together, and he lived with his mum), like me he's keen on those activities like exploring and orienteering, like me he'd time to fill before starting Uni, Bristol in his case. Yes, I know, he went out to Australia during his summer, while me, I only went to Shropshire, plus a few days trying to surf in Cornwall, but... shit, I'm well used to having a less exciting time than most of my contemporaries. It always works out that way. Anyhow Jamie – I think of him like that, like he's a friend – decided, once over in Australia to explore the Blue Mountains. And I must say from the pictures they look fantastic, awesome, I'd give a lot to go there. (Well, maybe after all this to-do, I wouldn't!) But obviously all those peaks and ravines and forest and wildlife appealed to him hugely as they would to me...

'Jamie checked into a youth hostel at Katoomba on July (see how every single detail's stuck in my head, Luke!). He was meant to go on a tour of the Jenolan Caves on July 4, but he didn't turn up, and the folk connected with the National Park hikes were worried. Especially when they found he'd left his mobile phone and personal papers behind in the hostel. A little later a couple came forward who'd definitely seen Jamie on July 3, on a lonely outcrop of rock, about to take a track even further into the wild.

So now everyone knew the last date he'd been seen alive, and that it had been in inhospitable country. They searched and searched, and his dad came out from England, the dad he'd never lived with! Bush-parties went out on foot, four hundred volunteers in all, and police helicopters, which took his dad on board, flew over enormous swathes of the National Park. But they didn't find him! He must have perished, they thought.

'Even his father – name of Richard Cass – came to believe he was dead, and that there'd be no point in any more costly investigations. He got a memorial-stone designed for the boy, and then prepared to fly back to the UK from Sydney. But on the very day of his departure – July 15 – in stumbles Jamie on some Blue Mountains campers, actually only four kilometres from the hostel where he'd been last seen. The campers made him welcome and took him to the police and safety – and to all sorts of official and medical inspections. He'd been missing twelve whole days. Without a compass he'd lost his bearings completely, and had not known which direction to take in such vast, totally unfamiliar territory.

'And then all the questions started in earnest. Did Jamie really got lost? Or was he pulling some kind of stunt? How could a boy, and a stranger to Australia into the bargain – it was mid-winter there, remember, with tough conditions in the Blue Mountains – possibly survive so long in that wilderness? What did he eat? Where did he sleep? The doctors who examined him all agreed he was suffering from dehydration and exposure, as well, naturally, from fatigue, and none of them has expressed any disbelief. Loads of other folk have, though. His father was furious with his accusers and sort of drove them away from bothering his son in his hospital bed. But before long things got bad between the two of them. Quite nasty, in fact. I hope they've made it up since though...'

'Money,' says Luke again, and this time it isn't an interrogative nor does he give any kind of smile.

'Dead right,' says Nat, wondering if staring this man with the vivid blue eyes hard in the face might be a good tactic, showing his own fearlessness. For he has now reached the crucial part, that which could get him into truly serious trouble. 'Money. *Sixty*

Minutes, a major Australian TV show did a feature on Jamie, for which he was paid £98,000. Agents started making a beeline for him, and even from his convalescent bed Jamie chose the best for himself. A celebrity agency reckoned his story could be worth some £500,000. His dad thought part of any money made should go to the search-and-rescue teams and also to himself, as someone intimately involved. Jamie had a different opinion here. Perhaps he's changed his mind since.

'But in the case of me and my dad, it's the father who never thinks realistically and creatively about money, and his inexperienced son who does – on his behalf. Always preferring to stock art-kites instead of the power-jobs, the sporting kind, where the money is! Often turning down – or as good as – or as bad as – guys with proper disposable money because he prefers to have another sort of customer, who share his Green Wave ideas. Who doesn't check the invoices with thorough regularity, or service his website, keeping it always up-to-date and interesting the way a business man these days should.'

His pulse has accelerated, and he can feel himself sweating anew. Luke Fleming sees this, and with an irrepressible rush of fellow-feeling with the boy, says: 'I get the picture! Got it a while ago! But let me say before you go on – I've done a little research of my own, and my own dad runs a shop too, as it happens, selling plants and flowers. Pete may be guilty of all the deficiencies you say, and this is no fun time for any of us. But I doubt there's need for quite all your worries about High Flyers. He's done okay up to now, hasn't he? Held his head way above water, and all that… But I can see how and why you wanted to help him; you've got a different approach to what a business should do from his… You wanted to be the Jamie Neale who actually gave the money to your dad. Who'd insist on larger sums than the media first offered, but for his sake, not out of any greed of your own. And you'd launch High Flyers into its greatest days of security and prosperity yet.'

'Right! That's right!' Nat respects the man for his ability to have grasped his ambition and to express it now without disapproval or mockery. Almost, it seems to him, with moral regard, if not admiration. And Luke is in fact comparing the boy before him with himself. While he never minded giving his father a hand with the plants, with the bags of compost, and the gardening equipment, he also got heartily fed up with helping him. And he has always, and conveniently, taken it perfectly for granted that his dad, under his mum's supervisory eye, knows what he's doing business-wise. Doesn't need any help from his son Luke.

'Yes, I said to myself, I will disappear like Jamie Neale. Like him, in somewhere wild and possibly dangerous. Not contactable by mobile. Nobody will know where I am. There will be search-parties, people will give me up for dead, just like they did poor Jamie. Papers will be speculating like fury. Wherever can he be? Has he been murdered? Has he taken his own life? Was he in trouble? Did he have enemies? Did he have love trouble?'

'I get the picture,' Luke feels like saying again here, a little taken aback by the cascade of bad predicaments tumbling from Nat Kempsey's mouth.

'And I have to say in this respect I succeeded. Most of those questions were asked in the tabloids – and in some of the broadsheets too. You even asked some of 'em yourself.

'The first decision I had to make was where to disappear. I wanted to be found, I had to be found to achieve my goal – though only after a lot of effort. So no good just leaving home and vanishing into the whole of Britain, as Dad apparently thought I might have done. Equally no good choosing somewhere very near Lydcastle either. Jamie Neale had caused me to set my heart on mountains, and – like the police – I first thought of Snowdonia, though I thought that might be too obvious and too well-patrolled. I also thought about Cumbria and the Cairngorms. Then I found that newspaper cutting about the 1974 UFOs and that suggested the Berwyns to me. The idea that it was somewhere Dad had been interested or possibly involved in gave it great appeal. When my dad takes an interest in something or somewhere, it's always worthy of attention. Think of this kite shop, think of South Shropshire in general and Lydcastle in particular. I even thought the Heights that my uncle Julian had spoken of in connection with my dad could refer to the Berwyns. And I was proved right, wasn't I?

'But though I was wanting to be thought lost like Jamie, I didn't want actually to *get* lost like he did. Besides how could I? Not only did I have an extremely clear idea of the whole area through conning the map repeatedly, the Berwyns are not the Blue Mountains. That hardly needs saying, does it? By British standards they're an impressive but compact range, and wild and enticing; by international ones they're pocket-sized, miniatures. Think what a comparatively short time it took the Eurocopter that picked me up to make her complete overhead tour of the Berwyns – even though it must have seemed eternity to those involved. The only thing for me to do, I thought, to earn myself a Jamie Neale-like story that would galvanise the press with its vast coffers, was to get injured. And in due course I would see to this myself. I didn't need to worry about that business until enough time had passed for the packet I'd given Joel to have arrived in Lydcastle. You were right, Luke, I put that arrival at Wednesday or Thursday not the Friday of reality.

'I really didn't think – maybe chose not to think – of the fear and worry I'd cause. I'd told Dad I was heading for the Heights. That could have been a clue for him as to where I was bound, though he didn't see it – but, with the xxxx that followed the message, I thought it was like a guarantee that I was in good spirits and not intending to do away with myself.

'Everything I did was after careful consideration. I even went to Shrewsbury a roundabout route in case I bumped into any people who knew me, wearing a baseball cap with its peak pulled far down over my forehead. Then I caught a bus to the Tanat Valley, and walked through Llanrhaeadr-ym-Mochnant all the way to Pistyll Rhaeadr. My good fortune in meeting Joel Easton there you know about – but maybe it wasn't such good fortune after all.

'I'd disposed of my mobile and my journal, and that gave me a marvellous free new identity. And I didn't plunge into some wild hermit's life either. I kept away from people, obviously, and sought out all the remotest stretches of the mountains. But I had lugged loads of good food with me, fruit and veg and bread and some ready-cooked meals, to keep me going for most of the time I was up there. I buried all the packaging. As I eventually did the Wallander thriller I'd brought with me, and read most of Tuesday and Wednesday… Towards the end, when I was getting distinctly worried about rescue, the provisions ran out; I could have saved more of 'em if I hadn't eaten so well at the beginning.'

'And the injuries?'

'Well, as it happened, I did twist my ankle – or something of that sort – you know, the way you can on hill paths. It swelled up a bit, and hurt quite a lot. I wrapped a handkerchief round it, and in due course it improved. But that little mishap was very useful to me when I was brought back to normal life. As I believe you guessed – and I take my hat off to you, Luke – I didn't give myself the serious injury, the broken ankle, till I saw the helicopter literally overhead. But doctors who examined me saw that I'd hurt myself in the same place earlier, and even if they were perplexed, they appreciated that I couldn't have moved all that far from the Pen-plaenau where I was discovered. End of, really.'

'And were you ever afraid up there? Alone and disabled!' Luke's tone isn't as mocking as the words might suggest.

'No, I wasn't. Towards the very end I was longing for discovery, I'll admit. But afraid, no.'

'Bored? Uncomfortable? Your ankles apart.'

'Not after the two days.'

'Not oppressed by your own company?'

'Own company? No!'

'Has it all been worth it?'

'Worth it? I haven't received a fucking fifty-pence piece, Luke!'

'In other ways apart from cash?'

Nat bats his eyelids as if trying to blink away pictures insistent on coming between him and the room he's now in. 'I dunno!' For there are some things he won't tell anybody.

'Perhaps we should ask your dad that question?' says Luke, who's been aware that Pete has heard the entire conversation he has just been conducting with Nat.

But – unlike the previous occasion – Pete doesn't burst in. He's busy with his own discomfiting reflections:

'Nat may believe he concocted his bizarre plan to help me, to redeem the fortunes of High Flyers, but that can't be the real explanation for his coming up with it. I know now that, deep down and desperately, he wanted and needed to find out that he was a unique person in others' eyes, and loved for himself. Terrible that he felt such love could be articulated only when he was feared dead.

'But by travelling those paths into that country I myself visited at his age, believing it to be Annwn, the Otherworld of peace, Nat has surely established not only his own right to be loved, he may well have won it for me also.

'And for his sake I'll get hold of a Spirit of the Air Power-Kite, and maybe for mine, he will join me in flying that rare, sacred, colourful Barroletta.

'But that's not an end to it all, is it?'

Two

Confrontations

The Town Hall clock strikes the quarter. 1.45. With Luke Fleming still out at lunch, and Nat deservedly, understandably and thankfully asleep, Pete feels he can remain within this early-afternoon hour just a bit longer, inside a quiet cell of time, more like what you'd find in a monastery than a police station, even if, after what he's overheard, he's only too aware of the latter. He can use this confined but calming space to gather fractured thoughts and feelings together, if that's at all possible. For the heavy blankness of exhaustion has taken him over... And now comes a knock-knock-knock on his shop door. Pete moves into the main part of High Flyers to answer it.

'Can't you bloody see I've turned the sign to CLOSED?' he silently demands of the unknown man of about sixty on the other side of the glass. In general appearance he's not so unlike himself: medium height, dark, grey-streaked, wavy hair, broad shoulders, and more stomach than desirable, though not as ample as many a male's in this age of obesity. I'll play the Man of Constant Sorrow, Pete thinks. And truly with Luke right now deliberating his professional duty, whether or not to publish the truth he has finally elicited from Nat, his sorrow does appear about constant. He could make his visitor feel he was acting selfishly to come bothering a man still in the public eye with his leisure-time requirements?

But as he undoes the door-catch, Pete knows for sure that here is no buyer-to-be. There's something too pleading about his smile.

'I'm shut,' Pete tells him redundantly, and in a huffier tone than intended, 'and I'm staying shut today. Far too much else on!'

'I believe you,' says the caller, 'and that's why I'm here. On an errand of sympathy.' His voice was warm, low, notably and incongruously intimate.

And who the fuck do you think you are, banging on a man's front-door despite the notice on it, just to show off your compassion, goes Pete to himself. However sympathetic he may feel, this bloke can't conceivably know about the heaving, stinking shit Nat has landed them both in. Nor the agony of having to wait till Luke has ransacked his journalist's conscience and come up with an answer. Something in the intentness of the newcomer's gaze, half softly sensual, half probingly puritan, compounded with his husky voice, reminds Pete of another occasion in his life, in precisely the terrible period he recreated for Nat and Luke upstairs. But it refuses to come to his bidding; Bob Thurlow wouldn't have tolerated such slowness, even at an audition.

'I haven't had the pleasure, have I?'

'I think you did once, without knowing it. I'm Don Parry!'

'Don Parry?' It has the sound of a name from a history book; it might have sprung out of G.R. Elton's *Reform and Renewal: Thomas Cromwell and the Common Weal*, for instance, which he'd been reading in his warm Woodgarth bedroom the night he was summoned to the Berwyns. Summoned because of the phone call to Sam Price this very man standing before him now, these thirty-five years later, had made.

'Well,' astounded, flummoxed, 'you'd best come in, hadn't you? I've been visited by God-knows-how-many different odds-and-sods these last days. But you're the very last person I've been expecting to see!'

Neither manner nor matter make this last remark complimentary. But this visitor in black cashmere jersey and cream chinos doesn't look put down. He steps confidently, even blithely into High Flyers, where he gives a swift look about him with evident admiration, which he also means Pete to see. 'A beautiful shop!' he exclaims, 'and I'll be honest with you, Pete. I've passed here a score of times, and looked through your window, and very impressed I've always been. But I've never had the nerve actually to come inside.' Pete thinks, if this guy's stupid enough to believe his chat-up line will disarm me, he has another thing coming!

'I didn't think I'd be welcome here, you see!' Don Parry adds.

Too fucking right you wouldn't have been, Pete remarks to himself. But today's visit's clearly no casual one, isn't inspired by curiosity as to whether the inside of the shop is as good as its outside. 'I guess you've come to Lydcastle over from Llanrhaeadr-ym-Mochnant?' he says. Happy if he'd never heard of that beauty-spot, which had wrought such havoc in two intricately connected lives! If this man now peering at the Chinese Butterfly kites and grinning sweetly at them like some soft-headed retard, hadn't bidden Sam to go to the little Berwyn town on the night of January 23, everything but everything would have been different. His parents and younger brother would not have been killed, he would have known his other brother Julian's whereabouts without having to read about them in his son's journal, he would have… he almost certainly would have… no, he probably wouldn't have… his head is afflicted with just such an onrush of giddiness as these last few days assails Nat, as a result of his own trauma. But Pete will press on regardless; sobbing was quite sufficient weakness for him to show in one single day.

His visitor is telling him: 'No, I haven't come from there! Well, of course I do go back to Llanrhaeadr quite often, though my mum passed away ten years ago, and I had to sell her nice house soon afterwards. I'm still attached to the place, I mean, who couldn't be? And I still do my paintings inspired by all the old tales of the district. But I've been living and working in Leominster almost since the time…'

And now memory strikes. No sliding of pertinent fact out of well-oiled mental grooves, as when Pete was young. No, what comes onto the outer layers of his mind is more like a whiplash. 'But you're Joe!' he objects, seeing the two of them together in that long-ago dawn ride, 'so how can you also be Don Parry?' And now recalls that the guy had told him Joe wasn't his real name, but never mind...

'Good, good, it has come back to you, that time we rode together; I wasn't sure how best to remind you of it... yes, you're right. The very morning after all the Great Events in the Berwyn Mountains our ways coincided. We met at the caff in Llanfyllin. But that cop you were with then had my name confused with my mate's, the one I was having a coffee with. When I drove you over to Leominster, I didn't know who I was driving. Just a lad who'd been worsted in a fight, I thought. I'd never met you, and Sam was usually too busy pumping me for info about women and the possibilities of the supernatural to talk much about the people he knew on his home turf. I'd no idea you came with him that night to Llanrhaeadr any more than I knew where the fuck Sam himself had got to – pardon my French!'

So Sam and Don Parry never met up that night. In the absence of any knowledge of Sam's activities after his assault on himself, Pete had always assumed they had. Despite all that he has been revealing of his past to Luke and Nat, he sees in a flash that there are very important things about that crucial occasion he doesn't, even after so many years, know. And this causes another ripple of giddiness to pass through his head. Pete realises that he must sit down. He doesn't do so immediately, still coy about showing weakness, so just props his back firmly against his counter. Some days of life, he thinks, are quite simply too much to bear. Indeed they can't be borne, and in all honesty never are; surviving them is just a question of disguise, pretence, self-suppression. This is the truth that people in every culture, every country, have gone out of their way to deny – as they feel they must, sometimes simply and sternly, sometimes with intellectual and emotional display – whenever they pronounce, as they do all the time, on life and God, and time and space, and the soul and the psyche, and morality and natural laws. And never properly acknowledge the outbreaks of the truly dreadful – which makes nonsense of everything that's helped till then to keep them going...

Just such a day which could not be properly borne was that on which Don (Don!) drove him back to Leominster, to learn that his whole family bar one had been wiped out. Just such a day, or as near a one as damn-it, was Tuesday last week – and Wednesday – and Thursday and Friday morning, all days when he woke up to see no logical reason why Nat shouldn't have joined those others he was kin to in extinction.

Today, however, is not one of this terrible sort, or not so far, Pete hastily checks himself: uncertainty is of existence's very essence. Nat may be both troubled and in trouble, but he's incontestably alive. And Pete's relationships with his fellow-townsfolk here in south Shropshire, with those customers who know him personally, and, even after all that has happened between them, with Izzie, his ex, are better, more beautiful, than ever they have been. And isn't that something! Not forgetting what's opening up, at long last, between Nat and himself.

'My son's sound asleep,' Pete says, 'in fact I gave him a tablet. We've had as gruelling a morning as you could ever not hope to have. We're not out of the woods yet, you see.' He despises himself for this last, overworked cliché, but then sometimes clichés are both useful and comforting as other more first-hand phrases aren't. They remind you how many countless others have been in your predicament, and have found it so hard to cope with that they couldn't come up with adequate original words to convey its quality. Anyway, isn't the present predicament really rather like being dumped in the middle of some dense, lightless, coniferous forestation, with no natural path out? 'So I think we'd better stay down here in the shop, Don,' he doesn't find the man's first name easy to deliver, 'where we can't disturb him. I can put the kettle on for us in the little kitchen back there, if you like... Tea? Coffee?'

'Tea'd be fine, Pete, but in your own time, man, in your own time. I'm in no hurry, though I wouldn't want to outstay any welcome you're good enough to give me.' He seems to Pete to be speaking without a hint of irony, let alone reproof. 'I'm really here as a messenger, Pete. As you've probably already guessed.'

I've hardly had the time to fucking guess anything, thinks Pete. But even as he articulates this to himself, he appreciates that there's no way Don Parry could have come over from Leominster on his own account.

'Sam Price?'

'Sam, yes!' assents Don Parry, clearly glad the name has been first uttered by Pete rather than himself. There's a look of strong resolve and optimistic good will on the man's somewhat florid face.

'Sam's followed the case of your missing lad, followed every bit of it,' says Don slowly, and his eyes give Pete's own now blanching face an unswerving attention that he finds both discomfiting and curiously tranquillising, 'and naturally when he heard where Nat was found... well, he was delighted on your behalf, of course. But he has his memories, you know.'

'I'll bet!' says Pete, 'and so he should.' Though – at least on that occasion – Sam himself never made it to Pistyll Rhaeadr and the mountains at its back.

Is it prevarication, or a stab of his former burning interest in that person, impossible for all its sorry associations now to resist, but 'Hadn't you better tell me a bit about Sam, Don? How he is now. What he's doing.'

'You don't know anything?'

'I'm hardly in the fucking mood today for asking idle questions to which I already know answers, am I? As I've told you, my son and I are not out of the bloody woods yet.'

'Well,' Don takes a deep breath – of personal pride, thinks Pete, 'Sam owns and generally looks after Price's Menswear with all its subsidiaries. And me, I'm the Leominster manager (though I may retire year after next), and on the Board too. We have branches now in Abergavenny, Monmouth, Newport (Gwent),

Ross-on-Wye, Gloucester, Stroud. Not too bad, huh?' Mouth stretches and pupils expand in satisfaction, and Pete realizes that Don too is glad of this interval in his narrative. 'Only all those shops have a different name. They're called Sartor (Latin for tailor). Sam thought Price's Menswear, though okay for when it started, was just a tad dull.' He laughs with something like irrepressible affection at Sam's – well, call them 'high-flying' – notions. 'So I expect you've seen a branch or two of us on your travels, without knowing you were looking at a business owned by your old friend.'

'Have I?' wonders Pete to himself. 'Clothes shops bore the balls off me. A long time since I felt good because of the trendy clothes old Ol had bought me! I go round more like an old tramp now, and that's how I like it!' Aloud he said, 'Old friend?' he expostulates, 'some old friend, him! You saw with your own eyes how he'd beaten me up that evening. In fact you remarked on it as we drove along. Thought it was two boys fighting over a lass. As if, incidentally, that'd have made him lamming into me any the better. I'm no friend to violence of any kind whatever.'

A pause, as well there might be. There's an animation in Don's face and voice that suggests he hasn't himself been a total stranger to violence – of feeling if not of deed, and of the past rather than of the present. 'Sam had treatment for those bad tendencies, soon after that episode,' he says in a soft, slightly injured voice, 'got them from his dad, we reckon. Not his fault. Anyway it worked. The treatment, I mean.'

'I'm pleased to hear it,' says Pete, 'makes me feel a bloody heap better about everything.'

Don puts out a hand, so it rests lightly on the dangling blue wing of a dependant paper-and-bamboo butterfly. Another pause. Then, somewhat to Pete's surprise says, with a definite contraction of that pleading smile (though it'll return in full very shortly), 'Sarcasm gets us all nowhere, Pete. And bitterness even less far… Sam wants so much to communicate with you. Needs to, you might say. He has the kite shop's email address – you're a famous establishment, after all – so he could have got in touch with you any time. But he thought it best not to, it might upset you too much. Make things worse by bringing back too much that was painful. Sam is not under any illusions. But he's been thinking and worrying about you, empathising with you, one might say... Until he begged me to go to Lydcastle on this mission. "See if you can effect a peace, Don," says he, "if *you* can't, nobody can".'

Well, that may well be true, Pete agrees. He's as good an intermediary as any – and has knowledge that others wouldn't have. But it doesn't mean he is going to succeed. Effect a peace, indeed! Makes it all sound like a relationship between retailers and suppliers. Perhaps Sam always was a businessman's son above everything else.

'Well, here you are, Don! You've carried out your mission!' Pete can't but entertain respect for the strong-willed yet plainly soft-hearted man in front of him, 'And I know that you did try to make peace once before. Sending me that cutting from *The Wrexham Leader* about the UFO sightings anniversary. Suggesting Sam and I met, and... buried the hatchet, I suppose. But it wouldn't have been possible. We were both so different. Sam had his course in medicine...'

'His heart was never in his medical studies, Pete. After Trevor Price's first stroke, giving them up and going into Price's seemed the obvious course. I'd already become Manager in Leominster. Sam's never regretted his decision, I know it.'

'...and I was just starting my delayed entry into the London School of Printing. And you never sent me any other – let's call them, olive branches, did you? So I don't know a thing about Sam's life, a subject I closed down in my mind long ago. But I can't object to opening it up now, at any rate for just a tiny while... Is Sam married? Does he have kids? Does he still live in Leominster?'

The smile (pleading no longer) comes back fulsomely: almost ear to ear. 'The answer's Yes to all those questions,' says Don with a look of personal happiness, as if he can take some responsibility for Sam's good life. 'Sam's been married to Giulia thirty years.

Met her when travelling to Italy – to Milan – on Menswear business. She comes from Bergamo, a marvelous old city – do you know it, Pete?'

'Never travel anywhere,' mutters Pete in reply to this parenthesis.

'And the two of them go out there and see family for part of every year. They have such a lovely apartment in the high part of the town, its old quarter; I sometimes stay in it myself, and I'm quite sure – if we have the reunion Sam's now set his heart on – that you could be his guest there yourself, Pete. Probably just what you need after all you've been through.' And he gives a persuasive little nod of the head, a salesman's gesture, thinks Pete, who has used it himself. 'And they've three beautiful children, Grazia, Lucía and lastly Ned, who's the image of Sam.'

Pete hardly knows whether, in this surge of reminders of past pains, he should be pleased at this last observation. 'Image', however, generally applies to externals. Outwardly Sam, as Pete knew better than anybody, was alluringly handsome as a youth. And for a few disturbing seconds his former friend's physical charm seems to advance towards him from across chasms of time and space – from a deserted car park, from the crest of The Stiperstones after speeding downwards from The Devil's Chair.

'And living in Leominster?'

'Where do you think in that town he lives, Pete?' Don's is a rhetorical question, for he's impatient to give Pete the joyful fact of the matter, 'why, The Tall House, of course. Poor Susan's been dead fifteen years – cirrhosis, sadly but unsurprisingly – and Trevor stayed on alone for a while, but then had to move to Sheltered Accommodation. Where he's doing pretty well! But The Tall House suits Sam and his family to a T.'

Why, the guy's talking about Sam as though he's in love with him, Pete comments to himself. And then – the guy *is* in love with him, of course! Sam was able to make people that way; I do believe, viewing it all from this remote perspective, now that I was in love with him too. In as much as I was able to be in that condition with anybody but my own self, the Wellerman-Kreutz

After Brock

wonder. But I was then a greenhorn of eighteen, and was always to go for women. In Don's case, am I not dealing with something more literally true? And more all-pervading? 'And how about yourself, Don? You married? You a family man?'

'No! I played the field as a young man,' I know, thinks Pete, Sam used that selfsame, idiotic, politically incorrect phrase about you, 'in fact I had quite a reputation – as you no doubt heard. But after – after that terrible day of the sightings, as I tried to tell you when we rode along together and you thought my name was Joe, I gave all that up. Took it for a warning that life's meant for more serious things.'

'What can be more serious than women?' asks Pete, a touch indignantly, even though he has behind him a marriage failed beyond any mending despite present mutual warmth. He couldn't ever be doing with misogynistic sentiment.

'More serious than the flesh, Pete, was what I meant,' says Don. And the sincerity of his tone enables Pete – to his aston-ishment, and for the first time during this, their one true encounter – to envisage him, without much strain, as a man who once believed (who maybe still believes) in Annwn, in other-worldly beauties and virtues, 'more serious than just fucking around. Which was what, God forgive me, I was doing. Life's been given us for hard work and for love.'

Both of which, I guess, he's found, thinks Pete. But he doesn't want now to hear any confession of devotion, which, enlightened though he is, would hugely embarrass him. Nor any correspon-ding recital of Sam's merits which would only make him suspicious. Anyway, since they have already alighted on that dark, significant point in the past, there's something he now greatly wants to hear. From as near the horse's mouth as makes no matter.

'Don,' he asks, 'what do you think about the night of January 23, 1974? You must have given it a hell of a lot of thought. Yours isn't the only life it changed.'

Don shifts the weight from one foot to another. Here they've been talking of momentous things, and yet both have remained

247

standing (half-propped-up in Pete's case). 'All I can say, Pete, so many years later, is, "I heard what I heard, and I saw what I saw." And I was so overwhelmed that I wanted my new friend, whom I'd taken such a shine to, as you might say, to share the aftermath with me. If you go onto YouTube now…'

And Pete shows by 'Mmms!' and a nod of the head that he has indeed done this, a fair number of times, 'You can still find people I personally know vouchsafing for the authenticity of their experience. But me – maybe I've turned dull in my old age; maybe years of managing men's clothes sales first for Trevor, then for Sam, has corrupted me – but me, I've come to think it was an earthquake, not so strange in this zone we live in, the Bala Fault and all that.' Exactly what I said to Sam when he first broke to me the occurrences in the Berwyns, thinks Pete, but it's carrion satisfaction. 'That accounts for all the tremors and great bangs, you see,' continues Don, 'and also for the many weird lights in the sky which seemed so awesome at the time. They frequently accompany upheavals below ground, but, us in Llandrillo and Llanderfel, we didn't know that. We were an ignorant lot, mostly, our heads fuller of science fiction and sensational stories in *The Mirror* or *The News of the World* than of geology.'

And, for all my conceit about my brain, I didn't have enough trust in my own knowledge to resist Sam that evening, Pete now reprimands himself. But then resisting him was the last thing I wanted to do then. Quite the contrary. I thought yielding to his will was a proof of my own testosterone. 'Sam, of course, had already seen, a UFO,' he reminds himself – and Don, 'at Darnton.'

Don at last removes his gaze from Pete's face, and casts it down to the well-swept wooden-boarded floor. 'Pete, I don't think so; I don't believe he did. He was an unhappy, mixed-up lad, and that day, on the long run, and feeling alone with his problems, he probably saw something a bit out-of-the-ordinary in the air, and it became something else in his imagination. Maybe it was a solitary bird, a crow or a magpie, which can give you a turn sometimes. Or maybe it was a child's kite like one of the fancier ones you sell here, adrift from its flyer. Who knows? But then when he read Jung's *Memories, Dreams and Reflections*, well…'

'"Well", indeed!' says Pete.

'Oh, come on, Pete Kempsey, youth's the time for fantasy, especially about oneself. And if you can't invent your own, then why not take somebody else's? Specially if he's a world-famous sage like Carl-Gustav Jung. What about you and those psychiatrists' tests?'

Touché, thinks Pete, even though the parallel surely is not exact. Besides, hasn't he held this interpretation of Sam's schoolboy experience far too long to be shocked by Don Parry himself cutting it down to size? 'And the event that got Sam chucked out of Darnton?' he finds himself asking. Its revelation to him was something he will never forget.

'That was a piece of schoolboy theatre. Got worse and worse in the telling. I reckon.'

'For Darnton it was no big deal?' Pete surmises, 'an almost routine piece of adolescent histrionics? That's why they took him back into the fold so easily.'

'Bang on, Pete! It was the right decision too; Sam was good at his studies, and actually the teaching at his old school, whatever he thought about the institution, was much better than at that crammer's in Hereford…'

What doesn't he know about Sam, Pete asks himself. Almost nothing. He knows so much, and in such detail, because… because he loves him. Probably has loved him since their first meeting, when Don was doing jobbing bit-work for Trevor. Sam had (has) Don Parry, and I had Oliver Merchant. Egotistic upstarts that we two boys were, sick of self-love as Shakespeare says, we didn't deserve all that steady service of the heart. Yet we expected it nonetheless. And therefore received it…

'Did I understand just now, Don, that you and Sam never met up that night?'

'We never did. I was with a bunch of mates, chewing the rag about what had been happening to us in the Berwyns. My old mum, who'd talked to Sam and thought him ever such a nice, well-spoken lad, was under the impression that he was coming back to ours to sleep. So we waited up and waited up... but nary a sign of him.'

'He drove all the way back to Leominster?'

'He did. Unwise of him to set out for so long a trip, I suppose, 'cause by then he'd had a few good deep smokes – you know the kind I'm meaning.' Pete hardly cannot do, seeing he is still enjoying these himself. So he merely nods.

'Would have probably got back to his house in Bargates – three o'clock, wouldn't you say?' Pete's heart is starting to pound fiercely fast. For in a sense these fast-approaching moments are ones he has waited these thirty-five long years for, and he cannot meet their arrival without fear – the fear of having hindsight imposed on him.

He makes himself continue: 'Sam'd have been home in The Tall House, sleeping off his night's misadventures, at the time you picked me up at the caff in Llanfyllin?'

Once again Don transfers his weight from one foot to the other, but this time it's a patent sign of awkwardness, even unease. The man has anticipated precisely this exchange but, now it's at last and irrevocably come, likes it every bit as little as Pete himself. 'I reckon so, yes.'

'This was all long before the time of mobile phones. But you know he was asleep at that hour because, Don, because he told you about everything?'

Don's eyes rather than his lips plead again. 'He did, yes, Pete. I was the big brother, you could say, in whom he – well, he was an only child – in whom he could confide. Confide what he was unable to tell Trevor or Susan. Or anybody else for that matter.'

'Me included, eh, Don? He was ungetatable ever afterwards. Mr and Mrs Price sent a wreath to my parents' funeral, but they never came to it; Sam himself sent me a condolence card – from London – and, later, another post-card of good wishes – from Darnton. But nothing more... But you know something, Don, I've got the strongest feeling, that even now we haven't got to the end of the whole dreadful business? There's a still grimmer truth you haven't yet told me. And that Sam has charged you to do so now. To make good the decades-long delay. So we can meet and be friends again...'

'And he'll do anything to be of help to you now, Pete.' Don steps nearer to him, you might say advances to him, as if to lay some assuring hand on him. Pete edges along the counter away from any demonstrativeness. 'He's a really wealthy man, Sam is, and deserves to be. Has a shrewd business-head nobody can rival, and works his arse off.'

I suppose this shrewdness has made him see the kind of difficulties Nat has plunged us in, thinks Pete. And he's offering to help. Guilt-money?

Or something handsomer, if you're prepared to forgive.

'Spit it out, Don Parry. I can't be waiting for you all bloody day!'

Don looks not at Pete but – oddly – at the debit-card machine on the counter, as if reminding himself of what his admired protégé could do for its owner – if only he could cleanse his heart. 'Before Sam left Llanrhaeadr – about half-past midnight he swears it was; he looked at his watch – he went into the phone box in the main street and rang...'

'My parents.' It's not a question now, but a statement of fact.

And had he somehow, somewhere, always known this?

'He rang up your home, Pete. He was sorry for what he'd done to you. And wanted to make amends.'

'Not sorry enough to turn his fucking VW back round, and pick me up himself?'

'Sam had a young man's pride, Pete, just as you had yourself. Proud young men don't do things like going back over their tracks and saying sorry. Would you not agree? You were like that yourself.'

The scene becomes – and is to remain – almost hallucinatorily clear to Pete. For years to come (with assistance from the one person who can know all its intimacies) he will regularly revisit it.

...Sam steps into the red telephone box, though it smells over-poweringly of vomit. Soon he'd be adding to this mess, for the cans of beer he's drunk with a few (already pretty sozzled) lads encountered near the British Legion have mixed unpleasantly with the dope he's himself smoked. He's in no state to re-present himself at Don Parry's house, and exhibit himself to Don's nice, hospitable mother. (And Don himself? Where is that fucker?) He dials the number he wants with an energy that surprises but pleases him, though several times his fingers slip out of the appropriate holes. And, at half past twelve am, he might well have to wait a goddam age for a reply. But wait he would. Wait he must. Eventually a voice comes on the other end of the line, and though drink and sheer exhaustion very nearly obstruct the tiresome business of inserting the coins (has he even the right ones to hand?) and the pressing of bloody fucking Button A, he accomplishes all this. 'Is that the Kempsey residence?' he shouts, and when Mr Kempsey (for him it must be) affirms in a slow, heavy, bemused but anxious voice that indeed it is, he bawls even louder: 'Mr Kempsey? Sorry to have woken you up in the middle of the night, and spoiled your sleep. But I thought you ought to know. I've just seen your son, Peter, lying on the side of the little hill road between Llanrhaeadr-ym-Mochnant and the waterfall known as Pistyll Rhaeadr. Looks as if he's been seriously in the wars. Hope he's alive still. I wouldn't like to say for sure, though.'

Then he hangs up – and to his profound shame and physical disgust – spews all down his bomber jacket and jeans, and then onto the floor... Gasping as he steps back into the keen January night air, the tears rolling profusely down his cheeks, he's tempted to turn round, re-enter the kiosk, ring the Kempseys' again, and inform them: 'Forget what you just heard. Just a drunken joke, by a stupid jerk who's going to feel even sorrier in the morning.' But he does not. For one thing, as he tells himself (and Don Parry) later, there's the reality of poor beaten-up Peter who, for aught he knew, might easily be lying there in exactly the same forlorn spot he's left him in.

After Brock

'So that's where my dad was driving them all to,' says Pete, and how right he was a few minutes back: life brings you things that quite simply cannot be borne, 'he was going to fetch me from Pistyll Rhaeadr. When the lorry jack-knifed into their Rover only a few miles out of Leominster, I was up on the Heights. And during the course of the night – according to those old legends you filled Sam's head with, Don – my family must have arrived there too. Isn't Annwn the Otherworld, the land of the Afterlife?'

He can't cry. He can't even be angry with this well-meaning soul who's been authorised to disclose things far better hidden.

'Those legends are metaphors, Pete,' Don's tone is so low Pete can barely catch the words, 'to help us in just such terrible situations as yours has been. They are things of beauty, to aid us and guide us and comfort us... Pete, think please that Sam was sorry that night. Think that he still felt himself your friend. Think that he wants to be your friend again. To assist you. To introduce you to his lovely, lovely family.'

Pete says: 'And my own lovely, lovely family? Dad, Mum, dead before they were fifty, Robin dead at age ten. Julian left with a tragedy that will stay with him for ever... So much silence, Don, so much conspiracy. You helped Sam to keep the truth of his absence in the Berwyns from his parents, from everybody. Just a lad, like every other red-blooded one, who'd been out on the tiles in his own town all night... But then Oliver Merchant performed the same service for me, so who am I to take the moral high ground? The moral fucking Heights.' He feels he might well break out now into a fit of insane laughter, like a character in some Jacobean drama, who would roll on the floor in a frenzy, gnashing his teeth and beating the floor with his fists. And whatever good would that do? It wouldn't even relieve the unnameable, indescribable emotions now threatening to take him over.

The only words he can find are, 'I know that in my own way I'm as guilty as Sam. At least I think so. If he can accept his wrong-doing, then I can accept mine, I guess. And if he's wanting to help me, then maybe somewhere inside me I'm wanting to be helped. Even by Sam Price... As for you, Don, I can't express, as well as I'd like to, my regard for you, for someone who actually came to confront me – ill-mannered bastard bound up in self even more than normal. As you well knew… Shouldn't we have that brew.' That's not really enough, but it's the best he can manage.

About half-an-hour later, Pete goes up to Nat's bedroom to take a look at his son. Who, though the afternoon sun is streaming strongly through the fabric of the drawn curtains, lies deep in sleep, on his right side but with three-quarters of himself above the duvet. His eyes being shut, no grey light shines disconcertingly from them; his mouth is half-open, but, from this angle, his row of ill-assorted front teeth is less conspicuous than usual. In the shadows that the curtains have caused to fall over the bed his tousled hair has lost its odd grey colour, seems the usual English mouse-brown. Why, he looks like practically every other youth, thinks Pete, like a couple of million others, at a conservative estimate. Ordinary enough. Still, he did a mad thing, did it deliberately and sustainedly.

Yet don't very ordinary people do very mad things? Think of me, Pete advises himself. I wasn't the High Flyer I thought, just a good average probably. But I carried out a surely extra-ordinary action – following someone through irrational devotion on a wild chase after UFOs which probably, it now seems, from as good an authority as I could have, weren't UFOs at all, just a geographical disturbance not so very remarkable in other parts of the world and scientifically explicable even in this one. But what I got at the end of my adventure, that surely was extra-ordinary? Enough so anyway to merit police inquiry and media attention.

Yet was it? Spontaneous heated action on the part of a father and mother who loved their child, and are therefore anxious about him, the deaths of several members of one family in a single accident – these don't really defy sensible canons for human experience. Watch BBC *Midlands Today* for just one week! Only to the bereaved individual who, because of his youth and narcissism, took for granted what should never be taken for granted, the continuance of life in all and any circumstances, could what befell the Kempseys those cold small hours of a January morning seem a defiance of probability, a violation of human rights, a breach of some contract you signed at birth.

A callow, inadequate notion, to put it mildly. Hasn't the Pete Kempsey of 2009 jettisoned it long ago? He now approaches life with unflagging, if not always obvious or even self-acknowledged, suspicion. Yet when Nat went missing, such a feeling of injustice came flooding back through him. It would return again if Nat were to have a serious relapse of health; it almost certainly will return, he admits, if, as a result of what he has just told Luke Fleming, he has to pay a severe penalty for his ill-begotten escapade, for activity in truth far 'madder' because more deliberate.

He tiptoes out of the room fearful of breaking a peace (born of relief and release) that Nat may well not know again for a long time. Let the boy sleep for every bit as long as he can. Now he begins the descent of the staircase. Nat always says it's like a ladder. 'Why it's worse than climbing down a fucking *ladder*!' he exclaimed, surprised by its steepness, on his very first visit to High Flyers, to be immediately embarrassed at having used such a word to his own father, an embarrassment that hasn't prevailed for many a year. And indeed Nat has a point. Even making his way carefully on his toes, Pete makes the narrow oaken rungs creak out. Maybe it's the tense stealth with which he is moving but all of a sudden it seems to Pete that he isn't in the eighteenth-century premises of his kite shop, in his early fifties and a tad overweight, but is a lithe youth creeping down a far broader-stepped staircase close-carpeted in turquoise, and trying not to rouse the Brats in their shared bedroom across the landing, engrossed in chequers. Yes, he is back at Woodgarth, and it is the evening of January 23, 1974.

Of course he will not resist Sam Price, either physically (that hand clapped over his mouth, that hard grip on his shoulders!) or psychologically – for how could any self-respecting young male pass up the chance to go haring off into the night after aliens – or even the attested possibility of them? Of course he will listen to Sam's Don-derived spiel as they drive north-west through the freezing dark, towards the Shropshire hills and the Welsh mountains beyond.

It is a while before the slopes of hills meet the road taken, but within forty minutes they do, bringing bursts of woodland, through which they see an owl making intent swooping movements. Pete's mind then travels back to that earlier Shropshire journey in Sam's VW, when Sam braked because a badger was crossing the road, and he was fearful of hitting him (or 'her' as Pete deduced). Appreciating the co-existence of the two of them, young travellers and native fauna with priorities and habits utterly their own, brings about a change in Pete's head. An owl, a badger, their own two essentially affectionate if also genetically competitive human selves – that's the reality that matters, not the appearance of weird shapes of shifting colours brought about (if, by now, they can even be apprehended) by some Will beyond any earthly comprehension.

And then, almost on cue, another badger arrives on the quiet benighted scene. Once again Sam has to brake while the creature, his great white frontal stripe a-glow, or as good as, in the darkness of his context (which includes, from where the boys are, his own body), crosses the road – with rather more sense of haste than his kin of earlier in the month. Sam is too concerned with what Don Parry has witnessed in the heavens to be as interested in the animal as he was that earlier time, though he handles the car with the same care for its safety, but Pete...

The Pete Kempsey recalling all this has by now successfully got to the bottom of the ladder/stairs. The sign on the shop door is still reversed, keeping any customers away. Any minute now this will swing on its string as Luke Fleming makes his entrance, and Pete's world will, more likely than not, undergo yet another upheaval, or even transformation... I now know, he thinks against his fears of a future only movements of watch-hands away, how things could all have gone differently, how if we'd attended to him properly, there could have been, after Brock, the triumph of the sanity that comes from respecting the ordinary.

After Brock

'Sam,' this other Pete – both of and not of the past – goes, 'stop the car, there's a mate! I must see that Brock really is making it to where he wants to go. Like we did last time.'

'But tonight we've got an assignation. With History.'

'Fuck History,' says Pete, 'if Martians really have landed, we'll all of us find out in good time. They won't confine themselves to the Berwyns, I shouldn't think. Wouldn't do their cause a lot of good to stick around somewhere as cut off as that. Far better for you and me to see to this one particular animal.'

'Okeydokey!' says Sam, if a mite reluctantly. So he slows down and then pulls up at the nearest gateway to a field, less than a hundred yards further on. The friends get out into the stinging night chill, and begin the walk back to where the badger had been traversing the road. Pete thinks he can descry lumbering movement in bracken and grasses ahead.

'Before we go on any further, I must tell you something,' Pete says, 'under your influence I chose UFOS for my High Flyers Special Subject, and then was too shy – or possibly too scared – to tell you. But I am not going ahead with it.'

After a long, for Pete, nerve-racking pause Sam says, 'So what subject will you choose, Pete? You really don't have too much time left.'

Pete laughs, and puts a finger to his lips, for maybe their voices are too loud and their footsteps on the frost-bitten tarmac too hard. 'Well, how about badgers?' he says, 'I've a week to gen up on them, and anyway we might learn something new tonight?'

No panic-stricken Llanrhaeadr-ym-Mochant. No blurting out of the unpalatable truth on an unknown lane leading away from there to heaven-knew-what bizarre visitants. No fury from Sam, no assault, no abandonment, no possible visit to Annwn, and… after Brock, might it not have been Pete himself who made the phone call to Woodgarth, ending in a blast of righteous anger over the receiver but no alarmed journey out of Leominster by Jim Kempsey, with wife Marion, and sons Julian and Robin aboard? After Brock there would have been life.

Julian and Robin. In the tiny interval between now and Luke Fleming's return Pete knows what he wants to do. He goes to his computer, and, having already memorised the address, types on the keyboard: 'jul.pringle@yahoo.com'

'Dear Julian,' he now writes, 'Hi! The journal Nat keeps – which I have read – has supplied your email address as well as a great many facts about your life – Ilona's worrying illness, for instance – that I am hugely ashamed I was ignorant of. Maybe you are in Hungary right now, as you intended. If you are, you may well not have heard of Nat's mission to bring us both money and himself fame by "disappearing" into the Berwyn mountains. It didn't result in either, I have to say, just in enough attention for me to resent the business heartily, and exposure to the elements and an injury to the foot that are keeping him bed-bound for the time being. These may not be the only bad consequences of his ill-conceived venture. Just at the moment I can't ward off ideas of a prison sentence being handed the lad for the wild goose chase he's led everybody. That'll bring satisfaction to *The Daily Mail* and further heartache to Izzie and me and everybody else who cares for him. Thank you for your own friendliness to Nat. It makes me bold enough to suggest we see a bit of each other. There's no reason why we shouldn't, is there? The terrible thing that divided our lives after I was "on the Heights" mustn't determine the rest of them. I remember…'

But he can't complete the sentence. Because what he is remembering is his own exclamation to Julian as he lay there on the hospital bed: 'I was up there on those Heights – those Heights in Wales, and they took care of me after my accident. What had I done to merit those Heights?' And this makes him recall Julian's letter to Nat, 'I prefer to let Peter stay up on his Heights, and not drag him down…' Heights, always that word Heights!! And suddenly a truth breaks on him which it amazes him it has taken decades to see.

With his regaining of consciousness Julian did recover memory; though he was declared to have amnesia, he knew perfectly well why the family had left Woodgarth at so unprecedentedly unusual an hour. But had chosen to keep quiet. He had wanted to spare Peter, to ensure that he did not suffer any more than he was already doing, that he was not troubled by further questions from authority or by more stabs from his already disordered conscience.

Kept quiet then, at a time when he must have wanted to cry out in protest at what had happened to him, kept quiet after that, for all the long years since.

Pete draws back from his computer, to place his head, eyes closed, in his cupped hands, consumed by an emotion so strong, so devouring that it defies naming – and maybe it will never quite let go of him. He is wondering how he can bear this new revelation – far more disturbing even than what he's heard about Sam from Don, asking, as it does, gratitude from him to someone he's rarely bothered himself about – when he hears a knock on the glass of the door. It is, of course, Luke Fleming returning from his lunchbreak.

Nat wakes up from his brief but deep sleep to hear this knock, realising who is responsible for it. But I'm ready, he tells himself, ready for absolutely anything, and I mean ready. And why? Because just now he's been reliving in his unconscious head those experiences in the Berwyns which he regards as far and away the biggest favour life has yet done him. Having received this – and treasured it, and stored it safely in his mind, to draw on for sustenance whenever he wishes – he is surely protected against whatever unkindness and suffering are to come his way. He doesn't feel disposed to telling anybody about it all yet, certainly no journo (even if this particular one, Luke Fleming does the kind thing and keep Nat's secret *secret*!), nor his mates, even Josh, nor Dad who certainly does respect animals, nor Mum who so loves, and seeks out, peace and harmony. The day may indeed come when he wants to share with others, but it will be for their sake, not his own.

He has already composed a poem – well, it's more of a psalm really – about all he witnessed up on the lower slopes of Pen-plaenau, but new verses for it keep on occurring to him, even now, in the interstices of stretching himself further awake and hearing Dad and Luke mount the precipitous ladder-like stairs to give him the news:

'You, all of you up there, I could never say anything to you. One syllable aloud, and the whole wonderful atmosphere – with me hidden, spellbound, you venturesome and active – would have been destroyed. You have not great reason to think kindly of my species, but there are some of us – and not a few – who wish you well, who delight in you.'

It was by chance – in surely a double sense – that Nat had come across the badgers. It was the evening of his first full day in the Berwyn Mountains, his first, that is, to start with him waking up there, a bit stiff and slightly damp.

Twice in its course he'd glimpsed people in the distance, making their way along a path leading between two peaks: a walking party in the first instance, a tall young man with an Alpenstock (hopefully not a rival, some fellow recluse or hide-away) in the second. But he'd espied both these human intrusions from behind an outcrop of siltstone rock; there was no likelihood of having been seen, but anyway, to be thoroughly sure, he'd retreated, bent more or less double so that he covered ground like a deer or a less massive wild boar, further uphill. Though his twisted ankle was still hurting, he was filled with general satisfaction, not least at himself. By now he had arrived at the lower reaches of Pen-plaenau, not so far indeed from where, four days later, he was to be spotted and rescued.

He had slept pretty well the previous night. To his relief. Unlike Pete in 1974, he had a sleeping bag with him; he'd bought it in Shrewsbury on his way over. When eventually he was rescued, as a hardy, plucky, stoical casualty, nobody would hold this invaluable piece of equipment against him; rather it'd confirm opinions of him as a sensible, well-prepared, countrywise lad who'd been undeservedly unlucky and suffered a serious tumble. He'd fought against admitting to himself any worry about the night (inability to achieve restful sleep apart) which had occurred to him when hatching his plan: that he might be disturbed, even frightened by all the noises of predators and victims issuing from the dark into the dark. But he needn't have doubted himself so. Maybe his nocturnal escapades in South London seeking foxes had steeled him. Instead the problem he faced in this twilight hour was: however to pass the sizeable time before sleep, even if fitful, delivered him from his immediate surroundings and carried him on to the burgeoning light of the next calendar day, in his own unadulterated company?

The light was dimming, but surely more gradually, more subtly, than Nat had appreciated in his urban life. One kind of greyness would hold for a while, as though it intended to stay forever, and it came, even to the intent watcher such as himself, as something of a surprise when it yielded to another deeper shade. The colours, this second evening of this mountain country – light green (turf), dark green (clumps of woodland), light purple, deep purple (all the heathers), brown (bracken), grey (the shale) – were, he thought, maintaining themselves so well that this time maybe they might win against the descent of night, and remain intact… Impossible, of course – though *was* it? Up here his mind was surely changing its set, and shedding its former certainties.

Not enough light for him to continue with Henning Mankell's *Sidetracked*, though its ever more horrifying unfolding of violence in the Swedish coastal town of Ystad had left him on tenterhooks, on which he would gladly impale himself next day. And his torch simply wasn't strong enough to illuminate page print; anyway stupidly he'd forgotten to buy new batteries, and mustn't let these ones run out. Just as he was despairing of hitting on any compensation for forgoing the Wallander mystery – and no speculations about UFOs! he commanded himself – he noticed an all but hidden little path which somehow appealed to him. It led up from the ledge on which he was now standing towards a rock crevice, its surface beaten hard and dry by constant use by some regular. He would follow it, but walk on the sheep-cropped grass to its right rather than in the wake of any discernible tracks, whose makers might notice and fret.

The path ended in a huge mound of slightly sandy soil, fresh and perfectly clean, thrust up by claws from the earth all around the crevice's base. Nat looked down. A large hole opened some inches from his calves, about ten inches across, and shaped 'like a D lying on its side'. The comparison came to him from some book he'd read about British wild life and its habitat a few years ago. Therefore… yes, this was the entrance into, the exit out of a badgers' sett, and the Berwyns, it was a well-attested fact, firm in his own head, were home to many badgers. The fissured rock directly above him would give the creatures excellent protection, and shield just such a reliable look-out post for them as he himself had needed earlier in the day.

Soon there could be no doubt. Here were three similarly shaped and formed holes, but slightly smaller, more like six inches diameter. At the end of one he could make out a descending passageway; no doubt if you edged along through it, you would arrive at the very same chamber as through the first opening. Nat would examine the first more closely but from an oblique angle. Remembering his successes with London foxes, he was wary of putting himself about too comprehensively, and was faithful to his wariness even at the cost of uncomfortable bodily contortions.

All round the hole, he saw, was a pattern of parallel lines, the work indubitably of the same sharp claws responsible for the pile of earth. Then, raising his head he saw the same pattern repeated, only much more deeply etched, on the rock fissure itself. Next he noticed several little bundles of dry grasses, placed by the entrance surely deliberately. Why, I'm an archaeologist but of the living, said Nat to himself, or a discoverer of some remote tribe, and somehow this was a pleasing thing to think, when all these months, until the Great Plan occurred to him, he'd been feeling rather bereft of satisfying pictures of himself. (His good A's had made strangely little difference here.)

How orderly, how well cared-for it all was. Nat had arrived, he felt, at a secure outpost of true civilisation kept up (over centuries, not to say millennia) in territory that – those peaks so stark now against the gathering dark – was capable of turning inimical, hostile.

The evening was virtually windless. And warm too, especially considering the altitude of where he was. Good, very good! No elemental reasons for any anxiety... I shall shift myself over to a slab of stone on that little rise just there, said Nat to himself and maintain a position that allows my scent to float way, way above the levels of the animals emerging from the bunker beneath. And I'll just wait and wait and wait.

Which is what he did. From where he was stationed he could look down onto a line of weather-stunted hawthorn trees marching, evenly spaced and still laden with berries, towards a little stream now silvering in the valley as dusk perceptibly thickened. What remained of the day's sun was blocked from his view by a gaunt, desolate-seeming ridge on his left. It was a waiting, in-between time. Still too light apparently for these badgers underground, preparing for their night activities well below, and dark enough for natural objects that only a short time ago had seemed comfortingly dependable in their distinctness to be camouflaged.

What is it that I really am doing up here in the Berwyns? Nat asked himself as, oddly, he hadn't done most of that day. Have I some deeper purpose behind all my carefully worked-out strategies and my flight into the unknown? Perhaps something you only attain when you've broken free of other people's definitions of your self and what you can or cannot do: the getting of grades, the finding of jobs, the building-up of businesses...

Typically, it was while his thoughts were taking him away from his – interesting and dramatically new – surroundings and into surely rather pointless speculation that the very first badger did venture into the open, from that first hole, the one closest to the crevice. And here she was – for Nat, like his dad before him, knew the first badger out any evening to be invariably a female – lifting her shining white-striped head into the air. Up went her snout, she sniffed the air, once, twice, thrice, as one ascertaining there was no danger nearby. (Either she failed to detect Nat's presence, he having placed himself so judiciously and motionlessly, or she didn't rate him as danger!) This done she must have given a signal (some combination of shuffle and the lowest of grunts) which this time quite eluded him, keen though he was, because next – and this time Nat saw it all – out came two rather smaller animals. Were these her cubs? They had sturdy little legs, and short, strong, low-held tails, and markings were definite enough. But there was something about these creatures that suggested they hadn't yet arrived at a maturity of either feature or movement.

At their arrival a snorting noise issued from the sow-badger, a pleased but purposeful sound, even an authoritative one, a kind of nasal cough. Then off the three went, at a trot, down the very path that Nat had come up. But they branched off from it some fifty yards later, onto a little track that he hadn't been aware of. This, it was apparent from up here, would take them to the stream.

So badgers had appeared only to disappear! Just his luck! But just as he was lamenting this, two more badgers came out of the sett. Not literally simultaneously, but in such quick succession, that this was how it seemed. These newcomers must have heard and attended to the sow-badger's signals and trusted her, for unlike her, they gave no apprehending, interrogative sniffs into the air, but, in no time at all – why, get this! – were rolling about on the earthen plateau below the main entrance. They gave the loudest grunts of the evening so far, and turned themselves over and over, revealing their somewhat squat bodies to be remarkably elastic, blissfully contracting and expanding (so it looked) as if to usher in the night with all its invitations and rituals. This, no doubt of it, was fun and games, there were rules to be followed but there were also moments of total and merry abandon. The animals might have been himself and Josh and their mates, a summer ago, down on the beach at Whitstable. Theirs were the wriggles and half-leaps and backward turns of purest enjoyment, and Nat could see the pair knew each other so well that theirs was a veritable unison of antics. And he started to make a verse out of his observation:

'Yours are the wriggles and half-leaps and backward turns...'

No two ways about it. Day was over, discarded. Its colours had ceased to stand out any longer against the sky, but had surrendered themselves up till next morning to the darkness now in charge... The two youthful badgers proceeded to lose themselves in their own liveliness for far longer than Nat chose to measure by his watch, though when he did eventually look at the luminous dial, three-quarters of an hour had gone by. For here were the sow and the two cubs back uphill from their drink. He positively had to check himself from stepping forward to greet them. Momentarily the boy-badgers (as Nat now called them to himself) stopped their frolics, then, seeing approval in the sow's benevolent beady little eyes, resumed them. One of the returning cubs picked up a bundle of withered grass in its mouth and disappeared with it, back into the hole, showing perhaps a natural bent for sett husbandry. But 'it' (sex was impossible to determine) was back almost straightaway.

Again some signal to the tunnels beneath the ground must have been given – but how by so small a member of the tribe – for now other badgers started to come outside, and were joined by some from the second biggest exit/entrance just below Nat's stone. The clan had gathered, Nat reckoned – for with so much movement of such a lively kind, counting was hard-to-impossible – that at least a dozen animals assembled.

Nat breaks off from his memories abruptly. The voices in the shop below – his dad's and Luke Fleming's, which have been in colloquy for quite a few minutes – are, all of a sudden, clearer, louder, nearer. A decision has surely been reached, even the method of turning it into the best words for its object has been agreed on. Very soon the men will walk over to the staircase up to his bedroom.

What can Nat do but continue with his thoughts? 'Were you ever, any of you, aware of Nat Kempsey, Human Being, so careful to remain out of sight and even scent? Did you somehow sense my good will, and bask in it? No, I don't think you did, even though it's a great idea. But there's one possible exception, though this animal didn't do any basking…'

'That exception. My very last night I placed myself closer to the sett even than I had done before. Sleep left me, though not quite fully, in time for me to see your mass return home for the day, your work (digging and eating enough earthworms, sometimes 120 per badger, to add to your fat and to help you through oncoming winter) and your revels (all those games I watched with such relish and admiration) truly done. Over in the direction of England, beyond the shale and bare mountain-shanks, I saw in the sky's sandwich-like layers of green, rose and yellow the first stages of dawn. I surely wouldn't be seeing another one break in the Berwyns – not for many years, at least. Then I looked down. I saw a young badger, clearly a straggler from the group, running really quite fast up the path towards the sett's main entrance. I must hurry, I must join the others at once, he (for I was sure it was a 'he') was obviously saying to himself. Then he stopped, only inches away from his destination, tilted his head so that his stripe was brilliant in the lessening darkness, and his snout began busily to quiver. He must, he surely must, have sensed my presence. And judged it benign, for he went back inside after a satisfied little shake of his body, away from the dangers of dawn into the happy security of his fellows and the earth in which they had their being.

'I felt that badger was myself.'

Nat raises himself up into a sitting, receiving posture. His father and the journalist are mounting the ladder-like stairs, and he must be composed and dignified, ready for them.

About the Author

Paul Binding has lived in South Shropshire for twenty years. He has worked as a literary editor and a university lecturer, and is a frequent freelance contributor to newspapers and journals. His interest in the culture of Scandinavia and the Low Countries, about which he regularly writes articles and reviews, makes him a frequent visitor to both. Animals are of the greatest importance to him, and he cannot imagine a life without their company.

Also by Paul Binding

Novels

Harmonica's Bridegroom
'A disturbing dark novel and an auspicious debut' – Brian
Moore
'A carefully husbanded talent with skill and sensitivity' –
Jonathan Keates

My Cousin the Writer
'Paul Binding has produced an original masterpiece... an
exquisitely crafted novel' – Zelda Longmore in *The Spectator*

Memoir

St Martin's Ride
'One of those rare masterpieces... Literary art of a very rare
kind' – Sir Stephen Spender
'A book as profound as it is beautiful' – Theodore Zeldin

Literary Criticism

With Vine Leaves in His Hair: the role of the Artist in Ibsen's Plays
'Richness of insight and style... The more you read this book,
the more you are convinced of Ibsen's depth and humility.' –
Murrough O'Brien in *Independent on Sunday*.